Dangerous Disguise

by

Tesa Devlyn

This is a work of fiction. Names, characters, places, and incidents are either the product of the author's imagination or are used fictitiously, and any resemblance to actual persons living or dead, business establishments, events, or locales, is entirely coincidental.

Dangerous Disguise

Contact Information: info@thewildrosepress.com

Cover Art by *Angela Anderson*

The Wild Rose Press
PO Box 708
Adams Basin, NY 14410-0708
Visit us at www.thewildrosepress.com

Publishing History
First Cactus Rose Edition, 2012
Print ISBN 978-1-61217-025-1

Published in the United States of America

Why had she made such an impulsive decision?

"What have I done?" she murmured…

Glancing around for her trunk, she froze.

Seth Morgan, his black Stetson tilted back on his head, his hands on his trim hips, stood next to the depot, scanning the area with dark, narrowed eyes. A shorter man in a suit and bowler stood next to him, chattering away.

"Oh no," she whispered. Could Hope be his destination, or was he stretching his legs? Kate's mind raced. Could she be arrested for impersonating Mary Catherine? Even if she had permission? She couldn't run off and leave Mary Catherine's trunk on the platform. Seth Morgan would chase her to Seattle and arrest her. She'd be suspected of murdering poor Mary Catherine.

She had to get her trunk back on the train and hide in her compartment. She turned away and started toward the attendant who'd tried to help her.

"Excuse me, Miss Leary. You staying in Hope or going to Seattle?" Morgan's voice reached her before she'd taken more than a dozen steps.

Her shoulders sagged with resignation. She turned as his long strides ate up the weathered platform between them. Damn. Her chance to get back on the train undetected vanished under his sharp eye.

Kate pasted a smile on her face. "Mr. Morgan, what a pleasant surprise. What brings you to Hope?" The train rumbled beside them, the crew racing to fill the water tanks from the lake.

"I'm the new sheriff. Guess we didn't talk about our destinations back there, did we?"

"No, I guess we didn't." Kate wished the man would disappear. If she was any judge of character, he'd stick to her to like honey.

Dedication

This book would never have survived
without the support and love of my husband, Don.
He's truly the stuff heroes are made of.
Nor without the enthusiasm of
my three daughters and their charming husbands,
and my awesome RWA group; IECRWA!
Thank you for helping my dreams come true!

Acknowledgements

Hope, Idaho, was built with the construction of the Northern Pacific Railway in 1882 and soon boasted many businesses which terraced the hillside overlooking beautiful Lake Pend Oreille. With the completion of the Idaho line, the roundhouse was moved to Montana, but in 1888, a drought hit, forcing the railroad to move their division back to the shores of the large lake.

In researching the history of this scenic place, this author found the setting of a drought around a lake with 44 miles of shoreline fascinating, not to mention the diversity of the people who built Hope: the railroad and the people who chose to stay. I took liberties with the layout of the town for the sake of my story. I used the Hope Hotel as the premier lodging of that era, when some accounts name the Highland Hotel as the place General Sherman was reputed to stay. I also created Mrs. White's Boarding House and Café and inserted a road up the side of the hill from town to the meadow where my characters Kerry and Janet Malone lived.

Today, Hope is a peaceful and very beautiful resort town that maintains its history and pride in having some of the most stunning views of the lake and the mountains of North Idaho.

Chapter One

New York City, 1888

Kate's heart raced and her eyes teared from the anger and fear surging through her body. *How dare he? How dare he do this to me?* She grimaced at the deep burn in her back and shoulders, caused by her marginal control over the racing pair of geldings, as they thundered through the narrow crowded streets of New York City.

The wheels rattled over the cobblestones, jarring her teeth and blurring her vision. With her last ounce of strength, she brought the dappled grays to a clattering stop in front of Ross William's prestigious, three-story law office.

The door man, his eyes wide and face pale, hurried forward to grab the harness and calm the team. "Miss McShane. You drove up like you was being chased."

"I am." Kate glanced around, then grabbed the heavy folds of her day dress and scrambled off the high seat. "At least I was."

She hung onto the carriage for a moment, allowing her heart to steady and her knees to support her. "Please watch my rig and beware of a man dressed in dungarees and a red-striped shirt. He's very dangerous."

"Sure thing, Miss." The man nodded and cooed to the horses as she ran past him and wrenched open the heavy, carved door.

Slipping inside the richly appointed reception area, Kate took a deep breath. She was safe. At least for now.

"Miss McShane. My goodness, what happened?" Ross's assistant, Mr. Gibb, hurried around his desk. "You look rather disheveled. Are you quite all right?"

Her chest still heaving, Kate bit back the retort, hell no, she wasn't all right. She paused a moment then answered the rather effeminate man. "I need to see Mr. Williams. Now."

"Mr. Williams is with someone at the moment but—"

Kate pushed past the slack-jawed assistant and threw open the inner office door.

"For the love of—" Ross shot up from his seat behind the massive desk, his brows smoothing when he saw her. "Kate, what is it?" He fastened the buttons of his perfectly cut suit jacket and brushed a golden curl off his forehead.

"Katie?" Leland Cook, her father's long time foreman twisted in the wing-backed chair then pushed out of the leather confines and hurried to her side.

The assistant huffed behind her, clutching her upper arm. "I'm sorry, Mr. Williams. I tried to stop her."

"Unhand me." She glared over her shoulder. He released her and stepped back. "Ross, please call off your watchdog. This is an emergency."

Ross nodded at his assistant, dismissing him with the wave of a hand. The moment the door closed Kate's knees buckled. She sank against the closed door and covered her face with both hands.

"Katie, for heaven's sake what's wrong?" Leland said, his expression etched with alarm.

"Oh, Leland." Kate threw her arms around the older man's neck. She didn't want to crumble in front of her advisors. She needed to appear strong and in control, but she couldn't hold back with Leland, who had always been like a second father;

even more so since her father had died six weeks ago.

Ross touched her shoulder. “Tell us what happened. Heavens, your dress is torn and dirty.”

“Give her a minute, Ross.” Leland patted her back.

Kate longed to stay in Leland’s arms and sob out her fright and frustration, but she couldn’t weaken now. She stepped away from the older man and sniffed. “I narrowly escaped being kidnapped; that’s what happened! That scoundrel Jeb Walker has to be behind it.”

“Good God, Kate, are you sure?” Leland’s thick, white hair was mussed, and his normally youthful face drawn and tired. His sharp blue eyes appeared dull.

She glanced at Ross. Heavens, more than one blonde curl was out of place as if he’d been raking his hands through them.

“What did I interrupt?” She looked from one man to the other.

“We can fill you in later. First tell us how this happened.” Ross slid his hands up and down her arms. His cologne surrounded her, his golden eyes captured her attention and made her wish she could settle for less than mad, passionate love and marry Ross.

He stepped back a proper distance. Still the suave man he’d been when James McShane hired him fresh out of law school, Ross’s career in the courtroom and law office hadn’t added an ounce of excess flesh to his tall, slender frame.

She cleared her throat and stepped away from his touch. “Jeb proposed to me again. I refused and left the office. I didn’t notice the driver, until we were deep into the dock area.” Chills scattered up her arms and neck at the memory of looking out the window of her carriage to discover she wasn’t on her way home. Kate swallowed and continued. "Someone had switched my driver for a hideous creature who dragged me into a disreputable establishment on the water front."

"Katie, my god, this is unforgivable. Did he hurt you?" Leland urged her to sit in the seat opposite the one he'd occupied.

"I'm bruised, shaken up, and angry, but he didn't take advantage of me, if that's what you mean." Kate raised a brow at Ross, who hadn't bothered to ask after her welfare. He appeared rather calm over what had been a life threatening situation.

She arranged her skirt around her and continued. "We were at the office. I had a particularly difficult meeting with the board of directors. They laughed at my idea to clean up the dock. Then Jeb sided with them." Kate pressed her fingers to her forehead and fought back tears of frustration. "After the meeting, I confronted him about not backing me, and he said I should give up the ridiculous notion of running the company and marry him."

"I assume you refused?" Ross tented his fingers under his chin and walked around the desk to reclaim his chair.

"Of course I refused."

"But you're sure Jeb's responsible for the kidnapping attempt?"

"Who else could it be? He has the most to gain, doesn't he?"

"Kate, you're a very wealthy heiress. There are multiple people who would want you." Ross propped his elbows on the desk. "We need to get to the bottom of this atrocity."

Kate rubbed her forehead, determined to continue without breaking down. "At the least!"

"How did you get away?" Ross narrowed his eyes

and drilled her with a less than sympathetic look.

"He dragged me into a place called The Goose Down. I struggled, but no one came to my aid. He took me behind the bar and into a small room. I didn't know how to get away, then I remembered my derringer." Kate hesitated, emotion choking her. "I pulled my gun and waved it at him. He backed away, and I ran outside and climbed on the carriage."

Leland glanced at Ross, his mouth turned down, his blue eyes shooting fire. "Ross, you're the Executor of the McShane estate, get to the bottom of this! The driver needs to be arrested."

The memory of helplessness swept over her. Kate shivered.

"I'm pouring you a sherry." Leland rose and hurried to the sideboard and the impressive display of crystal.

Kate leaned back in the soft leather chair and sighed. "Mercy, I can't believe what's happened since Father died. My entire world is crumbling."

Leland handed her a delicate crystal glass. Kate thanked him and took a sip of the sweet, amber liquid, relishing the immediate effect of soothing warmth through her blood.

She closed her eyes, but the disgusting face of the kidnapper flashed through her mind. She snapped them open, sat up straight, and pushed back her hair.

"I must look a fright." She pressed her hand to her chest. "If a street brawl hadn't broken out right behind me, the henchman would have caught the carriage."

"Good Lord, this has gone too far." Leland paced between Kate and the sideboard. "A woman of your standing in The Goose Down!"

"Have you heard of it?"

"We've, ah, certainly heard of it and its reputation." Ross shifted in his chair and cleared his throat.

Kate pursed her lips and raised one brow at the discomfort on both men's faces. "Hmm, it appears you have heard of it."

Not for the first time that day, she realized how much her father had protected her from the darker side of life. "Well, it's certainly not someplace I want to see again." Kate gulped another drink of sherry and swiped at fresh tears. "I've never driven a team before, but I had to escape."

Ross planted his palms against the shiny desktop. "I'll confront Walker right now."

"No." Leland stopped pacing. "We can't forget the plan."

"I thought we had more time."

Kate glanced from Ross to Leland, her stomach queasy. They acted as if she wasn't in the room.

"So did I, but he's moving faster than we figured." Leland eased into the chair.

Fear gnawed at her. "What do you mean? Are you referring to Jeb? She scooted forward and set the crystal glass on the desk. "Tell me what plan you're referring to."

Leland and Ross looked around the room then glanced at each other. Kate shot them both what she hoped was a scathing look.

"You two know something, and I demand you share it with me."

Leland sighed. "Yes, Katie, Jeb's up to no good, but we hoped he'd wait a more respectable time after your father's death."

"There's nothing respectable about Jebulin Walker." Kate's voice trembled. Oh, how she wished her father was still alive. She picked up the glass of sherry and drained it. Smacking her lips, she glanced from Leland to Ross and back. "Now, who is going to tell me what's going on?"

Leland cleared his throat. "We believe Jeb's

responsible for your father's death."

"What?" Kate stared at Leland through a gray tunnel. All strength left her body, her fingers released the crystal glass, and it hit the thick carpet with a thud.

"No." She pushed to the edge of the chair but couldn't stand. "What are you talking about?"

Ross walked around the desk and kneeled in front of her. "You were right, Kate. Jeb has the most to gain by either marrying or eliminating you. You are now the only thing blocking him from sole ownership of McShane Walker Shipping."

"Yes, but resort to murder?"

"James was the main obstacle to his ambitions. The more Leland and I discuss it, the more your father's death makes no sense. One thing we're fairly sure of is that Jeb was the last person to see James alive."

Kate covered her face with both hands. "I've felt so guilty about being in Europe when he died," she whispered.

She'd traveled with close family friends but would never have gone if she'd had an inkling her father wasn't well. By the time her ship docked in New York Harbor, her father had already been buried with the service the following day. "I was too overcome with grief to ask for details."

"Kate, you couldn't know what we suspect."

"Did anyone else see Jeb with my father? We can't make assumptions and make them stick."

Ross pursed his lips, then rolled them back. "No. Jeb was alone."

She clutched her throat, swallowing down the reoccurring nausea since she'd stood at her father's grave and read his name etched in stone. Just like that, he was gone, and she was alone. She'd questioned her family doctor about his diagnosis. He'd been sure of it being a heart attack.

"Kate, are you all right?" Leland squeezed her hand. "You look pale again."

"It isn't right. Something isn't right."

"Exactly." Ross slipped his fingers into the square pockets on the front of his suit jacket. "Our first priority has to be your safety; however, we need to step up our investigation of Jeb."

"I'll be fine at home with the servants, and I'll make sure someone accompanies me to the office." She'd be damned if she would hide away and let Jeb win.

"No, Kate. That's not good enough."

"Of course it is." Kate stood and brushed out her skirt, cringing at the dirt smudges and tears on the green, sprigged cotton. "I'm going home. That is, if one of you gentlemen will escort me. I'm not up to driving the carriage any farther."

Leland nodded and took her arm. "I'll drive you. Jeb might be waiting for you."

"I'm coming, too," Ross said, striding toward the door. "To keep a strong front, we should all have dinner at Delmonico's, act as if nothing's wrong. Word will travel back to Jeb."

"Good idea." Leland handed Kate through the doorway and into the outer office.

Ross's assistant jumped to his feet.

"Relax Gibby, I'm escorting Miss McShane home then out to dinner. You may close the office thirty minutes early."

"Yes, Mister Williams." Mr. Gibb hurried to the outer door and opened it for the three to pass.

True to his word, the doorman stood guard at the horses' heads. "No sign of your henchman, Miss."

"Good." Kate shuddered. If she never saw that man again, it would be too soon.

Within minutes, they arrived at the McShane estate, and Ross helped Kate from the carriage.

"Where is Spears?" She hurried up the wide

steps and waited in front of the carved double doors, a strong feeling of foreboding settling over her. She'd never personally opened this door.

Ross reached around her and grasped the brass handle, squeezing the lever; he pushed it open. Silence.

Kate shivered, then stepped into the two-story foyer, her boot heels clicked against the marble floor and echoed against the plaster walls. Still silence.

"Where is my staff? Spears commands that door like a military post, and Mrs. Haskins always greets me with dinner plans." Kate pushed through the French doors leading into the library. No one.

Frustrated, she stomped one foot. "Where in the world is everyone?"

Ross circled the room, glanced out the window facing the stables, then back to Kate and Leland. "My bet is, Jeb gave them the afternoon off so they wouldn't miss you as soon."

Kate frowned. "Does the man know no boundaries? If you're not going to confront him right now, I will."

Leland shook his head. "No, you can't. We have to remain cool. I'm sorry you were frightened, Katie, but we can't act on emotion."

"Emotion? Emotion? I was kidnapped, and now I learn someone has disposed of my staff." She jammed her hands onto her hips ready to do battle, but what she really wanted to do was crawl up to her room and hide in her fluffy goose down bed. Goose Down! The term made her blood run cold. She'd never again think of her wonderful bed in the same way.

"Katie." Leland slid his arm around her. "You should go to Erin's while we investigate the whereabouts of the staff."

"I won't endanger your daughter and her family." Erin had been Kate's best friend since childhood, was married to a wonderful man, and had two adorable sons.

"If Jeb's responsible for what happened this afternoon, I'm sure he didn't count on your strength." Leland chuckled. "Your father would be proud, Katie."

"He would be proud," Ross interjected. "However, he'd be making plans to send you somewhere safe. You're square in the middle of the trouble."

Kate laughed in frustration. "Isn't that the truth? The old goats on the board bucked everything I said today." She closed her eyes and lowered her voice. "I know how to make this company grow, but thanks to closed minded men and Jeb's influence, I'm not being given a chance."

"Your safety has to be our first concern. Leland and I will find the staff and corner Mr. Jebulin Walker. He's dangerous, Kate. I concur with Leland. You need to go somewhere until we have the evidence to arrest Jeb."

Kate slumped on the chaise. "I can't leave my company to that greedy, power hungry, egotistic—well, you know what I mean. He'll think I've done something like join the Ladies Aid Society!"

"Katie." Leland kneeled in front of her. "If you won't stay with Erin, then go to your uncle's in Chicago."

Kate sighed. She'd worked too hard to live up to her father's expectations and gain the respect of at least the majority of the crew. But what if Jeb convinced her crew she wasn't capable of running the company? They still treated her like the young girl who had tagged to the office with her father and visited them on the docks. She hadn't been in charge long enough to prove her mettle.

But murder. She'd suspected Jeb of many things, but never that. Especially her father's murder. That changed everything.

****

The Chicago bound train rocked and clattered down the track carrying Kate away from New York, her home, and her business.

After finding the household staff gone, Ross and Leland had accompanied her to Erin's house to rest while they located Spears, Mrs. Haskins, and the rest of her staff.

Their suspicions were correct. Spears had received a note from Jeb Walker, stating that he and Kate were spending the evening with friends, and they could all take the evening off.

Once that part of the mystery was solved, Ross and Leland escorted her to Delmonico's for dinner, determined to show a brave front. Her safety was in question, and she needed to hide until they found enough evidence against Jeb that the law would protect her.

They planned her departure, deciding not to alert her uncle since the wire could be intercepted. She would use the name, Elizabeth Downing. Where that name came from, Kate had no idea, but it made sense for her not to use McShane. Jeb no doubt had spies everywhere.

Once settled in the private compartment on the train, she buried her nose in the latest detective novel written by her favorite author. No matter how enthralling, she couldn't keep her mind on the story and off her problems. She rested her head on the back of the velvet-upholstered couch and stretched, then laid her book in her lap and gazed out the window.

She fingered the square cut emerald ring her father had given her on her sixteenth birthday. The birthday right after her mother left them for the Parisian social life and never returned. Weeks later her father received a packet from her mother's lawyer asking for a quick divorce.

She recalled the pain etched deep in his face, as he explained how people could fall out of love and Kate wasn't responsible. Her heart still ached when she thought of the far away looks her father would get from time to time. He'd given her mother everything any woman could possibly want, but she'd wanted something more.

Now her father was gone, and she was free to stop wearing the reminder of her mother's abandonment. Why hadn't she put it away? It had to be because her father picked it out and gave it to her out of his love and dedication for his daughter.

Outside, the coal-fired engine burped black smoke that curled over the cars, casting a shadow on the passing landscape.

She supposed there were diversions in Chicago, a society of sorts she could blend into, but it would be nothing like New York. She had no desire to spend the winter in Chicago or anywhere other than home. She prayed Ross and Leland produced enough evidence to arrest Jeb. Her company needed her.

But Jeb was a desperate man with motive and no conscience. A deadly combination.

She pulled her hair over one shoulder and combed her fingers through it, cringing at the grit of coal dust. What she wouldn't give for a hot-scented bath.

"Oh Daddy." Kate pushed her hair back from her face. "If only I'd stayed home from Europe to be there for you. You said I could do anything I set my mind to, Daddy, and that's what I mean to do."

She shook her head. Any more deep thinking and she'd go crazy. She needed a change of scene and fresh air. Ross and Leland ordered her stay in her compartment and asked the conductor to escort her to the dining car. She'd be damned if she'd make a spectacle of herself by asking for help every time she turned around.

Kate swung her feet to the floor and stood, then wound her hair and pinned it on top of her head. Glancing around the compartment to make sure her belongings were secure, she slipped into her lightweight wool coat. The air was hot and oppressive, but she'd stashed the money she'd withdrawn from her bank in the lining of the coat so she couldn't leave it unattended.

Tired, nervous, and discouraged, Kate giggled. She'd taken the idea from a character in one of the many novels she loved. A woman traveling alone was vulnerable enough without being a target for thieves. Besides, Ross had suggested a bank draft in Chicago could alert Jeb to her location.

Opening the door just enough to peek up and down the passageway, Kate stepped out and locked the door, slipping the key into her coat pocket. With no one in sight, she hurried toward the door at the end of the sleeping car and opened it.

Air rushed up, snatching her breath. The connectors clanked and swayed, and the tracks raced away below her feet. Transfixed for a moment, Kate nearly changed her mind, but to reach the rear of the train and fresh air required walking between several cars.

She scurried over the metal walk and burst into the next car, slamming the door shut.

Passengers glanced up at the noise. Panic filled her. What if the henchman was on board? She searched the curious faces, but no one resembled the man who'd driven her to The Goose Down Pub.

Kate walked down the aisle, grasping the back of each seat as she passed to keep her balance. She opened the door at the rear of the car and braved the rocking bridge, entering the next car with less drama. She pulled her handkerchief from her pocket, dabbing the perspiration from her forehead. The white linen came away coated with dust and grime.

The prospect of fresh air only two cars away made her stuff the hanky back into her coat pocket and hurry through the din of travelers.

Chapter Two

From one train car to the next, Kate noted the same things—curious glances from tired eyes, wreathed in weary faces. Fellow travelers who slept on hard seats and ate food out of baskets prepared days before.

Few passengers were fortunate enough to stretch out at night on anything resembling a bed let alone eat freshly prepared meals in the dining car. A twinge of guilt for her good fortune settled in the pit of her stomach. Was it due to the swirling odors of unwashed bodies and leftover food?

Kate quickened her pace. With one more car to pass through before she reached the caboose, she stepped into a cacophony of children. Younger ones flooded the aisle, shrieking and racing back and forth. Small ones curled in their mother's laps, thumbs or fingers latched in their mouths as they watched her pass with big round eyes.

She dodged and veered, nearly colliding with little bodies. Some women chatted amiably while others stared sightlessly out the windows, weary from days of travel.

The cloying air and constant rocking and noise threatened to make her swoon. Kate threaded through the children and scattered luggage and hurried toward the back of the car. Glancing to her left, Kate slowed her pace. A woman of about Kate's age, with auburn hair and a light dusting of freckles shadowing her creamy skin smiled. The woman's green eyes sparkled with good humor.

Kate hesitated. "Excuse me, have we met?" She

gripped the back of the nearest seat to steady herself against the sway of the car.

"I don't believe so," the woman called over the din of laughing children and murmured conversations. She had a pleasant tone and smile so she surely couldn't be a spy for Jeb Walker.

Kate leaned closer to the woman. "What's your destination?"

"A small settlement called Hope."

The car lurched. Kate stumbled and tightened her grip on the seat. She stepped aside to avoid a small child running up the aisle and chuckled at the wild blonde curls and delightful shriek.

"Hope sounds like a good destination. I'm in search of open air. Would you like to join me?"

The friendly female face made Kate's heart ache with longing to talk about things men didn't understand. She'd only been away from New York for a short time, but she already missed her dear friend, Erin.

"I'd love to." The woman's smile widened. She took a moment to ask the older lady across from her to watch her satchel, then stood and followed Kate.

Once in the empty caboose, they stepped out the door onto the small platform. The track raced out beneath them, and the train rocked and clattered, but fresh air and open countryside unfolded around them.

"Ah, this is much better." Kate closed her eyes and drew in a deep breath. Tension flowed out in a big sigh. Over the past few days, she'd been proposed to, nearly kidnapped, and discovered the startling theory that Jeb might be responsible for her father's death.

She opened her eyes, tightening her grip on the railing. Even out here in the middle of the country, far from New York, she must keep up her guard, watch and wait for Jeb to make another move.

Vulnerability swept over her, even more so than when she'd found her entire staff missing.

"Yes, it's wonderful," the other woman answered, startling Kate out of her apprehension. "Are you all right?" She laid her hand on Kate's.

Battling the panic threatening to envelop her, Kate lifted her face to the sun. "I'm fine. I'm just heady with fresh air and freedom. At least temporarily."

The woman laughed. "Since this train originated in New York, you haven't been cooped up for too long. Is that where you're from?"

Kate smiled at her. "Yes, but I'm not good at being cooped up. Tell me, where's Hope and what's taking you there? It sounds like an intriguing place, something I could use right now."

"It's in the northern part of Idaho Territory. Why am I going there? Well, it's a rather unusual story."

Kate laughed. "Believe me, my life has become an unusual story. Please, share it with me."

The woman sighed and gazed out over the open land. "I was born and raised in Boston, the daughter of a dock worker and a dressmaker. Both of whom are now gone."

"I'm so sorry." Kate could sympathize with the loss of her father so fresh. She squeezed the other woman's hand. "I lost my father six weeks ago." The words still didn't sound real, but they stung her eyes with tears and made her shoulders slump with loss.

"I'm sorry to have upset you." The other woman swiped at her own tears and turned to Kate. "By the way, I'm Mary Catherine Leary." She held out her hand.

Kate accepted her hand shake. "Kathleen McShane, but please call me Kate." Alarm bells sounded in her head. She'd used her real name and not the alias of Elizabeth Downing.

"It seems we both have very Irish names." The woman's eyes sparkled again, and her mouth curved up in a wide smile. "How interesting." Mary Catherine looked down at their clasped hands. "My what a beautiful ring!"

Kate fingered the emerald and smiled. "Thank you. My father gave it to me years ago." The warm sun rays dimmed.

Kate glanced back at Mary Catherine. "I think we share more than our names." She laughed. "I realize why you seem familiar. It's because you and I look very much alike! Maybe we're long lost relatives?"

"That would be wonderful, wouldn't it?" Mary Catherine slipped her hand out from under Kate's and patted it.

"Please continue with your story." Kate prided herself on being a good judge of character, and Mary Catherine didn't seem in the least like someone who would assist Jeb or the henchman.

"I'm an only child. My mother had a lengthy bout with consumption, and anything of value was sold to pay for clinics and medical attention." The increasing wind whipped a strand of hair from Mary Catherine's severe hairstyle. "As a result, I had very little left when she passed away."

"How sad."

Mary Catherine nodded. "My father was killed when he stepped in front of an ice wagon. My mother died a few days later of a broken heart. It turned out so different from how we imagined it would." Her chest lifted and she released a long, deep sigh. "She'd been sick for so long, I never dreamed Daddy would go first."

"Oh, Mary Catherine."

Pain filled her companion's eyes, and Kate was struck with a dose of reality. She may be without family, but money and position secured her in this world. Mary Catherine had nothing.

Mary Catherine sniffed and pulled a handkerchief from her threadbare jacket to dab her eyes. "It's so good to talk with someone who cares."

"Do you have other family?"

"Distant, yes. My relatives didn't help us when we needed it, and I have no intention of showing up on their doorsteps now as an object of pity, or scorn."

"But why travel so far away from home?"

"Marriage."

"You don't sound happy about it. Is he someone you met in Boston?"

The loosened strand of hair turned to reddish gold in the sunlight and slapped across Mary Catherine's face. She tucked it behind her ear. "No, the only man in Boston I'd ever marry has no interest in me." The clatter of metal against metal increased, forcing her to shout. "I answered a newspaper advertisement placed by a gentleman looking for a wife mainly to care for his son."

Kate tore her gaze from the soothing grass covered hills and blinked at Mary Catherine. "You responded to an advertisement?"

Mary Catherine shrugged. "There are plenty of mail-order brides who find contentment."

"But you're in love with someone else."

She turned away. "He doesn't love me. I can't afford to wait on the chance he changes his mind. I'm nearly penniless since paying for my parents' burials and the remaining debt." She lifted her face to the fresh wind.

"There's always another choice," Kate said, reminded of her escape from Jeb. "Traveling three thousand miles to marry a man you've never met is frightening."

"I have no other options."

"What's his name, this man in Hope?"

"Ethan Howland. He has a seven-year old son

named Will and owns a ranch. From the pictures he sent, he's a very handsome man, though not in the same way as Frank."

"Frank?"

"The man in Boston."

Kate couldn't believe her ears. There had to be other options for this poor young woman. "Perhaps someday we'll meet under better circumstances." Kate patted her hand.

"I would like that." Mary Catherine's eyes lit up.

"Have you spoken to Frank about your feelings?"

Mary Catherine gasped. "Talk to him about it? Why I couldn't just come out of the blue and tell him how I feel."

"Why not? You'd rather travel to the backside of nowhere and marry a stranger than take a chance?"

"I love Frank with all my heart, but I'm afraid to pressure him. I don't have your courage."

Kate decided to drop the matter. She didn't want to pursue her love for Frank, so Kate had to respect her decision.

"I think I'll return to my seat." Mary Catherine turned to Kate and smiled. "Thank you for asking me to join you, it's been lovely. I hope we meet again. Maybe you'll tire of Chicago and travel farther west."

"Perhaps." Kate turned to soak up the passing scenery and enjoy the fresh air. It really was glorious to be out of the train for a few minutes, even on her own.

The wind picked up and whipped the pins from her hair. She attempted to restrain the thick mass from completely coming undone and failed.

Lost in her conversation with Mary Catherine, then her own thoughts, she hadn't noticed the gathering black clouds roiling across the sky. The train was headed straight into a storm.

"Drat, I don't want to go back inside." A flash of

lightning filled the air. Kate jumped back from the railing with a shriek. Thunder cracked and boomed over the noise of the train. She stepped back again, feeling behind for the doorknob, her eyes on the sky for another terrifying flash of lightning.

Instead of the door, Kate's hands encountered fabric. She turned and a scream tore from deep in her body. She leaped against the rail.

The driver, the henchman who had taken her to The Goose Down, stood in front of her. Even in the shadow of his hat, the jagged scar running up one side of his face pulled the corner of his mouth into a cruel smile.

Kate's heart threatened to explode. She was trapped.

"Thought you could pull one over on me, didn't 'cha?" The henchman leered, exposing tobacco stained teeth. "Well, you was wrong. You and me are gettin' off this train in Chicago and catchin' another one back to New York."

"I'm not going anywhere with you," Kate said, her voice squeaking as she lifted her chin and willed her knees not to buckle.

"You made a fool of me once, lady. Yer not gettin' away with it again. There's nowhere to run this time."

"I'm sure you've been ordered not to kill me," Kate said, scrambling for a trump card.

"No, I can't kill ya," the man said, his tone a long drawl. "But there are other ways, better ways to get what I want." He trailed his forefinger along her jaw line.

Kate gagged and jerked away. "Don't touch me."

"Oh, I'm going to touch ya all right. It's a long way from here to New York." He moved closer.

Her heart pounding, Kate edged along the rail of the platform, inching her way to the door. If she could get around him, she'd run into the train for help.

"What do ya think yer doin'? Yer not escapin' me again, missy." The man stepped closer, close enough for her to smell the oily stench of his unwashed body. She took shallow breaths, working to slow her racing heart.

How would Sherlock Holmes, the character in the new book she should have kept reading instead of coming outside, have handled this predicament? Heavens, he was too smart to be in this predicament.

"I'm tired. I want to return to my seat." Kate wasn't strong enough to fight him off, but she could outsmart him. "I have a private sleeping compartment."

He grinned and gripped her upper arm. "Now yer talkin', sweetheart. But I'm warnin' you, pull that little popper at me again and I won't be nice."

"Oh, no. Please, come with me." She slowly reached for the doorknob, fighting the urge to be sick.

"No, allow me. I'm a gentleman ya know." The henchman flashed what he must think a charming smile.

Kate's legs quivered, her thoughts raced. Ross and Leland were too far away to help, and she had no desire to endanger Mary Catherine Leary.

She stumbled into the first passenger car and choked down the fear bubbling into her throat. Her chest tightened. Her life was in danger, but at all costs, she had to protect the innocent women and children filling the car.

The noise dimmed, and the activity around her blurred. Stiff with fear, she moved toward the other end of the car.

They passed Mary Catherine, who had settled back in her seat and conversed with the older woman sitting across from her. She smiled at Kate but didn't seem to notice the henchman. Kate smiled and kept moving.

Good heavens. She'd always been calm, collected, but the man pressing against her back made her want to run and scream. She'd escaped him once before; she could do it again. Think, Kate, think.

She couldn't think. She needed someone strong, damn it, she needed a man to help. It irked her. She was as capable and intelligent as any man, and she had her derringer, but she couldn't risk shooting an innocent bystander in the struggle.

They passed into another car. Without slowing her pace, Kate searched out the passengers lining both sides of the aisle. Her gaze lit on a particularly well-built man slouched in a seat facing the rear of the train. His black Stetson shadowed his eyes. She couldn't tell if he was awake or napping, but she was encouraged by his broad shoulders and square, whisker-roughened jaw.

She slowed her steps, the henchman nudged her. Blood roared through her ears, and panic blurred her vision. This sleeping stranger might be her only chance to escape.

Kate stopped. The henchman growled and shoved against her. She sidestepped, slammed against the edge of the seat, then toppled into the stranger's lap.

"Ohph! What the hell—" The man jerked straight up, the Stetson slid to the back of his head, and his arms came around her.

Kate didn't have to pretend to gasp. "Oh! I'm so sorry."

Deep, dark, brown eyes pinned her like a butterfly on a board, her stomach fluttered and she nearly panted. He was the most masculine, most handsome man she'd ever seen.

He lifted a dark brow. "Are you all right?"

She released a sigh then remembered the

henchman and rolled her eyes to one side, hoping to convey her distress. The stranger looked over her head toward the awful man. Thank heavens he got the message.

"I'm terribly sorry. I was so clumsy," she chattered on, sliding her hands up his hard chest for leverage to push out of his lap. Under the black leather vest, something sharp pricked her finger. A pin. A piece of metal. She traced the shape like a blind person. A star. She'd landed in the lap of a lawman.

"Come on now, leave the nice man alone." The henchman pulled on Kate's arm. "Sorry sir, the misses is kind of clumsy these days. Delicate condition ya know."

Kate blanched. The very idea of expecting a child with that odious man made her want to wrench, but she needed to buy time for the lawman to surprise her kidnapper.

The train swung with a bend in the tracks throwing Kate back into the lawman's arms. She whispered in his ear. "He's kidnapping me."

The lawman's expression didn't alter. His dark brows stayed straight above his eyes.

Kate pushed out of his arms. Damn, he didn't believe her. She was on her own. His large capable hands went around her waist and helped her to her feet. The henchman wrenched on her arm.

Losing her balance, Kate fell into the empty seat across the aisle and grasped the arms of the chair to steady herself. A scuffle began behind her.

She moved as quickly as the small space and her skirts would allow.

The lawman towered over her erstwhile kidnapper. He backed the smaller man into the seat with his fists. She should run to her compartment and lock the door, but her legs wouldn't obey.

Gripping the vacant seat, she stood aside as the

two men scuffled in the narrow space. The lawman may be the larger and stronger of the two, but fear of arrest fueled the henchman's strength.

The henchman slipped the lawman's hold. Kate shrieked as he ran down the aisle to the rear of the train. The lawman ran after him. Kate chased the lawman. She had to make sure the henchman escaped or was knocked out.

If he told the truth about her identity, her disguise would be over. She'd be forced to return to New York. Wait a minute. Kate slowed her pace. Would going home be so bad? Wasn't that what she wanted?

Shaking her head to clear it, Kate caught up with the men in time to watch Jeb's hired man jump off the platform she and Mary Catherine had enjoyed a short time ago. The storm was in its full fury. Rain pelted the pristine black of the lawman's new Stetson and soaked her coat.

The would-be kidnapper hit the muddy ground rolling.

Kate gripped the rail. "Is he alive?"

The lawman remained quiet, his eyes narrowed against the wind and rain. The henchman stopped rolling and pushed to his feet in slow pain-filled movements. He looked toward them as the train continued its way down the track, then turned, and limped away.

"I guess that answers your question."

Kate's knees buckled. She tightened her grip on the railing and leaned against it. For now, she was safe. "I can't thank you enough for coming to my rescue."

The lawman looked down at her, water running off the brim of his hat. Kate shivered as the fear left her body and cold entered it. He took her arm and hustled her into the caboose and out of the storm.

He stepped away to take off his hat and shake

off the moisture. Creased by the hat band, his dark hair curled over his ears and brushed the collar of his blue shirt. Dark lashes framed his dark eyes.

Everything about this man intrigued her.

"Why did he want to kidnap you?"

Kate swallowed hard and drew in a deep breath. "I do appreciate your help, but honestly—is it sheriff?"

"Yes, it's going to be sheriff when I reach my new town. Now back to that man." He lifted his chin toward the end of the train. "What was that all about?"

"I—I was getting fresh air, right out there." Kate pointed to the platform. "When that horrible man accosted me! I didn't know what else to do, so I followed his orders. I'm so thankful you were on the train."

The sheriff narrowed his eyes and stared down at her. "You said he was kidnapping you. Why?"

"Did I say that? Oh dear, I guess I didn't know what else to call it. I was so frightened." Kate mentally scrambled. "I appreciate your quick thinking, Sheriff."

"You're the one with quick thinking. How did you know I was a lawman?"

"I didn't. I took a chance. You looked young and strong; that was my main objective." Kate's face grew warm, and she switched her gaze to the passing scenery, noting that the terrain was beginning to subtly change.

"Look," the sheriff said, pointing in the direction they were traveling. "We'll reach Chicago early in the morning. I can send a wire to nearby towns, but I need to know why."

Kate glanced up at him. A dark shadow brushed his jaw, testifying to the hours since he'd last shaved. His tanned skin stretched over high cheekbones and a wide forehead. There was no doubt about it; the man was handsome and rugged in a way that sent thrills from her toes to her scalp.

But she wasn't looking for a man. She was looking for a space of peace while Ross and Leland found a way to outsmart Jeb Walker.

"I really must return to my car; I'm feeling quite tired after my ordeal."

"I don't doubt it." He drilled her with his dark eyes. "I want some answers. Why would he kidnap you?"

"Sheriff, I explained why I used that word, didn't I?" Kate's voice squeaked.

"Yes, Miss, you did. I've learned people speak the truth when they're caught off guard."

"I only assumed his intent." Kate shivered at the memory. "If you'll be so kind as to excuse me, I do need to lie down. Thank you again for your help."

"My pleasure." He tipped his hat. "If you change your mind…"

"I'll let you know." Kate turned away before she changed her mind and confided in him. His rugged handsomeness and slight southern twang made her want to throw herself in his arms and ask him to protect her.

What had happened to the independent business woman? The past six weeks had been spent convincing the men on the Board and the men who worked for the company that she had the strength and capability of any man.

Kate looked straight ahead as she hurried into the first passenger car.

"Kate, are you all right?" Mary Catherine stood next to her seat, her auburn brows knit together.

Kate cringed. She'd slipped and used her real name with her new acquaintance. "Yes, I'm fine." She explained what happened after Mary Catherine returned to her seat.

"I'm so sorry. I didn't realize you were in danger

until that man ran through my car with the other man chasing him. What happened to him?" Mary Catherine kept her voice low, yet loud enough to be heard over the hubbub of the passengers and the clatter of the train.

"He jumped off the back of the train but got up and walked away." Kate looked around to find the other passengers returning to their own business. "I'd rather not discuss this here. Someone might be getting off in Chicago, and my uncle doesn't need the scandal. Please don't mention our conversation to anyone."

"You have my word."

"Thank you. I hope you won't think me rude, but I need to lie down and rest." Kate smiled to soften her words. Her head spun with the events of the past fifteen minutes. Mercy, she never would have dreamed of so much happening to her!

"Certainly. You need to rest." Mary Catherine laid her hand on Kate's arm, her face wreathed in regret.

Kate hugged the other woman, then hurried to her compartment. Two people had offered to help her in the last few minutes. Maybe she wasn't so alone after all.

But she couldn't let her guard down. Jeb Walker had tracked her to the train. He must know about her assumed name. She should either return to New York or take on a new identity and destination. At this moment, the henchman was on his way to the nearest town where he'd send a telegram to Jeb. She'd be a prime target when she detrained in Chicago.

She walked through the car where she'd landed in the sheriff's lap and stared at his empty seat. He hadn't passed her while she spoke to Mary Catherine. She frowned. Where could he be? Shrugging, she continued through to the next car.

She couldn't become distracted with anyone, no matter how handsome he was. Oh, and the sheriff was handsome. And masculine beyond belief. Mentally slapping herself for slowing her step, Kate hurried to her door.

Her father always told her to glean the particulars and turn them to her advantage. Life handed you experiences to profit by. Of course her father had turned a tiny shipyard into a multimillion dollar enterprise.

At this moment, her father would say, "Katie girl, you have to think each move out completely."

She smiled as she recalled his soft Irish brogue and how he'd always called her "Katie Girl." Her heart squeezed hard. She missed him so much; she could close her eyes and smell his scent of fine tobacco and leathery cologne. She could still imagine his voice and the way his green eyes sparkled when he teased her.

She swiped at an errant tear. Her father had taught her to use her wits and to think things out. She had to make an alternate plan.

Mary Catherine Leary.

The name echoed through her mind as she stepped into her compartment.

Mary Catherine was traveling west to marry a man she didn't love, had never met. She loved Frank, but Frank was in Boston, and Mary Catherine didn't have money to stay there long enough to convince him of her love.

Kate had money. Plenty of money. She could fund Mary Catherine's return to Boston and take her place as the mail-order bride. They resembled each other.

Hurrying back through the train to Mary Catherine's car, Kate took her arm. "Mary Catherine, please come to my compartment. I have an idea you're going to like."

Chapter Three

Kate closed the door and wrapped her arms around her fluttering middle. Mary Catherine loved her idea to trade places. The plan was crazy but brilliant at the same time.

Tomorrow, when the train left Chicago, Kate would be on it. She'd change trains in St. Paul, Minnesota, and travel to Idaho Territory. At the first opportunity, she'd wire Ross and explain the needed change of plans in some cryptic language.

The thought resounded through her brain and gave her goose bumps. She'd faced danger and without the help of any man, she'd created an alternate plan. Well, almost by herself.

The sheriff had rescued her from her abductor, but Kate wasn't convinced she wouldn't have thought of some means of escape before they reached her compartment.

She flopped down on the couch that folded out into a bed and laid her head on the red velvet upholstery. What a day! At least it had taken a minimum of convincing to make Mary Catherine take her offer of return fare to Boston and money to tide her over until she could find a seamstress position.

Feeling too warm, Kate doffed her cumbersome coat. The letters from Ethan Howland to his mail-order bride were stuffed in her deep skirt pocket. They'd be the script for the part she'd play when she left the train in Hope.

****

Seth Morgan stepped from the caboose to the

open platform and gripped the rail. He inhaled the fresh evening air then reached for his breast pocket and the cheroot James McShane had given him the last night Seth saw him alive.

He dragged a match across the sole of his boot. The sulfur flared in the dark night. Seth touched it to the end of the cigar and drew in several quick, deep breaths. The end of the cigar caught and glowed. Shaking out the match, he flipped it over the railing. No danger of fires after the storm they'd passed through.

Stars twinkled overhead, dotting the soot-colored sky. Never one to travel on a train, Seth couldn't wait to reach his new assignment. The confinement and boredom of the trip had only been broken by the beautiful and very puzzling woman who landed in his lap.

His body tightened as he recalled her firm bottom against his thighs. Damn, it'd been a long time since he'd held a woman. Her fragrance still clung to his shirt.

Too bad he couldn't forget his decision to stay away from women and join her in her fancy compartment. He'd learned long ago there was no such thing as easy come, easy go. Women either wanted security or money, and he had neither.

He'd have to be wet behind the ears to believe she didn't know that man. Yet, the way she'd dodged his questions told him she wasn't a pro.

He'd bet she was running from an abusive father or husband.

The hired man he'd chased off the train could be in a town right now, contacting whoever sent him. Chances were, by the time they reached Chicago, her father, husband, or whoever the heck she was running from, would know her location.

Seth puffed on his cigar, relishing the expensive blend of tobacco, and thought back when he'd met with James McShane about Allen Johnston, the wayward employee of McShane Walker Shipping. Johnston had worked out of the Houston office until he caught wind of Seth's investigation into a string of robberies involving the Santa Fe line.

When Johnston slipped out of Houston, Seth chased him. He'd ended up at the docks in New York. Docks belonging to McShane Walker Shipping. James McShane was an affable and intelligent businessman who Seth liked immediately.

Finding James dead, slumped over his desk, still felt like a punch in the gut. Another good man gone.

Since Seth had been with James the evening he died, the police had questioned him. Satisfied with his answers, they released him to leave town anytime he wanted to. He'd remained in New York, combing the streets and waterfront for Allen Johnston.

The man was not only a thief and wanted in New Mexico, Arizona, and Texas, but he'd employed the man who killed Griff, Seth's mentor and old friend.

He ground his teeth against the cigar and shook his head. Well, that chapter of his life appeared to be over. Alan Johnston was nowhere to be found. Seth resigned from the Texas Rangers and accepted the sheriff job out west. He didn't belong in Texas or New York.

He stubbed the cigar out on the iron hand rail and flipped it into the darkness. The crisp, moist night air flushed out the smoke and relaxed him. Open air. It's where he belonged, not in the train car and not in the city.

****

Morning broke after a long, restless night on her fold-out bed. Sunlight spilled over the prairie turning it to mellow tones of gold and yellow.

Kate finished dressing as the train pulled into

Chicago, the last mark of civilization before she traveled west.

Misgivings coursed through her. She was headed into the unknown—to a land where no one knew her…no one cared about her.

She shoved her clothes into her satchel. If she hurried, she could have a conductor unload her trunk, the trunk she'd traded with Mary Catherine. She'd still pay Mary Catherine's way back to Boston, but Kate would stay in Chicago as planned.

She pushed her arms into her coat and leaned down to look out the window. The platform swarmed with people, some were leaving the train, others boarding. She didn't see her attacker. There must be cabs close by. She'd hurry across the platform and find one to take her to her uncle's house.

Her hand on the doorknob, goose bumps prickled the back of her neck. Kate turned back to the window. A lone man stood close to the train, looking up and down the platform. He wasn't the henchman who'd kidnapped her in New York and followed her on the train, but he was looking for someone.

He could work for Jeb. The henchman could have wired him about her escape.

She'd be nabbed the moment she stepped off the train.

She released the handle, and the satchel fell to the floor with a thud. She couldn't change her plans now. She had to stay on the train and continue with the brilliant plan to take Mary Catherine's place. As a mail-order bride.

Her stomach churning, she sank to the bed. The reality of what she was about to do paralyzed her.

She pressed her hand against her breast. Miles and miles existed between here and Idaho Territory. Too long to stay cooped up in this compartment. She'd wait until they pulled out of the station, then pay for the additional fare and find something to eat. Frightened out of her wits, she'd skipped dinner last night.

Voices echoed down the hall outside her door. Kate sprang off the bed and braced the only chair in the compartment under the doorknob. She fumbled with her coat and retrieved the derringer, her fingers wrapping around the cold metal.

Curling up on the couch, she laid the gun next to her and began to sort through Ethan's letters. She might be forced to continue the masquerade, but she'd end the ruse soon. In the meantime, she'd learn more about the man whose life she was about to invade.

The letters laid out the plan for their nuptials to take place one week after her arrival. One week! That certainly didn't give her much time. Arrangements were made for her, or rather Mary Catherine, to stay with his friends, Kerry and Janet Malone. The Malones lived in town, while Ethan lived a couple of hours away on his ranch.

The train lurched, the coupling between the cars clanged. Kate gasped, then rested her head against the seat. Never in her life had she been so jumpy.

The train jerked forward then picked up speed as it rolled out of the Chicago station. Her heart fluttered, and a weight settled in her chest. She'd give Ross and Leland a few weeks at the most to accomplish the task of removing the threat, then she'd return home. She had no intention of spending the winter in some Godforsaken backwoods.

She yearned for a cup of coffee and some breakfast, but someone may have boarded in Chicago and be combing the train for her at this very moment.

An image of the handsome lawman flashed through her mind. That was another reason to use caution. He clearly suspected her of no good. Right now, a good guy could be as dangerous to her location and disguise, as a bad guy.

Footsteps sounded outside her door. She held her breath, letting it out when a pounding sounded on her door.

"Conductor here. Ticket please."

Kate scrambled off the couch and moved the chair, opening the door just a crack.

"Hello. I've decided to travel to Hope, Idaho Territory. How much do I owe?"

"Pay me through St. Paul then buy a ticket when you change trains." The man named the fare, and Kate turned her back and retrieved the correct amount from her coat lining.

The man thanked her and turned away.

"Wait." Kate stuck her head through the opening and looked up and down the hall.

"Yes?"

"I had some trouble with a passenger yesterday. He jumped off the train, but I'm still a little reluctant to leave my compartment."

"Ah, you must be the woman the Texas Ranger told me about."

Kate blinked rapidly. "Texas Ranger?"

"Yes, the Ranger who saved you from the kidnapper. He told me about the incident."

"Oh, well, what I wondered was if you or someone could deliver a breakfast tray? A pot of coffee too, please. I'm nervous about venturing to the dining car just yet."

Her stomach rumbled. The conductor smiled. "Of course. I'll have someone bring it right away."

"Thank you so much." Kate smiled and closed the door, her shoulders slumping on a big sigh. At least she wouldn't starve.

Hmm, a Ranger. That explained his rugged, outdoor look. But handsome or not, he posed a threat to her safety.

She sat on the couch and watched the passing scenery. It'd be miles and miles before they reached St. Paul. A thought crossed her mind. She sat up straight and pressed her hand to her throat. Oh dear. What if the conductor connected her with her ticketed name? What if he mentioned it to the Ranger?

A tap at the door had her grabbing for her derringer.

"Miss Downing, I have your breakfast."

Kate pushed off the couch and fumbled with her coat to withdraw more bills.

"One moment, please." She slid her derringer into her dress pocket and moved the chair. A young man smiled, his hands full with a large tray, holding a plate of eggs and bacon, a plate of toast, and a small pot of coffee complete with cream and sugar.

"Oh, my, it looks wonderful." She stepped back and motioned for him to enter the compartment and set the tray on her small side table. "Thank you so much. Will this cover it?"

The young man took the bills and nodded. "Just fine, Miss. Let me know if you need anything else."

"I will, thank you, again."

Once he left, Kate closed the door and propped the chair under the handle. One meal down and several to go. She'd go out later, but she wouldn't make the mistake she'd made yesterday. She'd be sure never to be alone.

The day crawled by. Kate spent her time watching the changing scenery, studying the letters, and napping. When darkness fell, she lit a lamp and went back to the letters, memorizing every detail. She pondered over the new land ahead of her and the people she would involve in her deception. Dishonesty didn't settle well with her. Jeb Walker would attest to her straight forward way of approaching a matter.

Kate set the letter beside her on the red velvet couch she'd later make out into her bed. Breakfast had worn off long ago, and it was well past the dinner hour. Surely there'd be something in the dining car. Regardless of the risk, she'd die of boredom if she didn't get out of this compartment for at least a few minutes.

Despite the cloying heat in the room, Kate slipped into her coat. She slid her derringer into a pocket and cracked open the door. Not another soul appeared as she hurried from her car forward into the dining car.

Checking behind her, Kate slipped into a booth the moment she arrived. She glanced toward the window and gasped. Then giggled nervously and shook her head. She'd been frightened by her own reflection against the inky night. Damn Jeb Walker for putting her in this position.

"Miss?"

Kate glanced around, her heart pounding.

The same young man who delivered her breakfast hours ago, smiled at her, then concern drew up his brows. "I'm sorry, Miss. I didn't mean to startle you."

Kate pressed one hand against her chest, willing her heart to slow. "Hello, again. I realize it's past the dinner hour, but I'm afraid I slept through it. Is anything available?"

"I might be able to make a sandwich."

"That would be wonderful." She gripped the edge of the table as the train rounded a curve in the track.

"I'll be right back."

She turned back to the window and groaned over her bedraggled reflection. Smoothing her hair with both hands, she turned her attention to the unoccupied car. White linen covered tables lent an air of expectancy for the next meal when passengers would converge for breakfast.

The late hour and solitude sent a chill up her spine. At home, staff hovered over her night and day. She not only missed them for convenience, but also security. For the first time in her life, she was on her own.

"Miss, here's a roast beef sandwich."

"Oh!" Kate shook her head in disgust for over reacting to everything. "I'm sorry. I was lost in my thoughts."

The steward smiled sheepishly and set a plate in front of her. "Will this do?"

Kate's mouth watered at the generous slices of bread and thickly sliced beef and cheese. "It looks wonderful, thank you."

The attendant poured a glass of water and a cup of coffee. The aroma curled around her, beckoning her to take a sip, relishing the full flavor.

She glanced at her young companion, finding him at a table near the other end of the car, polishing a mountain of silverware.

The sandwich tasted as good as it looked. Heavenly. Amazingly, everything tasted good when you were truly hungry. She closed her eyes and chewed.

"That good, huh?"

Kate snapped her eyes open, gasped, then coughed as the half-swallowed bite lodged in her throat. Her eyes watered and panic set in. She worked the food down her restricted throat and patted her upper chest. The glass of water appeared in her hand, and she took several sips, focusing on each breath.

A look of alarm on his face, the Ranger who had occupied far too many of her thoughts, patted her back.

She coughed again, then dabbed her eyes with the white linen napkin from her lap. Her throat still hurt, but the food had continued its journey to her stomach. She leaned back in the chair and glanced at him. Her mouth went dry.

The Ranger sank to one knee beside her. Being this close to him made her feel very small and defenseless. What if he wasn't who and what he appeared?

"Yes, I'm fine as long as you quit sneaking up on me."

"I assumed you were getting off the train in Chicago."

Kate mentally scrambled. Had she mentioned leaving the train in Chicago? "No, I'm traveling farther west."

He slowly nodded, still in his kneeled position, his hand on the back of her chair.

"I've recovered, so you no longer need to hover." She leaned back, hoping he'd stand and give her some room. Better yet, that he'd leave the dining car.

He slowly nodded and stood to tower over her. "It appears my job on this trip is saving damsels in distress. Have you remembered anything about the man who tried to kidnap you? Anything that might help the law capture him?"

The fact he was the most handsome man she'd ever met became irrelevant with each pushy, nosey word.

"To tell you the truth," Kate said, tearing her sandwich in two. "I've tried to erase the pathetic man from my mind. I'm sure you can understand I don't want to dwell on the episode."

"Don't blame you." The former Ranger slid onto the seat opposite her. "But people are kidnapped for a reason."

Kate deliberately took her time chewing a bite of her sandwich. Could the man not take a hint?

"I appreciate your concern, but I have no desire to involve myself with that—that—man again. We saw him jump off the train. He's no doubt heading back where he belongs." She picked up her glass of water, irritated when her hand trembled.

"Well, Miss, uh, it appears we've never exchanged names." He planted his elbows on the table and leaned on folded hands.

Kate ran her tongue over her teeth, pursed her lips and smiled. "Mary Catherine Leary." She held out her hand.

"Seth Morgan."

His large hand enveloped her much smaller, pale one. Her breath caught at his touch, his callouses a contrast to her soft skin. She mentally searched for the composure she drew on when facing down the board of directors, and Jeb Walker.

"Mr. Morgan, I'm grateful for your help and your concern, but please forget what happened yesterday."

He slowly released her hand and leaned back in his seat. "I'm not giving up on this case."

"I'd hardly call it a case." She waved her hand, then spread her napkin on the table and laid her sandwich on it. "Do whatever makes you happy. I prefer not to think of it again. Now, if you'll excuse me?" She left the dining car, her back ramrod straight. She couldn't wait to be away from Seth Morgan. The man unsettled her far too much.

Chapter Four

Seth Morgan stepped off the train and nudged his hat brim. Black smoke puffed from the engine's stack sending a fine coat of dust over the surprising number of people crowding the platform.

Damn, it felt good to stand on solid ground.

He searched the faces of travelers and the people greeting them. He couldn't remember the last time someone met him at the train, or anywhere for that matter. In his telegram, the mayor said he'd meet Seth at the station. If he didn't show up, Seth would find his new office.

"Coming through!"

Seth stepped to one side, narrowly missing a porter with a steamer trunk. The burly man set it on the platform with a thud.

"Damn women," the man muttered. "They pack enough for two people."

"They're something all right." Seth spotted Mary Catherine, down the platform several car lengths, looking like a rose in a field of daisies. So, she'd traveled clear to Idaho. The conductor had mentioned the name, Miss Downing, not Leary.

Strange. The whole thing was strange. What in tarnation was she doing in a rough western town? She wasn't an innocent victim, he was sure of that. No one was randomly kidnapped.

Unless the man was after a wild tumble in the sack. Yeah, that could be. She was a looker, no doubt about it. His instincts had always served him well, and they told him there was more to her than met the eye. He planned to keep a sharp eye on Mary

Catherine Leary, or whoever she was.

"Sheriff Morgan?" A man's voice snapped Seth out of his surveillance of the woman. He turned to face a short, rotund man wearing a bowler. Dressed in a wool suit, starched collar, and string tie, he carried a coat of dust from head to foot.

"I'm Seth Morgan."

The man held out his hand. "Samuel Ellis, Mayor of Hope. Very happy to make your acquaintance, Sheriff."

Seth nodded, allowing the smaller man to pump his hand with exuberance. "Likewise. I see your letter was accurate, Mr. Ellis. There's a drought all right. Amazing when you consider the size of that lake." Seth turned and looked out over the glistening, blue and green body of water. "Nothing like that in Texas. How's the fishing?"

"Marvelous, my man, marvelous! Yes, indeed the fishing's grand. So is the drought. Come along and we'll talk on the way into town. You know, you aren't the first illustrious visitor Hope has had this year, no sir. General William Tecumseh Sherman graced us with his presence for most of the summer. Stayed at the Hope Hotel."

The mayor motioned for Seth to follow him, starting a litany about the railroad moving its Rocky Mountain Division Point back from Montana. He'd covered all the information in a letter, but Seth half listened to the repeat of what a teaming town Hope had become. The other half of his attention was fixed on seeing who met Mary Catherine.

The Mayor stopped walking. "Sheriff, is something wrong?"

"No." Seth slowly shook his head. "I'd like to wait and make sure one of my fellow travelers is all right."

"Certainly. I'll meet you at the sheriff's office in thirty minutes. You can't miss it. Take the stairs up the hill and turn right on the main street."

Seth nodded and watched Miss Leary. She still stood alone on the platform, looking around. He turned back to the Mayor. "I appreciate you meeting me, Mayor Ellis. I'll get my gear and horse off the train and find my way."

****

Kate waited on the platform while passengers streamed around her, some to stay in Hope, others stretching their legs before re-boarding the train for the continued trip to Seattle.

She might be the new chairman of the board of one of the largest shipping companies on the east coast, but leaving the train scared her to death. It'd become her refuge since leaving New York.

Since that night in the dining car, she'd done her best to avoid Seth Morgan. She was grateful for his rescue, but she couldn't risk his interference with her plan.

"Someone meeting you, Miss?"

Kate started, then turned to face the train attendant. "I think so." She glanced around the platform and expelled a breath of exhaustion. Was someone meeting her? The letters to Mary Catherine said Ethan would meet her, but the crowd on the platform thinned.

She walked toward the end of the puffing engine and stood in awe over the view. Lake Pend Oreille.

She'd read about it in Ethan's letters. Breathtaking, from its deep shades of blue-green to the steep, heavily treed mountains jutting at a sharp angle along one shore. Small islands dotted the waters, and another range of mountains framed the western horizon.

Turning back toward the town perched on the hillside above her, she let out another long breath. East of Chicago, this had been a carefully devised plan. Now, she stood on the edge of the frontier town of Hope, gazing over the awesome lake and acre after acre of forest covered land, and the hastiness of the plan hit her. She glanced around, her heart beat quickened, her palms grew damp. Shops and restaurants were her territory, not this vast wilderness.

"What have I done?" she murmured.

"Help you, Miss?"

The attendant remained at her side. The cautious expression in his eyes, confirmed Kate's suspicion. She was crazy.

"I'm fine. I'll be just fine." The reassurance was more for her than the nice man. "Tell me, do you know the Malones?" Kate's heart pitter-pattered.

"Do you mean Kerry Malone?"

"Yes." Kate nodded.

"Sure I know Kerry. He came with the railroad and owns the Smithy. They your family?"

"No. They're—they're friends." The ruse began. She'd stepped off the train into the life of a mail-order bride. She could only hope to contact Ross soon and convey the urgency of her return to New York. "Could you direct me to their home?"

Her mind fogged, and the blood rushed through her ears. She tried but couldn't absorb a word the man said. Could she really pretend to be Ethan Howland's fiancée?

The man stopped talking. Kate blinked out of her inner debate. "Thank you for your help."

The attendant walked away, but Kate didn't budge. She could change her mind. The train still sat on the tracks, idling, until the water tanks were filled and the wood boxes full. She'd journey on to Seattle. Yes, that's what she'd do.

Glancing around for her trunk, she froze.

Seth Morgan, his black Stetson tilted back on his head, his hands on his trim hips, stood next to the depot, his dark, narrowed eyes scanning the area. A shorter man in a suit and bowler stood next to him, chattering away.

"Oh no," she whispered. Could Hope be his destination, or was he just stretching his legs? Kate's mind raced. Could she be arrested for impersonating Mary Catherine? Even if she had permission? She couldn't simply run off and leave Mary Catherine's trunk on the platform. Seth Morgan would chase her to Seattle and arrest her. She'd be suspected of murdering poor Mary Catherine.

She had to think. She had to get her trunk back on the train and hide in her compartment.

She turned away and started toward the attendant who'd tried to help her.

"Excuse me, Miss Leary. You staying in Hope or going to Seattle?" Morgan's voice reached her before she'd taken more than a dozen steps.

Her shoulders sagged with resignation as she turned to see his long strides eat up the weathered platform between them. Damn. Her chance to get back on the train undetected vanished under his sharp eye.

Kate pasted a smile on her face. "Mr. Morgan, what a pleasant surprise. What brings you to Hope?" The train rumbled beside them, the crew racing to fill the water tanks from the lake.

"I'm the new sheriff. Guess we didn't talk about our destinations back there did we?"

"No, I guess we didn't." Kate wished the man would disappear. If she was any judge of character, he'd stick to her like honey.

"What brings you to such a remote place?" He crossed his arms over his chest and rocked back on the heels of his scuffed boots.

"I'm here to get married." She shoved the words around the guilt surging through her body. "I'd appreciate it if you didn't mention the problems on the train to my fiancé. It's silly to worry him over something that's done and gone."

Those dark eyes drilled her. "I wouldn't let my guard down, Miss Leary. That man could find his way to Hope."

"Mary Catherine?"

Seth glanced over her head and tilted his chin. "I think he's here for you."

Kate shook off the spell Seth seemed to cast over her every time he was near and turned to face the tall, lean man, with the charming British accent. His dark hair swept back from a high, broad forehead, dark eyebrows arched over brilliant blue eyes and a straight nose led to a sensuous mouth.

"Yes?" Her voice squeaked, and her mind went blank. She'd lived twenty-four years without meeting a single man who tempted her. In the space of a few days, she'd met two very handsome, very tempting men.

Behind her, Seth blew a breath of disgust.

"Mary Catherine, I'm Ethan. Ethan Howland," he added when she didn't respond.

"Ethan." This was the man who'd advertised for a bride? His photograph hadn't done him justice. What was wrong with the women of Hope? The man was handsome and quite suave, even in his western clothes.

"I apologize for being late; the wagon lost a wheel on the trip into town." Ethan looked over her head, a frown creasing his broad forehead. "Can I help you?"

Her astonishment over Ethan had taken her mind off Sheriff Morgan and the fact he stood behind her. She turned to face the dark, rugged man, who had become a thorn in her side. "I'll be fine now, Sheriff. Thank you for waiting with me."

Morgan continued to size up Ethan and Ethan, Seth Morgan. Good crimany! They were staring each other down.

"Ethan, Sheriff Morgan was kind enough to wait on the platform with me until you arrived. We traveled on the same train." She couldn't help babbling the explanation. If Morgan mentioned anything about the attack, Kate's plans would be crushed.

"I see." Ethan frowned. "Where's your jurisdiction, Morgan?"

"Here. I'm the new sheriff."

Ethan's expression eased, his attention fully on Sheriff Morgan. "In that case, welcome to Hope. I'm Ethan Howland." Ethan held his hand out past Kate. Morgan accepted it in what looked like a very firm shake.

The two didn't look trustful of each other, but after reading Ethan's letters and how his wife had run off with his best friend, she couldn't blame him for being leery when the tall, handsome sheriff had traveled west with his fiancée. What was the sheriff's excuse?

"Ethan, I'm sorry you had such a difficult trip into town. I'm sure you're eager to be on your way, shall we gather my things?" Kate wanted to get as far away from the sheriff as possible.

"Certainly." Ethan looked down at her as if seeing her for the first time.

What a loss for Mary Catherine. Kate hoped Frank Settler was everything Mary Catherine believed him to be, or she'd made a big mistake. Of course, looks were far from everything.

Ethan raised a dark brow. "Are your things in the depot?" He walked past her before she could respond. So much for niceties.

Kate gathered her skirts and hurried to catch him. She might look bedraggled and puff coal dust with each step, but that was beside the point. She wasn't used to being walked away from. My, but manners were certainly lacking here.

"That's my trunk," she called to his broad back, pointing across the platform where the old trunk holding her borrowed finery lay.

"Miss Leary, you need to tell him."

She turned to find Seth Morgan on her heals.

"I appreciate your discretion." Kate glanced over her shoulder at Ethan who stood with his hands on his hips, talking with the young conductor about her trunk. The first order of business was persuading him to extend the wedding date. She needed a week or two, then she'd return to New York, a much wiser woman.

"You're making a mistake. The train and the telegraph run between here and Chicago. This isn't the old west."

Kate glanced around at the rustic town and wilderness. "It isn't?"

"Miss Leary, that man could show up in a few days, and Howland would be caught off guard. Are you sure you don't know the attacker?"

"Yes, I'm certain," Kate said, as Ethan walked toward them, her trunk hoisted on his shoulder. "Please let it go. Now if you'll excuse me, Sheriff, my fiancé is ready to leave." Kate gathered her skirts and hurried after Ethan, who maintained a brisk pace to the waiting wagon. By the time she reached his side, Kate was breathless from struggling with her heavy coat and carpet bag.

Accepting his assistance, she climbed onto the high seat of the wagon, adjusted her skirts, and waited until he'd settled beside her before broaching the subject of the wedding.

"Ethan, I know we've barely met, but I think we need to discuss the wedding."

"That's fine. What is it?"

"Do you really feel a week is long enough for us to get acquainted before we marry?"

He picked up the reins. “That’s what we planned through our letters.”

“Yes, of course, but wouldn’t it be prudent if we took more time to get to know each other? Maybe two or three weeks?”

His shoulders drew back, and a frown puckered his broad forehead. “I had considered it settled. Janet and Ruth have made the arrangements. The entire town is planning for next week.”

“The entire town?” Kate swung around to face him and nearly fell off the edge of the seat.

He shrugged. “That might be an exaggeration, but many of us wouldn’t have made it here without helping each other. A wedding is something we share.” He snapped the reins and clicked his tongue. The pair pulled on the traces and set the wagon in motion.

Kate grabbed the edge of the seat as the wagon turned, and they started up the hill away from the depot and the lake. She glanced over the rustic little town terracing the hillside, the main street facing the lake, with a couple more rows of buildings behind it.

She sighed and glanced at the man beside her. He handled the team with a practiced ease, his elbows resting on his long thighs, the reins threaded through his fingers. His brows still pulled together in a frown.

She’d upset the apple cart. He’d made this plan with Mary Catherine, and she’d questioned it. If he didn’t agree to the extension, she’d be pressed to contact Ross immediately. Which was a possibility. Ethan Howland wasn’t like the young men in New York who allowed her to manipulate them. This entire situation couldn’t be resolved fast enough for her peace of mind.

Kate gripped the edge of the hard wooden seat as the wagon rumbled and lurched up the winding road. According to Ethan, the Malone family lived very close to town so they should arrive soon.

She searched for her self-proclaimed calm, but she'd left it hundreds of miles up the tracks where she'd impulsively changed the original plan. The right front wheel hit a hole. Kate lost her balance and slammed against the broad shoulder next to her. Ethan shuffled the reins to one hand and gripped her upper arm with his long fingers.

"Are you all right?"

Kate swallowed against the tightness in her chest. "I'm fine, thank you." She wasn't all right. She was in the middle of a deception of her own making. She'd acted rashly, without thinking the plan completely through.

He released her arm and returned his attention to the road.

The unseasonably warm autumn sun heated her back. Seagulls swooped over their heads, screeching for a handout. She had to stay calm, regain control of her emotions. This would all work out.

"I didn't expect seagulls so far from the ocean."

"It's a large lake." Ethan looked down at her with a half-smile. The change in his expression erased some of the tension between them.

"They act like they're hungry."

"Don't feed them, or you'll have every gull for miles following you around. They have plenty to eat. The lake's full of fish, and they feed off the garbage heaps behind the buildings in town."

"Huh." Kate wrinkled her nose. "Garbage heaps?"

Ethan glanced down at her nose and grinned. It quite transformed his face.

"Vegetable trimmings, food scraps."

"Oh." She nodded and fell back into silence.

The hill they'd climbed since leaving the depot crowned, and the terrain opened up into a small meadow. A whitewashed two-story home welcomed them with its glazed windows. It looked more prosperous than the buildings in town and shared the magnificent view.

Ethan pulled the team to a stop and wrapped the reins around the brake handle. He jumped down and dust poofed around his boots. Dust seemed to coat everything, including the people.

Kate glanced down at the traveling outfit she'd worn since boarding the train in New York. She'd planned to leave the train in Chicago so only packed nightwear in her carpet bag. After leaving Chicago with Mary Catherine's trunk, she feared if she asked to access it, it would draw too much attention, so here she sat, dusty, stained, and travel worn.

"Mary Catherine?"

Startled, Kate realized Ethan had rounded the wagon and waited, his arms extended, seriousness wreathing his face again. She placed her hands on his shoulders and leaped to the ground. Her legs wobbled and she stumbled against him. Impressions flashed through her mind; strength, warmth, male. Taller than Seth but not as solid.

Seth? Where had the comparison to Sheriff Morgan come from?

Kate glanced up at Ethan and blinked to clear her mind. She was simply tired and confused over all the new emotions running through her.

Ethan cleared his throat and glanced around. "Why do you want to postpone the wedding? We discussed it in our letters. You were concerned about staying longer than needed with the Malones." His voice low, he kept his hands on her arms.

"I—" Kate took a deep breath. "Why are you in a hurry? Now that I'm here, I feel we need some courting time."

Ethan looked around, anywhere but her face. He shifted from one foot to the other. "I have concerns, too. That's why we scheduled the wedding for a week after your arrival. I want to see you for a few days before you meet Will. I won't have my son hurt."

"I agree. I don't want Will hurt either. Can't we give our courtship more time? Letters are hardly a way for two people to become acquainted enough to marry."

Dear God, she didn't want to hurt the child. Her stomach roiled. She'd love to turn back the clock and get off the train in Chicago. Facing the henchman seemed preferable to lying to these good people.

"Sharing a house is a quick way to get to know each other," Ethan said, his eyes intent, the warmth of his body sending images of them living together through Kate's head.

And sharing a bed. Kate had barely been kissed in her twenty-four years; she knew little of what happened between a man and woman behind closed doors. Only what her close friend Erin had blushingly imparted.

"I understand this is unexpected." Kate searched her mind for a logical reason to ease Ethan's mind. "I want you to be sure I'm the woman you want to marry."

"I thought I made it clear in my letters. I need a caring woman to run my household and raise my son so Ruth can move to Boston and marry Horace."

"Your housekeeper."

His frown deepened. "Yes, my housekeeper, however, Ruth's much more than that. She's like a mother to Will. It'll be difficult for him to let her go. Your presence and role as his stepmother could soften the blow."

Kate's heart ached for this man and his son and what she was about to do to them. The impact of her decision to trade places with Mary Catherine hit her with both barrels. Never before had she been cavalier but now... She swallowed hard. "Of course,

I'll do my best. Where is Will?"

"He's at the ranch. To tell you the truth, I seriously expected you to change your mind at the last minute." He narrowed his eyes. "Why did you come?"

Kate recoiled. Did he see through her disguise? "What do you mean? You sent for me. We agreed to marry."

"Yes, that's what you said in your letters, but I sensed a doubt. Now, I want to know why you really came." He stepped closer, his arms folded over his chest.

Kate sucked in a sharp breath. The man was handsome, but he was a cynic through and through.

"Ethan, I have no intention of hurting your son. I came to marry you and start a new life. I had nothing left in Boston. No one." She was sure Mary Catherine would have said the same thing.

"Good. Just don't forget. I'll be watching you." He turned and guided her toward the house.

"Oh great," Kate said before she could stop herself. Two men watching her and a third one after her company. The spinster now had three men after her, each one wanting something different.

Ethan stopped and turned her away from the door, his voice low. "As arranged, you'll stay with the Malones until the wedding. My ranch is a two-hour ride from here. I'll spend as many evenings as possible. Winter's coming, and there's a lot to do before the snow hits."

"How romantic," Kate murmured.

"I thought you understood romance had no part in our agreement." He turned away and continued to the end of the house facing the thick forest. A clothesline loaded with clothes flapping in the warm breeze ran parallel to the house. Chickens clucked and pecked under the laundry.

"If I didn't understand before, I do now." She

waited while he rapped on the screen door. In only a few seconds, the door swung open.

"You've arrived!" A voice filled with sunshine greeted them. "Bring her in Ethan. Don't stand on ceremony." Janet Malone stood aside, gesturing for them to enter the house.

Ethan urged Kate to enter the kitchen first. She hesitated and took a deep breath. Fresh baked bread. Her stomach growled. The train food had become so monotonous she'd eaten very little over the past few days. Travel and the anticipation of taking over another woman's life had dimmed her appetite.

"Mary Catherine." Janet took Kate's hand and smiled. "I'm so glad you're here. You must be hungry and tired."

"I am. Thank you for asking." Kate couldn't help but smile at the cheerful Janet Malone.

"Of course, dear. Boston's a long distance from Hope."

"Oh I—" Kate caught herself before she corrected Janet on the origin of her trip, remembering Mary Catherine was from Boston.

"Yes, dear?"

"I was just going to say I enjoyed seeing all the country between here and there." For the most part she had, other than her brush with Jeb Walker's minion.

"Well, you have fortitude. I like that." Janet turned to Ethan. "She's no wilting flower is she?"

"No, I'd say she's not. Is Kerry at the smithy?" Ethan prowled around the room, obviously at home as he lifted the lid on a stock pot and smelled something simmering inside it. "Umm, your famous stew."

"Of course. I knew you'd be here for dinner. Kyle and Maura will be home soon. Why don't you unload Mary Catherine's trunk and hurry down to the smithy? If you don't light a fire under Kerry, he'll be late for dinner."

"But, Mary Catherine—"

"Will be just fine, don't you worry. Run along now and let us get acquainted." Janet turned back to the dinner she'd been preparing before their arrival as if the matter was settled.

Ethan looked startled by Janet's declaration but didn't object. He raised a dark brow at Kate, tapped his hat against his thigh, then turned to collect the trunk.

Kate resisted breaking out in laugher. So, big tough Ethan Howland was biddable after all. At least by a woman he respected.

Janet chatted on about her children, Kyle and Maura. Fifteen-year-old Kyle would be home soon from the school by the lake, and nineteen-year-old Maura worked at the mercantile. In the short time it took for Ethan to come through the door with the trunk, Kate's mind was buzzing with information.

"Take it upstairs, Ethan, to the bedroom you stay in when you're here." Janet gave a bowl of rising bread dough one last punch and the stew one last stir, then turned to Kate. "Of course, he won't be staying there tonight."

"I didn't think he would." An image of Ethan Howland in her bed flashed through Kate's mind as she listened to his boots hitting the bare wood stair treads. Not that she had a reference point of course.

Ethan strode down the stairs and into the kitchen, stopping in front of Kate. "I'll be back later with Kerry. Will you be all right?"

Well, forbidding he may be, but Ethan Howland at least redeemed his lack of manners at the train depot. "I'm fine. I'll see you later."

"Ladies," Ethan said with a quick nod, then went out the back door. Soon, the wagon lumbered down the hill.

"Hope you don't mind me sending him off," Janet said, laying her hand on Kate's shoulder. "I figured some time away from your fiancé would be welcomed. If for nothing else than to take a deep breath. It can't be easy, traveling all this way to a man you've never met."

Kate appreciated the woman's caring and candor. "It's unsettling, but I'll adjust given time."

Oh my gosh, she couldn't do this; she couldn't keep lying! Guilt heaped on her in waves. She had no intention of marrying Ethan Howland. What had started out as a simple ruse to let Mary Catherine return home and give Kate a new alias to escape Jeb Walker suddenly became very complicated.

Janet placed teacups and saucers, a plate of scones, and cream and sugar on the round pine table dominating the center of the kitchen and motioned for Kate to sit with her. "A strong cup of tea will set things right."

Kate smiled. "Or make me feel more like talking." How could anyone resist Janet Malone? Kate had to. Janet may be forthright and open, but she wouldn't be happy when Kate told the truth. Just a few days, that's all Kate needed.

Janet chuckled. "You caught me. Yes, I'm hoping to get to know you. Ethan is a dear friend to Kerry and me. When we came to Hope, he befriended us and helped us build this house. We had little more than a wagon load of furniture and two growing children."

"I have no intention of hurting Ethan." Kate patted Janet's hand. The words twisted in her stomach, making her lightheaded. She'd always prided herself on being as honest and forthright as Janet. When her disguise was revealed it would only confirm Ethan's opinion of women. And Seth's. She frowned. Why did the irritating sheriff keep popping into her mind?

"What a remarkable ring!" Janet took Kate's hand and examined the emerald.

"My father gave it to me for my birthday years ago."

Janet's lips pursed then worked to one side. "I take it your family had ample money at one time."

Kate grappled for an explanation. She wasn't used to hiding her wealth. When she went to her room, she'd hide the ring in her satchel.

"I hope you don't find me too forward," Janet continued, "but I am worried about Ethan." She glanced around the room as if searching for the right words. "His first wife hurt him terribly. She left shortly after little Will was born."

"He wrote about it in his letters. I can't imagine a woman willingly leaving her baby." In her heart, Kate knew if she ever met someone she loved enough to marry and have a child with, she'd face the devil himself to keep her child.

"Yes," Janet said, her voice low. "She ran off with a neighboring gentleman farmer. Ethan's close friend."

"No wonder he's so angry with life." Kate shook her head.

"You sensed that, did you?" Janet laid her hand over Kate's and squeezed it. "I could tell the moment I looked into your eyes that you're a caring person. Ethan's a lucky man."

Kate smiled, the knots in her stomach tightening. Good Lord, what had she gotten herself into?

After tea, Janet wrapped toweling around both hands and picked up a kettle of steaming water. Kate followed her up the stairs into a sunny, cheerful room. Yellow curtains framed the single window and a matching quilt covered the four poster bed. Fresh flowers filled a vase on the dresser and lace trimmed towels lay on the washstand.

Kate smiled and thanked Janet who left her to wash and rest then turned toward the trunk at the foot of the bed. Mary Catherine's trunk. Filled with Mary Catherine's clothes. All but the under things. Kate refused to wear anything but silk against her skin, so the two women had made their way to the baggage car and switched out the items they couldn't part with.

Lifting the lid, Kate gasped. A confection of ivory satin and lace lay folded in frothy layers. She lifted it out, sighing as the fabric whispered open in front of her.

Mary Catherine should have kept her wedding dress for Frank Settler; Kate had no use for it.

Unable to resist the poignancy of the dress, Kate held it up to her front, tucking the neckline under her chin as she turned toward the cheval mirror. She and Mary Catherine were of similar size and were certainly similar in coloring. The dress would no doubt take a few tucks here and there, but it would fit her.

"Dream on." Kate spun from the mirror and hung the dress in the wardrobe. She'd keep the dress safe and see it returned to its rightful owner when this was all over. It only took a few minutes to shake out several of the simple cotton dresses and hang them next to the wedding gown, then choose a cream colored dress with sprigs of peach blossoms to change into for dinner.

Kate washed thoroughly with the washcloth and hot water. The lace edged towels were soft and soothing. Exhaustion rolled over her. She slipped off the emerald ring and added it to the rest of the jewelry she'd packed in a satin bag.

Laying the dress over the footboard, she slipped into the inviting four poster and snuggled between the cotton sheets. No rocking, no noise, just peaceful stillness.

Images of the last few days fluttered through her mind settling on a tall man with compelling dark eyes, his dark brows raised in suspicion. Seth Morgan.

Chapter Five

"Mary Catherine." A woman's pleasant voice pulled Kate from a sound sleep.

"Yes?" Kate sat up in bed, the covers falling off her bare shoulders. She shivered and pulled the soft cotton around her.

"Dinner's ready. Are you rested enough to join us?"

Kate blinked. Was she dreaming? For a moment she puzzled over the simple yet comfortable bedroom. No fireplace with a carefully banked fire, and where was her maid, Clarice?

Her head seemed full of cotton wool and confusion, then clarity set in. There wasn't a fireplace because she wasn't in her room at home. She was in Hope, Idaho Territory about to take on the act of her life.

Janet Malone was on the other side of the door summoning her to dinner. The one person she may not be able to fool with her borrowed identity.

"I'll be right there." Reluctant to roll from the warm bed into the chilled evening air, Kate gritted her teeth and planted her feet on the small rug next to the bed. She pattered to the door and opened it a crack.

"I need to dress and freshen up. Please don't hold dinner on my account."

"There's time. The men are still out." Janet turned and hurried down the stairs.

Kate closed the door and leaned against it. It appeared that when Janet Malone spoke, it was law.

Kate glanced around the room, tempted to crawl

back into bed, and pull the covers over her head. Feeling foggy, she splashed her face with cool water from the bowl on the washstand and washed her hands. More shivers danced down her back.

Maybe this was all a dream, and she'd wake up in her bed at home. Jeb would be back in Houston minding his own business, and her father would be alive and running the shipyards.

A bit of flannel pressed to her face, Kate paused and stared into the mottled mirror.

Where had that thought come from? She desperately missed her father, but somehow she'd save the shipyards from Jeb's greedy clutches.

The borrowed dress skimmed over her figure and clung a bit too snug over her breasts. Clarice would have snipped a few stitches before buttoning her up and twisting her hair into a French knot.

While she struggled through the preparations for her first dinner in Hope, her stomach roiled with the anticipation of facing Ethan again. She prayed he'd agree to postpone the wedding for at least another week. He'd made it clear he didn't want love, didn't want an emotional entanglement, so why be in a hurry?

Voices drifted up the stairs from the kitchen. She glanced in the mirror, nibbled at her lips and pinched her cheeks then stepped toward the door. "Just breathe," she lectured herself. "He's just a man, and he's not your man."

Downstairs, the sound of a family conversing after a long day apart filled her with warmth. She missed having a family. Her father had always been such a lively dinner companion, even after her mother left.

Emotion choked her. Kate gripped the doorframe and worked to gather herself. Control. She had to maintain control, stay composed, and work through the predicament she'd firmly planted herself in.

Kate gathered her skirts in one hand and descended the stairs. The moment she stepped into the kitchen, all talking and laughing stopped, and all eyes focused on her.

A surge of disappointment engulfed her. She'd prepared herself for seeing Ethan, but he wasn't in the room.

"Come in, Mary Catherine. The men stepped outside, but Kyle and Maura are eager to meet you." Janet beckoned her toward the table.

Kate smiled at the open expression on the teenaged boy's face, then turned to Maura and almost flinched. Smoky blue eyes shot daggers at Kate. The younger woman was clearly not happy to meet her.

"It's a pleasure to meet you, Miss Leary," Kyle said, touching her hand.

"Maura Malone, where are your manners?" Janet prodded her daughter, a puzzled expression on her face.

"Hello, Miss Leary," Maura said, her tone stiff.

Kate nodded a greeting, puzzled over Maura's clear dislike when they'd just met.

"Please call me Mary Catherine, better yet, call me Kate," Kate said, eager to be identified by something familiar.

"Do you commonly go by Kate?" Janet tilted her head in question.

"Since I was about two and my father said Mary Catherine was too much of a mouthful."

"We'd love to call you, Kate, wouldn't we children?" Janet ran an expectant gaze over her children's faces.

"I'm not a child, Mother," Maura said, her voice stilted.

Kyle asked about her trip and about Boston. He'd been born there but hadn't seen it since his family moved west. Kate had visited Boston on several occasions so didn't have to fabricate the descriptions.

The scrape of boots against the boardwalk out back announced the men's arrival.

Kate clasped her hands together then moved to Janet's side to offer her help with dinner. The problem lay in the fact she'd never prepared food in her life. Maybe an omelet, yes, she remembered Erin showing her how to make an omelet one rainy Saturday afternoon.

She didn't want to be idle when Ethan appeared. He offered a challenge—one that dared her to prove not all women were deceptive and self-centered. Never mind that she was lying to him about her very presence in Hope.

The back door opened, and Ethan stepped through the doorway, then paused, his arm braced against the frame, his hand tapping against his thigh.

He'd taken off his jacket and rolled up the sleeves of his blue shirt. His ruffled hair made him look much more relaxed. The two top buttons on his shirt lay open, revealing the tanned column of his throat and a hint of dark hair. Her gaze swept over his strong chin and straight nose to settle on his blue eyes. She swallowed.

"Madam, you look more rested." His faint British accent washed over her like a warm rain shower. Goose bumps skittered up her back and spread over her breasts. To think she could be married to this man in one week and share his life, his bed.

"Stop," she said.

"I beg your pardon?" Ethan straightened in the doorway, his head brushing the top of the frame. His dark brows met over his jewel tone eyes.

"I, uh, I meant." She looked around the room at

the startled faces. "I was referring to my mind, racing with so many impressions of life in Hope." Yes, there was her ability to cover when she needed it. She couldn't allow this very large, very imposing man to learn she was deceiving him.

Janet patted her hand and smiled, then turned to Ethan. "Kate barely rested while you were gone. You should sit and visit while I finish dinner. Where's Kerry?" Janet bustled around like a military commander.

Lips pursed, Ethan walked toward the table, gesturing for Kate to join him. "He's putting the horses away."

Kate's heart pounded as she sat next to Ethan, all too aware she was playing with fire.

Maura sat on a chair on the other side of Ethan. Her eyes had softened and could even be described as smoldering. Ah, ha. So that was the lay of the land. Maura had a crush on Ethan. No wonder she didn't like her.

"Kate, is it now?" Ethan leaned back in his chair. His eyes twinkled, and his sensuous mouth turned up in a beguiling smile.

"Mary Catherine sounds too formal." Kate found her breath catching at his closeness, his intensity. No wonder Maura adored him. When not being serious and cynical, the man could be quite charismatic. Oh dear. She couldn't keep acting like his fiancée.

Unsettled by her lack of emotional control, Kate turned back to the table and arranged her soup bowl, bread plate, and silverware in front of her. She glanced at Janet who bustled between the stove and the table. "Can I help with something?"

"Oh, no. You relax with Ethan. Kyle, wash up for dinner, darlin'. Your da will be in soon." Janet set sliced bread and a dish of butter on the table.

Maura didn't offer to help her mother but stayed

in her chair, hanging on Ethan's every word while Kate struggled for something to say. "Did you help Kerry at the smithy?"

"I helped out a bit. I'm not good at waiting around."

"I'm sorry I upset your schedule today." Why did he make her feel like she was such an imposition when he'd been the one to send for her? Well, he'd sent for Mary Catherine.

He looked away and stood, moving toward the door. "I'll go help Kerry with the horses."

Kate sighed. So much for trying to converse. She wasn't a deceitful person; how had she ever thought she could pretend to be someone else? She nibbled on her bottom lip and gave Maura a side glance. The young woman looked away, then got up and started helping her mother put dinner on the table.

Minutes later, the back door opened, and a man stepped in with Ethan behind him.

"Kerry, you must come meet our guest." Janet looped her arm through Kerry's and urged him across the room.

"Hello, Mary Catherine." Kerry smiled at her, then at his wife as he smacked her with a kiss, then untangled from her grip. "I need to wash up my sweeting. Supper smells mighty good."

A knock sounded at the door. Ethan turned and opened it. "Sheriff, what can I do for you?" His tone didn't exactly sound friendly.

"The Malones invited me to dinner."

Kate's heart fluttered, then sped up when Seth entered the kitchen, his fathomless dark eyes focusing on her. She dropped her gaze to the black leather vest covering his broad chest and remembered being pressed against it. The resolve to be indifferent waned.

All right, so she couldn't be indifferent to him, and it irritated her. He rankled her like no man ever had, and she wanted nothing more than to convince him and herself that he didn't affect her.

Ethan crossed the room and reclaimed his chair next to Kate. "You make quick acquaintances, Sheriff."

Seth turned his charming smile on Janet. "I met Kerry at the smithy. I hope it's not an inconvenience, Mrs. Malone."

Janet flitted in front of them. "Of course not, Sheriff. I'm happy to have you at our table. It's the least we can do for the man who will straighten out our little town. Consider it a standing invitation."

"That's very generous of you, ma'am."

"Please call me, Janet. Now have a seat there on Kate's left. I'm just finishing up with setting the food out."

Kate scooted toward Ethan. He glanced at her, with a raised brow. Maura's curious gaze at Seth switched to Kate with a glare.

She subtly shifted away only to be assailed by Seth Morgan's unique, spicy scent.

He accepted a mug from Janet and added cream and sugar. Spell bound with his every move, Kate watched as he lifted it to his mouth and his lips fastened to the lip of the cup; his Adam's apple bobbed as he swallowed the coffee.

Dear heaven's, the man may infuriate her, but he entranced her at the same time. First thing in the morning, she'd make a trip into town and send a telegraph to Ross. She was in over her head.

Thanks to the woman sitting next to him, who now called herself Kate, Seth barely tasted Janet's cooking.

She spent the meal shifting back and forth in her chair. When her shoulder touched his, she'd jump like she'd touched a live coal. Then, she'd slide closer to Ethan.

The woman was up to something. She'd gone

from Elizabeth Downing to Mary Catherine Leary somewhere between New York and Chicago. Around the time she was kidnapped, as she put it.

Even more odd, Howland didn't look like a man chomping at the bit to marry. He no sooner finished his dinner and he was on his feet.

"Janet, thank you for the wonderful meal, but I must return to the ranch."

"You haven't had dessert." Janet appeared surprised at his announcement. "I made apple pie."

Kerry nodded and wiped his mouth with a blue gingham napkin. "Yes, Ethan. Travis can handle things just fine, and Ruth is with Will."

Interesting. Evidently Ethan normally lingered after dinner with the Malones. He was on fire to get away tonight. Seth couldn't say he was sorry. If Ethan left early, he might have a chance to question Kate. He'd break her down and get the truth.

"I'll have a piece of that pie," Seth said. Kate visibly stiffened. Yeah, he made her nervous all right. Maybe for more reasons than her fear of the truth coming out. He'd be lying if he didn't admit she rattled him. But he couldn't afford to get involved with her. He had unfinished business beyond being the sheriff of Hope.

"I'll see you to the door, Ethan." Kate jumped up, her chair skittered backward. Seth caught it before it hit the floor. Kate wasn't going farther than the door to bid her fiancé goodbye. He'd relish his pie while she did her duty. Not for a minute, did he believe she really cared about Ethan.

Ethan nodded and motioned for her to lead the way.

A bite of rich cinnamon coated pie halfway to his mouth, Seth acknowledged the twinge in his gut was jealousy. Kate disappeared out the door and into the dark autumn night.

The Malones remained at the table, their

expressions showing their unease over Ethan's early departure. Except young Kyle, who dove into his pie like most growing teenage boys. Maura had a look of pure dislike on her pretty face. She wasn't happy about Kate being outside in the dark with Ethan.

Seth studied her while he slowly chewed the last bite of pie.

"Sheriff, how'd you hear about Hope?" Young Kyle broke through Seth's mental conflict between wondering what Ethan and Kate were doing and pretending not to give a damn.

"Saw an ad in the newspaper, Kyle." Seth set his fork down and picked up his coffee cup. "You'd be surprised what you find in the papers back east."

Kate stepped out the door and turned to face Ethan. He put on his hat. "It's dark, Kate, you shouldn't linger. I'll see you at dinner tomorrow."

"All right," she said, her voice unintentionally soft. She looked at his mouth, wondering what it would be like to kiss such a handsome man. "I think we should talk about the wedding." Would he kiss her? Maybe if he did and she liked it, she'd enjoy the situation she'd placed herself in.

"What's there to talk about? The date is set."

"I asked you about giving us an additional week, remember?"

"How could I forget?" He propped his hands on his hips and blew out a breath that turned to steam in the chilly night air. "The explanations will be awkward, but I agree, we need an additional week. I'll let everyone know."

"I can't imagine people not understanding. Marriage is a great commitment. People should take time to get to know each other."

Ethan's tight expression turned into the semblance of a smile. "You're not at all what I expected, Kate Leary. Your letters made you seem quite different."

Kate felt like the lowest of low. She looked through her lashes at him. "Is that a bad thing?"

"Not necessarily." Ethan took her hand and squeezed it. He smiled, then turned to leave.

No kiss.

"Ethan, can I talk to you before you leave?" Kerry's voice boomed through the screen door, startling Kate.

Kate stepped aside and let him pass then turned toward the kitchen door. She hoped no one in the kitchen had overheard their conversation.

She hesitated a moment to smooth her ragged nerves before she faced Seth. The moment she reentered the kitchen, her gaze met Janet's and her head began to hurt. She had a feeling nothing slipped by Janet Malone.

Seth remained at the table, relishing what must be a second piece of apple pie, chatting with Maura and Kyle. Why wouldn't the man leave?

Maura seemed interested in his conversation, but her gaze kept straying toward the door behind Kate. The one Ethan had just left through.

Chapter Six

Ethan sighed, eager to be on his way. He stopped at the head of the team, giving both of the geldings' noses a quick rub as he waited for Kerry to say what was on his mind.

Kerry patted the roan's neck. "You've never turned down Janet's pie. Something wrong?"

"Not at all."

"You're not changing your mind about Kate, I hope."

"I don't plan on it." Ethan laid his hand on his friend's shoulder. "I apologize if I seemed abrupt."

"She's quite the woman, isn't she?" A grin wreathed Kerry's ruddy face.

Ethan pulled his hand away and took a step back. "She's not what I expected."

"She seems kind. I can tell Janet likes her, and I trust my wife's judgment."

Ethan looked up at the star-studded, violet sky. "I want someone to raise Will, be the mother he needs, but I don't need a woman in my life."

"Many a lonely man has sent for a mail-order bride, but you're not like them. You won't settle for marrying a stranger." Kerry took a step closer to Ethan and gripped his shoulder. "Trust her, man, get to know her first. Give this more time. She can stay here as long as it takes."

"Interesting you should say that. Kate asked for more time, too."

"It's not so strange. She's travel weary and from the city to boot. She needs time to adjust and so do you. You're a good man, a good friend. Don't hurry things and chase her away."

Ethan frowned. "Chase her away? What makes you think she'd change her mind?"

"There's a fire in her eyes, Ethan. She's a woman of deep feelings, and she wants to be more than a convenience."

"You're turning into quite the philosopher." Ethan untied the traces and walked around the team to the wagon, more than ready to return to the ranch, kiss his son goodnight, and crawl into his lonely bed.

"Call me what you want, but if you don't change the course you're on, you'll spend the rest of your life a lonely man. I've said enough; I'm going back inside to my family."

Ethan reached out to shake Kerry's hand. "I appreciate your friendship. I'll think about what you've said. For now, we're taking it a week at a time."

"Good," Kerry said. "Very good."

Ethan climbed onto the wagon seat and clicked to the horses. He urged the team to pick up the pace, passing through town and up the narrow road to the ranch. While Kate adjusted to life in Hope and to him, he'd make several late evening trips home in the dark.

Maura's image flashed through his mind, her expression crestfallen when he'd told her Kate had arrived. Damn, he didn't need the complication of her feelings for him. Or his for her.

The glow of lamplight through the trees beckoned him to the ranch he and his brother-in-law, Travis, had spent years building. A lantern illuminated the barn and lamplight the kitchen. Warmth stole over him. Home. He'd never expected to feel so at home in this wild, rugged land. Virginia had been home with its rolling green meadows and deciduous trees.

Travis walked out of the barn, wiping his hands on a rag, when Ethan jumped from the wagon, his boots thumping as they hit the dry ground.

"You're home early."

"Doesn't seem like it." Ethan led the team out of the traces and into the barn.

"What's she like?"

"Not what I expected," he said for the third time that night. He pulled the tack off the horses and hung it on the wall.

"Ugly is she?" Travis chuckled and stepped in to help Ethan take care of the horses.

"Definitely not."

"So, she must be a looker, or you wouldn't be so edgy. How did Maura take to her?"

"Travis, when I want you to interfere with my personal life I'll ask." Ethan gave the geldings one last pat and turned toward the door. "Did all the horses come in from the meadow?"

"Of course," Travis said, following him out of the barn toward the house. "You changed the subject. Maura might be only nineteen, but she loves you, Ethan. I don't understand why you advertised for a wife."

"Maura's thirteen years younger than I am. She's the daughter of my good friends."

"She's a grown woman. She knows her own mind." Travis stopped. "Do you really think Kerry would object to you marrying his daughter? A man he admires and respects?"

"I'm not going to find out. End of subject." Ethan stopped in front of the house and turned to face his best friend. Travis had stood beside him when Natalie left. His sibling loyalty weakened by her desertion.

"If I've made a mistake, it will soon become apparent. Her meeting with Will will be the real test. For now, I stand behind my decision."

"Foolish pride." Travis shook his head.

Ethan turned toward the door and entered the house. "Good night, Travis."

Ruth, his longtime housekeeper and nanny to Will, sat by the fire in the kitchen, the needle in her hand passing up and down through a small, torn shirt.

"How did the evening go?" She glanced up from her sewing.

"Fine." Ethan reached for the kettle of hot water Ruth kept on the back of the stove.

Ruth set her sewing aside and stood to put more wood in the cook stove. "What's she like?"

"She's nice enough. We'll see how Will takes to her."

"How could a woman not love little Will?" Regret clouded her eyes the moment the words left her mouth.

"Ruth, we both know what Natalie did and how she left. It's time to let it rest."

"I'm more than pleased to hear you say that." Ruth clasped her hands in her lap. "It's time you went on, made a fresh start."

"I'd like to." However, he had a penchant for falling for the wrong woman. Maura Malone's hurt-filled expression, when he'd announced his plans to advertise for a bride, settled in his mind.

"With Mary Catherine Leary?"

"Of course." He looked away and raked his hand through his hair. "I don't want you to worry over each word that comes out of your mouth. Will and I would have been lost without you. You sacrificed your happiness to come west and care for us. You've been everything a mother could ever be to the boy."

"I love that child and always will. It's what makes leaving so hard."

"You've fulfilled your obligation to us and then some; it's time you resume your life."

"I'll leave when the new Mrs. Howland is settled, and not a minute sooner. Horace understands my sense of responsibility to you and Will."

"We appreciate Horace's patience. Please give him my regards the next time you write." Ethan smiled at her, then set about brewing a pot of tea. Picking up a cup and the steaming pot, he turned to leave the room.

"Sleep well, Ruth."

Time had come for Ruth to marry Horace and have children of her own. When Kate settled in, Ethan would buy a train ticket for Ruth to join Horace in Boston.

He set the teapot on a trivet he kept on his desk for late evenings such as this one, when a cup of tea soothed him enough to go to sleep.

Who was he fooling? Tonight was nothing like other nights. Kate was in Hope, summoned by him and more beautiful than a mail-order bride had a right to be. She was nothing like she'd sounded in her letters. She wasn't the mousy, spinster he'd envisioned. Not that he respected those traits.

He filled his cup with fragrant tea and blew on it before putting it to his mouth.

A homely woman was more likely to serve as the caretaker he needed for Will.

"Ouch!" The tea burned his upper lip. He licked it and set the cup down.

Dammit, why hadn't he simply advertised for a nanny to replace Ruth? A wife would expect so much more of him. But would a nanny have been willing to travel so far without the prospect of marriage?

Ethan shoved his hands through his hair. If only Maura wasn't so young and the situation so complicated. No use traveling down that road. When he'd sent for Kate, he'd made a commitment, and he was bound to stand by it.

****

Seth Morgan turned the key to the sheriff's office and stepped inside. No one occupied the single cell, so he'd have some peace, time to think. Hell, he'd spent many a night with his feet on the desk, tipped back in the chair, taking a few winks.

He'd rented a room at Mrs. White's boarding house, but he wasn't ready to face the well-meaning lady. He didn't want to face anyone until he got his equilibrium back.

Kate Leary was different from any woman he'd ever met. She did crazy things to his mind. One minute he wanted to haul her in for questioning; the next he wanted to kiss her.

He still didn't believe her story from the train. Things like kidnapping didn't randomly happen to people.

He'd grown up in the streets of Austin, his mother a prostitute in one of the largest houses of ill repute. At eight years old, he had divided his time between doing chores at the house and running the streets, stealing and making mischief.

His early years had given him a perspective of women. They were all after something, and if they didn't get it by trading their bodies, they traded their fortunes or housekeeping skills. He couldn't pin point Kate Leary quite yet.

The moment she'd fallen into his lap on the train, he smelled trouble. That and her sweet fragrance. She'd looked like a frightened doe, her green eyes wide. He'd expected her to leave the train in Chicago and was surprised to find her, late the following night, in the dining car, gobbling down a sandwich.

Just his luck she'd chosen to live in Hope. Of all the towns between here and Boston, she picked Hope to settle down in and get married.

Leaning back in his chair, he planted his booted

feet on the scarred oak desk and clasped his hands behind his head. Yeah, for some reason the marriage part really needled him. He couldn't say why. She sure wasn't his type.

Poor Howland. The man could get his heart ripped out over such a beautiful woman. Kate Leary wasn't the typical penniless spinster from Boston or anywhere. His first assignment in Hope was to keep a close eye on her and uncover whatever mischief she was up to.

Chapter Seven

The sunny, yellow curtains lifted from the chilly draft seeping around the window frame. Kate scrunched farther under the quilts, listening to the faint sounds of activity downstairs. The Malone household was awake.

Her night had been filled with fitful dreams, and it felt good to wake up and face the day. Almost.

"Seth," she said, her voice hoarse with sleep. Her dreams had been filled with pursuing henchmen and Sheriff Seth Morgan. He was more of a man than any man she'd ever met. All the more reason to avoid him.

Her stay in Hope was temporary. New York held her home, her business, her life. She didn't need any more complications.

Poor Ethan. Kate rolled over to her stomach and bunched the pillow under her head. He was either blind to Maura's feelings for him or didn't want to see them.

Poor Maura. How long had the younger woman tried to make Ethan notice her? Maybe, just maybe when Kate confessed the truth, he'd wake up and realize the woman for him had been under his nose all along.

She stared at the whitewashed wall and sighed. Her first mission today was to send Ross a telegram. He and Leland believed her to be safely in Chicago with her uncle. Should she telegram her location? What if the message fell into the wrong hands? Jeb seemed to have eyes everywhere.

Kate pushed off the covers and swung out of

bed, her feet hitting the cold floor. She wasn't at home anymore. Clarice wouldn't be bringing her morning tea and rolls.

The chilled air pushed her to quickly dress. She brushed her hair and wound it in a simple knot at the back of her neck. Setting her brush on the bureau, Kate walked to the window and pushed aside the curtain.

One look at the view took her breath away. No wonder the Malones chose to live here. Early morning sunlight glistened off the crystal blue waters of the vast lake and turned the islands and mountains behind it into shades of aquamarine not seen since she'd visited the jeweler at home.

Beautiful it may be, but with the strokes of fiery red and orange, fall had already made its mark on the land. Before long, the snows of winter would set in and strand her in Hope.

Eek. The thought of spending the cold, snowy winter in the backwoods town, no matter how beautiful the scenery, held no appeal. She had no time to waste.

Buttoning her black leather boots, she hurried from her room, anxious for a cup of Janet's tea. Dear Janet, she could tell something was wrong, and Kate's heart weighed heavy with the need to tell her the truth.

Halfway down the stairs, she hesitated. Would it hurt to tell the Malones who she really was? Of course, they'd want to tell Ethan, then her disguise would be gone. Oh dear. Not only was her independence in danger, but her life could be as well. She didn't know how far Jeb would go to gain control of McShane Walker Shipping.

She sank to the bottom step, both hands on the walls to keep from falling over in shock. The magnitude of her situation became as clear as the blue sky above. If Jeb had killed her father, would he hesitate to kill her?

She took a deep, steadying breath. Think Kate, how can you get out of this mess without putting everyone in danger? She pushed off the step and walked into the kitchen.

"Good morning," Janet greeted.

Maura stood by the door, coat on and satchel in hand, while Kyle stuffed half a biscuit in his mouth, his cheeks bulging.

"Off to school?" Kate asked, genuinely interested in the daily life of the Malone family.

Kyle's eyes lit up when he saw her. Oh dear, a young man's infatuation. Maura remained silent. Kate wanted to tell her not to worry about Ethan, but she couldn't. Ethan had made his decision to marry and hadn't proposed to Maura.

"Yes," Kyle said, swallowing the bread. "I'm going to school, and Maura's going to work."

"I look forward to seeing you tonight," Kate said, charmed by the youngster. When she looked at Janet, she was met with a pleased expression.

"Kyle, mind to your studies and listen to the teacher. Don't dilly-dally after school. Come directly home." Janet gave her son a quick hug and closed the door behind him.

Kate found the teapot on a cast iron trivet on the back of the stove. "Have a cup with me?" She glanced at Janet and held up the pot.

"Ah, I'd love to. My cup is there, next to the plate of side pork." Janet accepted the tea and took a sip then smiled at Kate.

"You just made Kyle's day you know. Having a beautiful newcomer pay attention to him."

Kate laughed. "Kyle's only fifteen."

"Nearly sixteen and ripe for romance, but then, you're already spoken for, aren't you?"

Kate frowned and gripped her cup. "Of course. That's why I'm here."

"Is it?"

Kate faced Janet, uncomfortable with the tension between them. "I don't know what you mean."

Janet walked toward the stove. "I didn't sleep well last night. Something isn't what it seems."

"I've just arrived; I need time to adjust." Kate tried to laugh off the awkward moment. She'd send Ross a telegram the moment she went into town. He'd respond with the news Jeb had confessed, and then she'd tell everyone the truth.

"That's true. Still…?"

"My father came from Ireland. When did your family arrive?" Kate sipped her tea hoping she could divert the conversation in a subtle way.

Janet narrowed her eyes as she lifted the cup to her lips. "My grandparents came over after the famine, believe it or not. They managed to survive starvation, but when other relatives sent word from the states, they chased the dream of America."

Smoky blue eyes, much like Maura's, drilled Kate for a moment, then Janet seemed to relax and return to her efficient and motherly self. "You should have breakfast. I kept a plate in the warming oven for you."

Janet dished up a generous serving of oatmeal, dressed it with molasses and cream, then set a small plate of side pork next to it.

A few minutes ago, Kate couldn't have managed to eat a bite. Her stomach had burned with the revelation of her precarious situation. Now, she was starved, and the sight and smell of the wholesome food made her mouth water.

"You're such a good cook, if I'm not careful, I'll have to let out my clothes." Kate buttered a thick slice of bread. The simple cooking wasn't what she was used to eating, but was delicious and substantial.

Janet puttered around the kitchen, not saying a word. Somehow, Kate doubted the other woman stayed silent to give her peace to eat her breakfast. Janet wasn't buying her story.

"When I'm through with the washing and have set the bread to rise, we'll go into town. You'll be wanting to see the shops, such as they are. It'll help you feel like you belong." Janet pulled out a large tub and a wash board.

Finished with her breakfast, Kate carried the dishes to the counter. She'd offer to help with the laundry or the baking, but she had no idea how to do either.

Last night, Janet poured hot water over the dishes and added soap, so Kate did the same. Then she picked up a rag and began to wash the plates, cups, and saucers. She didn't remember how the soap was rinsed off and started to panic when Janet appeared at her elbow, filling a pan with more hot water and dipping the dishes in before laying them on a towel.

"You should wear an apron if you're going to work in the kitchen." Janet glanced at Kate, a smile tipping up the corners of her full mouth.

"I'll be careful." Kate no sooner said the words when she splashed soapy water on the front of her dress. She glanced at Janet, expecting an "I told you so."

Janet laughed. "Kate, I have the feeling you don't know a lot about housework."

Kate nibbled on her lip, then smiled. "You would be right. I don't know how to wash clothes or bake bread either."

"Didn't your mother teach you?"

"My mother wanted to take care of my father and me, so I wasn't allowed in the kitchen."

"What did you do when your mother became ill?"

"I, uh, bought bread from a neighbor and hired a

girl to clean."

"Oh," Janet said. "That could be expensive. I imagine Ethan will hire someone to help with the housework. He came from a well-to-do family, so he'll understand. If you can finish here, I'll start the wash."

Kate finished washing the dishes, then wiped down the counter and the table. In one corner of the room, Janet rubbed the soiled clothes on a ribbed board, alternately dipping the garment in the tub of steaming water and lathering it with a cake of soap. Kate had never seen laundry being done, so she watched with fascination.

Janet hummed as she worked, creating a rhythm of scrubbing and sloshing. Kate was reminded of her housekeeper at home who hummed when she didn't think anyone was around. The memory sent a twang of homesickness through her, and her eyes pricked with hot tears. She didn't belong here. Her home was a large estate in New York City, and her work was in the office on the docks.

By the time Janet piled the last piece of clean, wet clothes in a basket, her hands were red and chapped. Guilt over her inability to help made Kate ask if she could hang the clothes to dry.

"The basket's heavy. Are you sure you can lift it?"

Kate bent over the heaping basket and braced herself before lifting and settling it on one hip. "I have it."

Once outside, she set the basket of clothes next to the line and began to shake out each piece, fastening them to the rope with a wooden pin. By the time she'd hung the last pair of work pants, her back muscles burned and ached.

She took a step back, dried her hands on her skirt, and surveyed her handiwork. Not one day in the boardroom had given her the satisfaction she experienced over hanging up three lines of wet clothes.

When she returned to the kitchen, Janet had bread dough on a board, working flour in as she folded and kneaded it. Kate stood just inside the door mesmerized by how rhythmic Janet made everything she did.

"Hanging the clothes saved me a lot of time." Janet smiled at her over the lump of dough. "If you would fill the kettle and set it to boil, we can have a quick cup before we leave for town."

Kate nodded and added water to the kettle, before setting it directly on the hot stove top. If she wasn't careful, she'd learn how to take care of herself and shock the servants when she returned home.

Water bubbled from the spout, just as Janet picked up the large batch of dough, formed into a ball, then set it in a greased bowl. She placed a damp towel over the top and set the bowl on the warming shelf above the stove.

"You learn quickly. Never underestimate yourself." Janet washed her hands in the dish pan and smiled over her shoulder at Kate.

"You're very gracious." Kate took the pot and cups to the table. "You work circles around me."

Janet smiled. "I give you credit for not complaining. You did your best, Kate."

Kate washed her hands then settled at the table with her tea, pleased over her small victories. How different her life was from Janet's. Kate spent her days in the business world waging verbal wars with men who thought she should be at home doing needlepoint.

No wonder the average woman had no desire to become involved with business. They didn't have time. Every day was filled with cleaning, cooking, laundry, mending, and sewing the clothes. No time existed to think about anything other than homemaking.

Through all the work, she could also see the sense of accomplishment on Janet's face when they were cleaned up and ready to go into town. The clothes on the line flapped in the afternoon breeze coming off the lake. The bread was rising in a very large bowl, filling the air with a yeasty scent. The entire house smelled of lemon wax and fresh air.

The family would return home later that day to a clean, cozy house, smelling of fresh baked bread and dinner simmering on the cook stove. They'd wrap themselves in the security of knowing Janet was home taking care of them.

A lump lodged in Kate's throat as they closed the door and walked toward the hilltop overlooking the town. She may never know Janet's sense of accomplishment. At twenty-four, she doubted she would marry and start a family.

Along with the advantage of being born with a silver spoon in her mouth, also came the stark disadvantages. Men wanted her for her money and position. She had a company and an estate to maintain and a power hungry monster after her. She would have no peace in her life until Jeb Walker was stopped and even then, she'd return to a solitary life, filled with employees and servants.

The brief trip through Hope the previous day hadn't prepared Kate for the roughness of the teaming railroad town. Dust from the streets soon covered her boots and hem.

Janet narrated the origins of Hope, as they walked down the hill and onto the main street, perched just above the tracks that rimmed the lake.

The railroad had built the town in the early eighties. The track was completed in Gold Creek, Montana, but the roundhouse had stayed in Hope for a while. Later, the officials moved operations to

Heron, just over the Montana line until the drought hit. Along with the return of the roundhouse and new buildings, the railroad also brought gamblers and ruffians.

"Lucky for us, we have the new sheriff," Janet said, stepping onto the rough-cut boardwalk that lined the dusty street. For being such a small woman, she walked fast, and Kate pushed to keep up. Following her into the general mercantile, Kate hesitated to drink in the charm of the country store.

Rough planks covered the floor, and shelves ran clear to the ceiling, groaning with the bounty of stock. A counter paralleled one wall, and banded barrels and crocks filled with salted meat, pickles, and cabbage ran down the center of the room. The store smelled of dust, wood, and brine.

Kate smiled, her heart lightened with the adventure of it all. She walked through the store, smelling, touching, and feeling the ambiance of the quaint western town. Pioneers had begun moving west over the past fifty years, and their fortitude had always fascinated her.

This was the store Maura worked in, and Janet was busy with her daughter picking out fabric for a new dress and linen for kitchen toweling.

She could picture Janet cutting out new hand and dish towels, hemming them and embroidering flowers on one end to add that special touch. The towels in Kate's room even had tatted lace on the hem. Life here might be rough, but Janet brought gentleness into their lives.

Kate turned away; the sad knowledge she wouldn't be here to see the new towels and their delicate trim washed over her. She wove around barrels and pyramids of canned food, stopping at Janet's side.

Maura's eyes met hers, and her mouth tightened. Kate laid her hand on Janet's arm.

"Excuse me, Janet, where's the telegraph office? I'm going to let my ad—" she'd almost said advisors, then remembered Mary Catherine wouldn't have people advising her. "I need to send a message to my dear friend in Boston to let her know I've arrived."

"Of course." Janet turned to her with a smile. "It's in the post office just down the street. Go outside and turn right. Cross the road we walked down, and you'll see it next to the sheriff's office."

The dratted man was everywhere she turned. "Thank you, I'll be as quick as I can."

"Take your time. I'll meet you there if I finish before you return." Janet went back to her fabrics and threads.

Once outside, Kate paused, taking a deep breath of fresh mountain air. She hated lying to everyone. How would she get through the next week?

Then, there was Seth Morgan. She couldn't go more than a few minutes without him either walking through the door or into her dreams.

Last night, she'd rolled over in her sleep and was back in his arms on the train, running her hands over his chest, begging him for help. But the begging didn't make her moan in her sleep. It'd been the memory of his hard-muscled chest beneath her fingertips, the spicy scent of his clothes and warm skin.

"Urrr." She growled under her breath and stomped one healed boot on the rough lumber walk. She had to make the best of her time in Hope and stay out of Sheriff Morgan's way.

Part of her energies could be spent bringing Maura and Ethan together. She'd given it some thought while she hung the wet clothes on the line. It would be a way to make her presence in Hope and in their lives have a purpose.

She managed to enter the telegraph office without being detected. The entry was narrow and faced a partition with a counter.

"Can I help you?" A balding man with a dark green visor pulled down to his eyebrows and garters on the full sleeves of his white shirt appeared behind the counter. Behind him, pigeonholes lined the wall, and a small table held the telegraph machine and a stack of paperwork.

"Yes, please. I'd like to send a telegram."

"Where to?" The man slid a paper and pencil toward her.

Kate stepped closer and picked up the pencil. "New York City to Ross Williams, Esquire, of McShane Walker Shipping." The hairs on the back of her neck prickled. She glanced behind her, but no one was there.

"Haven't seen you around here before." The little man narrowed one eye.

"I arrived yesterday on the train."

"What brings you to Hope?"

Kate sighed. "Mr…."

"Smith. Josiah Smith."

"Mr. Smith, I'd like to send my telegram now."

"Yes, ma'am." Mr. Smith's barely visible brows crinkled. "What's your message?"

"Here it is." Kate handed him the paper. She'd tried to be as cryptic in her wording as possible, just in case Jeb Walker got his hands on it. She hoped Ross understood.

"McShane Shipping, eh? I've heard of that company." He took the paper and began to tick out the words that would hopefully reach Ross with quickness and a hint of urgency.

"You've heard of McShane Shipping? From way out here?" Kate tried to sound nonchalant.

"Hmm." The man scratched the back of his scalp under the banded visor. "What's this word?"

Kate leaned over the counter. "Results. I'm sorry. Your counter is hardly conducive to good penmanship."

"Yeah, well this ain't New York." Mr. Smith frowned.

"Oh, I didn't mean to offend you. I think Hope is charming. Can you read the rest of my writing?"

"Why don't you read it aloud for me, and I'll tap it out."

"Fine." Kate glanced around to make sure no one was near the door. "Need results quickly. Am safe for now. Please answer. Kate."

Josiah Smith sent the message and absently crumpled the paper. Panic threatened to engulf her. Ross had to realize the urgency of her situation.

"Kate?"

She spun around in the small entry and right into Seth Morgan's arms.

"Easy there. I didn't mean to startle you."

She looked up into his dark eyes, the dreams of last night warming her. "I'm fine." Her voice quavered.

"I saw Janet on the street. Did your message get sent?"

"Yes, thank you."

"Ma'am, there's a fee for sending a telegram." The postmaster said in a droll voice from behind his counter.

"Of course." Before leaving the Malones, Kate had taken a fifty dollar bill from the lining of her coat. She laid it on the counter.

"Wooeee, I haven't seen a bill that large in these parts for a while." Mr. Smith fingered the bill before counting out change and reverently tucking the currency into his cash drawer.

She turned to leave; her gaze met Seth's. One corner of his mouth turned up in what might pass as a smile. He'd been suspicious enough of her, now he'd have one more thing to question her about.

Taking hold of an elbow, Seth ushered her out

the door and into the sunshine. His rugged good looks and size sent a flutter through the region of her stomach.

"Janet said she'd meet you at Mrs. White's for tea. Mind if I join you?"

"It's a free country, Sheriff." Oh my word, she had to get over this breathless, fluttery feeling each time she stood near him.

"As free as you can get." Seth guided her across the street. "I could have delivered a telegram for you after dinner last night."

Kate hesitated to answer, focusing on the echo of his boots against the rough planking. He swung around in front of her, his chest inches from her face.

She swept her gaze over his corded throat, determined jaw, and into his deep dark brown eyes.

"I'd hate to impose on you, Sheriff."

"I'm here to serve, ma'am." He stepped a fraction closer, his arms open as if calming a nervous filly.

"To serve the people of Hope, not deliver telegrams for someone who is perfectly able to take care of her own business."

"Are you able?"

Kate lifted her chin. "Of course I am. I—" She almost blurted how she ran a large shipping business, but she couldn't tell him the truth yet. Furthermore, hiding out in a remote western town, while someone else straightened out her problems, didn't demonstrate her professional abilities.

"Are you shopping for your wedding?"

"Wedding?" Kate repeated, startled from her thoughts.

"Your wedding's next week, remember?" One eyebrow cocked, he stepped closer. "Have you changed your mind?"

His spicy scent enveloped her. Damn the man for disconcerting her with his masculine presence one minute while he treated her like a criminal the next. Was he trying to trick her into confiding in him?

"No." Kate steeled herself against the urge to turn and run away, as much from her traitorous response to his nearness, as his incessant questions. "Of course I haven't forgotten about the wedding. However, we've postponed the ceremony for a week."

"Oh really?" One dark brow rose. "How'd that happen?"

"We agreed we need more than one week to get to know each other. Letters are hardly enough."

Seth nodded. "Waiting longer is a good idea."

Kate blinked in surprise. "You're agreeing with me?"

"Sure. Marriage is a big step, at least it should be."

Mesmerized by his nearness and deep, gravelly voice, Kate stared into his dark eyes, seeing a warmth incongruous to the toughness he exuded.

She drew in a deep breath of fresh lake air. "Ethan's first wife hurt him deeply. I'll do everything in my power not to do the same."

Seth held out his arm. "Shall we join Janet for tea?"

Kate laid her hand on the proffered bicep and tried to ignore the strength in his arm, the warmth through the layers of fabric. He hadn't commented on her vow not to hurt Ethan. She ground her teeth. Never mind the fact that Ethan would be hurt in the end. If this was a real engagement, she'd never hurt the man she loved. Not intentionally.

A Chinese man crossed the street in front of them, pushing a large wooden cart filled with potatoes. A long queue lay on his back, and the handlebars of a thin, black mustache framed his chin. Dust clouded around him, coating his black clothes.

Kate coughed and covered her mouth with a handkerchief. Keeping it there as a muffle for her words, she tilted her head toward Seth. "I'm surprised to see so many Chinese in this area."

Seth nodded. "From what I understand, they came with the railroad construction in eighty-two. A few stayed." He lifted his chin toward a Chinese woman who hurried down the street, a laundry basket balanced on her head.

"So much culture in such a remote place." Kate was accustomed to seeing people of all origins in New York. A port town, it had welcomed newcomers for two hundred years. Out here, well, she hadn't thought about the people who would settle a northwestern town.

They continued down the sidewalk, side by side. The people they met nodded, some smiled, but curiosity wreathed their faces. Guilt wrapped even tighter around Kate. She was Ethan's bride to be, and there'd soon be a wedding. Why was she on the arm of the new sheriff?

Seth stopped a couple times to introduce himself and Kate to his new fellow citizens. Uncomfortable, she wanted to hurry on their way. Once the truth came out, and it would, the people of Hope wouldn't be so welcoming.

Outside Mrs. White's café and boarding house, Seth reached around her to open the door and guided her inside. She'd been on men's arms for most of her adult life, but she'd never wanted to be even closer.

From her seat at a small round table covered with a floral cloth and a full tea service, Janet smiled at them. "I see Seth found you."

"Yes, what a surprise." Kate forced a smile.

Seth pulled out a chair next to Janet's and gestured for her to be seated. "Hope's a small town. It's not hard to find someone."

"Well, we're glad you're here, Sheriff. Aren't we, Kate?" Janet signaled a woman in a blue gingham dress, generously covered with a white apron, to bring another setting. "The better we get to know you, the safer we'll feel." Janet introduced Kate to the proprietor, Mrs. White, then turned back to her tea. "Kate, do you need anything for the wedding?"

The wedding. It loomed in every conversation. And if she heard how great Seth Morgan was one more time, she'd scream. An image of standing at the altar with Ethan, while Seth watched her every move, flashed through her mind.

Kate took a sip of the strong tea. Maybe it would clear her mind of all wild images. She'd refused to marry Jeb to save her company, and she'd refuse to marry a rancher in the wilds of Idaho Territory, even to save her life.

But what to do with Seth Morgan? She pretended interest in the flakiness of the scones, but she couldn't ignore the man sitting next to her. He was far too sure of himself. Downright cocky. At every turn, he waited to catch her in a web of deceit.

"I really must go home." Janet opened her reticule and took out a coin.

"Allow me." Seth pulled money from his pocket and handed it to Mrs. White.

"Why thank you, Sheriff. I didn't invite you to join us in order for you to pay."

"It's been a pleasure." He stood and pulled Kate's chair out for her. "Would you like to take a walk?"

The man may as well have asked her to dance.

"Why don't you two take a stroll around town?" Janet hurried toward the door. "He will see you home, won't you, Sheriff?"

Kate couldn't believe how adeptly Janet maneuvered them into spending more time together, and Seth fell right into the plan. What had happened here? Janet shouldn't be encouraging her to spend time with a man other than her fiancé.

"I should help Janet with the bread." Kate attempted to gracefully decline.

"Absolutely not." Janet waved as she sailed from the café.

"Looks like you don't have a choice." Seth took her arm and escorted her to the door. They stepped out into the sunny, late morning. "Janet Malone's a determined woman, so you might as well accept her plan."

"Plan?" Kate glimpsed Janet as she turned at the end of the boardwalk and disappeared. Her heart leaped in her throat, and her hands grew damp.

"Don't tell me you don't see it." He covered her hand with his.

"See what?" Another display of his arrogance. He thought he saw things she couldn't. "Janet's testing your affections for Ethan. I have a feeling she knows you're not who you claim to be."

He didn't look at her, instead gazed out over the lake, his dark eyes narrowed against the glare of the sun on the water.

"You should say, you don't think I'm who I claim to be. Don't use Janet Malone as an excuse." Oh dear, pretending to be someone else was getting more difficult by the minute. "I came here to marry Ethan Howland, and that's what I'll do."

Seth speared her with his intense gaze. "What's the old saying? 'The lady doth protest too much'?"

Lost in his dark eyes, Kate swayed toward him until her chest brushed his leather vest. Seth cupped her elbows, bringing her even closer. Kate gasped when sensations darted through her and her blood warmed.

Around them, the town dissolved; the passersby disappeared. She and Seth were alone in the world. She'd give anything to be able to press her lips to his, see how that slightly fuller bottom lip felt against her mouth. Experience what it was like to be in the arms of a strong man, who didn't know who she was, didn't want her for her money and position.

"Am I interrupting?" A familiar deep voice said from behind her. Kate hurtled back to earth like a burned out star. Twisting out of Seth's grasp, she turned to face Ethan. His blue eyes blazed with suspicion.

"Not at all," Seth said, a twinkle in his eyes. "Kate was feeling a little unsteady and stumbled on our way back to the Malones."

"I came into town early to talk with you, Kate. I was surprised to meet Janet walking home alone." He didn't sound angry, but his voice held an edge.

"All is well now that you're here." Kate pulled her disguise tightly around her. "Sheriff Morgan suggested a tour of the town, but I began to feel overly tired. Now that you're here, I'd love for you to take me home." She moved to Ethan's side and took his arm.

"Certainly, Miss Leary." Seth tipped his hat to her then nodded at Ethan. "She's all yours." He turned and walked toward his office.

Kate schooled her breath and blinked against the stars in her eyes. Never had she come so close to fainting as she did then. The pressure of keeping up this pretense threatened to turn her into a wilting flower. A trait she'd never admired.

She could only imagine what Ethan thought about finding his fiancée in the arms of the sheriff.

Chapter Eight

Ethan watched the sheriff stroll up the street to the edge of town where his office and jail stood. What was the man up to? He was affable enough, but he didn't like that Morgan and Kate had traveled many miles together on the train. He glanced down at the woman he'd agreed to marry but knew very little about.

"Shall we walk?" She smiled, her lips twitching just a touch. A nervousness that could be attributed to the newness of their relationship. Or was it something else?

"Are you feeling well enough, or should I get a buggy?"

"I think the exercise might help."

He didn't reply but turned with her toward the hillside leading to the Malone house. "Kate, exactly how did you and the sheriff meet on the train?"

Her hand tightened on his arm, her entire body tensed. Kate cleared her throat.

"There was no real association with Sheriff Morgan. He was simply a fellow passenger as were many others."

"He indicates there was much more." He longed for her to prove him wrong in his suspicions. He didn't want to be right. Right about women and their inability to make a lasting commitment to a single man.

Kate glanced at him, holding his gaze for several heart beats.

"Let me assure you, there was nothing of a personal nature between Sheriff Morgan and myself." She looked away. "He helped dispose of a rather obnoxious man east of Chicago."

"Did someone accost you?" Ethan stepped around to face her, ready to protect her even if he didn't fully trust her.

"Not exactly, but I had reason to believe he would hurt me if I didn't get away from him. Sheriff Morgan came to my aid and made sure the man was removed from the train."

"I worried about you traveling all that distance alone. Dammit, I should have made the trip and escorted you here." Ethan stepped closer and ran his hands up her arms from her elbows to her shoulders.

Kate stiffened.

Ethan frowned. "I didn't mean to offend you with my language."

"It's not that. I should hurry home to help Janet with the household chores."

"Janet said you were very helpful with the laundry." He held out her hands. "Such delicate skin. Not that of a working woman."

Kate pulled her hands out of his. "Just because someone works hard doesn't mean they have to let themselves go."

"True enough." He couldn't erase the suspicion that all was not what it appeared to be.

"I'd like to check in with Kerry, see if he needs some help. If I take you as far as the Smithy on the edge of town, can you continue to the Malone's without me? It's nearly within sight."

"Of course." Kate smiled. If Ethan didn't have Maura's smoky blue eyes fixed in his mind, he'd be enchanted with the green ones sparkling at him now.

****

Kate walked as fast as her legs would allow up the steep slope. She was a city girl, and the forested countryside intimidated her, making her heart pound and her ears pick up every sound. Perspiration spotted her dress by the time she opened the kitchen door of the Malone home.

What had she been thinking when she agreed to walking from town alone? Furthermore, what had she been thinking when she leaned into Seth Morgan's hard, so very male body? Right in the open where anyone in town could see.

Ethan no doubt witnessed the entire scene.

Janet was forming loaves from the risen dough. The tea kettle steamed and spit on the back of the stove and a teapot stood at the ready.

"You're home sooner than I expected." Janet set the pans of bread dough on the warming shelf and covered them with a dish towel.

"I met Ethan, and he walked me as far as the smithy."

"Ethan's in town this early? That's unusual." Janet washed her hands in the wash pan and dried them on her apron. "I'm brewing tea, would you join me?"

"We had tea at Mrs. White's." Kate smiled and shook her head, unable to resist teasing the other woman. "Don't you mean you want all the details?"

Janet smiled and held up her hands. "You already know me so well! Yes, I do want all the details. Starting with where you were when Ethan met you."

Kate strolled to the table and rested her hands on the back of an oak chair. "Which leads me to ask, why would you suggest I walk with Seth when I'm engaged to Ethan?"

Janet busied herself at the stove, adding a stick of wood to the crackling fire. "I fixed tea because we didn't really have lunch. Only Mrs. White's delicious scones."

"That was fine for me." Kate worked her mouth to one side. Who was she to press Janet for the truth when she'd been lying since arriving in Hope? If she was on a journey for the truth, she should be first. She released the chair and started toward the back door. "I'm going to check on the laundry. Some of it must be dry."

"Please don't worry about those," Janet called, but Kate walked out the door to the clothes line.

How could she continue this charade? Her second day in Hope, and she'd planted more doubts in Ethan's head. Seth's, too, for that matter. If Ross gave her the slightest encouragement, she'd confess to the entire town of Hope and leave for New York.

Janet followed her outside. "How did Ethan react when he saw you with Seth?"

"Not well. He didn't say anything in anger, but I could tell by his expression he wasn't pleased." Kate removed the clothes pins from a pair of pants and shook the stiff fabric to remove some of the wrinkles.

Janet gave her a little half smile. "Jealousy is a wicked thing."

"How can he be jealous when we've just met? You have to have feelings for someone to feel jealousy."

Janet narrowed her eyes and planted her hands on her hips. "You don't feel anything for Ethan?"

Kate draped a dress over her arm and smoothed it with her free hand. "I don't know him. That's why I asked him for an extra week before we marry."

"Are you worried about running his household? Don't forget what I said about Ethan being willing to hire help. His main concern is providing a mother for Will."

The laundry basket piled high, Kate carried it into the kitchen.

Janet followed and filled the teapot with boiling water then wrapped it in a cozy. "Just set the laundry in the corner. Tomorrow morning we'll heat up the flat iron."

Kate grimaced. She'd never picked up an iron in her life and would probably burn holes in the clothes.

Ignoring Kate's objection to another tea break, Janet placed a tray with milk, sugar, and sliced apples in the center of the table.

Kate picked up an apple slice. "Do you think Ethan realizes he made a mistake?"

Janet stirred a heaping spoon of sugar into her tea. "I think he's starting to realize sending for you might not have been the right thing to do. Nothing against you, of course. Just marrying a stranger is never good. Especially when he sees you with another, very charming man."

A bite of apple halfway down, Kate coughed and patted her chest.

"That bad, eh?" Janet handed her a cup of water.

Kate sipped the water and cleared her throat. "Seth and I were looking at the lake and talking. I lost my footing and Seth caught me. I'm sure when Ethan saw us, it looked rather compromising."

"Really?" Janet paused with her cup halfway to her mouth. "That could be bad."

"Oh, Janet. The last thing I want to do is hurt him."

Kate set her cup on the table and rested her forehead against her palms. Janet was an intelligent woman and had to know her daughter loved Ethan. Why wouldn't she do everything possible to bring them together?

Could that be why she invited Seth to dinner last night, then asked him to join them for tea at Mrs. White's? No, Kerry had invited the new sheriff to dinner last night.

Then, Janet asked Seth to show Kate around town. All of this was very strange and could only point to one thing; Seth was right. Janet wanted to test Kate's affection for Ethan. If all went right, she'd break them up so Ethan could marry Maura.

Janet dropped the subject and asked Kate about her family and Boston. More than once, Kate caught herself beginning to confess the truth. When the teapot was empty, Janet stood to clear the table and began dinner preparations.

Kate insisted she help, so Janet showed her how to peel potatoes while Janet prepared apples to bake for dessert.

"You're not only more beautiful than I'd expected, but more determined as well." Janet laughed. "Just try to get more peel than potato in the chicken feed."

"You feed the chickens potato peelings?"

Janet stopped washing apples, her mouth gaping. "I feed all of our fruit and vegetable scraps to the chickens."

"Oh, that's a good idea. Umm, baked apples. I haven't eaten them since my mother died." Kate picked up the paring knife and started peeling potatoes.

Her servants would be amazed if they could see her helping with the wash, the household chores, and now preparing dinner. They'd always taken care of her and probably didn't think it proper for a woman in her social station to do such menial work.

Kate enjoyed it. She liked the earthy, scent of the potatoes and the sense of accomplishment when she stepped back and saw what her two hands had done. Even if some of her peelings had more potato than the potatoes.

Kyle burst through the door; his school bucket in hand, his eyes wide, his face pale.

"Good heavens, Kyle. What's wrong?"

"A man followed me. He was outside the school when I left. I didn't think anything of it, until I saw him following me through town."

Kate's heart leaped, the room tilted.

"Did he do something? Why are you scared of him?" Janet hurried to her son and clasped his shoulders. "Are you hurt?"

Kyle visibly swallowed and shook his head. "I'm not hurt, Ma. He just scared me. When I turned around, he'd act like he was doing something else, then he'd follow me. When we reached the hill, he darted in and out of the trees."

Kyle was a strapping young man. He wouldn't be frightened by just anyone. The warm, pleasant day disappeared into a cloud of fear. It could be the henchman, or another of Jeb's minions looking for her. Could he have found her so soon?

Maura walked inside and glanced between her brother and mother. "What's wrong?"

"Kyle was put off by a man who followed him home. Did you see anyone outside?"

Janet was clearly concerned, and Kate wanted to cry. This was what she'd feared since arriving in Hope. Surely though, Jeb couldn't track her this quickly.

"No, I didn't see anyone." Maura laid her hand on Kyle's arm. "Did he hurt you?"

"No, I'm fine. I thought he'd attack me, but he'd—he'd disappear, then step out of the trees again."

"I want you both to stay inside until your da comes home. Kyle, check the rifle and make sure it's loaded." Janet's voice was calm and firm. She returned to her dinner preparations.

"Kate, go ahead and cover those potatoes with water and set them on to boil."

Kyle took the rifle off the pegs over the back door and checked the chamber. "It's ready to go." He leaned it against the wall.

"Darlin' sit down at the table and have some tea and a scone from Mrs. White's. You've had a fright."

"Thank you, Ma." Kyle settled in at the table,

and true to most growing boys, promptly devoured a scone.

"I'm going to change, Ma. I'll be back to help with dinner." Ignoring Kate, Maura left the kitchen, her footsteps echoing as she climbed the stairs to her room.

"Don't mind her, Kate. She's been a bit unsettled lately."

Kate pressed her fingers to her temples. "I don't blame her." The last thing she wanted was to embarrass Maura. She busied herself gathering plates and silverware for the table.

Boots scraped outside on the porch. They all stiffened and stared at the door. It swung open and Kerry walked in, with Ethan behind him.

"I see the bride to be is helping with supper." Kerry smiled at Kate as he looped an arm around his wife.

"Thank heaven, you're home." Janet laid her head on her husband's shoulder.

"What is it, Sweeting?"

"Someone followed me home, Da," Kyle spoke up.

"Someone? Who was it?" Kerry's jovial expression turned to concern.

"That's just it, we don't know. Kyle didn't recognize him." Janet draped her arm around her son's shoulder. At fourteen, the young man stood a head taller than his mother, but that didn't stop Janet from wanting to protect him.

"He darted in and out of the woods, Da. I thought it was strange, so I hurried home."

"Son, you did the right thing." Kerry rubbed his hand over his face and shot a glance at Ethan.

Ethan clamped his hand on Kyle's shoulder. Kate couldn't help but think what a good brother-in-law Ethan would make.

"Stay alert, Kyle. Some unscrupulous people

have moved in since the railroad returned."

"I will, Ethan." The boy nodded. "I'm not a kid anymore, but he scared me."

"Even a grown man gets scared now and then. Never be afraid to heed your instincts. It could save your life." Ethan squeezed with affection, then let his hand drop to his side.

"We'll let the sheriff know about this. Seth can look into it." Kerry moved to the washstand and began to clean up.

At the mention of Seth's name, Kate glanced at Ethan. His mouth tight, he stared at her for a moment, then washed his hands and dried them.

Janet set out cups and made more tea.

The tension from Kyle's experience mellowed, and the men soon began discussing the coming winter. The subject of snowfall reminded Kate she had to leave this wild and beautiful place soon or risk being snowed in.

Maura chose that moment to return to the kitchen.

Ethan glanced up, his expression brightening. There was no doubt in Kate's mind; Ethan wanted Maura, but something stopped him from acting on his desire. Clearly Maura wanted him too, so why in the world had he sent for a bride? Ethan shuttered his expression and turned his attention to Kate.

When the men left the table and moved into the parlor to visit while dinner preparations were completed, Kate sighed with relief. She'd rather learn to cook than experience Ethan's sharp looks of scrutiny.

Janet soon had the venison carved and showed Kate how to drain the hot water off the potatoes and arrange them on a platter. The apples continued to bake, filling the kitchen with the delicious scent of cinnamon and pungent fruit. Kate's stomach growled.

Janet laughed. "I think you've worn off the scones and apple."

Kate smiled. "It's your fault for making the kitchen smell so good. I can't wait to taste it all."

She was hungry, but she was also distracted with the need to know who the man was who followed Kyle home. Any measure of peace she'd begun to feel since arriving in Hope vanished. For that reason alone, she wished Seth would come through the door.

Janet's voice, calling the men back into the kitchen to eat dinner, jarred Kate out of her racing thoughts. Could she sneak out after dinner and find the sheriff? He needed to know that Jeb's hired man or some other hireling of Jeb's might be in town.

Maura continued to ignore her, making a wide berth when they met at the table; Maura with gingham napkins, Kate with the butter dish. Maura took the seat at Ethan's right, while Kate sat to his left and bowed her head as Kerry asked a blessing on the meal. Whispering amen, they all looked up and began to pass the platters and bowls.

From the corner of her eye, she caught Ethan watching Maura slice a piece of venison into bite size pieces. Oh dear, he was in love all right.

Maybe having another woman in the picture would force Ethan to act on his feelings for Maura. Kate's presence could be a physical barrier to their love, making their feelings more forbidden and sweeter. She planned to do all she could to get them together.

When the baked apples were eaten, Kerry and Ethan returned to the parlor with Kyle on their heels.

Kate and Maura helped Janet clear the table, at least Kate tried to. At every turn, Maura elbowed her aside and took over her intentions. Kate finally gave up and leaned against the table, while leftover food was covered to be taken to the spring house.

"Kyle?" Janet called to her son who was no doubt hanging onto the men's every word.

"Yes, Ma?"

"Please go with Maura to the spring house. I want you to carry the rifle."

The brother and sister nodded and took the leftovers out to be stored for the next day in the cool interior of the spring house. Not a bite of food could be wasted. Scrapes were fed to the dog and cat.

The moment they were outside, Janet glanced at Kate. "Don't be too hard on her. I'm sure you can see her feelings for Ethan."

"As plain as day." Kate set the dirty plates in the bottom of the wash pan and ladled hot water over them.

"It's a sticky situation," Janet continued. "I don't want Maura to be hurt, but Ethan made his decision, and we have to honor it."

Kate didn't know what to say. Until Jeb was arrested or cleared, she was bound to her disguise.

Maura and Kyle returned to the kitchen.

"See anything unusual?" Janet picked up a wet plate and dried it with a hemmed square of flour sacking.

"Nope. It's quiet. I'm sure Randy would've barked." Kyle lifted the rifle over the door and rested it on the wood pegs. "He might be old and lazy, but he wouldn't let anything happen to us."

The old dog had been very mellow since Kate arrived. She wasn't as convinced as Kyle that he'd become aggressive enough to scare a stranger away.

"I don't want either of you outside without someone else and the rifle until we find out more about the stranger."

Both Malone offspring nodded.

Maura left the room to return with a sewing basket. Kate wiped off the pine table with the soapy dishrag and finished cleaning up the dishes, while Janet turned up the lamp and Maura laid out quilt pieces.

"Kyle, do you have homework?" Janet called into the parlor. Kyle appeared his mouth in a tight line.

"Yes, I have to finish my arithmetic, or Mrs. Collins will lecture me for a week."

Kate laughed. "It sounds like teachers haven't changed since I finished my schooling."

Janet lifted her chin toward the parlor. "Kate, go ahead and sit with Ethan while I help Kyle."

"I'll help him, Mother," Maura offered without looking up from her sewing.

Impressed with Maura's thoughtfulness, Kate followed Janet into the parlor. The male voices stopped. Janet settled in next to Kerry. Kate stood just inside the doorway, her stomach in knots. She would have rather retired to her room to think about how to extricate herself from the mess she was in, but Kerry smiled and waved her into the room.

"A whiskey, Kate? It's the good stuff, straight from Scotland."

Since turning eighteen, Kate had often enjoyed a glass of sherry after dinner, but she'd never tasted whiskey.

Ethan relaxed on the settee with one leg crossed over the other, a glass of whiskey resting on one thigh. He glanced at her, waiting for an answer. Did he expect her to accept or decline the drink? Kate had only been here for two days, and she was already tired of walking on egg shells.

"Thank you, Kerry, I'd love to have a drink."

Kerry poured a couple fingers of whiskey into a cut glass goblet and added a splash of water before handing it to Kate. She smiled at Kerry, then turned toward Ethan. The man had the bluest eyes she'd ever seen. His mouth softened a margin, before he raised his glass to his lips.

Suddenly a pair of very dark, fathomless eyes flashed through her mind. Damn Seth Morgan for haunting her day and night. How many men had pursued her since she entered society? She'd managed to ward them off without a second thought, convinced they were all after her money.

Seth didn't know she had money. He thought she was a criminal. So, why did she allow him so much space in her thoughts? It had to be the wildness of the west and his rugged handsomeness.

"Kate, please have a seat and relax." Janet motioned to the settee Ethan occupied, his large frame taking up most of the seat.

Kate smiled and instead chose a small chair across from him.

The next hour was spent fielding questions about her life in Boston. Since she had stayed in Boston on several occasions, she could sound authentic. Except the accent. She was surprised the Malones, who were from Boston, didn't question her highly educated New York speech.

"Oh, by the way." Janet sipped her whiskey and swallowed. "While I waited for Kate, Mrs. White and I had the most interesting discussion with Sheriff Morgan." Kate's stomach fluttered and Ethan's jaw stiffened.

"He's quite a handsome man," Janet went on. "Mrs. White is pleased to have him as a boarder."

"Is that right?" Kerry winked at Kate. "I guess I'd better be watching my women folk."

"Kerry Malone, you're full of malarkey. You know you have my heart. It's your daughter you have to watch. Maura's a beautiful young woman." Janet sent Kate a faint wink.

Eager to change the subject, Kate fidgeted in her chair. "With the lake and the creek around us, it's hard to believe there's a drought. Except for all the dust of course." Anything to direct the conversation away from Seth. Ethan had yet to mention finding her and Seth together on the hillside. Not mentioning it made Kate more uneasy.

Janet raised an auburn brow and went on. "Sheriff Morgan said there was trouble on the train east of Chicago, and he came to Kate's aid."

Ethan nodded, his lips pursed. "Kate mentioned the incident to me."

And was she glad she had. One less thing for him to be suspicious of. She turned to Janet and Kerry, "A man tried to accost me. Sheriff Morgan dispatched the man who escaped out the rear of the train."

"That's terrible!" Kerry's thick, dark brows met above his gray-blue eyes. "Were you hurt?"

"No, just frightened and very angry." She returned Ethan's suspicious stare. "I don't take intimidation well. I saw the sheriff on the train and was able to gain his attention."

Ethan stood and crossed the room to set his empty glass on the side table. "I should return to the ranch."

Kate and Janet exchanged puzzled glances. He was leaving, just like that. Even though she'd assured him there was nothing between her and the sheriff, he still harbored doubt. Kate stood and set her glass on a side table. The room gently tipped to one side. Mercy, that small amount of whiskey had gone to her head.

"Thank you for dinner." Ethan picked up his hat and nodded at Janet and Kerry then turned his stunning blue eyes on Kate. "I think it's time you met Will. Time for you to see the ranch."

Somehow, through her growing irritation with his wounded façade and his unreasonable sensitivity, she felt reluctant to let him go without clearing up the matter. No Kate, a voice chirped in her mind despite the waves of whiskey. Don't say another word.

All eyes were on her. Kate found it hard to breathe. They were all waiting for her to respond to his suggestion. The deception continued.

"I'm eager to meet your son and see the ranch." That was at least the truth. She loved children, had envied her friends, who all had several children. Her dinner roiled in her stomach. Meeting Will ensured the boy would be hurt when she left. She shivered. Unless Maura stepped in as the new Mrs. Howland.

Ethan cleared his throat, pulling Kate back to the conversation. "The challenge is, I'm bringing in the last of the winter hay. I don't have time to fetch you tomorrow."

Fetch her? Kate was hardly Randy, the old dog, waiting for a pat or a meaty bone. She grasped the back of the chair she'd been sitting in.

"I can take her to the ranch." Janet spoke up. "I haven't seen Ruth in a long time."

"Thank you, Janet. Ruth would welcome a visit." Ethan's gaze didn't leave Kate's face. Two thousand miles away, this had seemed like such a brilliant plan. Reality crashed around her. She was going to meet his son and the nanny.

"I thought you wanted to wait a week before introducing me to Will." Kate massaged the back of the chair, hoping she could hold her emotions together until Ethan left and she escaped to her room.

The effects of the whiskey threatened her self-control, and her balance. The contents and people in the room started to waver. Kate stumbled backward. Ethan moved to her side and clamped his large hand on her arm to steady her. "Are you all right?"

"I think so." She put her hand to her forehead.

Ethan raised a dark brow. Kate's stomach sank. She remembered her married friends experiencing dizziness when they first learned of their pregnancies. Surely, he didn't think…

"I'm fine. I think the whiskey went to my head."

Kerry guffawed. "Of course that's it, Kate. I should have cut it with more water."

Janet was at her side in a moment. "You've had a long day, and it's catching up with you. Nothing a good night's sleep won't fix."

Kate's anxiety eased. Janet always came to the rescue. She had no idea how she'd continue to fool Janet Malone, nor did she want to.

Kate said goodnight to the men and allowed Janet to guide her into the kitchen while Kerry walked with Ethan out the front door.

Maura worked on her quilt pieces and Kyle on his arithmetic.

"How about a soothing cup of tea before you turn in?"

"That sounds wonderful. Maybe it'll cut the effects of the whiskey." Kate tried to laugh the episode off, but one look into Janet's eyes, made Kate wonder if Janet thought she was expecting a child.

Flustered and overwhelmed by the events of the day, Kate turned her attention to Maura's colorful quilt pieces. They were coming together, beautifully stitched by Maura's skillful hand.

"Oh, my. You're a very talented seamstress, Maura."

Maura glanced up, surprise widening her smoky blue eyes. "Thank you. I'm not nearly as good as my mother."

"That's not true." Janet added tea leaves to the ceramic pot, then steaming hot water. "Your work is marvelous."

The shiny needle in Maura's deft hand slipped easily through the soft blue calico and back up. If Kate had a prayer of bringing Maura and Ethan together, she had to break down the wall between them.

Janet set a cup of tea in front of Kate with a fresh pitcher of milk. "I'm going with Kate to the ranch tomorrow so she can meet Will."

The shutter went back over Maura's eyes.

"I'm hoping Maura will accompany us." Kate spoke up before she could change her mind.

Maura's jaw dropped.

"What a wonderful idea." Janet glanced over her shoulder, from where she washed the glassware they'd used for their after dinner drinks. "Little Will loves her. Better yet, Maura, why don't you take Kate, and I'll stay home. I don't feel good about leaving the house unattended when a stranger is hanging around."

Kate picked up the dish towel to help Janet. "I don't mean to leave you out of the excursion, Janet. I thought this would give Maura and me some time to get better acquainted."

"I have a job." Maura objected. "I can't leave Mr. White shorthanded at the mercantile."

"Oh, Mr. White will let you have the day off," Kyle interjected, obviously finding the women's conversation more interesting than his homework.

"Kyle, mind your own business." Maura glared at her little brother.

"Now, Maura, I'll have none of your bickering." Janet squeezed soapy water out of her dishrag. "Kyle's right. Mr. White will let you have the day off to go with Kate. If you walk to the store early in the morning, you can ask him."

The matter seemed to be settled, but Kate wasn't sure how Maura would act during the ride to the ranch.

On the edge of an inappropriate giggle, Kate said goodnight and took her tea to her room. In light of her very limited experience with whiskey, she couldn't guarantee what she'd say.

Chapter Nine

Cool and crisp, the morning air washed over Kate in welcome relief. She'd spent another night with Seth Morgan encroaching on her dreams. She had enough to deal with, without adding an attraction to the suspicious and very handsome sheriff.

She'd risked traveling far from home for one reason and one only, to hide out until Jeb Walker was arrested.

She opened the wardrobe doors and cringed. She hoped Mary Catherine was enjoying her tailored dresses, made from the finest fabrics and in the latest designs from Paris, because Kate missed her clothes. Mary Catherine's humble, ready-made clothing, chipped away at Kate's already reduced self-esteem.

Resigned to having no other choice, Kate washed and slipped on a dark green cotton shirtwaist. She twisted her hair and pinned it into a chignon. It would have to do.

Entering the kitchen, she found Janet alone, with Kyle and Maura already gone.

Janet glanced up from her ironing. "Looks like you could use some coffee. Did you have a restless night?"

Kate filled a cup from the pot on the back of the stove. "Yes." She breathed in the aromatic coffee before taking a sip. "Ah, just what I needed."

"Too much on your mind?"

"Hum." Kate took another sip, wishing she could discuss the man who occupied her thoughts and dreams. But she was supposed to be in love with Ethan.

"I'm so grateful you suggested Maura take you to the ranch." Janet slammed the hot iron onto the cotton dress.

"I want her to know I'm not her enemy."

Janet stilled. "Land's sake, why would she feel that way?"

Unable to stay idle, Kate picked up the dishcloth and began to wipe off the table. The deception was wearing on her; she had to begin addressing the issues.

Kate turned to Janet. "She's in love with Ethan, and I believe he's in love with her. Why wouldn't he court her instead of advertising for a bride?"

Janet's bright blue eyes lit on Kate. "I've wondered the same thing."

Kate's stomach flip-flopped. She hadn't expected Janet to be so candid. Since arriving at the Malone home, they'd played cat and mouse with everything from Kate's motives to Janet's opinions. "Do you and Kerry think Ethan's too old for Maura?"

Janet twisted her mouth to one side. "Mercy no. He's settled, has a growing ranch. And he's as handsome as the devil. No, wait." She cupped her chin with one hand. "Seth Morgan better fits that description, don't you think?"

The back door opened, and Maura hurried into the kitchen. "Mr. White grumbled a little, but he let me have the day off and tomorrow, too, in case we stay at the ranch. I'm ready to leave whenever you are."

Kate worked her mouth but nothing came out. Maura didn't realize it, but she'd saved Kate from committing herself on the subject of Seth Morgan.

Maura assessed Kate, from the lace neckline of her dress to the velvet edged hem.

"Isn't that dress too fancy for a trip to the

ranch?"

"It's the best I can do, Maura. I'm not as suited to the frontier as you are." Kate smoothed her hands over the front of the dress. "How long is the ride?"

"It's two hours each way, and I don't want to drive back after dark. We need to leave right away or spend the night there." Maura went from resentment to amazement. "You don't have sturdier clothes?"

"Kate lived in the city and lived a much gentler life," Janet interjected. "Now, let her eat breakfast, and you can be on your way." She set a skillet on the hot stove and added a pat of butter.

"Please scramble my eggs, Janet, and I'll make a sandwich. I don't want to waste part of our day." She didn't want Maura even more irritated by making them late.

Kate stood to one side of the wagon and ate her sandwich while Maura and Janet hitched the team of bays to the wagon.

Janet completed the last buckle and turned to Kate.

"Flossy and Fiona can be jittery, so Maura will drive. Please give my best to Ruth. She's given up a lot for Ethan and Will."

Kate nodded, gathered her skirt to one side and placed a foot on the step. With a push off the ground, she swung onto the hard seat with a thump. She gritted her teeth until the pain in her behind abated.

Forcing a smile, she settled her skirts around her and squared her shoulders. "I'll certainly give Ruth your best."

Maura climbed onto the seat next to her and took hold of the reins. She clicked her tongue and lifted her hands, letting the leads come down on the horses' backs.

The wagon ambled down the narrow, hillside road toward the blue-green waters of the lake.

Crowning the hill, they looked down on the town and four sets of Northern Pacific Railroad tracks, man's mark on the land. A sharp pull on the traces turned the team left onto the main street of Hope, in the opposite direction of the sheriff's office.

Several Chinese residents crossed back and forth as the team passed up the street. Railroad officials strolled along the boardwalk, their suits freshly brushed, tipping their bowlers to the few women on the street at this time of the morning.

"My, she is the most prosperous looking woman I've seen in Hope." Kate lifted her chin at a woman capturing attention from every man she passed, the bustle of her gold taffeta dress swishing with exaggerated movement.

"Most prosperous, but not from doing good." Maura shrugged.

Kate glanced at Maura. "What does she do?"

"Let's just say, she manages the rooms over the Mangy Moose Saloon."

"I see." Kate shuddered. "Mangy Moose, Goose Down."

Maura maneuvered the team around a group of young boys playing ball in the street. "Goose down? What do you mean by that?"

Kate twisted on the seat to look over her shoulder just to make sure Seth wasn't spying on her. "It's a bad memory that reared its ugly head for a moment."

"I don't see the sheriff this morning," Maura said, glancing at the boardwalk. "Maybe he's on one of the back streets, questioning Miss Candy's girls."

Kate blinked at her, then turned toward the mercantile as they passed.

"I hope Mr. White could truly do without you today."

"He said he could."

A thick tension lay over them as Maura

carefully navigated the busy street to avoid running over children who didn't attend school or were too young.

Kate steeled herself from looking for Seth. Maura could be right about him being with a less than respectable woman. After all, he was extremely handsome and had the normal needs of a man. At least, that's what she'd overheard the dock workers talking about over the years. Kate gasped and gripped the edge of the hard seat. Startled, Maura jerked on the reins. The horses whinnied and sidestepped.

"What's wrong?" Maura brought the team back under control.

"I'm sorry." Kate pressed her hand to her throat, her heart pounding like a run-away team. "I could swear I saw the man from the train."

"I heard you talking about him last night. Is it him? Should we find the sheriff?" Maura pulled back on the traces and guided the team to the outside of the street.

"No!" Kate's voice quavered. Was it possible the henchman had reached a track in time to catch a train and follow so closely behind?

"Sheriff Morgan would want to know." Maura twisted on the hard seat to look behind them. "Oh, there's the sheriff!"

The anticipation of seeing Seth after the realistic dreams of the night before made her fidget until she nearly fell off the seat. Maura grabbed her arm and pulled her from the edge. "Maura, please don't say anything about that man."

Maura frowned. "Why? Aren't you afraid of him?"

Seth was within hearing distance. "There are other things that scare me more," Kate whispered. She smiled at Seth over Maura's shoulder. "Good morning, Sheriff."

"Morning." Seth touched the brim of his black western hat. The flash of his strong white teeth sent butterflies through Kate's midsection. How could she be so enamored with a man who suspected her of criminal acts?

Seth continued to her side of the wagon and leaned against it, his hands inches from Kate's bottom. Kate scooted back.

"Miss Malone." He nodded at Maura. "Where are you ladies headed on this fine day?" His hand remained much too close to Kate's hip, and his magnetic presence threatened her breathing.

"We're going to Ethan's ranch. He's expecting us for tea, so we need to hurry." Kate twisted her hands in her lap.

"Sounds good. I haven't visited Ethan's ranch yet, mind if I join you?"

"Of course not," Maura piped up.

Kate struggled for a reason why he couldn't possibly accompany them. Her mouth opened and closed. "Surely you're too busy, Sheriff?" she finally croaked.

Seth squinted against the morning sun as it crested the hill. "I always have time to get acquainted with my upstanding citizens."

"Would you like to ride with us?" Maura held out the reins.

"I'm certain the sheriff would prefer to ride his horse." Kate forced a smile to soften her words. If Seth took offense, he didn't show it.

"Kate's right." Seth stepped back from the wagon. "You go ahead. My horse is at Kerry's livery."

"Glad to hear that." Maura raised a brow at Kate. "We'll be happy to wait, won't we Kate?"

"Of course." Kate understood Maura's motive. She might be only nineteen, but she recognized Kate's attraction to Seth and would do everything she could to promote it, and stop the planned marriage to Ethan. Like mother-like daughter.

****

In a matter of minutes, Seth had his horse saddled, bid Kerry a good morning, and rode up the street toward the waiting ladies. He chuckled at his own wit. He knew darned well he had Kate tied up in knots. She'd looked like a scared fawn when he said he'd like to go with them. The woman was up to something all right. He'd sent telegrams to the contacts he'd made while in Boston and New York but hadn't heard a word.

He reined in beside the wagon and tipped his hat. "Ready?"

Kate nodded, then turned away.

Maura clicked at the horses and guided them to the end of the main street and onto the narrow road that led southeast along the lake.

Plodding along with the wagon, Seth marveled at the beauty of this remote place. Even with the drought, the trees were green and the mountains a blue-green. Flicks of orange dotted the mountainsides, but Kerry had explained that the trees weren't dead, but were Larch trees going into hibernation. The lake narrowed, and the trees thickened at its shores.

His mind wandered from the beautiful scenery to the fetching, deceptive woman bouncing on the buckboard seat. She might be charming and beautiful, but she wasn't who she claimed to be. She was the typical woman, selling her self-respect for some end goal.

The wagon wheels kicked up a billowy cloud of dust, coating Kate's dark green dress. Why did he have to notice what she wore?

Grit coated his teeth, and he rolled his tongue through his mouth to moisten it, then spit past the toe of his boot.

Kate turned toward him and frowned. "Really,

Sheriff, is that necessary?"

"It is, if I don't want to eat a pound of dirt." He chuckled at the way her nose crinkled and her lips curled in repulsion. Oh yeah, the dust covered beauty intrigued him even while she mystified him.

"This is the mouth of the Clark's Fork River." Maura yelled over the noise of the plodding horses and metal rimmed wheels, crunching against pine cones and rocks.

It only took an hour into the trip for Seth to realize he'd been crazy to tag along. Kate's henchman was in Hope. He should be tracking him down for questioning, not traipsing after Kate like a lap dog. Once the ladies were safely at the ranch, he'd return to town and find the piece of scum.

"We're almost there." Maura's announcement broke into his self-reproach.

Seth tore his attention from Kate's shapely backside and looked around the clearing. Howland had quite a spread. The ranch house sat ahead and to their right, slightly angled so the back of the house paralleled the river. A barn, with the wide doors flung open, sat to their left bordering the line of thick trees and another large barn edged a meadow straight ahead.

All the buildings showed the relative newness of the ranch. Howland even had a lawn and flower beds edging his house with a vegetable garden on the south side.

Kate should be impressed. The thought irritated him.

She straightened her posture on the bench seat and brushed at the dust on her clothes.

Seth guided the gelding next to the team and stopped at the hitching post. The front door opened, and a woman who looked to be in her thirties stepped out, her dark skirt short enough to show the ankles of her low-healed black boots.

"Maura, I'm so glad you came with Kate." The woman hurried down the steps to Kate's side of the wagon. "I'm Ruth."

Kate smiled and held out her hand. "Ruth, I'm so happy to meet you. Janet sends her best."

Ruth grasped Kate's hand and looked into her eyes for a moment as if taking measure of her. Seth would love to know what Ruth thought of the beautiful woman, and if she looked like mother material for Will, or heartbreak for Ethan.

"I've been eager to meet you, Kate. Please come in the house. I've just finished brewing tea. Ethan tells me you're from the city. Boston, isn't it?"

Kate grinned. "Yes, I'm from the city, but it's a pleasure to be here."

Maura climbed off the wagon and walked around to meet the older woman, enveloped her in a hug, then turned toward Seth. "Ruth, this is Sheriff Morgan. He wanted to see the ranch and was kind enough to escort us."

"Welcome, Sheriff. Ethan said Hope was lucky enough to have a former Texas Ranger as a lawman." She shook Seth's hand, then gestured toward the door. "Please come in. You can wash up while I set out tea. I'll ring the bell for Ethan and Travis. They're gathering in the last of the hay." Ruth walked toward the covered porch and pulled the rope on a brass bell hanging over the railing. The clanging reverberated off the tall trees surrounding the clearing.

Seth wrapped the reins around the hitching post. He started to follow Ruth and Maura inside the house, then turned to see Kate still sitting ramrod straight on the hard seat. "Need some help?" Without waiting for an answer, he approached the wagon and held up his hands.

"I'm sure I can make it on my own." Kate clenched her teeth.

"Don't be stubborn. Your posterior's numb, and I'll lay odds the moment your feet touch the ground, your legs'll give out." Seth narrowed his eyes, then shrugged and lowered his hands. "Have it your way."

Not a word. The woman was as stubborn as they came. He walked toward the door that Ruth and Maura disappeared through, then slowed his pace. Halfway up the steps, he paused.

"Coming?" He braced his hand on the whitewashed upright post.

"Of course," she called back, her voice quavery.

He turned toward the yard, pretending to survey Ethan's property, watching her from the corner of his eye. She rocked on her bottom, inching toward the edge of the seat, then stuck her booted foot on the notched step and started to swing around. Her straight teeth bit into her bottom lip, and she cringed with pain.

He couldn't do it. He couldn't leave her to her own stubborn devices even if she did deserve to land on her ass in the dust.

His boots hit the gravel, and he reached the side of the buckboard in three strides. "Silly stubborn woman."

She opened her eyes, the green irises watery. Her pride wasn't the only thing making her hesitant to accept his aid. There was something strong between them, and it shook her up.

Kate braced her hands on his shoulders. He bracketed her waist and lifted her off the seat and to the ground. She started to step away and stumbled. Seth caught her closer to him.

"Leg asleep?"

"Um-huh." Her breath caught. "Both of them."

"Lean on me for a bit until they wake up." He kept his arm around her waist and led her toward the porch. The flowery scent of her hair drifted up to confuse him even more. Her soft warmth tested his resolve to never dally with another man's woman.

He wanted to pull her close and bury his face in her auburn hair, soak up her softness, but he steeled himself, drawing on every inch of restraint he possessed. Dammit, this wasn't a loose woman he could play with and leave behind. She might not be telling the truth when it came to her reason for being in Hope, but he didn't believe for one minute that she'd purposely made him want her like he'd never wanted a woman.

Chapter Ten

Kate's shortness of breath and pounding heart had nothing to do with the pinpricks darting through her legs and hips. Not even Ross, with his careful guidance and charm, could compare with the tough lawman who emanated strength and courage, along with his spicy scent.

She stepped away and grasped the porch rail. "Thank you. I think I can make it now."

He loosened his hold on her waist but didn't remove his hands. She looked into his eyes, over his strong nose and stared at his full bottom lip. She'd never seen a mouth so sensual and yet so masculine. Air rushed from her lungs.

He raised a dark brow and let his hands fall back to his sides. "Do you ever let people see who you really are?"

"I don't know what you mean." She sounded like the debutante she'd never cared to be. Being weak and dependent on a man had no place in her life as owner of McShane Walker Shipping.

Seth wrapped his fingers around her upper arm. Without saying a word, he escorted her up the steps and through the door and into the foyer.

"Oh, my."

The care she'd seen the moment they'd arrived at the ranch carried into the house. It may not compare to her home in New York, but for being in the rugged setting of Idaho Territory, it was beautiful in its own right.

A bank of windows lined the back wall and displayed the most lush, green lawn she'd seen since her arrival. The lawn sloped, then rolled to the riverbank of the lazily flowing Clark's Fork River.

She'd love to stroll over the green lawn, let the peace of the moving water carry away her problems, but Maura and Ruth were talking from somewhere to her left, and Seth stood beside her. She glanced at him. "I'm sorry, it's just so peaceful."

"Don't apologize." Seth gestured for her to lead the way down a short hall and into a warm, inviting kitchen. A large table dominated the center of the room, where Ruth had set up a matching tea set on a flowing, white linen cloth. Sunlight streamed through several windows, turning the wood floor into a mellow gold.

"The house is beautiful." She stopped at the table and smiled at Ruth, then Maura.

Ruth smiled. "Ethan will be happy you like the ranch. Please be seated, and I'll serve tea. Will ran out to make sure his father heard the bell."

Kate carefully settled into a chair, reluctant to place her still tingling behind on another hard surface. She inwardly grimaced, when Seth pulled out a chair right beside her and sat down. His signature spicy scent played with her senses, and she barely heard the conversation around her. Against her better judgment, she glanced his way, noting how his shoulders strained against the blue chambray shirt. He'd taken off the black leather vest he normally wore, and the top two buttons of his shirt were unfastened, showing tanned skin.

From somewhere outside, came the giggles of a child. Kate took a sharp breath as the reality of her deception pounded through her heart, in unison with the boots stomping on the steps. The kitchen door swung open, and Ethan stepped into the room. Another man, she assumed, Ethan's friend Travis, followed with a young boy on their heels.

Will's soft, dark curls bounced against his

forehead, and his dark blue eyes sparkled. He was a young, innocent version of his father. Will glanced at her, grinned, then dashed through the room, disappearing somewhere in the house. Oh my, she pressed her hand to her chest, hoping her heart would slow its erratic beat before she fainted. The boy was delightful. The thought of hurting him with her lies made her eyes burn.

"Kate, Maura," Ethan nodded to them. "Sheriff, I'm glad to have you join us."

Seth stood and held out his hand to shake Ethan's. "Thank you. I met the ladies on their way through town. Thought it was a good chance to see your spread."

"It's not as vast as you're used to in Texas, but it's beautiful."

Ethan jerked his thumb toward the man standing next to him and grinned. "This is my foreman, and longtime friend, Travis Connor."

Travis shook Seth's hand, then stepped forward to take Kate's. "It's a pleasure to meet you, Miss. How do you like Hope so far?"

"It's beautiful. Different from what I'm used to, but charming."

Travis' eyes danced as he looked at Kate, sure he was checking her out from head to foot. He looked like he wanted to say more but turned to Seth.

"Sheriff, I'm sure Ruth has some coffee hiding out if you're not a tea drinker."

Seth grinned. "Everything looks so good; I'm not going to be picky."

"Now, Sheriff, I won't be offended if you prefer coffee." Ruth set a coffee pot over a burner on the large, polished wood stove. "It'll just take a few minutes. Travis drinks coffee, too."

"I'm not a dandified Englishman like the boss." Travis chuckled.

The men washed up at the washstand next to

the back door, then joined them at the table. "Where's Will?" Ethan looked around the room, with a frown.

"I'm here!" Will dashed into the room, his hands behind his back.

"What are you doing? You need to meet our guests." Ethan motioned for Will to join them at the table.

"I want to show Maura my new lesson book." Will grinned and pulled a large, tooled leather book out from behind his back.

Maura smiled at the boy, and Ethan shifted in his chair.

"It's beautiful! I've never seen such a grand lesson book." Kate ran her hand over the tooling, thinking it interesting that he specifically mentioned showing it to Maura.

"Uncle Travis made it for my school work."

The boy's exuberance was contagious, lifting Kate's heart. His little chest puffed up as he held the book up for all to see. His attachment to his uncle came through loud and clear. He hurried to Maura's side and handed her the notebook.

"Will, I don't blame you for being so proud of your book." Maura touched his head, her heart in her eyes. "Uncle Travis is very gifted, isn't he?"

Will nodded, his entire body swinging back and forth.

"Will, please properly shake hands with Miss Kate." Ethan eyed his son as the boy carried out the instruction.

"Hello, Will." Kate smiled. "I am very pleased to meet you."

"Hello, Miss Kate," he answered in his childlike voice. "Did you have a pleasant journey from town?"

"I had a lovely trip, thank you." Kate's heart squeezed and a lump grew in her throat. Will deserved a mother who would love him without reserve. Someone like Maura, if only Ethan would give her the chance.

Kate found it hard to continue her act as Ethan's mail-order bride. But if she hadn't changed places with Mary Catherine, there wouldn't be a chance of Ethan and Maura coming together.

Forcing herself to relax and remain alert to what happened around her, Kate caught both Seth and Ethan studying her. Were they waiting for her to make a mistake?

Ethan filled Kate's teacup. "What did you think of the ride from town?"

"I've never been in such a beautiful, yet wild place." Seth's dark brows lifted. Did he think she was pretending to like the area for his sake?

Ethan picked up his cup, then set it down without taking a drink. "After tea, I'll give you a tour. We're fortunate to be right on the river."

"I noticed how close the house is to the river the moment I walked through the front door! The view from the parlor is spectacular." Kate glanced at her companions.

Maura stared at her plate, her body still, her shoulders slumped. Ruth glanced uneasily at Maura then Kate. Did Ruth know about Maura's feelings for Ethan?

Kate glanced away and caught Travis gazing at her over his coffee mug. Did his expression hold typical interest or admiration? Feeling like she was under a microscope, she smiled, then glanced at Seth. He eyed her with suspicion. Did he imagine her flirting with Travis?

She fought an urge to throw her tea in Seth's face, straightened her shoulders and lifted her chin. "My but the ground is dry." The weather had always been a safe subject.

"It is." Seth took another scone off the platter in the center of the table and set it on his plate. "The lack of rain has taken on a life of its own in Hope. It's all the town's people talk about. Being a Texan I'm used to the dust."

Ethan rolled his lips together. "I've been here for six years, and while it gets hot for a few weeks in the summer, I've never seen it this dry."

Kate nodded, relieved the conversation had rolled along and she was no longer under scrutiny. "It's very dry and dusty. It seems to be half of what I eat every day."

Everyone chuckled, but Kate hadn't meant to be funny. She missed her long, oil scented baths; having help with her dress and hair. She could imagine the shocked look on Ross' face if he arrived to find her smudged, creased, and wrinkled, sipping tea in a remote ranch house.

She bit into a tender biscuit, smothered in strawberry preserves and cream, and sighed. Ross wouldn't walk through the door anytime soon, and even if he did, Kate would challenge him to criticize her choices.

She ate the last bite of her biscuit, brushed the crumbs off her fingers, and took a sip of tea.

"Very well." Ethan pushed his chair into the table. "Are you ready for the tour?"

"Certainly." Kate started to get up. Seth quickly stood and pulled the chair out of her way. Stunned over his attentiveness, she thanked him and smoothed her skirt to hide her trembling hands. This crazy response to him had to stop.

Halfway to the door leading into the parlor, Kate realized Seth was right behind her. The man had more nerve than anyone she'd ever met. Well, beside Jeb Walker. She shot a glance at Travis. He raised his brows, shook his head, and set down what was left of his third biscuit.

"Uh, Sheriff, how about a tour of the stables? We've got some fine breeding stock." Seth hesitated, then nodded and propped his hands on his hips. "Sounds good, Travis. Guess I should let these two lovebirds spend time alone."

The walls closed in on Kate. She glanced at Maura, her heart squeezing at the pain on the younger woman's face. Sweet little Will continued to devour his biscuits and jam while Ruth began to clear some of the dishes.

"Maura, I'm sure Ethan and Kate wouldn't mind if you went with them."

Bless Ruth's heart, she already saw the lay of the land. Kate certainly didn't want this opportunity to pass. "Yes, Maura, you should walk with us. When were you last at the ranch?"

"I hardly think we need a chaperone." Ethan braced his hands on either side of the doorway. His brows creased.

"I wasn't suggesting we did. I thought Maura might like some fresh air and see the grounds, too."

"I'd love to come along." Maura's expression brightened. She picked up her plate and cup and set them on the counter.

Kate glanced at Ethan in time to catch the tightening of his mouth. This day could turn out to be very interesting.

"Maura, run along with Ethan and Kate. I'll clean up and start dinner." Ruth used both hands in a shooing motion.

"Oh, Ruth, I should help you." Maura looked torn, and Ethan looked hopeful.

Kate chuckled when Ruth persisted. "Nonsense. This is your day off. Enjoy it. Will can help me, can't you Will?"

"Sure." Will's lip jutted. "But can I go to the stables with Uncle Travis and the sheriff when we're through?"

"That sounds like a marvelous idea. Why don't you run along?" Ruth smiled at the boy.

Seth looked as pouty as Will did but patted the boy's head and lifted his chin toward the back door. "Let's go partner. I need you to show me the livestock. Travis might forget where they are."

Will giggled. "Uncle Travis knows where they are!"

"Shall we?"

Ethan's voice brought Kate's attention back to the doorway and the man who believed she was his mail-order bride. He stepped to one side and motioned for her and Maura to walk ahead of him into the hallway.

Kate wished she was going to the stables with Will and the other men, and let Ethan show Maura around. She'd stirred the pot by encouraging Maura to join them. Ethan was doing everything in his power to avoid the younger woman, and Kate was determined to bring them together.

French doors opened into a formal dining room. A bank of windows captured the same view Kate had seen upon entering the house.

"Oh Ethan, it's so beautiful!" Kate admired the brilliantly hued birch tree, sporting its fall colors, the branches bowing toward the lush green grass. Two fat deer with glossy coats, grazed on the riverbank, unconcerned with the house and the people who watched them.

"I've set up a siphon system out of the river to water the grass." Ethan's face softened and a smile tipped his lips. "It gives me a touch of my Virginia home and civilization."

"It's lovely and such a relief from the drought."

"It's my refuge after working in the dry heat all day."

Maura hesitated at the window, seeming to drink in the view. Was she imagining herself mistress of this ranch, this house? They continued into the next room, the one Kate had seen from the front entry.

"This is the parlor." Ethan gestured in a sweeping motion toward the Persian rugs and elegant, yet comfortable furnishings. He'd managed to bring the refinement and gentility of his Virginia home without losing the rustic beauty of the Idaho Territory ranch.

She glanced at Maura. The longing to live here with Ethan was written on her face. She repeated her earlier question. "Maura, when were you last here?"

Maura ran her hand over the brocade of a high backed chair. "A couple of months ago with Ma. I've never seen this room."

"Really?" Kate glanced at Ethan who hadn't moved since they'd entered the parlor. "I have noticed that most socializing out here is done in the kitchen."

"Very true." Ethan moved to her side. "Customs here are different." He shifted from one foot to the other, his hands behind his back, his fingers clasping and unclasping.

He'd no doubt intended to use this tour to talk about the wedding, and she'd ruined the opportunity by inviting Maura.

A band formed around Kate's head and pain shot through her left eye. She closed her eyes and took a steadying breath. If only she could confess her deceit immediately; tell them to quit playing games and admit their love for each other.

She opened her eyes and turned in a slow circle, struggling to overcome the headache and tension. "Ethan, you've put your heart and soul into this place."

"It's my dream to turn this land into a profitable ranch." He quit fidgeting and propped his hands on his hips. He shot a side glance toward Maura, then looked down at Kate. "I need to know something."

His voice low, he dragged his hand over his face. "How do you really feel about Hope? You've seemed, I don't know, like you've made a big mistake coming here."

Kate's heart contracted with sorrow over the lies she'd told and would have to continue to tell until she knew Jeb Walker was behind bars. These good people didn't deserve her deception.

"I love Hope."

Strangely, it was true. There was something about the quaint, rustic town that captured her sense of adventure, and the people she'd met were so open and kind. She pressed her hands over her heart and swallowed hard. Hot scented baths and maids aside, she did love it here.

"Are you all right? I didn't mean to upset you." Ethan touched her arm, his brows drawn over concerned eyes.

"I'm a little overwhelmed at the moment."

"It's not what you expected?"

"Oh Ethan, it's so much more than I expected." She glanced at him. His brow smoothed, and he blinked away the shutter normally masking the beauty of his dark, blue eyes. The poor man. He'd been worried that she wouldn't approve of his home. Natalie had scarred him forever, and Kate would soon enforce his belief that women couldn't be trusted.

Oh, but she had no choice. Staying wasn't an option. She wasn't Mary Catherine, wasn't the woman who'd left her home to travel west to marry this man. Instead, she'd brought danger to his peaceful home. She'd only thought of herself.

"Shall we go outside?"

Not waiting for a response, Ethan slipped his hand to the small of her back and guided her though the French doors and out onto the lush green lawn. The river flowed along, deep green and nearly silent in its power and depth. The deer glanced up then moved farther down the bank.

Maura strolled behind them, quiet and tense. Kate longed to bow out and leave them alone to enjoy the warm autumn day, the mesmerizing effect of the river and the forest beyond.

They walked along the grassy bank on a path Ethan had created through the trees, winding around to the barn where Travis and Seth discussed different breeding techniques. Seth drilled her with a look of suspicion. Kate wished she could tell him to mind his own business and leave her alone.

She tore her gaze from Seth and turned to the horses. Ethan began to describe the bloodlines of each mare. Since her father always kept a high quality stable, Kate was familiar with several breeds. However, Mary Catherine probably wouldn't know a great deal about horses, so she smiled and pretended ignorance.

"Kate, will you be all right while Travis and I finish bringing in the wood we cut this morning?"

"Of course I'll be all right. Maura, shouldn't we return to town?" Kate was exhausted from pretending to be someone she wasn't.

Maura looked somewhat relieved. "Yes, the days are getting shorter, and I don't want to drive home in the dark."

Ethan turned his sapphire eyes on Kate. "I'm sure Ruth is cooking a special dinner. I assumed you'd spend the night."

Kate's chest tightened. An entire night of pretending. "I wouldn't want Ruth to go to so much trouble."

"Me either." Maura almost shouted, her smoky blue eyes wide with apprehension. "Besides, Kate and I didn't pack over-night bags."

Kate found Maura's near panic surprising. A chance to spend more time with Ethan, even sleep under his roof should be delightful and yet, she wanted to leave right away.

Noticing Maura's trembling hands, Kate stepped in. "The Malones won't know if we're safe or in trouble along the way."

"No problem," Seth said. "I'm returning to town; I'll let them know you're staying here tonight."

Maura and Kate exchanged looks, comrades for the first time. "Well, I suppose in that case we can't refuse the invitation." Ethan wasn't taking no for an answer, so Kate was at a loss. She waited until the three men stepped out of earshot, then turned to Maura. "I'd love to look at the river again. Do you think Ruth would mind if we didn't hurry back?" She wanted to confide in the younger woman right now, let her know she didn't have to fear, Kate wouldn't be marrying Ethan.

Maura tore her gaze from Ethan's retreating back and glanced at Kate. "Ruth wouldn't mind, but I'd feel bad if I didn't help her."

"You're right." Kate drew a stabilizing breath. "We can walk later."

Once in the kitchen, Maura began to peel potatoes. Enchanted with her, Will stayed at her side, chattering about his new kittens and the puppy his papa had promised him. Each moment spent with the younger woman convinced Kate she had to bring Ethan and Maura together before she returned to New York.

Ruth asked Kate to mix up a batch of biscuits. Kate broke out in a cold sweat. "How about I peel the potatoes and Maura can make the biscuits?"

Maura smirked, her hands flying as she made short work of the potato peelings. "I've got this, Kate. You go ahead with the biscuits."

Ruth assembled the bowl and ingredients. Kate had no choice but to try.

"Kate dear, you have to cream the lard, sugar

and eggs before you add the flour." Ruth took the heaping cup of flour from Kate's hand and set it aside, cracking a couple of eggs over the lard.

Kate cleared her throat. "Ruth, I'm not familiar with baking, but I'm willing to learn."

Ruth studied her for a moment, a smile tilting one corner of her mouth. "I'm sorry, Kate. I didn't mean to make you uncomfortable. I assumed," she went on in a lower tone, "you knew how to cook."

"My mother took care of the cooking before she became ill. Then my father hired a woman to help out."

"Hmmm." Ruth continued to mix the biscuit dough for Kate.

Maura murmured something, and Will giggled. Kate smiled. "It must be hard to say goodbye to Will. You've been such a large part of his life."

"It will be, but I've put Horace off for nearly seven years. I stayed with Natalie when pregnancy hit her so hard. It's time I settled down and started my own family before I'm too old." Ruth's eyes nearly glazed when she mentioned Horace.

"I understand. I hope Will accepts the changes."

"He'll be fine." Ruth chuckled. "Have you seen the way he stares at you? I'd say he's more than ready to welcome you into the family."

Queasiness washed over her. Would Will understand when she told his father the truth about her identity and why she came to Hope? Why she lied to everyone?

Yearning for a family, a child of her own sliced through her and the beauty of the day dimmed.

"Are you all right?" Ruth laid her hand on Kate's shoulder. "You look pale."

"I'm fine. Just a little overwhelmed."

"I have just the thing." Ruth wiped her hands on her apron and hooked her arm through Kate's and led her into the parlor. She let go long enough to fill a crystal flute with sherry.

Kate accepted the amber liquid with a smile and took a sip, rubbing her lips together. “Mmmm. Thank you.”

“There, your color’s returning.”

Kate glanced toward the doorway leading to the kitchen, then back at Ruth. “I hope you don’t think I normally enjoy spirits this early in the day.”

“Piffle.” Ruth patted Kate’s arm. “You’ve been through life changing events and need a minute to catch your breath.”

Kate giggled, then covered her mouth. If she wasn’t careful, she’d be spewing the truth to this kind lady before she thought out the consequences.

Ruth winked and took the empty glass from Kate. “See, you’re already more relaxed. Just what the doctor ordered. We’ll slip back into the kitchen with no one the wiser.”

Kate laid her hand on Ruth’s arm and gave her a gentle squeeze. “I can see why Maura loves to visit the ranch.”

Ruth twisted her mouth to one side and peeked at Kate through one eye. “I think we both know why Maura loves to come here.”

Kate nodded. “You do know.”

“Anyone with eyes should see Maura loves Ethan.” Ruth glanced over her shoulder to ensure no one stood within hearing distance.

Ruth evoked such a sense of trust and understanding, that the moment Kate could safely tell everyone who she was, she’d personally visit Ruth to explain why she’d done such a thing.

But not today. Today, she’d continue the ruse of being Ethan Howland’s fiancée.

They returned to the kitchen and finished the biscuit dough. Kate watched while Ruth rolled out the dough and cut rounds with a glass. She wished life was really this simple.

Heavy boots against the board walk outside the kitchen door, followed by the deep tone of men's voices, dissipated the new found relaxation. Ruth looked up from carving a roast of beef.

"Here they come, starved no doubt."

"It's time to eat dinner?"

Ruth chuckled. "Yes, on the ranch we have dinner mid to late afternoon. We often have something light to eat later in the evening, but this is our main meal."

Accustomed to dining after seven, the Malone meal schedule was enough of a surprise to Kate. Now, yet another difference between her life in New York and life in Idaho Territory.

The men entered the kitchen and took turns washing at the fully stocked washstand. Kate caught herself staring as Seth lathered his hands, wondering what event had caused the tiny scars on his thumb. His fingers were long and large, capable. She tingled at the memory of those hands on her waist when he helped her from the buckboard.

Ruth and Maura carried heaping dishes of food to the formal dining room. Kate blinked and jerked her attention away from Seth Morgan and back to the activity around her.

"Oh!" Coming to her feet, she pushed the chair into the table and hurried to take a basket of bread off the kitchen table. "Please, allow me to help."

One corner of Seth's mouth lifted in what she viewed as sarcasm. He seemed to be a witness to every faux pas she committed. She huffed and turned away, but not before Travis saw the exchange. There was someone else who had to know Ethan and Maura belonged together.

The food was plain but delicious, the company delightful. Kate smiled at the banter between Travis and Ethan. The old friends seemed to bring out the best in each other. It became clear through the table conversation that Travis was Ethan's former brother-in-law. Natalie's brother. Had that very important fact been mentioned in Ethan's letters to Mary?

Seth joined in on the banter from time to time, accepted as if he were an old friend. He had a way of blending in where ever he went; along with standing out like no other man she'd met.

After dinner, the men retired to the window-lined parlor for a brandy. Kate helped Maura and Ruth put away leftovers and wash the dishes. Maura left the kitchen to retrieve the last dishes off the dining room table.

"Ethan's a wealthy man, Kate. He can hire kitchen help after the wedding," Ruth said in a low tone.

"I'm obviously inept, aren't I?" Kate dried her hands on a towel and smiled at the other woman.

"Clearly, you haven't had much time in the kitchen. Kate, don't be what you can't be. You'll learn as you go along."

Kate looked into Ruth's clear, honest brown eyes. "There's a lot about me no one here knows, Ruth. I'm—"

"Here are the last of the dishes." Maura's appearance cut Kate short. What was she thinking? The sherry, food, and relaxing dinner companions had thrown off her guard. This deception couldn't end fast enough.

Chapter Eleven

The various chores on the ranch were done before dark. Travis retired to his cabin, and the sheriff returned to town, but Ethan needed to clear his head. The barn with its fragrance of hay, tinged with clean animals and fresh manure calmed him like nothing else. He loved this ranch and never wanted to leave.

He'd been stunned when Maura accompanied Kate to the ranch. Kate and Seth Morgan. The man was likable, there was no doubt about it, but he was also a shadow to the woman Ethan intended to marry.

He'd made it clear in his letters that the marriage was an arrangement for Will and nothing more, that he didn't want to become intimately involved with Kate.

Then, reality hit. He was about to marry someone he didn't love. That could make for a very long and unhappy life. Fate had dealt him a cruel hand. He'd found the girl of his dreams, watched her grow into a beautiful woman, but he couldn't have her.

Ethan leaned against the top rail of the corral and rested one booted foot on the bottom one. A low whinny rumbled through his gelding's throat, and the horse ambled across the corral for attention.

Ethan shook his head. If only his life could be so simple. All Maximillion had to do was eat, run, and sleep. What insanity had possessed him to invite them to stay overnight? At this moment, Maura was in the guest room getting ready for bed—changing into a nightgown, brushing out her thick, chestnut hair. Desire thundered through his body, and he gripped the split rail. Had he sentenced himself to a loveless marriage when he could have spent the rest of his life with Maura?

Will had been the center of his life since the day Ruth placed the red, squalling baby in his arms. His son had been the reason for sending for a wife, and Ethan couldn't forget that. Will needed a mother.

Yearning to give his son one last hug goodnight, Ethan left the barn and reentered the quiet house.

As usual, Ruth left a lamp burning in the center of the kitchen table, turned low. It cast the rest of the house in shadows. He blew out the flame and walked by memory and feel through the dark house to the stairs. He wanted to see Maura before he turned in, but why torture himself with what he couldn't have?

The door to Will's room was ajar and soft voices drifted into the hall.

His heart pounded as he pushed the door open and stopped. The scene before him, wrapped around his heart like a warm blanket.

Maura perched on a small chair beside the bed. Will, snuggled in his pajamas and blankets, raptly listened to Maura read, his eyes alight and a smile stretching his mouth into the deep dimpled cheeks. Maura made sound effects and changed the tone of her voice with each character. She had Will, and Ethan, totally captivated.

"Papa." Will sat up, noticing his father in the doorway.

Maura stopped and turned, her eyes met his. Ethan's breath caught in his throat, and his legs went weak with things he wanted and couldn't have.

For an instant they were like parents, smiling over the preciousness of their child.

That was not possible.

Maura could never be Will's mother. Ethan couldn't allow himself to entertain the dream. His fiancée slept in the next room.

He cleared his throat, moved to the other side of the bed, and bent to ruffle his son's hair. "So, it looks like you talked Maura into reading your favorite story."

"Maura wanted to read me a bed time story." Will propped himself on his elbows.

"Will's right, I volunteered." Maura stood and smoothed her skirt, her index finger still in the book holding her place.

Seeing her in the intimacy of the bedroom, with only the glow of a lamp, crumbled some of Ethan's resolve.

Maura may be inexperienced, but she was nineteen years old. She was young, but a grown woman. Someday, a man would speak for her, and Ethan's dreams would be crushed. Dammit, he didn't want another woman to read his son to sleep, kiss him goodnight. Nothing melted a man's heart faster than watching such a beautiful woman fuss over his son. She could be Will's new mother, and more children to come. It would be so easy…

He cleared his throat and shifted from one foot to the other. "Did I disrupt your story or were you finished for the night?"

"I have a couple more pages, then I promise I'll let Will go to sleep."

"Oh!" Ethan laughed, his head back. "So that's the way it is, eh? Will's suffering through the story so you can read it."

Maura smiled. "I don't think either of us is suffering."

"Do you want to have children, Maura?" Will asked, his eyes wide.

Maura gripped the back of her chair. "Yes, Will, I'd love to have children."

"My daddy was married before to my real mother."

"I know, pumpkin." Maura sat back down and stroked his hair away from his smooth forehead. "I know about your mommy."

"Can you be my mommy instead of Kate?"

Maura gasped and glanced up at Ethan. "No, honey. Your father has decided Kate will be your mommy." She opened the book. "I think we should finish the story so you can go to sleep. It's getting late."

"Good idea," Ethan said, his voice gravelly, his heart breaking. He bent and pressed a kiss to Will's forehead then straightened to leave. "Maura, I'll be in the parlor, if you'd like to share a night cap."

Maura looked around the room instead of at him. "I think I'll turn in when I finish reading to Will."

"Fine. I'll see you in the morning." He turned on his heel and left the room.

"You can go if you want to spend time with Papa." Ethan heard Will say, as he turned down the hall toward the stairs. He slowed his steps, a masochistic urge to listen, tearing him in two.

"No, I want to finish reading," Maura said, her voice soft. "I like this book, and I like spending time with you."

"Papa gets lonely sometimes. That's what Ruth says."

Startled, Ethan pressed his hand against the wall and took a deep breath. His son was very wise for seven-years-old. He sensed his father needed company, maybe even Maura's company.

His mind spinning, he made for the parlor in a fog. He wanted something far more intoxicating than the drink he'd offered her.

He lit a lamp in the corner of the room and poured a whiskey. Shadows spilled through the room like strokes of a paintbrush dipped in the richest tones of midnight.

He wandered to the windows and stared out at the star-studded sky. Light footsteps announced her. His body tightened; his teeth clenched. "You changed your mind."

"I decided it was too early to turn in."

"That wasn't the reason I hoped for." He turned toward Maura, his hands deep in the pockets of his black trousers. He really hadn't expected her to join him, so he'd gotten comfortable. He was barefoot, and the white shirt he'd worn for dinner was open to his chest. He hoped he didn't scare her off.

"Maybe I shouldn't have come downstairs."

"Don't apologize." He motioned to the bar in the corner of the room where the glasses glistened in the soft lamp glow. "Can I pour you a drink?"

"Thank you. Water please."

"Probably a good idea," Ethan mumbled under his breath as he walked to the bar. Moonlight and Maura could be a dangerous enough combination. One of them had to be strong and clear headed.

The water in one hand and his whiskey in the other, he joined her in front of the windows. She took the glass, giving him a glance with her thank you and turned back to the view.

He never tired of the view. A full moon hung low in the sky, casting a silver swath over the waters of the Clark's Fork River. Dew coated each blade of grass between the house and the riverbank turning the yard into a million fairy lights.

"It's beautiful." Maura tipped her head back and gazed into his eyes, her mouth slightly open. His insides tightened with need. Why couldn't Kate affect him like this?

"I'm glad you approve." Ethan took a sip of his drink and stepped closer to her side.

She blinked. "Does my opinion matter to you?"

"Absolutely." Spell bound by the deep, dark water reflecting the magic of the moonlight, and the beautiful woman, Ethan moved closer, his arm brushing hers.

"You're making fun of me because I don't drink spirits." Maura didn't pull back from his nearness.

"I would never make fun of you." Her fresh, floral tinged scent wafted around him. Her practical dark blue dress could have been a ball gown, she looked so lovely.

Why couldn't they be closer in age? Maybe then, he wouldn't feel like he stepped over the line each time he thought about loving her.

A single tear escaped and rolled down her cheek.

"What's this?" Ethan caught the tear with his index finger. He kept his touch gentle, his voice soft, but she continued to cry.

"I'm sorry."

"Don't keep apologizing. What do you have to be sorry for?" He took the glass from her trembling hand and set it on a nearby table, then returned to her side and slowly pulled her against him.

He was lost the moment her cheek pressed against his bare chest and her arms wrapped around his waist. Holding her felt so right, like he'd waited all his life to be here in the moonlight with her.

It would be so easy to take this all the way, forget his integrity. Forget his obligation to Kate.

The tears continued uncontrollably, and she trembled against him.

"Tell me what's wrong."

"You'll never ask me to the ranch again." Maura chuckled through her tears.

"What do you mean?" His voice drug through his throat. He breathed in the sweet scent of her hair and brushed his lips over her forehead.

"Maybe I should have had whiskey, so I could blame this on it." She tightened her hold on him, her breasts pressed against him, her legs interlaced with his.

"The alcohol only lets out what's yearning to escape." He'd combust in a minute if he didn't put some distance between them. But he wanted to combust. He wanted to get even closer, and go up in flames.

When she pressed her lips to his bare chest, he moaned. "Sweetheart, you don't know what you're doing to me."

Maura leaned back in his arms and looked up into his face. Moonlight washed over her delicate features. Illuminated her blue eyes. "What am I doing to you?"

"Making me want to forget my integrity and my commitments. You make me want to change everything." He cupped the crown of her head and brought her forehead to his chest. He couldn't look into her face, or he'd be lost. He let his hand slip down her scalp to the back of her neck and pressed his lips against her head while his hands explored her back and hips.

She lifted her face to his and stared up at him as he lowered his mouth to hers. He just wanted to taste her, just this once. Later, he'd beat himself up for taking advantage of her, but tonight, with the moonlight and the whiskey, he wanted Maura.

She didn't pull away when he increased the pressure, or when he ran his tongue over the seam of her mouth. When she opened her lips and allowed him entry, Ethan came apart.

Tentatively, Maura ran her hands over his shirt. Ethan cupped her bottom and brought her against him. He'd hate himself in the morning, but tonight, he needed this memory.

He groaned and claimed more of her mouth, pulling her closer until he didn't know where he ended and she began. She was a proper woman from proper society, but she also had a passion he'd never guessed. He wanted to show her the mysteries between a woman and a man.

Ethan gasped. "Oh Maura, I want you in a way I don't have a right to take. We have to stop."

"I don't want to stop, but you're right." She slid her hands back to his chest to gently push him away. "We have to stop before we do something we're sorry for."

"I'd never be sorry for tasting what you have to offer, Maura. But I sent for Kate." His chest heaved with each breath. Even in the dim light, jealousy flared in her smoky blue eyes. Damn, she wanted him too, and it was too late.

He threaded his fingers through her lustrous chestnut hair, allowing his hand to slowly fall to her shoulder, then bracket the back of her neck, pulling her toward him until her forehead touched his chest, much like they stood before comfort became passion.

Instead of it being a prelude, it gave them time to slow their breathing, slow the heart rate, slow the passion that had nearly carried them into his bedroom, where they would have consummated a marriage that could never take place.

"Yes, you're marrying Kate." Maura choked out the words. "I should go to my room."

"I'll see you to your room where you can lock me out." He took her elbow and led her through the French doors into the entry and up the stairs.

They were silent as they passed Will's door, then Ruth's. Kate's door was closed, but Ethan felt the weight of Kate's closeness as much as he was sure Maura did.

Outside the guest room Maura would use, Ethan pressed a quick kiss to her lips and backed away, before his aching body changed its mind and followed her into the room. "I'll see you in the morning."

****

Kate stretched and sighed, luxuriating in the comfort of the feather bed beneath her. She burrowed farther under the comforter, her eyes shut against the day and the realities ahead of her. She'd prefer to live in a dream world where all would turn out as she wanted it to.

How should it turn out? Her logical mind was at battle with her heart.

Seth.

Since she met him, an image of Seth appeared in her mind each morning upon waking. How could she think so much about a man who didn't trust her? Probably didn't like her. Yet the thought of him sent thrills through the entire length of her body.

Kate sat up, clutching the comforter to her breasts. She couldn't deny it. The man sent her senses into a whirl wind of emotions. The way he felt, the way he smelled, the way his hands had bracketed her waist while he helped her from the buckboard. She couldn't think about being in his lap on the train, without getting hot all over.

She'd been sorry to see him leave last night, but she understood. He had a responsibility to the town.

She glanced at the window. The drapes were drawn, but a narrow shaft of sunlight signaled another sunny, dry day. Time to get up and face Ethan and another round of lies.

Kate slid out of bed and washed and dressed. In her mind's eye, she could see her maid, Clarice, cringing at the lack of amenities.

Her haphazard chignon looked fine for her life in Hope. There were no board meetings, teas, or shopping with friends. She'd only been away from home and her maid's assistance, for a short time, but she was adjusting to taking care of herself.

Kate looked in the mirror and smoothed the strands on either side of her face, tucking them into the chignon. Smiling at her reflection, she nodded in satisfaction for the job she'd done.

The smile slowly faded, and she blinked with realization. She'd always thought of herself as an independent woman; she'd never needed a man in her life. But she did. She'd had her father paving the way for her, and then Ross and Leland leading and guiding her. Being in this rustic society brought home how dependent she'd been all her life. She'd just emerged from a fog and suddenly everything became clear. She certainly wasn't Mary Catherine Leary, but she wasn't the Kate McShane she'd believed herself to be either.

She couldn't do it all on her own, she needed help.

A new resolve bloomed in her heart. Seth suspected her of something anyway; why not tell him the truth? He was a lawman, and she a law abiding citizen, she'd done nothing wrong. She was the innocent one running for her very life. She'd find a way to make him understand she'd had no other choice but to hide away in Hope until home was safe once more.

At the bottom of the stairs, Kate paused, her hand on the painted wall. Ross should have received and answered her telegram. Once she checked in at the telegraph office, she'd find Seth and tell him the truth.

Eager to put her plan into motion, Kate hurried through the foyer and into the parlor. A shaft of sunlight cast a beam though the small window next to the front door and illuminated the wood floor. The large trees outside the French doors cast soft shadows across the furniture and floor with leafy and bough-like designs.

It really was beautiful here; Ethan had done a beautiful job of building and furnishing his home. She took a moment to drink in the soothing view of the mossy green grass, the sloping bank to the river, and the passing waters. The sky was a sharp azure, and autumn fully hung in the air. Part of her wanted to walk along the river, linger and forget her troubles.

"Sleep well?"

Ethan's deep voice startled her. She turned to face him, pasting her lips into a smile. "Yes, very well, and you?"

"Fine, thank you." He stood in the dining room doorway, the top of his head nearly brushing the frame. He looked splendid from the tips of his shiny black boots to the soft blue shirt hugging his broad shoulders and tucked in at his flat stomach.

Life would be so much easier if she could love this man and be satisfied as a rancher's wife. But she didn't love him. Maura did.

"Kate, I think we should postpone the wedding for an additional week."

Was she hearing him correctly? "I thought we already did."

"I mean a third week."

Kate was speechless. This was too good to be true, but she couldn't act too happy or he'd grow suspicious.

"You said you wanted more time to get to know me. I've given it some thought, and I agree with you."

"I'm just surprised." Had he and Maura talked when no one was looking? Maybe late last night? "What made you change your mind?"

He gazed over her head, a faraway expression in his blue eyes. "It came home to me last night. We need more time to make this large commitment."

Kate folded her hands in front of her and nodded. "I've enjoyed my time at the ranch and meeting Will, Ruth, and Travis. You've been blessed, Ethan, to have such caring people around you."

He rolled his lips together, exhaled and nodded. “Extremely blessed under the circumstances.”

Infused with new confidence that things might work out as she planned, Kate stepped closer to Ethan. “I’ve found that things happen for a reason, good and bad. Natalie leaving like she did was painful for all who cared for her, but out of that experience you discovered the friend you have in Travis. Ruth stepped up as Will’s surrogate mother, and by moving out here, you met the Malones.”

He riveted his eyes to hers, their intensity drilling through her as if he wanted her to go on so maybe she’d continue and include Maura in that picture, but Kate stopped. One step at a time.

“I’m expecting a telegram from my dear friend in Boston, so I’d like to return to Hope right away.”

“I do have some work to catch up on today. Ruth always insists that we rest on Sunday.”

“Oh, do you attend Mass?”

He tilted his head and narrowed an eye. “Was that something we failed to correspond about? I’m Anglican. We have a service on Sunday, right after Mass. In this small town, it will be a while before each service has its own building. I sense that you’re Catholic?”

Kate chuckled. “Irish Catholic through and through. You’re right. We didn’t discuss our religious background. Is it a problem?” Another obstacle for Maura to overcome?

“Not especially. This is a free country and freedom of religion was at the base of its structure. There’s no reason why Will and any other children can’t learn both faiths.”

Kate smiled in relief. “You’re very generous.” She turned to take one more look out the windows overlooking the river. She wished life were as simple as that winding, flowing body of water. No evil plots for her money and power, no deceptions. Life would be like the river, gathering water from streams along the way and eventually emptying into the lake.

"Kate? Are you all right?"

Kate turned to face him; the war between what she'd chosen to do and what she should have done threatened to over whelm her. "I'm fine. Shall we join the others?" She was eager to return to town and the man who held a bigger than life reputation.

Chapter Twelve

Hope hummed with Saturday activity as the buckboard rumbled through town. Kate smiled at two small boys who chased a ball down the dusty street, shrieking and darting from side to side. Maura jerked on the reins to narrowly avoid them.

"Oh my gosh! I thought we'd hit them!" Kate gasped and pressed her hand to her chest.

"Those two are always playing in the street, so I keep an eye out for them."

"Don't they go to school?" Kate shook her head, and they went on playing as if they didn't nearly get run over by a team of horses.

"Not all the children in the area attend school. Some of the mothers teach them at home, others, well, there are some others who don't pay attention to them at all."

"How sad." Kate turned on the seat and watched the ragamuffins dart in and out of the people on the boardwalk.

Merchants, laborers, and gamblers milled around, all tipping their hats as they met women dressed in their next best to Sunday clothes, baskets on their arms.

Kate touched Maura's arm and lifted her chin toward the building that doubled as a telegraph office. "Would you mind letting me off at the post office? I hope a message from my friend has arrived."

Maura pulled back on the right rein, guiding the pair to the hitching post in front of the whitewashed building, then pulled both traces to stop the team. "Here we are. I'll wait in the wagon."

Kate smiled at the younger woman, puzzled over her change in manner. Since meeting in the kitchen that morning, Maura almost seemed resigned to Kate marrying Ethan. Kate tried not to imagine what may have transpired last night. Ethan had also seemed different.

"No need to wait for me. You're eager to get home, and I can walk the rest of the way."

Maura's expression turned serious. "Kate, there tends to be trouble on Saturdays. It's the precursor to Saturday night, and you know what they can be like."

"Wild, huh?"

"Very. That's why the decent townspeople were so excited to hire Seth Morgan. He has a reputation of being a tough Texas Ranger, and that's what we need to stop this crime wave."

Kate wasn't as brave as she wanted Maura to think, but she had to check for a message from Ross. If none had arrived, she'd have to send him yet another one, and she didn't want to worry about Maura walking in on the process. "Don't worry, I come from the big city, and I'm used to rowdy people."

"Good morning, ladies."

Kate and Maura both swiveled on their seats.

"Sheriff Morgan." Kate's breath caught, and her heart fluttered at the sight of him.

"Hello, Sheriff. I was just telling Kate that it's not a good idea for her to walk home from town alone."

Kate tried not to tighten her mouth. Why was Maura all of a sudden concerned with her safety?

"I agree, Maura. No decent woman should walk alone on a day like this. I'm suddenly feeling useful." He glanced up and down the street. "When I arrived during the week, I thought the conditions had been exaggerated."

"We've had an exceptionally quiet week."

"Then why do your parents allow you to walk to work alone?" Kate regretted her retort the moment it left her lips. She'd been gaining ground with Maura, and she may have just ruined it.

"I don't. Either Da or Kyle walk me home."

Kate nodded and folded her hands in her lap. "Well, it seems I'm outnumbered. I'll hurry."

"Better yet." Seth laid his hand on the edge of the seat not two inches from Kate's bottom. "I'll escort you home when you finish your business."

Kate's head swam. "I couldn't possibly infringe on your time, Sheriff. As you pointed out, today's a busy day for you." Kate shifted away from his hand and bumped into Maura. Seth raised his hands.

"Let me help you down, Miss Leary."

Somehow the name sounded like an endearment on his sensuous lips. Her hands trembled with apprehension and excitement as Kate placed her fingers on the sheriff's shoulders and allowed him to lift her off the seat. Unlike the last time he'd aided her, her legs held.

"You're stronger this time." Seth smiled his irresistible grin. Now he could read her thoughts.

Her emotions threatening to bubble over, Kate twisted out of his grasp to face Maura. "Thank you for taking me to the ranch."

Maura sent Kate a rare smile. "I'll see you at home." She clicked her tongue and tapped the reins, urging the team to move up the street.

Kate looked at the man who plagued her dreams and too many of her thoughts. "I may be a few minutes. Would you like to meet me somewhere?"

"I don't mind waiting for you." He tipped his hat, his slightly narrowed eyes daring her to object. "It can't take too long to check for mail."

The man didn't trust her for a minute. If she didn't hurry, he'd check on her for sure. Kate nodded and went into the tiny building.

"Can I help you?" Mr. Smith still wore the visor and the grouchy look. She'd offended him with her remark about his counter, and he seemed none too happy to see her.

"Have I received a telegram?"

"This ain't the big city, ya know. Things don't move as fast out here."

Kate swallowed, then took a deep breath. "I understand, Mr. Smith. I'll check later."

"Now just hold on there. I didn't say you didn't get one." Mr. Smith laid a ratty looking piece of paper on the counter. "Came this morning."

Kate's heartbeat quickened as she picked it up and read the choppy words. Where are you? Be safe. Stay put. Can't move yet. The nearly illegible words sent Kate's hope plummeting. The message must mean Ross and Leland hadn't found enough proof to convict Jeb.

She was the major stockholder of the company; why did she have to hide out, posing as another woman?

She crumpled the message and tossed it on the counter. "I'd like to send another telegram."

"It's your money." The man pulled the visor down to shade his eyes.

Kate shook her head at his eccentric behavior. "Please say, 'Will stay but need quick resolution.' "

"What? What was that word?" Mr. Smith poked his visor back with an ink stained index finger and squinted at her.

"I'll write it down. Then finish it with, situation urgent, Kate."

"Situation." Mr. Smith labored over the words, a frown arching his brows. Kate tapped her nails on the counter. Mr. Smith looked pointedly at her hand. Kate stopped tapping.

"That'll be two dollars."

"Two dollars? You only charged me seventy-five cents before."

"Price went up this week."

Kate fumbled with the drawstring on her purse, found her money and counted out two dollars. She thanked him and stepped out into the warm autumn day.

"Get something?" Seth took her arm the moment her boots hit the boardwalk.

"I did." Kate allowed him to lead her toward the end of the boardwalk, where the road branched to run up the hill, ending at the Malone's. Her pulse quickened, but not from the brisk walk.

It wouldn't be long before they crowned the hill and were in sight of the Malone home. If she didn't confess her identity to Seth right away, she'd lose the window. Her nerves seesawed. Was this the time to tell him? Out in the open where anyone could walk by and find them in an intimate conversation?

"I doubt I'm in any real danger, Sheriff, but I do appreciate your time."

Seth laughed. "Don't underestimate your draw. You attract plenty of attention." He didn't ease the hold on her arm.

Kate sighed and fell into step beside him. She hated the way his spicy, warm male scent heightened her senses. This crazy attraction complicated her plan to trust him with the truth. Nothing was plain and simple with Seth Morgan.

****

Seth kept a firm hold on Kate's upper arm, afraid she'd bolt if he eased up. The woman was trouble, plain and simple. She looked like an angel and smelled twice as good as any flower. The top of her head reached right below his shoulder, just the right height to pull close and envelop in his arms. His body battled with his suspicions of her.

His contacts back east hadn't responded to his

telegrams, so he was still in the dark when it came to Kate Leary. He'd been a lawman too long to be fooled by a pretty face.

Poor Howland. Heck of a decent guy, but he'd been bamboozled by a beautiful woman. If Kate Leary was a penniless spinster, he was Wyatt Earp.

Seth slowed his pace and closed the scant distance between them. She wanted him to let her walk the rest of the way alone. With the scum from the train in town, he decided to escort her a little farther.

"Are you a native of Boston?"

Kate stiffened.

Ah-ha, he'd hit on a sensitive subject.

"My, uh, parents and I relocated from Boston when I was ten. I finished school in New York City."

"Then you moved back to Boston?"

"Why do you ask?" She looked away, pretending to study the backs of the buildings below them. Had she seen her kidnapper from the train? Seth hadn't seen him since yesterday, but he had a feeling he was still around.

"I heard somewhere you're from Boston."

"I recently moved to Boston. Most of my life has been spent in New York. That's where I feel at home."

"I understand both your parents are dead?"

"Sheriff, you are full of questions."

"Just trying to be friendly, ma'am. Since you're a resident of my jurisdiction, I'd like to get to know you."

"Fine." Kate huffed and started up the hill. "My father was run over by an ice wagon, and my mother died after a lengthy illness and a broken heart."

Seth quirked a brow. The words were sad, but the tone lacked sincerity. As if she was reciting rehearsed words.

Kate glanced at him, her mouth drawn into a

tight line. "You don't believe in broken hearts?"

"I don't believe it's a physical condition. People can't die of sadness. It takes a bullet or a knife. It takes an illness that can't be cured."

He didn't mean to ramble on. Losing his mother to pneumonia had just begun to heal when the bullet found Griff's heart.

"Really, Sheriff, you do sound cynical. You must never have been in love."

He clutched her arm and stopped her. "Have you?"

"Been in love?" She gazed into his eyes, sending his heart for a race through his chest. Damn the woman was beautiful. Too bad she was a liar, and who knew what else.

"No, I haven't been in love, but I miss my father so much at times I can't breathe when I think of never seeing him again." Her voice lost its edge, softened, and her chin quivered.

No matter her other faults, he could tell she wasn't pretending to grieve for her father. Seth resumed walking up the hill.

"Really, Sheriff, I can walk alone from here. There's no one in sight."

Seth looked around, ready to object. She was right; there wasn't a soul in sight. Damn, she made his guard drop. And that wasn't good. She couldn't have seen the man from the train, or she'd never suggest walking home alone.

"I'll escort you to where the hill crowns and we can see the Malone's." The telegraph office beckoned him. Smith was obligated to give him any information he asked for, and he wanted Kate's messages.

"That's fine." She picked up her skirt and looked straight ahead.

Reaching the crest of the hill, Seth stopped and touched her arm. She looked at him, her accelerated breathing lifting her breasts against the dark green bodice. Perspiration beaded on her forehead and upper lip. Seth glanced around. No one in sight and not far from the Malone's. "I want you to walk straight to the back door, no detours."

"No detours," Kate repeated, laying her hand on her chest.

Seth backed up a few steps, reluctant to leave her. The woman attracted trouble like steel to a magnet. To be honest, her safety wasn't the only reason he wanted to be near her. "I'll see you soon."

"Is that a threat, Sheriff?"

Seth looked at her and closed one eye at her drollness. "I mean it, Kate. Go straight to the house."

"I will, uh..."

"Yes?"

She sighed, looking like she wanted to say something more. Seth hesitated, but when she didn't speak, he tipped his hat and turned to leave.

"Since you're in a hurry, can we talk later?"

Seth stopped and turned to face her, hoping his eagerness didn't show on his face. Could she be ready to confess to something?

"I'll see you at the Malone's for supper."

"Do you have a standing invitation?" A smile curved Kate's beautiful mouth.

"I do. Come this weekend, I'm riding up that mountain." He lifted his chin to the mountain behind the Malone's house. "I'll bring out one of the big elk I've heard about. That should restock what I've eaten."

"I'm sure Janet will be grateful."

"I'm grateful for their friendship. See you tonight."

Seth hurried down the hill and back onto the main street. He bee-lined to the telegraph office.

"Smith, you here?"

"Right here, Sheriff. What can I do for you?" The

balding man poked his head around the corner, peering out from under his visor.

"I want all of Miss Leary's telegrams. Outgoing and incoming."

"Why Sheriff, that's private information." The man puffed his chest out. "I can't break my oath. This is a federal institution."

"Smith, I'm a peace officer for that government. Those telegrams are part of an investigation I'm conducting."

"Is Miss Leary an outlaw? Wouldn't surprise me. Those easterners come out here in their fancy clothes, talking their fancy words and flashing money. Big city people with big city ideas." Mr. Smith handed over three pieces of crumpled paper. Seth glanced at them, then thanked the man and walked out the door, making it clear he wanted any other correspondence relating to Miss Leary.

Seth reached under his black leather vest and slipped the papers in the breast pocket of his shirt. Planting his hands on his hips, he looked up and down the street and blew out a breath. Did he really want Kate Leary to be an outlaw? No, but he was a lawman, and his job was to protect the law.

****

Kate clutched her purse, waiting while Seth Morgan strode down the hill toward town. The man looked as good from the backside as he did from the front. Narrow hips, wide shoulders and a lean waist.

A breeze blew off the lake, kicking up a cloud of dust. She blinked, her eyes watering from the grit. That's what she got for sneaking a peek at the sheriff. She pivoted on the heel of her black leather boot and resumed her short journey to the Malone's.

What had happened to her resolve to confess everything to Seth? The moment he stepped to the side of the buckboard and planted his hands near her derriere, her tongue had tied and her confidence fled. Walking home with him would have been the perfect time, but he was in a hurry to get away, and she couldn't seem to gather her thoughts fast enough.

Dabbing perspiration from her face with a white, lace-edged handkerchief, Kate pushed her thoughts of Seth Morgan to the back of her mind. The good news was Ethan's request to postpone the wedding even longer, giving her two more weeks to resolve her issue with Jeb Walker and return home. It also gave her more time to play matchmaker with Maura and Ethan.

And explore her attraction to Seth Morgan.

For some strange reason, she could picture Seth in the McShane Walker Shipping boardroom. The room would be filled with his presence and self-confidence. From the head of the long, polished table, he'd overrule those musty, rusty old board members who didn't think her capable of running a company.

A strong hand gripped her arm from behind. "What's your hurry?"

Kate's heart leaped into her throat, and she whirled in the attacker's grip, clutching her purse to her chest.

"Unhand me!" She'd expected to see the man from the train, but she'd never seen this man in her life.

He tightened his hold on her arm but didn't take her purse. Kate slid her hand down her dress, into her pocket, and wrapped her fingers around the comforting metal of her derringer.

Dressed in a black suit with a white shirt and black string tie, the stranger didn't wear a hat, but the crease of a hat band, marked his dark blonde hair. She glanced at the hand clutching her arm. Clean, trimmed nails, no callouses. He must be a gambler.

"Settle down, little lady. I'm not going to hurt you. At least not today." He moved closer and ran his lips over the side of her throat. "Today, I want to make you feel really good."

Kate gagged and jerked away. "Leave me alone. You couldn't possibly make me feel anything but revulsion."

Rage over being a victim yet again gave her the strength to stand strong enough not to faint.

"I think I can change your mind." He slipped his arm around her waist and pulled her against him.

Kate's hold on her derringer slipped as she strained away from him. She pounded on his chest with clenched fists. "Leave me alone!" Desperate to escape him, she stomped her boot heel down on his instep. He yowled and jumped back, rage replacing his playful demeanor. "You bitch. This could have been good."

Kate clutched her purse and turned to run. He grabbed the neckline of her dress and wrenched. The row of buttons down the back of her bodice popped off one by one. He didn't stop until the waist seam gave away, and the bodice hung from her arms like a strait-jacket.

"Beautiful." He breathed the word, his hands like bands of iron on her arms. The assailant yanked her against his body. His lips connected with the tops of her exposed breasts.

Tears stung her eyes and her breakfast roiled. What possessed her to think she could defend herself?

"Oh my God, Seth, where are you?" The words escaped her lips on the wave of panic.

"Seth Morgan can't take care of you like I can. Forget him." He nipped her tender skin. Kate screamed.

"Shut up!" He glared at her and connected the back of his hand with her cheekbone.

Star bursts exploded in her head, blinding her to everything but the pain and humiliation of the violation of her tender breasts.

She hadn't saved her virginity and innocence all these years for some stranger to take them. Kate drove her knee upward, connecting with the man's aroused crotch.

He yowled, cursing her with foul words she'd never heard on the docks.

Tearing out of her tattered sleeves, she plunged her hand into her pocket, gripping the derringer like her life depended on it.

It did.

He straightened and moved toward her, fury contorting his face. Kate backed away and jerked the gun from her pocket, leveled the barrel at him and squeezed the trigger. The derringer popped and blood bloomed like a red rose over the shoulder of his suit.

"My God, you've shot me! You hell cat!" The stranger staggered toward her, stunned and bleeding.

Kate backed away, then turned and ran across the meadow, fueled by pure fear.

"I'm going to get you!"

The blood roared through her ears and tears poured over her checks.

"Dammit, I'm bleeding, I need a doc!"

Kate stopped at the hitching post in front of the house and clutched her aching side with one arm, aiming the empty derringer with the other. Her chest heaved, her consciousness faded in and out.

"I'll be watching for you, you bastard!" Her voice crackled, but she held the gun steady and stared down the attacker until he stumbled over the edge of the hill. The moment he disappeared her knees gave way and she crumpled to the rocky ground.

"What in the world?" Janet slammed out of the

back door, a rifle in one capable hand. She kneeled at Kate's side. "What happened? Are you all right?"

Tears of rage and fear welled in her eyes and streamed down her face. "I was attacked. He was there." She pointed across the meadow. "Waiting for me."

Janet glanced around the meadow and the line of thick forest. She hooked her free hand under Kate's arm. "Let's get you into the house."

Kate allowed the older woman to help her inside the cozy, secure house. She had traveled so far to be safe. But she'd learned no place was safe. The kidnapping attempt in New York, the one that drove her from her home, flashed through her mind. If not for her derringer, she would've been left in worse shape.

"Maura, I need your help!" Janet guided Kate to the rocking chair in the corner of the kitchen and helped her ease down.

Kate whimpered then sobbed. "No, please, I don't want anyone else to see me like this." She pulled her torn bodice around her bare flesh.

Maura hurried down the stairs and across the kitchen. The color left her face as she sank to the floor in front of Kate.

"What happened?" Gone was any suspicion or resentment. "I should never have left you! Where's Sheriff Morgan?"

Kate laid her hand on Maura's cheek and shook her head. "It's not your fault;, it's mine. My pride caused this."

The tenuous bit of control she'd used to escape snapped. Pain stored since her mother left, then her father's death, released in a flood of tears.

Janet enveloped her in her arms and patted her back, while Maura held her hand until the tears slowed. Kate hiccupped and took a deep, quavering breath.

"Kate, can you tell us what happened?"

"I insisted I could walk home alone, but Seth wouldn't leave me until we crowned the hill, and he looked around the meadow. It seemed all right. I—I waited for a minute, looking at the view." The view of Seth's backside. "Then I started across the meadow, lost in my thoughts. He grabbed my arm and pulled me against him." She hiccupped again and more tears welled. "He wanted—he wanted." She couldn't voice his intentions. She fingered the flap of material that had once covered her camisole. "He tore my dress and touched my breasts."

"Kate, did he do more?" Janet smoothed Kate's hair from her face. "I know it's hard, but you need to tell me."

Kate sucked in gulps of air. "Nothing more." He'd kissed her where no man had ever seen, let alone touched and it appalled her.

"How did you escape? Oh my Lord, I wish I heard you sooner. I would have shot the bastard."

Kate grasped Janet's arm and shook her head. "Don't blame yourself. My self-confidence got me into this pickle. When I couldn't make him stop touching me, I shot him in the shoulder with my derringer." She covered her face with both hands. "He said he wasn't through with me. I ran to the house and he left."

Janet patted Kate's arm and kneeled in front of her. "Land sakes, girl. You carry a derringer? Kate, you're a wealth of surprises."

Kate swallowed and hiccupped. "My father taught me to shoot at a young age."

"Smart man, your father. Now, we need to tell Sheriff Morgan what happened."

"No!" Kate sprang, ramrod straight on the edge of the rocking chair. "We can't tell the sheriff, he can't know about this, no one can."

"Kate, this might be the same man who followed

Kyle home." Janet took her hand. "I know you're upset, but the man's dangerous. I can't leave you and Maura alone, but the sheriff should be here for dinner. Now what you need is a hot bath. Maura, darlin', please take that pan of hot water to Kate's room, and I'll grab the other one. It won't be a deep, luxurious bath, but it'll soothe you."

Kate rotated her sore shoulder. "You're so good to me."

"I have just the ointment for that shoulder, too. When you've soaked, I'll rub it in."

Kate followed them up the stairs and leaned against the doorframe while they dragged a copper slipper tub into her room and dumped in the pans of steaming water.

Janet added a bucket of colder water, and sprinkled a handful of bath salts. The relaxing scent of lavender swirled through the room.

Kate sighed. This wonderful family didn't deserve her deceit. She simply had to tell them the truth and soon.

They left her to bathe with the promise of a strong pot of tea when she came downstairs.

Kate eased into the bath, sighing as the stress and pain drained away into the scented water. She'd claimed to be a strong woman, strong enough to stand up against the stiff-necked board members who didn't believe a woman belonged in the business world. Strong enough to reject Jeb's proposals of marriage; strong enough to change her escape plan and trade places with another woman.

But she'd left her home to hide out; the henchman was in Hope, looking for her and a stranger could have overpowered her had she not shot him.

Her arm throbbed. She glanced down and gasped at the red teeth marks on the swell of her right breast. Her stomach roiled.

Downstairs, the kitchen door opened and shut. It could be Kerry, or Kyle. Maybe even Ethan or Seth. Kate sank farther into the water. She'd wanted to tell Seth the entire truth, but he'd been in such a hurry, and she needed time to explain.

Pushing out of the cooling water, she dried off and dressed, grimacing when pain shot through her arm. Janet's ointment would have to wait until Kate had the chance to tell her story her way.

She wiggled her feet into her boots and peered into the vanity mirror. "Ekk." Her eyes were red and swollen, her throat chaffed. She resembled the breakup of a hard winter.

She leaned over the washbasin and splashed cool water over her eyes, then patted her face with the soft, lace edged towel.

Easing down the stairs, she hesitated in the kitchen doorway, one hand on the doorframe, one at her throat.

"Did you have a good rest, dear?" Janet greeted, her auburn eyebrows peaked over her warm hazel eyes.

Kate glanced around the kitchen, forcing a smile in response to Kerry's nod, and Kyle's adoring look. "I did, thank you. I thought the sheriff might be here."

"Kerry just walked in the door and said Seth had to ride to Sandpoint. He won't be joining us for dinner, but I think we should sit in the parlor so you can tell Kerry what happened."

Kate's skin heated and dampened with perspiration. "Can we wait until the sheriff is here so I only have to say it once?"

"No, dearie. Kerry has to know about this man. He could be a danger to the entire family."

"You're right." Kate reluctantly nodded. "I'll tell Kerry."

Oh, Seth, why couldn't you be here?

Emotion lay so close to the surface, she should be glad he wasn't here. She might do something foolish like fall into his arms, no matter who was watching.

Chapter Thirteen

Sunday morning arrived on a wave of cool air, but the sky remained the sharp blue it'd been since Kate's arrival in Hope. Entering the small church for Mass, Kate and the Malones were greeted by parishioners, all discussing the drought and the fear of fire.

Kate followed her hosts up the aisle of the charming, but rustic church. The floor was constructed of rough cut boards, and the altar sat on a plain box. Benches served as pews and formed two sections, leaving an aisle in the center.

She gazed toward the front row, remembering all the Sundays she and her father had attended Mass. Her father's position in the community and donations to the church had garnered them half of the left front pew. He'd taken great pride in the brass plate affixed to the dark polished wood at his shoulder, bearing the McShane name.

This roughhewn building bore no resemblance to the stone cathedral at home, yet her heart ached knowing she'd never share the pew with her father again.

She settled onto the hard bench, determined to keep her mind on the service when murmuring broke out behind her. Kate glanced over her shoulder. Seth had returned from his trip to Sandpoint. He stood out in the aisle of teaming church goers.

His damp, dark hair was slicked back, with one errant lock dipping over his forehead. His black trousers were cut from a high quality cloth; a crisp white shirt covered his broad chest, contrasting with his dark skin. A long black jacket swept down his tall form, the tails touching the back of his muscled thighs. The western formality was topped off by a black string tie at his throat.

Kate sighed. Seth Morgan presented a dichotomy of polish and tough western lawman. Her fingers itched to run over the fine fabric covering his broad shoulders. The mere sight of him filled her with heat and yearning.

Time stood still as she drank in his presence and bearing. One quick sweep of the room, and his gaze settled on hers. Another time, another place, and meeting him would have been the answer to her every dream.

But she was only here until Ross and Leland notified her of Jeb's guilt or innocence. Seth's attention stayed on her as he sat in the back of the room. The murmuring continued. Kate turned toward the altar. Panting over the handsome sheriff would only add to the scandal the Malones and Ethan would face when she left town.

The priest entered the church and began the Latin Mass. Kate opened her prayer book and followed along with the proper responses, shutting out her troubled thoughts for a few minutes, allowing herself to forget what brought her to Hope and the attack yesterday. She cradled her sore arm and let her mind float with the familiar cadence of the Mass she'd heard since she was a child.

With the last amen, Kate rose, genuflected and left the building, fully aware that Seth walked right behind her.

Stepping into the warm autumn sun, she descended the front steps and turned to wait for the Malones.

Seth stopped beside her. She gazed at him, squinting against the bright sun. "I didn't know you were Catholic."

One corner of his sensuous mouth quirked into a half smile. "I don't know that I am. I grew up on the streets of Austin, Texas, with Mexican boys. Going to Mass was my only connection to family."

Surprised he'd revealed something so personal, Kate stared into his dark eyes, searching for a glimpse of that lonely little boy. She couldn't see him. The boy had grown into a man, never to return. "Where was your mother?"

Seth glanced at the fellow churchgoers streaming out of the church. "She worked a brothel. I came and went as I pleased."

"Oh." Kate looked away, struggling to regain her composure. She wasn't sure how to respond to this information.

Her mother had left them for another life and later, another man, but her father had shielded her from the full harshness of the situation, until she was old enough to better understand it. Not that she ever did understand how a woman could leave a man who adored her and a child who needed her.

He glanced around. "Where's Ethan?"

"Ethan attends the Protestant service. I understand they're held about thirty minutes after Mass." Kate hoped Kerry and Janet lingered with other friends until Seth left. She wasn't ready to relate details of the attack to him. Not right now.

"See you later then." Seth tipped his hat and walked away.

Kate let out a pent up breath. She had a reprieve, but not for long. Seth had to be told the truth about her identity.

****

Seth walked away from the church, and the woman who filled his thoughts, day and night. He had rounds to make. There might be two church services every Sunday, but right about now, other sorts of people were waking up from a late night of gambling and carousing.

He flexed his hands and forced his thoughts from their first meeting on the train, and Kate's rounded bottom planted firmly on his lap. She'd left an indelible imprint on his senses. Damn, he had to get things into perspective. She might be a criminal, but he was the sheriff, and his duty was to uphold the law.

He raised his hat and forked his fingers through his hair then set his hat at an angle to shade his eyes. This town had an element he needed to fix his full attention on. He couldn't be daydreaming like a lovesick fool.

He'd returned from Sandpoint late last night. Too late to join the Malones for his standing dinner invitation. A lead on some missing railroad equipment had taken him out of town. But the trail petered out. According to the locals, Hope could be a rough town, but Sandpoint had more than its share of corruption.

"Sheriff!"

Seth tipped his hat. "How are you today, Mrs. White?"

"I'm just fine, Sheriff. I'm concerned about that sweet Kate."

"She seemed fine at church just now." A familiar chill of dread ran down his back. He'd spent most of his life hearing bad news and never got used to it.

"I'm so glad." Mrs. White planted herself squarely in front of him. He had no choice but to wait for her to impart her news.

"I'm not sure what you mean, ma'am." He was sure she itched to tell him.

"Well. I wouldn't normally say anything, but you are the sheriff and here to protect us. Otherwise I would never break a confidence." Mrs. White adjusted her sun bonnet and her ample bosom expanded like a banty hen ready to fly into a predator. "I had hoped your presence would discourage citizens of that type."

"I'm doing my best, Mrs. White. It'll take time." He'd learned a long time ago, if he waded through information he didn't want to hear, he'd learn something valuable. "How did you hear about Kate?"

"The Malones are very protective of her, but Maura works for Mr. White at the mercantile. Last evening, Kerry came into town, looking for you. He stopped at the mercantile, just as Mr. White was ready to lock up before the, well..." She pressed her embroidered handkerchief to her mouth, took a deep breath and pulled back her shoulders. "...less desirable persons of the town came out for Saturday night. Kerry told Mr. White to use caution for both he and myself because a violent stranger was on the loose."

The woman finally paused.

Seth's nerves twanged.

"And?"

"Well, Kate was walking across the meadow yesterday, mind you, right in front of the Malone's house and a man attacked her. Dear lady, thank heavens she wasn't seriously hurt, but very upset."

Seth set his teeth back. He should have walked her to the door and seen her inside instead of being in an all fired hurry to trap her in a crime. He'd left her at the top of the hill, thinking she'd be safe and made a bee-line for the telegraph office to question Mr. Smith.

Mrs. White looked around, then stepped closer to Seth. She pursed her lips before she spoke, her tone low. "I assume there's more to the story. Something she wouldn't want all over town."

Seth flexed his hands to stem the urge to grab this irritating woman and shake her. "I assume I can trust you to keep this information to yourself and not tell anyone. Else."

Mrs. White's graying brows shot up. Good, his point was made.

"Well," she huffed. "You can be assured I won't tell another soul."

"Thank you, Mrs. White, and thank you for trusting me with this information. I'll be the soul of discretion." Seth tipped his hat and moved up the street, grinding his teeth. Why hadn't Kate told him? Damn the woman. He'd play hell running to her. If she wouldn't tell him something affecting the well-being of the town, he'd make her wait until later, then leisurely appear at their doorstep.

****

No sooner had Janet taken the last batch of crispy, golden pieces of chicken from the large fry pan, when someone knocked on the back door.

Kate laughed for the first time since, well, since the attack. "Janet when you cook, people just appear!"

Janet smiled. "It is uncanny. Would you mind answering the door, dear?"

Ruth and Will stood on the other side of the screen. Her heart lurched at the eager look on Will's little face. Heartache spread out like the endless stretch of rails between Hope and New York.

"Good afternoon, Ruth. Will." Kate bent slightly to shake Will's hand. "Please come in."

"Yes, come in and make yourself at home." Janet hurried to her friend, wiping her hands on her apron as she went. "It's so good to see both of you! Where are Ethan and Travis?"

Ruth returned Janet's hug, then stepped back, a smile on her face. "Ethan's at the smithy with Kerry. Travis returned to the ranch to check on a colicky horse."

"Please tell Travis we missed him." Janet motioned toward the table. "Let's have a cup of tea while we finish up dinner." She returned to her chicken and potato salad, a pleased smile on her face.

Kate resumed the simple task Janet had shown her, chopping cabbage for cole slaw. Maura came in from the garden, fresh carrots dangling from one hand, lettuce in the other. According to Janet, normally by mid-September, frost would have killed everything but the root vegetables. Thanks to Janet's vigilant watering, she'd extended the life of her garden, despite the drought.

Maura had rinsed off the long carrots next to the well and would now scrub them in a pan of water, scrape off the outer layer and chop them into smaller pieces to cook. Kate had seen the process since arriving at the Malone's but was still fascinated with how her food reached the table.

Since Kate's attack yesterday, she and Maura had formed an interesting bond. Was it time to assure Maura she had no intention of marrying Ethan?

Will accepted a cleaned carrot from Maura and nibbled on it. Kate smiled. Maura loved the boy, and he adored her. No other woman could be the loving, dedicated mother Will needed. Or the wife Ethan needed.

Kate scooped the last bit of chopped cabbage into the bowl and tossed it with the mixture Janet had shown her to make with sour cream, sugar, and vinegar.

If only her life was as simple as learning to make a salad. She'd be engaged to a handsome, decent man. She'd have an instant family and wonderful friends. It would all be ideal, except for one thing. She didn't belong here, and she was insanely attracted to Seth Morgan.

She could only hope the reprieve Ethan had given her had to do with the realization he belonged with Maura, not a mail-order bride. Something had happened between Maura and Ethan at the ranch Friday night to change his mind about rushing into this marriage.

Sunday dinner was nearly on the table when the screen door swung open and Kerry and Ethan came in. The men took turns at the washstand, continuing to discuss the ramifications of the drought and how much rain and snow it'd take to restore the ground water supply. Kyle hung onto Ethan's every word and move.

Too unsettled by the inevitable conversation after dinner, Kate gave the cole slaw a final stir and carried it to the table.

"Ethan, how was church, today?"

Ethan looked surprised at her question, but his sudden smile indicated he was pleased about her interest. "Very good. Although I have to confess, I dozed through the last half."

"I thought confession was for Catholics." Kerry winked and chuckled.

"Kerry Malone!" Janet scolded her husband.

"To have one building for both faiths is so different, but interesting at the same time." Kate set the cole slaw on the table with a flourish, pleased with how good it looked.

Ruth smiled and nodded toward the cabbage, looking impressed with Kate's accomplishment. "I thought the same thing when I arrived, Kate. We're all used to going our individual ways on Sunday morning. In this new land, economy of building is the rule."

Dear Ruth. Kate smiled at the older woman. She was such a genuine person. Ethan and Will would miss her when she left to marry her sweetheart.

The blessing on the meal had been asked and the chicken platter on its first trip around the table, when boots sounded on the back step.

"Hello." Seth's voice carried though the screen, sending tingles of anticipation up Kate's back.

"Sheriff, please come in," Kerry called, as he pushed his chair away from the table and rose to greet the man at his door. "You're just in time."

Seth doffed his hat. "I couldn't turn down a Sunday dinner."

"We missed you last night." Janet hurried to meet Seth at the door.

Kerry motioned to Kyle who had settled in next to Kate. "Kyle, grab the apple box and let Sheriff Morgan use your chair."

The young man scrambled to retrieve a box and plumped down on it, looking none too happy at the rearrangement.

"Kyle, I can't—" Seth started to object.

"Yes, you can." Kerry motioned for Seth to take the seat.

Seth eased into the chair, and Kate's world shrunk to a whirlwind of spicy male scent and strong masculinity. She scooted over an inch or two.

He accepted the proffered platter of chicken, his long fingers wrapping around the edge of the stoneware. Kate stared at them, remembering how his hands clasped her waist when he lifted her from the buckboard. They were capable hands, with beautiful long fingers. He took a chicken thigh and set it on his plate.

Heavens, everything he did turned her world upside down. Did the Lord have a sense of humor and this journey was really about finally finding love? A love she couldn't possibly nurture?

Nonsense. She was here to preserve her freedom and save her company from a greedy murderer. Nothing more.

"Sheriff, while you were out of town yesterday, we had a close call." Kerry filled his plate, his expression serious.

Kate's throat tightened and her palms grew damp. Here, in front of everyone?

"Kerry, dear." Janet laid her hand on his arm. "That conversation should wait until after dinner."

Kerry looked at her for a long moment, then glanced at Kate. "Maybe you're right."

"Is something wrong?" Ethan glanced around the table, his attention settling on Kerry.

Kerry shook his head. "Not at the moment, but Janet's right. We should do justice to this delicious meal, then talk."

Kate wanted to hide. Her arm ached, and her head began to pound. She could barely swallow.

As head of the household everyone respected Kerry's decision to delay the discussion. Janet asked Ruth about her plans to travel east and the men discussed the drought, but the tension in the air spoke of anticipation.

After what seemed an eternity, Kerry pushed his chair from the table and nodded at Ethan's empty plate. "Get enough?"

"Quite enough," Ethan responded. "Excellent meal, Janet."

"Yes, delicious, and a treat to have the day off." Ruth patted Janet's arm and began to gather empty plates and silverware. "I'll wash the dishes."

"Ruth you will do no such thing." Janet started clearing the table. "Maura and Kyle can help. You relax and enjoy your tea."

"I insist." Ruth bustled to the stove and poured water from the steaming kettle to the wash pan. "It seems an important discussion is about to take place, so Maura, Kyle and I will clean up while you all take care of it. Will, you can look at Kyle's book on horses."

Janet smiled at her friend. "I'm so glad you're here, Ruth. I'll miss you when you go to Boston."

"And I you," Ruth sniffed and dabbed her eyes

with her dress sleeve.

Janet refilled Seth's coffee cup. "Sheriff, did you get enough to eat?"

Seth blinked a few times, then smiled. "Janet, if I keep eating your food, I'll look like Mayor Ellis." He smiled and winked at Kyle who still looked glum over moving away from Kate.

Kyle's expression brightened, and he grinned. Janet blushed at Seth's compliment. Seth Morgan was a charmer, no doubt about it. He could even flatter the faithfully married Janet Malone!

Prolonging the time until she had to tell the sheriff and Ethan about the attack, Kate grabbed the large pan holding the remnants of mashed potatoes. Pain shot from her wrist to her shoulder. She gasped and released the pan. It clattered and crashed to the floor.

Ruth and Janet rushed to her side. "Are you all right, dear?"

Seth stood, his chair screeching against the plank flooring. "What happened? Did you burn yourself?"

Tears pricked Kate's eyes. Since the attack, the Malone household had been jumpy and worried about what the stranger might do next. "No. I forgot my right arm was bruised. I couldn't hold onto the pan."

"Bruised?" Seth moved to her side and lifted her hand. "What happened?"

Janet wrapped her arm around Kate. "It's time we join Ethan and Kerry in the parlor. Kate has something she needs to tell you."

Kate longed to step into Seth's arms, lay her head on his shoulder, and lose herself in his strength. She lifted her gaze to his dark eyes and turned her hand in his to squeeze it. His brows arched. "Something happened yesterday, even Ethan doesn't know about." She took a deep breath and released his hand. "Let's get this over with."

She left Janet's comforting embrace and marched into the parlor. Kerry and Ethan glanced at her, Kerry with sympathy, and Ethan with suspicion. What she wouldn't give for a nip of sherry to give her courage.

Turning to face the three men and Janet, she clasped her hands behind her back and squeezed her fingers together. She'd faced down the board members of McShane Walker Shipping; she could disclose the details of an attack that wasn't her fault.

So why did she freeze?

"Go on, Kate. Tell Ethan and Seth what happened." Kerry settled into his favorite chair.

"If the law was broken, I need to know." Seth folded his large frame onto the settee, and sat forward, bracing his elbows on his knees.

"And as your fiancé, I have a right to know anything that affects you." Ethan sent a pointed look at Seth. He didn't seem inclined to sit and stayed in the center of the room mimicking Kate's stance.

Did Ethan want a reason to cancel the wedding?

Kate pushed her hope aside and recounted the attack.

"I should never have let you walk home alone." Seth stood and paced the room.

"You're right, Sheriff. You shouldn't have let her out of your sight." Ethan blamed Seth but drilled Kate with an admonishing stare.

Kate folded her arms under her breasts. "I should have insisted the sheriff walk me to the door. But I didn't, and he didn't and that's how this happened. But that doesn't preclude the fact that there's a dangerous man hanging about."

Janet stepped forward to lay a hand on Kate's arm. "Kate's right. The bigger problem is keeping the family safe. Kate, you said the man was a stranger."

"I'd never seen him before yesterday." Kate's voice cracked, and her chest tightened. This was the first pure truth she'd told these good folks.

"He's not the same one who tried to kidnap you on the train?" Seth moved toward Kate. "I saw that character in town yesterday. I've been looking for him since, but he's disappeared."

Kate shook her head. "He's absolutely not the same man. This man looked more refined, which surprised me given his actions." Nothing should surprise her after learning Jeb Walker had killed her father and tried to force her into marriage.

"The dregs of society come from every social status." Seth folded his arms over his chest and rocked on his heels.

He could be irritating and condescending, and create emotions and feelings she'd never experienced before meeting him, but he also made her feel safe. Kate lost herself in his dark compelling gaze.

"Men, back off and give Kate a chance to catch her breath," Kerry said, heading to the sideboard and the whiskey decanter.

What would she do without the Malones? They'd been stalwart friends through thick and thin. It hurt to imagine how they'd react when she told them her true identity and motives. Kerry handed her a heavy bottom glass of whiskey and water.

"Thank you, Kerry." She sipped the liquor and closed her eyes to absorb the warmth it created.

"Let's all sit down and give Kate time to collect herself." Janet gestured to settee and chairs.

Seth and Ethan sat on opposite ends of the room. They were very different, yet very much alike. Because of their histories, neither trusted that a woman could be simple and honest. Kate always had been honest and forthright, but through recent circumstances she couldn't confess everything she longed to disclose and it pained her.

Frozen to the braided rug dominating the center of the room, she clutched her glass, until Janet guided her to the most comfortable chair in the room. She moved behind the chair and laid her hands on Kate's shoulders. "I'm sorry you're on the spot, but that animal, disguised as a man, has to be dealt with."

"I just want to forget it happened." Kate sipped the watered down whiskey and sank farther into the chair. "But I couldn't bear if something happened to another defenseless person because I didn't speak up."

Seth narrowed his eyes and drilled her with his interrogative look. "Did he say much? I mean, other than make demands?"

Kate stared at the tiny white scars on his thumb, then straight into his eyes. "He said he could take better care of me than you could."

Shock registered in his eyes, but his body remained still.

"Better than Morgan?" Ethan stood and planted his hands on his hips. "What in the hell does that mean? Did you correct him? Tell him that I'm your fiancé?"

"Ethan, I was being assaulted. I didn't care about technicalities."

Seth held up both hands. "Settle down, Howland, we need to get to the bottom of this. He saw me walk Kate to the top of the hill. Depending on how long he's been in town, he'd know I'm the sheriff. I've made it my business to get acquainted with as many citizens as possible."

"He could be someone from your Texas days." After staying quiet for a while, Kerry entered into the conversation. "In your line of work, you've probably made some enemies."

Seth snorted. "No doubt about that." He stroked

his jaw, his calluses rasping against his whiskers. Seth could be clean-shaven in the morning and by mid-afternoon, black whiskers began to pepper his jaw.

Kate returned his probing gaze. "Anyone could have seen you ride up the hill on any given evening."

"It does appear to be a pattern," Ethan said, his tone droll.

Seth leaned back, drumming his fingers on one muscled thigh. "Only someone who watches, picks up routines. Someone who has a plan. Describe him."

"I did."

"Do it again."

"He was well dressed, his hair a dirty blonde or light brown." She frowned and stared off into space, conjuring up an image of the attacker. "He didn't wear a hat, yet there was a band mark around his head. Bright blue eyes, that would have been attractive, but they held a meanness that ruined his looks." She drew in a deep breath, her hands trembled and her stomach flip-flopped. She didn't want to remember him, or the fear still fresh in her mind.

"Any scars or marks?" Seth gazed at her as if they were alone in the room.

"Nothing I noticed." But you have a tiny scar on your upper lip. Kate could have described Seth down to the last dark eyelash.

"Somehow, you escaped." Ethan stopped pacing and stood in the doorway, his shoulder on the jam, like he was guarding the door, keeping Ruth, Will, and the Malone offspring safe.

"I escaped, because I carry a derringer, and I know how to use it." She looked down her nose at Seth and Ethan. "He, uh, pulled me into his arms, so I used my knee to temporarily distract him. I pulled the gun from my pocket and shot him. He ran."

Seth hooted with laughter. "You shot him?

You're a wild card, Kate Leary. Where was your pop gun on the train?"

Kate shook her head and narrowed her lips. "I didn't want to risk hurting an innocent person. Otherwise, I'd have used it instead of asking you for help." She stood and flounced to the door. Ethan started to step aside.

"Whoa, there lady. We're not through here." Seth grasped her arm with his strong hand.

Pain shot up Kate's bruised arm. She flinched and groaned.

Seth released her.

Kate spun toward him. "Excuse me, Sheriff, but is it your practice to punish the victim of an attack, or track down the criminal?"

"I don't mean to punish you, Kate, but it's my job to uphold the law. As you mentioned, he could hurt anyone in this room, or in town. I'm determined to find the man and get to the bottom of your incident and Kyle's, too."

Kate struggled to ignore the pain in her arm. She stared into Seth's eyes, hoping the daggers she shot with her expression hit their mark. "Thank you, Sheriff, for clarifying your mission. I'm relieved you don't hold one person higher than the other."

She elbowed past Ethan with her uninjured arm. She'd had enough of both of them. She couldn't wait until Ross gave her the all clear to return home.

One good thing came out of this episode. Whatever she'd thought attractive about Seth was gone.

Chapter Fourteen

"I'm relieved you don't hold one person higher than the other," Seth mimicked. Kate's condescending tone filled his head as he entered the north end of town. "The woman gets under my skin, and she's not telling me everything."

He strode down the boardwalk toward his office. What an evening! Ethan had looked ready to either banish Kate or slug Seth. He should have done both. Seth would enjoy a good fist fight right about now to work off the frustrations caused by her delectable body and sultry green eyes.

Unlocking his office, he shut the door behind him and stirred the barely glowing embers in the stove. He needed a strong pot of coffee, then, Sunday afternoon or not, he'd get Smith back to the telegraph so he could send out more feelers. Light a fire under his contacts in New York and Boston.

Kate Leary, or Downing, or whoever the hell she really was, remained a puzzle. She claimed her cultured accent came from going to school in New York, but if her parents had that kind of money, how could she be a penniless spinster? He'd seen the fifty dollar bill she'd used to pay for her telegram.

The latest attack didn't make sense either. He shook his head and snorted. How could a woman be attacked twice in the past few weeks by two different men? If this new character wasn't the man from the train, then who was he? Somebody was looking for Kate. A husband? A father?

He filled the coffee pot with cold water and threw in some grounds. Interesting how the attacker had mentioned Seth by name. Had Allen Johnston followed him from New York?

His skin crawled with the need for revenge. He'd tried to put away his anger when he gave up his search for Johnston and headed west. Ha! He'd been kidding himself. Johnston needed to face justice for his part in Griff's death.

Kate had her own deception going, of that he was sure, but he didn't want her caught in the cross hairs of his past. He couldn't blame Kate for not going into more detail with all of them hanging on her every word. For all her backbone, she was gently raised and not used to the profanities Johnston would have used, or the handling.

She was polished and beautiful and distracted Seth from his investigation. The foolishness had to stop. Johnston could be in town, and if he thought Kate meant something to Seth, he'd go after her again.

Seth slammed the coffee pot on the hot stove top and dropped into the chair behind his desk. Taking out paper and pen, he scratched out three messages. One for the Boston Chief of Police, one for the New York Police Department, and one for Leland Cook, foreman of McShane Walker Shipping in New York. He'd spent time with Leland while investigating his case against Johnston and liked the guy.

An hour later at the telegraph office, Seth listened to Smith grumble about opening on Sunday. The telegraph chattered, and Smith handed him a message from Boston. In his messages Seth had included all the names Kate had used since boarding the train along with her description.

According to the Chief in Boston, no one matched Kate's description, but he'd found a neighbor of a Mary Catherine Leary, who'd been born and raised in Boston. Both parents now dead, Miss Leary was believed to have left on a train west to marry a rancher.

Unlike his usual grouchy demeanor, Smith got excited about sending telegrams to big eastern cities for Sheriff Morgan and volunteered to deliver any message that came through. Later that evening, he burst through the office door.

"I got something Sheriff!"

"Who from?"

"New York."

Seth took the message and scanned the man's scrawling penmanship and frowned.

****

No word from Ross on Monday. Nor Wednesday, when Kate made an excuse to return to town with Janet and her shotgun as an escort.

Ethan had joined them every other night for dinner, and like clockwork, Seth showed up every evening. Janet took Seth's appearance in stride, and Kate wondered if she hoped he was courting Maura. He was very attentive to her, but then he was to Janet, too.

The thought didn't set well with Kate. He made her stomach flutter, and her body heat up. She bounced back and forth between wanting to kiss him and wanting to slug him. He'd shown her little affection, but she admired his treatment of everyone else in Hope. He might not care for her, but he was a good man.

Thursday morning, she helped Janet clear the breakfast dishes then asked Kyle and Maura if she could tag along with them to town. Waiting for news was wearing on her. She'd barely slept a wink since Saturday.

"If Kerry's too busy, I'm sure Sheriff Morgan will bring me home," Kate assured Janet as she walked out the door.

"Just don't walk alone." Janet's face creased with concern. "That good for nothing has disappeared, but he might be watching."

Kate shivered. "Believe me, I haven't forgotten the attack. I won't leave town without an escort."

Unlike the last time she sent a telegram, Mr. Smith greeted her with a smile, eager to help. The contrast in his behavior struck Kate as odd and made her suspicious of his motive.

She wrote out the message for Ross and handed it the clerk. If Ross didn't respond soon, she'd go crazy. She'd obeyed his instructions to lay low, but time was running out until the wedding day. More than anything, she wanted to be honest with Ethan, the Malones and Seth. Dammit, especially Seth.

Kate pressed her lace-gloved fingers to her throat. The attack on Saturday served to remind her of the danger still lurking. The despicable man could be in Jeb's employ.

"Mr. Smith, I'm going to the mercantile. I'll return for the reply."

Mr. Smith pulled the bill of his visor down and crossed his arms. "Nobody but the president could get a reply that soon. I'd check tomorrow if I were you."

Kate smiled. "Nevertheless, I'll check before I leave town, just in case."

"Suit yourself."

Kate left the building but hesitated on the front step. For the first time since her arrival in Hope, she was nervous about walking the streets alone. Even in daylight.

Her gaze rested on the new sign hanging above the sheriff's office. She smiled. Seth had been here for a little over a week, and he'd already made his presence known.

She stepped down to the dusty street. Maybe she should check with Seth about walking her home later, before she visited the mercantile. Then again, he might be irritated at her for making him look bad for not walking her all the way to the Malone's last Saturday. She could check with Kerry, but she hated to bother him. Was she just making excuses to see the irritating, yet compelling Sheriff Morgan?

"Hello." Kate walked into the sheriff's office. Silence. No one around, and thank goodness, no one occupied the jail.

She glanced around the small office, running her hand over the scarred desktop. Seth Morgan's desk. She thrilled at the risk of exploring his work place without his knowledge. What could she learn of him?

"What does Sheriff Morgan keep in his drawers?"

"Just ask and I'll show you." His deep voice drawled from the doorway.

Kate gasped and jumped. "Oh!"

"Sorry, but I couldn't let that one go." Seth leaned against the doorjamb, arms folded over his chest, ankles crossed.

Her face heated to the boiling point. "I didn't mean…uh, of course I was referring to your desk."

"Of course." Seth swaggered into the office.

"It's true!" She laid her hands on her warm checks. "I'm curious about the famous Texas Ranger."

"Hardly famous." He shifted through some papers on his desk. His powerful presence wrapped around her.

"That's not how the townspeople look at you. Kerry says they're in awe. I wonder what previewed your arrival."

"According to Mayor Ellis, I was the most exciting thing to happen since General Sherman ended his summer visit." He shrugged. "Exaggeration to say the least. I was a lawman in Texas. Nothing more." He glanced up. "What brings you to town and alone, I gather?"

"Not alone. I came with Kyle and Maura. I

assured Janet I wouldn't walk back alone either."

"Have you asked Kerry to walk with you?"

Kate longed to run her fingertips over his whiskered cheek, the dark day old growth looked bristly, but appealing.

"No, I decided to ask you first."

"Really?"

"Really."

"I can't help but wonder what your fiancé thinks of your trips to town. Every other day this week, unless I missed one."

"You've seen me?"

"It's a small town." Seth stopped shuffling through his paperwork and looked at her, his dark eyes penetrating. "You didn't answer my question about Ethan."

"Ethan surely doesn't mind if I become acquainted with the town."

Seth bit his tongue. Why wouldn't she tell him the truth? The telegram from the New York Police Department had revealed nothing about any of the names he gave them. But her telegrams, the ones she'd written for Smith to send, connected her with Ross Williams. The messages were cryptic. He hadn't pinpointed her relationship with Williams, but he knew the man and didn't trust him. Oh yeah, if she were his fiancée he'd want to be warned. He contemplated telling Ethan himself.

Without conscious thought, he moved closer to her. The rose scent of her hair played with his senses. He cleared his throat. "Are you ready to leave?"

Her lips moved but nothing came out. He took a quick breath then regretted it when her flowery scent filled his head. He backed away and tripped over his chair in the process. Damn, if he survived this woman, he'd be lucky. The prospect of her married to another man and living in Hope wasn't a possibility he wanted to contemplate.

Righting his chair, Seth walked around the desk and motioned for Kate to precede him out the door.

"I-I have to visit the mercantile first." Kate stuttered. Did he affect her like she did him, or was she nervous about being caught in a web of lies?

"Then what brought you here to rifle through my desk?"

Kate appeared to huff. Then puff. Seth wanted to laugh but restrained himself.

"I was not rifling. I explained my presence. I'm not ready to leave town, so there's no need to take you from your duties yet."

Seth nodded and placed his hand at the small of her back, holding his other hand out in front of her. "Shall we?"

"Really Sheriff, I have a couple errands, there's no need for you to accompany me."

"Part of my job is watching the town activity. I can do that while you shop."

Kate acquiesced and walked out the door ahead of him. He waited while she picked up some things at the mercantile for Janet. She paid for some lace trim out of her purse instead of applying it to Janet's store account. Curious.

This time she used a twenty-dollar bill. The money didn't mesh with the story he'd gathered about Mary Catherine Leary. The true Mary Catherine wouldn't have this much money.

Leaving the store, she hesitated in front of the telegraph office, then picked up her pace. "Sheriff, are you sure you should leave town right now?"

He dragged his attention from her swinging backside. "I won't be gone long."

Strolling up the boardwalk, Seth took her arm when Kate stepped down onto the dusty street. "Have you remembered anything more about the attack?"

She shivered, then stopped and looked at him, her eyes wide. "What else is there? I was attacked by a complete stranger. I described him as well as I can."

Seth tightened his grip on her arm. "I don't want to take chances with the safety of my upstanding citizens."

Kate exhaled and searched around as if looking for an escape. "Since you don't consider me one of that category, you don't have to worry."

"That's not true, Kate. I'm here to protect you as much as anyone." Maybe more. His body warmed and parts of him, that he'd rather not deal with right now, started to swell.

"How comforting. Nevertheless, I don't remember anything new. I've been assaulted three times in the last month, three more times than I ever believed could happen. I'm bruised and shook up, but dammit, I'll survive." She huffed again.

Three times? To his knowledge, she'd been attacked twice.

She glanced at him. "Since you're so concerned about the incident, have you found any leads?"

"Some possibilities." He itched to tell her, he had her telegrams. Why wouldn't she just tell him the truth? Maybe he could help her.

He rubbed his hand over his chin, the whiskers sounding like sandpaper against his callouses. "You flashed a fifty dollar bill the first day you sent a telegram."

She drew up short. "You think the attack had something to do with Mr. Smith?"

"No. Smith's an odd bird, but an honest man. Has anyone else in town seen you with a large amount of money?"

Kate looked at his hand, still resting on her arm. He liked touching her, even if fabric separated him from her soft skin. Maybe she should be afraid of him. If they were in a private place, he'd be hard pressed not to pull her into his arms and kiss her like he was sure she'd never been kissed.

"Of course not, Sheriff Morgan. My money's all gone. I'm penniless."

"You have nothing?" She'd used a twenty-dollar bill to pay for the lace in the mercantile.

Her lips quivered.

"I'm sorry, Kate. I don't mean to upset you. I was under the impression you came to Hope because you had no money. Yet, you rode from New York in a private sleeping compartment and ate in the dining car. Your clothes are typical, but your manners are of someone who's had the best education and society."

Kate gazed up the street. "Is money the reason you think I lied about the attack on the train?"

Seth looked across the untamed land, the awe-inspiring lake, and the tree covered islands. "I don't want to believe you've been lying to me, Kate, but some things don't add up."

She didn't respond. There were some things he wished she was lying to him about. Like her plan to marry Ethan in less than two weeks. Seth looked down at the top of her head. The morning sunshine sent fiery lights through her thick, shiny hair.

"Kate?"

She turned from gazing at the lake, her eyes met his. "My life is so complicated. Saturday, at the ranch, I made the decision to confide in you, but you were in a hurry to be rid of me, then the attack happened."

He tilted his head to one side. "You want to confide in me, and not Ethan?"

"It's complicated," she repeated, looking anywhere but at him.

Seth's lawman logic warred with the emotions this woman stirred in him. She'd tell him first and not Ethan. Not the man she'd traveled thousands of miles to marry.

He cleared his throat. "We'd better get you home before Janet sends out a posse." And before he threw away his scruples and pulled her into his arms.

"But I need to talk to you, Seth. If I don't tell you the truth, I'm going to explode."

Seth frowned. They were on the edge of town in full view of anyone who happened to pass by. Not the place for an in-depth conversation.

He studied her for a moment, then raised one brow. "So, you're ready to tell me who you really are?"

"I am. I need to." She closed her eyes for a moment then opened them, chipping away at his resolve to keep his hands off her, with her brilliant green eyes.

He crossed his arms over his chest. "This might be the time, but not the place." He glanced around. "Let's go back to my office."

He took Kate's arm and guided her to his office, shutting the door behind them. "Would you like to sit down?"

She shook her head. "No, I can't sit down until I've told you everything." She took a deep breath, her breasts straining the fabric of her dress.

Seth coughed. "Go on."

"Poor Ethan, the last thing I want to do is hurt him. My plan seemed like the only option at the time." She splayed her hands over her face. "I was so wrong."

"Tell me." He worked to keep the impatience and lust out of his voice.

Tears welled in her eyes. Kate impatiently swiped at them and stood straighter. "My real name is Kathleen McShane. Seven weeks ago, my father suddenly died, leaving me as Chairman of the Board of McShane Walker Shipping."

"You've got to be kidding me." The tie in with Allen Johnston became clear.

"You've heard of my company?"

"Heard of it? Of course I've heard of it. Jeb Walker runs the office in Houston." Seth wrung at the back of his neck with one hand.

Kate turned white and stepped back, grasping for the desk behind her. "He and my father were partners, but they didn't get along, so it made sense for Jeb to live in Houston."

Her face was tight with strain, but he wasn't backing down. The telegrams connected her with Ross Williams, but he'd never suspected her to be James McShane's daughter.

"Go on."

"I'm sure you're wondering what the heiress of a multimillion dollar business is doing in Idaho Territory, living under another woman's name, and preparing to marry a man she'd never before met."

"I am curious."

Kate let a sigh escape, and her shoulders slumped. "My company and my life are in danger. Jeb Walker wants full control, and he'll do anything to get it, even if he has to marry me."

She pressed one hand to her throat. "When I refused his third proposal, he had me kidnapped. I managed to escape, but Ross and Leland insisted I leave New York while they sort things out and hopefully find enough evidence to…" her voice broke, "…convict Jeb of killing my father."

"Whew." Seth whistled the word. "That's how you've been attacked three times." And how she was connected to Williams. But had she told him everything? Seth suspected Williams of being connected with Allen Johnston, and he didn't trust either one of them. "This is bigger than I suspected. Is there strong evidence Jeb killed your father?"

"Leland and Ross think so. Guilty or not, I want

the man out of my company and my life."

"Don't hang him until you have clear evidence." While in Houston, he'd spent time with Jeb. The man might be unscrupulous at times, but Seth didn't believe he'd kill his partner.

"I," she said, laying a hand on the breasts Seth couldn't seem to get his mind off of, "have no evidence. It just all made sense when Ross and Leland told me. With me either out of the way or under his control, Jeb could buy up my shares and have sole ownership of the company."

"So, Ross Williams is in charge of the investigation?" He couldn't leave his suspicions alone.

"Yes." She frowned. "You sound like you know Ross."

Seth pursed his lips and pushed a breath through his nostrils. "I met Mr. Williams in New York."

She frowned. "Really? How?"

"Since we're being straight with each other, I know Ross and Leland Cook."

"You do?" Kate sank onto the narrow, straight back chair in front of his desk.

Seth needed to verify some things before he talked too much about Williams and risked Kate tipping him off. Now that he knew Kate's identity, he'd contact New York again and dig deeper.

He narrowed his eyes and studied her expression. "To lay it all out, I met Jeb when I traced Griff's murder to Allen Johnston. Griff saved my miserable life more than once and was like a father to me. Johnston was the man giving the orders for the stagecoach robberies Griff was assigned to investigate. As far as I know, Johnston ordered his minions to kill any Ranger who got in their way." He took a stabilizing breath. Emotions he'd thought he had a hold on threatened to overtake him.

"Johnston worked in your Houston office. To get close to the shipping office and investigate Johnston, I pretended to court Trisha Walker, Jeb's daughter."

"You courted Trisha?" Her brows shot up under the soft auburn curls brushing her forehead.

"I pretended to. It seemed like a good plan at the time." He hoped she understood his motive for courting Trisha was a tool, just like Kate's plan to change places with Miss Leary. "Sometimes you do what you have to do."

"Sounds like torture." She bristled. "How did you leave it with her?"

Kate seemed more worried about his relationship with Trisha, than the fact that he knew key people in her company. "I told her I'd enjoyed spending time with her, but I had to move on."

Kate slowly nodded and looked around the room, seeming to gather her composure before she looked back at Seth. "I'm sorry about your friend's death. I know how it is to lose someone you love. But Ross and Leland are in New York. How did you meet them?"

"I had the connection with the company in Houston. Jeb put me in touch with them. He thought, as I did, that Johnston ran to New York, and the more help I had from the company, the better."

"I can't imagine Ross doing anything Jeb asked." She wasn't ready to hear his suspicions, and Seth felt a strange twinge of jealously over her loyalty to Ross.

"Kate, he was in constant contact with the Houston office."

She lifted her chin. "Exactly how well do you know Jeb Walker?"

"Not well." He slowly shook his head. "He's a powerful man in Houston. Your company's powerful. Which leads me to the question of how you came by this new identity?"

"I left New York as Elizabeth Downing, a name Ross concocted to get me to Chicago undetected. The plan was for me to stay with my uncle until the issue with Jeb was resolved." Her expression tightened. "Then right before the attack on the train, I met Mary Catherine Leary. We resembled each other. She was bound for somewhere she didn't want to go, and I needed a new place to hide."

"I remember her. I thought you were family. So, you gave her the money she needed to return to Boston, and she gave you her name and destination." Seth grinned. "Mercy, woman. Do you ever do anything in a simple way?"

She smiled for the first time since he'd discovered her in his office, going through his desk. "It seemed like a perfect plan. Then, after I arrived and met Ethan and the Malones, I realized I'd made a mistake, but I can't do anything about it until Ross tells me I'm no longer in danger."

She stood and stepped closer to him. Seth's blood warmed another notch.

"It isn't only me that I'm worried about. If my real identity is revealed too soon, it could put the Malones in danger. And Ethan's family. Even you."

"Even me," he repeated, wishing he could kiss the worry off her pretty face. "So, you're waiting for Ross to clear the way for you." Seth guiltily patted his breast pocket, where he'd stashed the telegrams he'd intercepted.

"I'm becoming concerned." She turned away and walked to the stove that hadn't seen a fire since early that morning. "I realize these things can take time, but I was under the impression, from Ross, that he'd be able to confirm his suspicions right away."

"How well do you know Ross?"

Kate faced him. "I've known him for many years.

He came to work for my father right out of law school. Why?"

Seth shrugged. "I've learned to look at a situation from all angles. Sometimes what we think is obvious, isn't."

Kate frowned. "If you're implying that Ross is somehow involved with Jeb, beyond the needed business, you couldn't be more wrong. He's been a very loyal retainer. The meetings he had with Jeb must have been sanctioned by my father."

Seth shrugged again. "Like I said, I've learned to look at all angles."

"Well, you're wrong about Ross." Kate smoothed her dress and hair. "We should leave. Janet will be worried about me."

"Yeah, you're right." He had to get away from her before he claimed her full lips. His glance must have given him away because Kate's cheeks glowed with a charming shade of pink.

Chapter Fifteen

Saturday rolled around, with no response from Ross. Kate was losing time, and the wedding date loomed closer. After her trip to town on Thursday and her conversation with Seth, she felt some relief, but all was not well until Ross confirmed it.

The mood at the dinner table that night reminded her of a performance she once saw with her parents at the theater. Maura flirted with Seth; Ethan glared at Maura. Janet watched everyone, while Kerry seemed oblivious to the tension. Kyle grinned at Kate every time she happened to look at him. She really must have a talk with the young man before she left about flirting with older women.

Seth acted as if he was involved in a crime investigation and everyone was suspect.

When the dishes were cleared and dessert over, the men went into the parlor to discuss the subjects they preferred. The type of talk Kate had listened to most of her life. The hum of male voices, the scent of spicy hair tonic, and the tang of pipe tobacco lulled her into a deep sense of security.

Missing her father terribly, Kate hurried to her room to splash her face with cool water. She blotted her damp face with a lace-edged towel just as Maura stepped into her room and shut the door. "What were you talking about last Saturday, when you told me not to worry about you marrying Ethan?"

Startled by the younger woman's fiery blue eyes, she stepped back and grappled for an answer without revealing the entire truth.

"I meant exactly that."

"The wedding day will arrive, Kate. Ethan believes you'll be at the altar. The entire town plans to attend. How can you change that now?"

"Maura, I know you love Ethan, it's very evident. You don't need to worry."

"I don't understand." Tears welled in Maura's eyes.

Kate wanted to hug her, but she couldn't let her guard down completely or she'd be sputtering out the truth and crying with the younger woman. "Right now, I can't tell why I won't marry Ethan, but the wedding will be cancelled in a few days. He loves you, Maura. You belong together."

Maura sank to the bed, tears rolled over her bottom lid to bead on her lashes. "I think so, too, but he's too honor bound to end his commitment to you." She threw her arms in the air. "He has this crazy idea that my parents would feel betrayed if he declared himself to me. He thinks he's too old for me. Can you imagine?"

"Ethan's a very honorable man. I'm sure the memory of Natalie's betrayal still hurts. He's determined to avoid heartbreak again."

"I don't understand." Maura glanced toward the door. "Why can't you tell Ethan now?"

"It's complicated," Kate said for the third time that day.

Maura shot off the bed. "I've loved Ethan since I knew about love. My heart broke when he told us he'd sent for a wife."

Kate sat on the bed. "I'm sorry I can't tell you more, but please believe when I say, I won't be marrying Ethan. If I have my way, you'll be filling that position. You're the perfect choice, he just needs to get over his ridiculous ideas and act."

Maura's eyes widened. "You'll help me?"

"Yes." Kate smiled. "But you have to swear you'll keep it between us."

Maura sat down next to Kate and ran her hand over the quilted bed top. “I’m sorry I was so mean to you, Kate. You didn’t deserve it.”

“I understand. If I were in love with a man and someone threatened to take him from me, I’d be angry too.” Like Seth? The name sang through her mind. She was falling for him. She’d been enraged with jealousy when he told her about courting Trisha, no matter what his motive. If only he fit into her real life.

Maura nibbled at her bottom lip. “I promise I won’t say a word.”

Kate sighed. She’d let down her guard, and now she hoped Maura could keep her confidence until Kate could tell Ethan the truth.

****

The warm Indian summer held as another Sunday morning dawned in Hope, Idaho Territory.

Janet had planned a picnic after church services to take advantage of the warm weather before winter set in. Kate suspected Janet had more on her mind than the chicken she’d been frying since before daylight.

She’d invited Ethan and his family to join them at a spot on the lake, not far from town.

No doubt Seth was also invited.

Kate sighed. The man tied her in knots. Yesterday, he’d acted like he wanted to kiss her, and today after Mass he’d barely acknowledged her presence.

Their mutual attraction was making her crazy and was obvious enough for Janet Malone to notice and possibly use to test Kate’s loyalty to Ethan.

The Malones packed the picnic supplies in the buckboard and drove to the lake. Waves lapped at the pebble-strewn shoreline, littered with driftwood and larger rocks. Though the scents of fall tinged the air, the unseasonal warmth of summer prevailed.

Seth arrived in time to help Kerry and Kyle unload the blankets and food basket, setting them in a partially shaded spot before attending to the horses. Janet spread out the blankets, then stood, her hands on her curvaceous hips, gazing out over the blue green waters of Lake Pend Oreille.

"Ethan will be here soon, Kate. It won't be long, and you'll be part of his family."

"Won't be long." A knot settled in Kate's chest. She glanced at Maura and flinched at the look of helplessness on the younger woman's face. She hoped her confession the night before would help her through the next week.

Maura turned and flounced away.

"Maura Malone, I did not teach you poor manners. You come back."

Maura kept walking along the shoreline.

"Trouble?" Seth asked, joining the women. The man had a penchant for walking into a sensitive conversation.

Janet shook her head and joined her husband and son, who were busy uncoiling fishing line and attaching it to the green, pliable lengths of Quaking Aspen they'd gathered.

"Not fishing with the men?" Kate crossed her arms over her stomach to keep from touching Seth.

"I think there's a bigger catch right here." Seth's voice was deep and low.

Kate shivered, wishing he meant it in a romantic way. "I'm not something you can simply reel in, Sheriff."

"I thought you were calling me, Seth."

"I'm an affianced woman, and therefore not free to call men by their first names."

One dark brow cocked. "Oh? Well, I think in private we can drop all that, don't you?"

The rumble of another wagon saved Kate from a reply. Ethan's group had arrived, and Kate smiled at

Will who stood in the wagon behind his father, clutching Ethan's broad shoulders.

"Is that smile for Will or Ethan?" Seth's voice came too close to her ear.

Goosebumps scattered over the back of her neck. She looked at him from the corner of her eye. "Of course it's for Will. You know I won't marry Ethan, so why do you persist in deviling me about it?"

"Humph." Seth walked away to help Ruth with her baskets. "I'll be damned if I know."

Janet helped Ruth set out their food, while the men moved the horses and wagons away from the picnic sight, taking the horse flies with them.

Ethan's blue gaze brushed over Kate, as she walked toward the blankets, then settled on Maura, who stood down the shoreline, staring out over the water. As if sensing Kate's attention on him, Ethan looked back at her, a hint of guilt in his eyes.

Kate smiled and walked to his side, looping her arm through his. "Beautiful day, isn't it?" She wanted to spare him the pain and regret he must be feeling. The intense look he'd given Maura told the story and confirmed Kate's decision. She had to get those two together before she left Hope.

Ruth and Janet arranged the food and called for everyone to join them. Kyle didn't hesitate to fill his plate, and Kerry and Seth were right behind him. Ethan gestured for Kate to take a plate.

"You go ahead." She laid her hand on his arm. "I don't think Maura heard the call for dinner. I'll go get her."

Ethan hardly looked at her. What would it take for him to realize Maura was the woman for him?

Seagulls swooped and squawked, hoping for a handout. The waves lapped close to her feet, making her want to keep walking, lose herself in the peacefulness of the water and sun.

"Maura, it's time to eat," she said, when she

reached Maura's side. As she had done to Ethan a few moments earlier, Kate looped her arm through Maura's. "I know this is hard, but you have to remember it's only temporary."

Maura turned toward her, tears streaking down her face. "Just because you're gone doesn't mean Ethan will propose to me. You can't make Ethan Howland love me."

Kate smiled. "He already does. We have to make him realize it. You should have seen the way he looked at you a moment ago. He's torn between what his heart wants and what his mind thinks is right."

"Grrrr, I'm so tired of his sense of honor! I want to shake him."

"I know." Kate turned toward the picnic spot, pulling Maura with her. "It's hard, but please hold on. If it helps, you can act like you don't like or trust me."

Maura sighed with frustration but walked toward the picnic with Kate. They filled their plates with chicken, potatoes and salads, then sat on a blanket. Seth and Kyle were bantering over the glamor of law enforcement. With the optimism of a youth, Kyle insisted he wanted to be a Ranger when he turned sixteen, just like he'd heard Seth had done. Janet jumped into the conversation with her objections.

Appreciating the chance to think of something other than her troubles, Kate scooted across the blanket to snap up another roll. She didn't see Will's glass of punch until it tipped over and soaked the skirt of her peach dress.

"Oh, dear!" Kate scrambled to her feet and fanned her skirt.

"Kate, I'm so sorry." Ethan blotted the fabric with his napkin without getting too close to her.

Kate pressed her napkin against the fine cotton, watching the peach and berry colors blend into a bright fuchsia. "You know, I like this color, maybe I should dye the entire dress." The events of the past weeks bubbled up inside her, and she began to laugh.

She glanced up to find everyone staring at her as if she'd lost her mind. Maura's blue eyes were wide in surprise. Ethan still dabbed at her skirt, fruitlessly attempting to remove the juice. Tears of mirth streamed down Kate's cheeks. She was losing her mind; she must be!

"Kate, are you all right?" Janet stood and wrapped her arm around Kate's shoulder. Kate saw this all as a perfect chance to give Ethan and Maura some time without her around.

"I'm fine." She sniffed and wiped at the tears. If they thought her upset over the silly dress so be it. She owned dresses far finer than this one. "I should go home and change. This dress is quite sticky."

"I have some soap that might take it out." Janet pulled the wet, sticky fabric from Kate's legs.

The sound of a sob took Kate's attention from the plan forming in her mind to Will, who sat on the blanket, his face puckered. "Oh, honey, I didn't mean to upset you." Kate crouched and put her arm around the small boy.

"But I shouldn't have put my cup there."

"Will, I tipped it over when I reached for one of Ruth's wonderful rolls. I'm not worried about the dress, sweetheart, but I do want to go home and change."

"I can take you." Ethan stepped forward. Kate could see his heart wasn't in it. Just like it hadn't been into each visit over the past week, but bless him, he offered.

"I can surely walk home from here in safety." Taking Ethan away from Maura would undo her plan.

"I'll see you home." Seth set his half eaten

dinner to one side and stood. "I can check on things in town while you change. You'll be back in time for pie."

"That's a wonderful idea," Janet piped up. "Go with Sheriff Morgan, and Ethan you can take Will wading to cheer him up."

Ethan visibly relaxed. "Very well. Thank you, Sheriff."

Her heart refused to beat right when Seth handed her up to the wagon seat. She scooted over, making room for his large frame, and fought to breathe when he sat next to her, his intoxicating male scent sweeping over her.

Life had suddenly become a stage, and she was playing the part of the deceptive woman who planned to marry one man under false pretenses, while in love with another one.

Love? She was in love with Seth Morgan? The truth tightened her chest and made her lightheaded. She was attracted to him; she had been since the first time she saw him on the train. She'd found trust in him, but love?

Seth clicked to the horses and turned them toward the hill. Kate grabbed the edge of the seat. She'd leave Hope heartbroken from falling in love with a man she highly respected, but who didn't fit in her life. Nor, did she fit in his.

The wagon rumbled up the dusty roadway toward town. Uncertain with her new knowledge, Kate looked at the passing scenery—the tall, tall trees, the blue sky, and the vast lake. Anything but Seth. She fanned her damp, sticky dress in the warm air.

Seth nodded at several citizens as they rumbled past his office and the telegraph office. He turned the wagon and started up the steep hill toward the Malone's. How many of these people had seen her and Seth together on other occasions? She cringed.

What would the townspeople say when the news of her real identity came out?

She sighed. Ross, where in the world are you?

The moment Seth guided the horses to the Malone's back door, Kate scrambled off the bench seat and hopped to the ground.

"Whoa, what's your hurry?" He jumped off the wagon seat and followed her to the door.

"I want to get out of this dress and rejoin the picnic." And I don't trust myself alone with you.

"What are you running from, Kate? Me?"

Kate hesitated, one hand on the back doorknob. "Seth, don't."

"Don't what? Don't follow you, don't touch you, don't make love to you?"

Kate's knees weakened, and she clung to the door. The thought of Seth doing those things drained her of all strength. She turned the knob and pushed against the door to escape the oh so masculine chest pressed against her back. His spicy scent blended with leather and warm man sent her senses reeling. She burst into the kitchen and hurried to the stairs.

"Why are you running like a scared rabbit?" His voice echoed through the house.

"I'm not running." She stopped at the bottom of the stairs her hand on the modest newel post. "I told you. I want to rejoin our group."

"I don't believe you." His dark gaze drilled into hers.

Kate hurried up the stairs and closed the door. Leaning against the wood panel, she took a deep breath, then groaned. How had things gotten so crazy? Oh yes, the company, Jeb Walker. That was the reason she'd assumed another woman's life and found herself lying day and night. She had never planned to meet Seth Morgan. The man was irritating and exciting all in one. She vacillated between wanting to slap him to wanting to kiss him.

He evoked a passion she hadn't known she possessed.

Kate stripped out of the sticky, stained dress. She might be able to get the punch out of the thin cotton, or she might throw it away, either way didn't matter. Mary Catherine had Kate's quality gowns to wear and would never know.

She dipped a soft cloth into the bowl of room temperature water and washed off the perspiration, dust and the remnants of Will's punch. With every swipe of the damp cloth, her awareness of being alone in the house with Seth grew.

She shook off her dangerous thoughts and took a mint green dress from the wardrobe, one she hadn't worn since arriving in Hope. Slipping it over her head, she ran her hands over the bodice and down the skirts, smoothing the fabric. A glance in the cheval mirror confirmed the color suited her auburn hair and green eyes. She'd been lucky to trade places with a woman whose coloring so closely matched her own.

Downstairs, Seth paced, his boots echoing off the wood floor. On impulse, she spritzed her throat and wrists with rose water. Patting her hair, she took one last look in the mirror and snapped up her shawl.

Seth turned and looked at her the moment her foot touched the plank floor.

"Lord a mercy." He breathed the words, sending a thrill down Kate's spine. Her breath caught at the effect one look from this man did to her body. Never had she dreamed of experiencing such powerful feelings. Her breasts puckered, and a ball of fire formed low in her stomach.

She tried to ignore the heat in his eyes, act nonchalant, but she couldn't. Nor could she keep from walking toward him, stopping when she could define his pupils. They flared. She moaned.

Before she could think or form words to stop him, his arms came around her, pulling her against him. His mouth came down over hers, possessing, massaging. She couldn't think; she could hardly breathe.

Her palms ached to touch him, learn things she'd never known, feelings she'd never imagined. Sliding her hands over his customary black leather vest, she slipped inside, seeking heat and something she didn't quite understand. Put her in front of a board meeting, and she was aggressive and knowledgeable, but in a man's arms she was a novice.

Moving her fingers over his cotton shirtfront, she outlined his ribs and muscled chest, hearing a crackling when her hand covered his breast pocket. His fingers encircled her wrist and pulled her hand away from his pocket.

A thread of curiosity fluttered through her mind. What did he have in his pocket he didn't want her to know about?

Her curiosity over the paper evaporated when his kiss deepened and he backed her against the table until she lay on the blue gingham cloth. He shoved the sugar bowl and butter dish aside and lifted her farther onto the sturdy pine table.

Kate gasped against his mouth, when his hardness conformed with her softness. Her head swam and body tingled with sensations she'd only dreamed of.

He bracketed her face and deepened the kiss, his tongue slipping between her lips, laving, tasting. Kate returned the action and was rewarded with a low, deep groan.

Heady with power, she bucked against him, instinctively searching for release from the tightly wound passion deep in her belly. His heat and spicy scent filled her head and overcame any last thought of stopping the insanity of making love on the Malone's dining table.

Kate's head bumped into the condiment dishes. She blindly pushed them farther out of reach, then gasped. He pulled his mouth from hers. Her heart skipped a beat at the heat in his dark, dark eyes.

"What?" His voice was as rough as the stones along the lake.

"I stuck my fingers in the butter dish." How foolish, she'd gone and ruined the moment.

Seth chuckled and brought her hand to his mouth. He sucked first one finger then the other between his full lips, eating the butter off as if it were the most delectable thing.

Kate turned to liquid.

Seth growled and rubbed against her lower body, pressing that mysterious, wonderful, hard, male part against her belly. His expression grew more intense, his eyelids heavier.

As quick as he'd laid her on the table, the kissing stopped. Seth moaned. "What in the hell am I doing?" He pressed his forehead against hers as he worked to slow his labored breathing.

Kate's heart sank. "Was it so bad?"

His delicious mouth turned up into a smile. "Ah, Katie, what am I going to do with you?" He pulled away, then pulled her off the table. "Your kisses drive me crazy. That's the problem."

She placed a hand on his chest, and his strong, steady heartbeat sent goose bumps up her arm. "I've never done that before—I never dreamed…"

He propped his hands on her hips. "I know you haven't. It's not like that with just anyone, Katie."

Kate lifted her chin. "I'm twenty-four years old, Seth, and I've never been so close to someone."

He pushed his fingers through his hair. "I can tell. I'm glad you haven't been—well—that intimate with anyone else."

"When this is over, when I can tell everyone the truth. What will happen between you and me?"

Seth drew in a sharp breath. "I don't know. We have things to work out."

Kate's heart sank just a bit. Was he leaving open a way to escape her? He said he appreciated her lack of experience; was there something else about her he didn't find desirable?

"Seth, I told Maura I won't be marrying Ethan."

"What? You told her?"

"Not about my true identity. She's so upset over this mail-order bride thing. I wanted to ease her mind. This ruse becomes more complicated by the day." Kate patted her hair and busied herself putting the table back to rights. Her body still tingled and ached at the same time.

Seth moved behind her and wrapped his arms around her waist. "A few more days and you'll be able to tell Ethan and the Malones the truth. I'll be there when you do."

****

Kate slept fitfully most of the night, with images of Seth laying her on the table, kissing her, pressing his body against hers, running through her mind. Then the image would change to Ross, an evil glint in his eyes. Doubts and passion took turns weaving through her dreams until they startled her awake.

She stared into the darkness, torn between wanting to lie in Seth's arms and yearning to be back in her own bed with her own life. The sky began to lighten when exhaustion overcame her, and she fell into a deep sleep.

When she awoke later, full sunlight streamed through the curtains. Kate hurried to wash and dress. Oh no! She had to check for a telegram and couldn't walk to town alone.

Rushing down the stairs, she stopped in the doorway, her fears confirmed. Kyle and Maura were already gone for the day. Only Janet remained in the kitchen, slicing up the late apples she'd picked yesterday after the picnic.

"I over slept."

"You were tired."

"I have to go into town. Right away."

Janet wiped her hands on the flour sack apron tied around her waist. "What's the hurry? If you need things for the wedding, we can go to town later."

"No, it's not the wedding. It's a telegram." At Janet's raised brow, Kate sputtered. "I hope my friend Erin can attend the wedding."

"You didn't mention your friend coming before."

Kate sighed. Another lie to add to the long string she'd already told. "I invited her, but she wasn't sure. I really miss her and at least want to know for sure." That was the truth. She desperately missed her dear friend, Erin, who would normally be her sounding board on her feelings for Seth.

"In that case," Janet said, untying her apron. "I'll walk to the top of the hill with you and see that you make it to the blacksmith."

"You'd be walking back to the house alone." Kate's heart lifted a bit, but she didn't want to risk Janet's safety for any reason.

"No, not alone." Janet took the rifle from the hooks over the back door. "I'll have Chester."

"The gun has a name?"

"He's part of survival in this wild country. He deserves a name."

Kate chuckled and followed Janet out the door.

Minutes later, she turned at the blacksmith to look up the hillside and wave at Janet.

She could be very close to returning to New York. Her step faltered. Leaving would mean never seeing all the wonderful people she'd met. It would mean leaving Seth, after all the time she'd waited for a man who moved her. The memory of what happened yesterday sent spirals of heat through her body.

She'd never forget the taste of Seth's lips, the warmth and strength of his body. Nor would she forget the fire in his eyes when he pulled away and looked at her. She'd willingly gone into his arms and returned his kisses, but she'd be leaving soon. She wanted her old life back, didn't she? She knew that life, understood it, but there'd be no Seth Morgan, no fire running through her veins from his touch.

Just below Kerry's blacksmith and stables, the train sat at the station. She could keep walking past the sheriff's office, past the telegraph office and buy a ticket; be on the train when it pulled out. No, she wasn't made that way. She couldn't skip out without an explanation.

Sighing, she walked up the boardwalk, taking a quick glance through the window of the sheriff's office. The memory of being in Seth's arms, kissing him, flashed through her mind. She tripped over the edge of the boardwalk, mumbling over not paying attention as she stepped into the post office.

"Mr. Smith, do I have a telegram?"

The balding man glared from under his dark green visor. Why he insisted on wearing the silly thing was beyond Kate.

"Nope. Nothing here."

"There has to be!" Kate leaned against the counter, her fingers gripping the edge. "Are you sure my messages are reaching New York?"

"I don't send failed messages."

"Then something else is wrong. I need to send another."

"Suit yourself." The man slid a piece of paper across the counter. "It's your money."

Kate picked up a pencil and began. *Ross, Please update. Urgent that you respond. Kate.* She slid the missive across the counter and waited while Mr. Smith sent it.

"All righty, it's done."

Kate paid him, then walked into the warm autumn air. She leaned against the front of the building and gazed across the wide expanse of water. Ross and Leland had to know something by now. Kate McShane didn't do well when she was left out of the business at hand.

She glanced up and down the street, sighing at the roughness of the town, the dust clinging to everything and everybody. They needed rain before a fire started and burned the place down.

With heightened senses, she glanced up the street. Seth stood in front of the sheriff's office, his arms crossed over his chest, his gaze fixed on her. Heat flared through her body that rivaled the warm day. She should hurry to the blacksmith shop and ask Kerry when he could take her home. Instead, she turned her back on Sheriff Morgan and walked to Mrs. White's.

Entering the café and bakery, she inhaled the scent of fresh baked bread and pastries. Her stomach growled. She'd slept past breakfast and hadn't wanted to take the time to eat.

No one else occupied the charming café with its round tables covered in bright floral patterned cloths.

"Miss Leary." Mrs. White bustled out of the kitchen. "What brings you into town today?"

"I had some business and missed breakfast. Your scones and tea came to mind."

"Please have a seat anywhere." The older woman indicated the small grouping of tables. "What kind of scone would you like?"

"The huckleberry, if you have them. I'd also like to take six home for the Malones."

"Lovely. I'll have your tea right out."

Kate sank onto the ladder back chair and sighed. Her nerves couldn't take much more of lying to everyone, nor this obsession with Seth. She couldn't trust herself not to fall into his arms, and that would only complicate things more.

She was running out of time. At the end of this week, the entire town expected her to marry Ethan. Maybe jumping on the train right now wasn't such a bad idea.

Mrs. White set out lovely golden brown scones, a teapot with a matching floral teacup and saucer, cream and sugar bowl. A glimmer of the civilized world. She smiled and thanked the older woman, then poured her tea, adding a spoon of sugar and a dollop of cream. Sitting back in the chair, she blissfully chewed on the tender pastries.

"Mrs. White, please change my order and box up a dozen scones if you can spare them. I know the Malones will enjoy them."

"I'll be happy to. I made a double batch just this morning. I must have known you were coming." Mrs. White wiped her hands on her apron. She wore a blue sprigged gown with tiny green leaves, the shoulders puffed and narrowed toward the elbow and tight at the wrist. The style was very close to the clothes Kate wore to the shipping office, practical, yet attractive enough to feel confident. "I've been concerned about you, my dear."

"Concerned?" Kate's stomach fluttered, her mind racing to think which situation would concern Mrs. White.

"About the attack, my dear." Mrs. White had the grace to look uncomfortable. "Mr. White met Kerry that afternoon. When Kerry came to the sheriff's office to tell Sheriff Morgan."

"Kerry told him what happened?"

"He was very worried about you, my dear, and the safety of his family. He actually warned Mr.

White to be on the lookout for that despicable man."

"Hmm." Kate stirred sugar into her tea, searching her mind for a tactful way to end this line of conversation. "I thank you for your concern, but I'm really quite well. My shoulder was sore for a few days, but it's much better now."

"I'm so glad to hear that."

"Mrs. White, where are you from?" Kate longed for simple social conversation where she didn't have to watch every word.

"Chicago." Elena White smiled as she poured Kate another cup of tea, then gently set the teapot back down. "I came with my first husband, but he died of influenza two winters ago."

"You stayed here alone?"

"I didn't have anything to return to. By that time the café was doing well. I have no family left in Chicago. They've scattered all over the west. Why go back? Then of course, I met Mr. White." The older woman fairly glowed at the mention of her husband and the owner of the mercantile.

"It's wonderful you met someone."

Kate's large house in New York might be filled with servants, but since her father died she'd felt alone.

The door opened. Booted footsteps echoed across the plank floor.

"Good morning, Sheriff." Mrs. White smiled over Kate's head. A thrill skittered across Kate's shoulders and compelled her to turn toward him.

"Mrs. White, how are you today?"

Seth Morgan stood, hat in hand, his hair still showing a slight impression of the hat band. His clothes were clean and wrinkle free but carried a slight coating of the dust that permeated the town. He looked indescribably handsome.

"Miss Leary." His eyes changed from a congenial twinkle to a flare of heat. Kate schooled her heart to slow, to not send a telling blush to her face.

"Sheriff Morgan." She nodded and returned to her tea, her hands trembling as she picked at her scone. Blood roared through her ears, but she heard Elena ask Sheriff Morgan to choose a table, and she'd bring him coffee and a scone.

The chair to her right scraped across the floor, and Seth settled in at the neighboring table. Other than a few minutes ago in the street, she hadn't seen him since he returned her to the picnic by the lake. He'd quickly made an excuse about returning to the office and rode out on his gelding without a backward glance.

Elena White left the room.

"Why are you in town alone?"

"How do you know I'm alone?"

"I watched you walk into town."

In that case, he more than likely saw her enter the post office. "I planned to stop by the smithy and have Kerry escort me home on his lunch break."

Elena returned with Seth's coffee and scone. Seth smiled and thanked her, then picked up his mug, and took a sip of the fragrant coffee. He relished the crumbly scone, as if he didn't have a care in the world and wasn't sitting next to the woman who drove him to cross a line of ethics he'd never crossed.

Her engagement might be a lie, but he'd nearly thrown up her skirts and planted himself deep inside her, right smack dab on the Malone's kitchen table.

He chewed the berry scone and washed it down with another swallow of coffee.

"I'll walk you home." He played with fire, but he couldn't help it. He wanted to spend time with her before she stepped on the east bound train.

Silence, then she nodded. "Thank you."

Mrs. White returned to the dining room,

refreshed his coffee, and refilled Kate's teacup. She must have sensed the tension in the air, because she said very little and hurried back to the kitchen.

Seth swallowed the last bite of scone and drank down the fresh cup of coffee. He pushed back his chair and stood. "I'll make another round while you finish up. Meet you out front?"

Kate nodded, her attention fixed to her cup.

Seth blew out a frustrated breath and tapped his hat against his thigh. He looked at her for another moment, then laid a bill on the table and turned to leave.

"I'll be ready in a few minutes."

His hand on the doorknob stilled. Tension coiled in his lower regions and heated to a slow burn. The woman didn't know what she did to him. Either that or she didn't care that the sound of her voice, the curve of her mouth, or a gaze from those deep green eyes made him crazy.

He opened the door and stepped out on the walk. The excuse to make another round of the town was just that, an excuse. He needed distance from her before he made a fool of himself. So, why in the heck had he offered to see her home? He needed to stay far away from the woman. He couldn't be trusted.

After wasting twenty minutes, he returned to the café. Kate waited, a bakery box in her gloved hands.

"Would you like for me to carry that?" He took the box, relieved to have something in his hands besides Kate. She'd do fine without his assistance.

They walked toward the road that cut off the main street and began the climb to the Malone house. Kate slipped. Seth juggled the bakery box and grabbed her arm.

A short distance up the hillside, Kate stopped and turned to face the lake. "I'm a little winded. Could we rest just a minute?"

"Sure." Was she loitering so they'd have more time together?

"I've never seen so many trees in my life. The scent of pine permeates the air."

He belonged in this half-wild, half-tamed land, but she didn't. She looked small and fragile against the rugged background, her auburn hair framed by the blue sky, the sun lighting a fire in her curls.

She looked at him, her green eyes smoldering. His body turned into a raging furnace. If she kept it up, he'd turn into a pile of ash. All he could think of was how she'd felt in his arms, how she'd tasted.

Kissing her hadn't satisfied his hunger, it'd only heightened his need to possess her completely. Pure old lust could get him in trouble. She may have confided in him, but he still wasn't sure what she was up to. Her trust in Ross Williams worried him.

She lifted her face to the sun and closed her eyes, breathing in the fresh, warm air. Her breasts strained against her dress until Seth thought he'd explode. Damn, the woman had way too much control over him.

His body warred to overrule his head. It didn't matter that she was pretending to be engaged to Ethan, or that she might be as crooked as her attorney. He burned for her, wanted to hold her, taste her. Maybe if he made love to her, he'd be able to walk away and do whatever the law required of him.

Grabbing her arm, he pulled her toward a path he'd explored last week after the attack.

"What are you doing?" Kate jerked against his hold.

His throat closed with emotion.

"Stop, you're hurting my arm."

He eased his hold, but didn't let go, or slow his pace. He held the branches so they wouldn't slap her and led her into a small clearing away from the road and town.

He was insane with need. Had he embellished the memory of holding her? Did she really smell like roses and taste like honey?

"Seth, where are we going?"

"To talk." His voice rasped through his throat, but it wasn't from the ever present dust in the air. The woods around them blurred; his mind, his senses were completely over taken with the thought of kissing this woman.

When they reached the small clearing, Seth set down the box of scones and stepped toward her. Startled green eyes looked at him, then her lips parted and her head tipped, offering exactly what he wanted. He groaned and pulled her against him. Damn, she did smell like roses. Double damn, her mouth tasted like honey.

Kate moaned, pushing him over the edge. He eased her back against the smooth bark of a birch tree and pressed his hot erection against the softness of her belly.

Kate should shove him away, stop this insanity, but she couldn't. This was the stuff her dreams were made of, when she lay in bed alone night after night, while her friends met the men of their dreams, married and had children. She'd always thought McShane Walker Shipping would be enough to satisfy her.

She'd been wrong.

The first time she lay in his lap on the train, Seth Morgan had chipped away at her decision to remain unattached. With each stroke of his hands and caress of his lips, he brought out more of her need to give herself fully to him.

Seth pulled back. "Oh, darlin', I want to make love to you right now, but I want the first time to be on a featherbed with candlelight and a good bottle of wine."

Kate shoved her fingers through his thick, dark hair, cupping his scalp in her hands. "The tough lawman is a romantic at heart." She kissed each side of his mouth, then pressed her lips against his. "What am I going to do? The wedding's almost here, and Ross hasn't answered my latest telegram."

"You have to tell Ethan, right away. You belong with me, Kate McShane, not Ethan Howland." He threaded his fingers through her hair, pulling it gently out of the chignon she'd hastily twisted it into that morning.

Kate gazed into his eyes, and her heart ripped in half. She wanted so much to make love to him, and not just once. It would be the beginning of something powerful, so powerful it scared her witless. Her desire for Seth didn't change the fact they came from different worlds, and she'd soon be returning to hers. The moment they left the forest, reality would return and the bond they'd forged would slip into a wonderful memory.

"I want to tell him right away, but is it safe for him to know, before we know Jeb's whereabouts?"

"Kate, you thought taking on this disguise would protect you and the people around you, but it won't. They need to know someone could show up in Hope looking for you. It'll help them stay out of the cross fire."

"Oh, Seth, I've made such a mess of things." She shook her head and gulped against the lump of sorrow in her throat.

Seth cupped her face and feathered his thumb over her lips. "Darlin', we both saw the man from the train, and I have a hunch it's Allen Johnston who attacked you on the hill." He raised his chin toward the road they'd just left. "Ethan needs to know so he can protect his family."

"You're right." She wrapped her arms around his neck and pulled his mouth down to hers.

His kiss was more delicious than Mrs. White's scones. Her legs trembled, and the forest swirled around them. She couldn't have stood on her own if she tried.

Seth tore his lips from hers and stepped back. His hands opened and closed at his sides; his chest expanded and contracted as if he'd been running. "Sweetheart, I shouldn't have brought you here."

Torment filled his eyes and warred with his desire to make love to her. He had to know they'd soon go their separate ways. Fighting her own desire to wrap her arms around him, Kate gripped the tree behind her, her sensitized palms tingling from the paper like birch bark. Everything around her seemed bigger, softer, brighter and more fragrant then before they'd stepped into the woods and kissed.

With a deep breath, she pushed away from the tree and smoothed her dress. She wound her hair into the chignon he'd destroyed, her breath catching when she caught Seth staring at her breasts, his dark eyes smoldering with the heat she'd come to crave.

Something rustled in the brush. Kate gasped.

Seth stepped between her and the noise, his gun drawn. Kate shivered at how quickly the mood altered, and the lover of moments ago turned into the hard edged lawman. She felt secure yet in peril, with her powerful feelings for Seth.

Silence. Then more brush rustled. A dark shape hurried away from them. Kate gasped again, her heart pounded. Seth held up a finger, then motioned her to stay put. He moved toward the noise.

Kate did as she was told and kept her back to the tree

Nearly silent, Seth returned to her side. "I lost him."

"Any idea who it was?" She caught herself

leaning toward him, needing his comfort to still her ragged nerves. But Seth's focus was on the man who could have attacked Kate.

"No, I couldn't see his face. Strange thing though, he was dressed in an expensive looking suit."

A shiver chilled its way up Kate's back. "Expensive suit?"

Seth's dark brows drew together. "Why, what are you thinking? The man on the train wasn't well dressed."

Kate slowly shook her head. "No, I don't think it was him. There are more affluent men looking for me. The man who attacked me was well dressed, too."

Seth propped his hands on his hips. "You think Jeb would travel this far?"

Kate took a deep breath and slowly let it out. "I don't know. Ross' last telegram instructed me to lay low. Could he be aware of the man who attacked me Saturday? Oh, Seth, I'm sorry to bring more trouble to Hope and to you."

He stepped closer, his hard chest brushing against her sensitive breasts. "I can take care of myself and you." He caressed a curl that had escaped from her hastily repaired hairstyle. "I'd face down anyone to protect you."

Kate shivered with awareness of the powerful currents streaming between them. "I have to go home, Seth. I have to go back to New York."

His long fingers stilled on her hair, then slipped up, to cup her chin and caress her jaw. "I'd expect you to go home and settle things. I might be crazy, Kate, but I want more from you then a quick meeting in the woods. I want the world to know you aren't engaged to Ethan."

"Oh Seth," she said, nearly breathless.

Through the trees separating them from the

road, came the rumble of wagon wheels and clip-clop of horse hooves. They stepped farther apart.

"I need to return to the Malone's."

"Well darlin', you're not getting out of my sight until you're inside the house."

Kate picked up her bakery box and accepted Seth's outstretched hand. He led her out of the woods at a much slower pace than they'd entered. He hesitated and looked around the deserted road, his hand on the butt of his gun.

He released her hand and grasped her elbow. "Ready, Miss Leary?"

Kate slowly shook her head. "Not really, and I can't wait to hear my real name."

"Me either."

Kate started up the hill with a sharp awareness of the man next to her. Since old enough to court, she'd maintained tight control on her emotions and actions. With Seth, she was ready to throw her reputation to the wind and go as far as he'd take her.

He didn't fit in her world, but he moved her more than any man she'd met. Whatever happened in Hope with Seth Morgan would warm all the lonely nights to come.

"Kate? Sheriff Morgan?"

Seth and Kate stopped and turned toward Kyle who trotted up the hill behind them.

Kate hurried toward the youth and grasped his arm. "What is it, Kyle? Why are you alone?"

"Ma would have my hide if she knew, but Mr. Smith gave me a telegram for you and said it was marked urgent." He held out a folded piece of paper, grinning from ear to ear.

Kate handed Seth the bakery box and opened the missive. *The fox has escaped, and there's a snake in the hen house. Please use caution and stay put until I know more...Leland*

Kate gasped. Leland? A snake? What was he

talking about, and why didn't Ross answer her telegram? She glanced around, unsettled over the idea of being tracked and watched.

"What is it?" Seth touched her arm.

Kate folded up the telegram. "Thank you, Kyle." She forced a smile to ease the concern on the young man's face. "I appreciate you bringing this to me. Now, shouldn't you be getting back to school?"

"Yes, ma'am." Kyle tipped the brim of his hat and swaggered back down the hill.

"Wait, Kyle." Seth grasped Kate's arm and walked after the young man. "Someone was watching us a few minutes ago. We'll wait at the top of the hill until you're on the main street. I don't want you walking home alone, do you hear me? Not until I track down whoever it is."

"Yes sir." Kyle hurried down the hill, then turned and waved at them when he was close to Seth's office.

"Thank you, Seth." Kate's heart swelled at the care Seth gave to the good people of Hope. "Kyle is such a good boy."

Seth turned her to face him. "What did the telegram say?"

"Seth really, I don't think this is the place to discuss it. Someone could come along and see us together. We've already been seen together too many times in town."

"You might be right, but I want to know what the telegram said."

With his investigative background, he might understand Leland's coded message, but they were in full view of Janet's kitchen window. She'd been watching the area with an eagle's eye since Kate's attack. "I promise I'll let you read it later, where we can talk in private."

A slow grin curved his delicious mouth. "We don't get much talking done when we're alone."

Kate sucked in a quick breath, tingling with the implication of his words. "We'll have to curb our inclination, Sheriff Morgan. I may not be who everyone thinks I am and not technically engaged, but when I tell everyone the truth, it'll be time to return to New York."

He pursed his lips. "We're not going to walk away from each other, Kate. I don't care who you are."

Kate's chest tightened at the intensity of his tone. No man had ever touched her like Seth, not only physically, but emotionally. She blinked back sudden tears. "We'll talk later."

Her heart was going to break when she left Hope and Seth Morgan.

Chapter Sixteen

Halfway through the delicately seared, roast beef dinner, Kate's head began to pound. A few hours ago, she'd been pressed between a birch tree and Seth's deliciously, hard body. Now, she sat between him and Ethan at the dinner table.

She yearned to tell everyone the truth, here and now. Maura kept glancing at her, expecting an announcement. Ethan's expression was down cast, as if he were headed for the gallows.

Then there was Leland's telegram. A fox and a snake on the loose? Leland had no way of knowing, but time was running out. In five short days, she was expected to walk down the aisle and commit her life to Ethan. Several hearts and her integrity were on the line. When she'd traded places with Mary Catherine, she'd never planned for things to go this far.

At least Seth knew the truth.

Kate carefully placed her fork on the half full plate. "Janet, dinner is delicious, but I have a terrible headache. I really need fresh air."

"Oh Kate, I'm so sorry." Janet patted her mouth with her napkin. "Ethan, would you mind walking outside with Kate? I'm still uneasy about us ladies going out alone, especially after dark."

Ethan glanced at Janet, then Maura, then set down his fork. "I'll be happy to take you outside, Kate." He placed his napkin on the table and stood, pulling out Kate's chair.

She had no choice. Her plea for escape had trapped her. "I don't want to interrupt your dinner."

“I’m sure Janet will hold it for me.”

Kate met Seth’s hard, dark look. It should have disconcerted her, but after being in his arms on two occasions, she realized it was jealousy, not distrust or dislike. His unhappiness over her going outside with Ethan gave her a little boost of self-confidence.

She preceded Ethan out the back door. Darkness fell early in late autumn, blanketing the hillside and the lake below, in varying hues of purple and made the glow of lamplight from the house even more welcoming. Silence filled the air, the birds and squirrels already snug in their nighttime habitations.

A breeze blew off the lake, bringing with it, the scent of pine and cedar. She was far away from the streets of New York and truly on her own for the first time in her life.

Unable to see Ethan’s expression, she kept her back to the house, in hopes he’d step in front of her, and allow the faint glow of light from the house to illuminate his face.

She had no doubt; he was miserable, but was too honor bound to call off the wedding. Honor meant everything to Ethan, so he planned to live with the regret of sending for her.

Kate took his arm and pulled him in front of her. Behind him, the last vestige of light swirled over the far mountains in a stroke of orange.

“Ethan—”

“Kate—”

They spoke at the same time. Kate released his arm.

Ethan shifted from one foot to the other. “Please, you go first.”

The nip in the air lent a sharp contrast to the warmth of the afternoon. Kate folded her arms below her breasts and cupped her elbows.

Was it time to tell him the truth, or should she

wait until Leland contacted her again? Seth believed everyone deserved to know the truth to protect themselves from Jeb, the henchman, and possibly Allen Johnston.

She pressed her fingers to her temples.

"Kate, are you all right?" Ethan's deep voice shattered the near silence of the evening and pulled her from her mental anguish. She'd lied to this honest, hard-working man and everyone in town. Her sense of honor demanded she take charge of her life.

"Yes—no, I'm not all right. I have something to tell you."

The moon crowned the mountain behind them and shed its soft silver light across the landscape, illuminating Ethan's crisp white shirt, and casting his handsome face in shadows.

"Go ahead, I'm listening."

She took a deep breath, then let it slip from her lungs like the evening breeze rustling the leaves of the nearby birch trees. "I don't know where to start."

Being a gentleman, Ethan took her hand in his and kissed her knuckles. "Take your time. The beginning is usually the best place."

Kate smiled at him, wondering if she was crazy to let such a handsome, honorable man out of her grasp. "I'm not penniless." She took another breath, then rushed on. "I'm the heiress of a very large shipping company in New York."

Silence.

"Please bear with me, Ethan. This is the only way my story will make sense. Are you all right so far?"

A chuckle rose deep from his chest. "I'm not sure yet. Please go on."

"Well, my mother left my father and me several years ago, and as his only child and heir to his shipping empire, he took me to the office every day. I was to take over running the company, far in the future when my father—when he was no longer with us." She flinched at the pain still fresh in her heart. "He, my father, suddenly died eight weeks ago."

"I'm so sorry." He caressed her hand, his tone genuine and patient.

She cleared her throat, blinking back tears. "He had some rough financial times during the late seventies and took on a partner. They didn't really get along, so Jebulin Walker set up his office in Houston, and my father continued to run the New York operations."

In the moonlight, the buttons on his white shirt turned to black dots. Kate focused on them, willing herself not to be overcome with grief. She had to remain strong long enough to rectify things. Later, in her room, she'd let down and cry herself to sleep.

"As the years passed, Jeb became more insistent with his ideas of how the business should be run and more abrasive to my father. My advisors, Ross and Leland, both believe Jeb gave my father something that caused a heart attack. Then Jeb turned his attentions to me."

"Oh, Kate," Ethan said, his voice rough. "He didn't—"

"No—nothing like that happened. He had the audacity to insist we marry. When I refused him for the third time, he hired someone to kidnap me. I barely escaped. I thought if I stayed home with a house filled with servants, I'd be safe until he could be dealt with. I was wrong." She shivered. "When I reached home, my servants were gone. I later learned he'd given them the night off! That was when I realized I couldn't fight him on my own." She paused for a moment, searching through the shadows for some indication of his expression.

"Go on." His soft tone gave her courage to continue.

"Ross and Leland suggested I go to Chicago and stay with my uncle while they put Jeb behind bars." She shrugged. "So I caught the train. That's where I met Mary Catherine. I didn't dream up this scheme to switch places with her right away. I thought I'd be fine with my uncle until things were resolved." She clasped her hands in front of her face. "But the same man who kidnapped me in New York was on the train. I'd been discovered and had to devise an alternate plan."

"You're not Mary Catherine?" Ethan's voice boomed through the darkness.

Kate placed her hand on his shirt front. "No, Ethan, I'm Kathleen McShane."

"McShane?" His voice boomed again. "Of McShane Walker Shipping? You certainly aren't an impoverished spinster."

"Not impoverished, but considered a spinster in my social circles."

Ethan blew a breath of disgust. "Exactly why I chose to move here. The upper social circles are ridiculous. But go on, I need to hear it all."

"After Sheriff Morgan rescued me from that despicable man, I asked Mary Catherine to trade identities. I had money to finance her return to Boston, and I could hopefully disappear until Jeb was stopped.

"You see, she was in love with someone in Boston, but he didn't return her affections. With her finances diminished, she was forced to respond to your advertisement. I can only hope her plans have worked out for her."

Ethan turned away.

"I don't blame you for being angry with me. I thought purely of myself when I traded places with Mary Catherine. I needed to save my company from Jeb Walker, and yes, myself too."

"How could you do this?" Ethan turned to face

her. "I believed you were the woman I corresponded with. I introduced you to my son as his future mother."

"That was the hardest part of all. I don't want Will to be hurt. Don't you see? Will loves Maura, and I believe you do, too."

His broad shoulders sagged, and he gazed at the emerging stars. "I can't believe I'm having this conversation with you. You've known the truth all along and have dealt with it in your mind. I haven't."

"I know this is a shock."

Ethan barked with humorless laughter.

"A shock? I'm confounded, woman!"

Kate searched her mind for something to make him see the best in this situation. "I'm not minimizing my deception, but you must admit my being here has forced you to spend more time in Maura's company. She loves you, and she'd be the perfect wife for you!"

"Kate, don't try to turn my attentions away from what you've done with the promise of Maura Malone."

"Don't you see? It's all part of why this happened. You didn't realize how perfect Maura was for you and Will, so you sent for Mary Catherine."

"You're amazing!" He clamped his hands on his hips. "You blithely come to Hope and deceive all of us, then try to make it look like the doing of a higher power!"

Kate matched his stance and stood tall. She still had to crook her neck to look into his shadowed face. "I'm simply pointing out the truth. I did what I had to do to survive. I'm not proud of concocting the story and deceiving all of you. It's been torture."

Ethan bracketed her arms and turned her into the glow from the windows. "Kate, I'm having a very hard time feeling sorry for you. Right now I'd like to turn you over my knee and spank you."

Kate raised a brow and set her mouth in a firm line to keep from laughing at his threat. “I’m not asking for your sympathy, Ethan. I simply had to tell you the truth in hope you’d see reason and live the life you’re meant to live. Far be it for me to keep pushing. You can live alone for the rest of your life if that’s what you want!”

She pivoted on her heel and marched toward the house. She’d taken the first step to clear the record, now to tell the Malones. Maura would be thrilled; Janet would nod, suspecting something like this all along.

Then there was Seth. Pain clashed with pleasure. Pleasure because Seth could kiss her without guilt. Pain because no matter how much truth she shared, Seth was still a man of the West and she was from the East. There would be no meeting in the middle.

****

Ethan spurred his gelding through the moonlit night, his usual, tight control slipping. Being engaged to Kate had saved him from acting on his true feelings for Maura. But now…now that Kate wasn’t his fiancée, he had to resolve his love for Maura.

He rode into the meadow and frowned. A light burned in the barn. Either Travis had carelessly forgotten to blow out the lamp, or he hadn’t turned in yet. Ethan wasn’t pleased with the thought of losing ten ton of hay or with discussing his eventful evening with Travis.

He ducked as the gelding passed through the double doors. Travis sat in front of the tack room nursing a cup of coffee and polishing the metal on a bridle. He glanced up as Ethan rode into the barn and dismounted.

“Sure don’t spend much time with that pretty lady,” Travis said, a big grin on his face. “I can’t understand why you come home in such a foul mood every time you see her."

"I'm not in the mood for sparring, Travis."

"Ouch, you're a real bear tonight. Anxious for the wedding?"

"Humph." Ethan heaved the saddle on a rail. "Not quite."

"So what's wrong?"

Ethan paused, one hand on the horn, one on the skirt of the saddle, and forced himself to relax. "Kate's not really my fiancée."

Travis set down the bridle and shot to his feet. "What?"

Ethan turned to face his old friend. Travis had been with him through thick and thin. Even when his own sister betrayed and deserted Ethan, Travis stuck by his side. "She traded places with Mary Catherine Leary on the train from New York. She's really a shipping heiress, running from a crooked business partner."

"My God, you have to be kidding." Travis nudged his hat to the back of his head. "Go on."

"There's not much else to tell. With the wedding only days away, Kate decided to be honest before she really had to marry me."

"I'll be damned." Travis propped his hands on his hips. "So the wedding is off."

Ethan nodded. "Her justification for the escapade is she thinks Maura and I belong together, and the real Mary Catherine would have prevented us from coming together."

Travis's mouth tilted in a grin. "Kate's one smart lady. I've seen something happening between you and Maura for a long time."

The frustration had run its course. Ethan relaxed his shoulders and took a long breath. "I can't deny my feelings for Maura. I thought she belonged with someone closer to her age, someone without a ready-made family and a shattered marriage in his past."

"I don't think Maura cares about your past, and she adores Will."

"She deserves every bit of happiness life can offer."

Ethan stared through the lamp light, watching the dust motes dance in the soft glow. He'd been attracted to Maura since she was sixteen, and he'd felt like a perverted old man. Granted he was only ten years older, but he'd lived so much more. He'd been married and fathered a son. Kerry and Janet were good friends from the time they had moved to Hope. Making an advance on Maura might betray their friendship.

Now, she was nineteen and a woman in full bloom. He couldn't deny his feelings anymore. "Kate made me madder than hell, but she also gave me some hope about Maura."

"You'd have to be blind not to see how you and Maura look at each other."

For the first time in hours, Ethan allowed his mouth to curve into a smile. "I guess we really didn't hide our feelings, did we?"

"Only from each other, Brother." Travis clamped his hand to Ethan's shoulder. "It's time you have the happiness you deserve, and Will, the mother he loves. Brush the dust of this mail-order bride thing off your shoes, and move on to the woman you're meant to spend your life with."

Ethan's smile widened. "I think you're right."

****

Seth laid awake half the night, thinking about Kate. Now that the truth was out, he could openly court her. As dawn brushed the sky, he rolled out of bed and threw on his clothes.

He tried to stay in his room until the town began to stir, but the rumpled bed reminded him of what he'd like to do with Miss Kate McShane, so he tiptoed out of the boarding house and walked around the quiet streets.

Sure, he could openly court Kate, but it would have been better if she really was a penniless spinster. Instead, she was wealthy and didn't need him or any other man. What would she want with the son of a prostitute? A former Texas Ranger who'd failed to keep his partner alive and was now nothing more than a small western town sheriff?

To compound things, she had complete trust in Ross Williams, a man who couldn't be trusted.

He peeked through the post office window. If Smith wasn't there, he'd drag him out of bed. Jeb and Ross were both missing, and Seth was determined to hunt them down. Jeb might be a hard-edged businessman, but he hadn't killed James McShane, of that, Seth was sure.

Ross Williams, on the other hand, would do anything if it meant feathering his own nest.

After telling Ethan and the Malones the truth of her identity, Kate had shared the new telegram with him. She was puzzled over the language of the message and that Leland had sent it, instead of Ross. She was an intelligent woman. Had Ross slipped down a cog or two in her estimation?

In Seth's pursuit of Allen Johnston from Houston to New York, he'd bumped into people who'd known a different side of Ross than the McShanes did.

"Sheriff, I saw something you might be interested in."

Seth turned away from the post office door and pushed his hat to the back of his head. "Morning, Kerry. What is it?"

"Two characters in fancy suits were just now behind the smithy talking. It's not often you see suits that expensive in Hope, and not at this time of the morning. After Kate's story last night, well, I guess I'm more alert."

"Hmm. Are you sure they aren't railroad officials?" Seth rubbed his bristly jaw. He'd been so eager to get out of his room he hadn't taken time to shave.

Kerry shrugged. "Could be, I suppose, but not likely. I don't imagine they'd meet behind the smithy just after dawn."

Seth nodded. "Between you and me, I expect trouble."

"I thought as much. Let me know if I can help." Kerry patted Seth's arm. "Be careful, Sheriff. We just got you, sure don't want to lose you."

Seth couldn't get to the depot fast enough. After spending the night dreaming about making love to Kate, he needed a mission to burn off some frustration before he exploded. Damn, he'd have to delay sending that telegram.

A conductor waited next to the rumbling train, getting ready for the morning departure.

"Morning." Seth touched his hat. "I'm Sheriff Seth Morgan, and I wondered if you could answer some questions."

"I'll try. What is it?"

"Can you recall who got off this train yesterday? Men, women?"

The conductor shifted his hat to one side and scratched his head. "One woman who I'd lay odds is a business woman, if you know what I mean. Five men. Two were gentlemen to be sure. Dressed like it anyway. The other three could be here for any reason."

Seth slowly nodded. "Thank you." Yep, there was going to be trouble, and he planned to be ready for it.

Chapter Seventeen

With Kate's confession the night before, Janet and Maura decided to leave early the next morning to visit Ethan's ranch. The purpose of the impromptu visit was for Maura to share her feelings with a now, unattached Ethan. Janet wouldn't let her go alone.

No longer the bride-to-be, Kate planned to move to Mrs. White's boarding house while the Malones were all gone. They hadn't asked her to leave, but it didn't feel right to stay. She'd begun her entire association with them on false pretenses. The time had arrived to set things straight and be on her own.

Leaving a note of thanks and farewell on the kitchen table, Kate lugged her carpet bag to the boarding house. Her trunk could be delivered later.

The moment the bell over the door tinkled, Elena White bustled out of the kitchen. Her white brows shot up in surprise. "Not staying at the hotel, Miss Leary? It's much finer than my rooms."

Kate tilted her head to one side and smiled. "I assume you know what's transpired?"

Elena smoothed her starched white apron. "Well, Maura stopped by the mercantile to tell Mr. White she wouldn't be working today. The news around town is you're an heiress and no longer engaged to Ethan."

"News travels quickly."

Elena shrugged and smiled. "We don't have much entertainment in these parts, Miss Leary, so please humor us."

Kate chuckled. "I'll humor you if you'll please

call me by my real name. It's Kate McShane, and please call me, Kate."

"I'm honored to, Kate. Would you like some tea?"

"I'll settle in first, Mrs. White. Thank you for asking. Kerry or Kyle will deliver my trunk later."

Settling into a comfortable room overlooking the main street, Kate decided to stay close to the boarding house. She could have stayed at the Hope Hotel. Elena was right; the hotel was grander than the boarding house. General Sherman had spent most of the summer there.

But Kate didn't need grand at the moment. She needed to be close to Seth, and he lived at the boarding house. She'd relax and wait for him to return. He was probably busy with his job, and she wasn't ready to test her new found freedom by tracking him down. Maybe he didn't want to spend time with her, and he'd be embarrassed if she waltzed into the sheriff's office.

Foreboding cast a dark shadow over her. What if Jeb was here to meet with his henchman? Her lies were laid to rest, but her life was still in danger.

Voices and commotion downstairs alerted Kate to the possibility of other guests arriving. A cold chill skittered up her body. For the first time since leaving the train, she was vulnerable to whoever came and went from town. Staying with the Malones had offered her a security she'd taken for granted.

She sat on the bed and wrapped her arms around her middle, staring at the door. Even if they only made love once, and it had to last the rest of her life, she still wanted to experience it. Give herself completely to Seth; store enough memories to last through all the lonely, dark nights ahead.

All he had to do was walk into the room and her stomach clenched and her body flared with an unfamiliar heat. He was a rough, yet gentle man, who probably belonged to an earlier era where justice was clear and the land still untamed. He didn't fit, nor did he care to fit, in her world with its cities, society and business. No matter how much she wanted him, Seth didn't want to be part of her life in New York.

She fell back on the bed and spread out her arms. Oh, but she needed to know what it would be like to lie with him on a soft bed, pressed against his strong body. To feel his arms around her, his legs tangled with hers. Her dreams last night had been so real, she could clearly recall the breathlessness, the tingling from head to toe, heat building in the intimate parts of her body. She longed to be wrapped in Seth's arms where she'd be safe from intruders, but in danger of losing her heart, soul, and body to a man she could never marry. The thought was delicious and frightening at the same time.

She moaned and rolled over, burying her face in the pillow. No use torturing herself over something she could never have.

If only her father were alive so she could talk to him. Most likely if he were, she would never have boarded that west bound train, would never have met Seth. He wouldn't have moved in her circle.

Tears burned her eyes. What a cruel trick fate had played. She'd found the man of her dreams at last, but there would be no happily ever after.

An hour later, her patience ran out. She could surely check in at the post office for a telegram. In daylight and in town, she should be safe. Kate rolled off her bed, straightened her hair, and dashed from her room.

****

Seth made a thorough inspection of the town but avoided the upstairs portion of the saloons. Since his feelings for Kate had moved from suspicion and distrust to lust and yes, even love, he'd been thinking a lot about his humble origins.

A young boy sleeping on a pile of sacks in the kitchen, listening to the comings and goings of the influential men of the city. A childhood spent trying not to think about what his mother did with one man after the other. Things no child should have to think of his mother doing at all. Those memories served to remind him of what different worlds he and Kate had grown up in.

His purpose-filled stride led him toward his office, his instincts alert to protecting Kate from greedy, ambitious men. He was sure Ross Williams was one of them.

Later, he'd walk to the Malones and tell Kate how he'd met James McShane in New York; how he'd seen him hours before his death. He'd attended her father's funeral and had seen the heiress to McShane's vast fortune, swathed in black from head to foot. If he'd seen her beautiful face, he'd have recognized her immediately on the train. There was no way he could ever forget Kate McShane.

Tired, dusty and sweaty, Seth unlocked the office door and threw his keys on the desk. They skittered across the scarred wood surface to the floor. He swore and retrieved them, sinking back into the chair behind the desk.

Damn, he was frustrated. He'd spent the morning searching for the two finely-dressed men Kerry told him about. They had to be connected to Kate, or could they be connected to Allen Johnston? Ironic how his enemies crossed over to hers.

He could ask the mayor for help, but for all his pompous attitude, Ellis didn't have much experience in keeping the peace.

Seth leaned forward and propped his elbows on the desk, resting his chin on folded hands and stared at the telegrams Kate had sent and received. They were the main reason he had locked his office. All he needed was for Kate to find the evidence of his snooping. She was a determined woman and wouldn't take kindly to him kissing her one minute and spying on her the next.

Damn the woman drove him crazy. Never had he struggled to keep his mind on his duty like he had since meeting Kate McShane.

Since he'd turned sixteen and Griff had taken him under his wing, the law had come first. The law was still important to him, but he also wanted to test his feelings for Kate.

The door swung open.

"Sheriff! We need you at the saloon. There's a fight!"

Seth pushed his chair back and stood, grabbing his hat as he left the office. "I'm right behind you."

Thirty minutes later Seth marched the bastard who'd kidnapped Kate in New York, then again on the train, to the jail. His hand on the doorknob, he swore. Damn! He'd been so distracted with his feelings for Kate, he'd left the door unlocked.

Sweeping the door open, Seth shoved the miscreant ahead of him and froze. Kate stood behind his desk, the telegrams mere inches from her hand.

Her green eyes wide, she gasped. "Seth!"

His heart sank. Had she recognized them?

He kept a tight grip on his prisoner, who'd finally tripped up due to his weakness for liquor and fast women. Securing his prisoner in the cell, Seth braced himself for Kate's temper.

Seth stepped into the outer office. Kate's glance darted from him to the door he'd locked behind him. "It's him! It's the henchman!"

"You have a nicer name than the one I just called him. But you're right, it is him. Pure dumb luck we have him behind bars. He started a fight over a woman in the saloon." Seth hung the ring of keys on a nail behind the door.

Kate collapsed into his chair. "I can't believe you

have him."

Seth glanced toward the heavy door, separating the jail cells from the office. "You'll need to swear out a statement to send to the circuit judge. If we can make the charges stick, he'll be shipped out to a federal prison. If we can't, well, he'll be free again." Seth folded his arms over his chest, bracing himself for her reaction to the telegrams.

Kate didn't budge from his chair. She ran her hands over the surface of his desk, her fingers straying ever closer to the crumpled bits of paper. He swallowed hard. A large square cut emerald graced her right ring finger. The same ring she'd worn on the train, but he hadn't seen it since. Who had given it to her? Williams?

Exhaustion swept over him. Seth glanced down at his dusty, sweat caked clothes then back at Kate. "You'll have to excuse my appearance. I've been busy."

One corner of Kate's mouth tilted in the whisper of a smile. "You look like you've had a rough day."

"Yeah." Seth couldn't make his brain work. He wanted to open up and tell her everything, then after she'd forgiven him, he'd take her in his arms. Yeah, right, Morgan, happily ever after isn't meant for you.

"I came to see you." Kate's gaze never left his face. "I moved to Mrs. White's."

His heart skipped a beat. "You what?"

"I moved to the boarding house."

Seth rubbed his hands over his face, grimacing at the sandpaper beard and grit. "What happened with the Malones?"

"I couldn't keep intruding on their hospitality. I came under false pretenses. Now that they know I'm not Ethan's fiancée, it's time for me to stand on my own again."

Seth blew air into both cheeks then let it slowly

escape. He was beat and grimy, and dammit, he'd wanted to be clean and rested when he met with Kate. They needed to talk about them.

Seth reached into his breast pocket to pull out a heart shaped locket he'd bought in the mercantile during his rounds, then stopped. The humble locket paled next to the rock on her finger.

"Nice ring."

Kate smiled and toyed with the stone. "My father gave it to me years ago. Right after my mother left."

His locket was hardly in the same league. It didn't match the quality of her other jewelry. At least her father had given it to her, not Williams. He'd better quit tripping over his stupid pride and give her the damned necklace.

Seth sauntered toward the desk, scooped up the telegrams, and stuffed them in the top drawer, then dangled the locket in front of her. Kate's eyes opened wide, and she reached out to grasp the shiny gold heart.

"It's beautiful!"

"Since you're no longer engaged, I figured I could buy it for you."

"It's for me?" She stood and stared at him, her lips parted in surprise, her brows raised.

"Yeah, it's for you," he said, his voice rough.

She fingered the locket, and he let loose of the chain, letting it fall over her hands. "Would you help me put it on?" She handed it to him, then turned, smoothing the hair that had escaped the knot of shiny auburn hair.

He ached to press his lips to that peach-tinted skin. Nuzzle the soft curls that were so like the woman who owned them, too determined to stay confined. He ached to press against her bottom. Ached, hell, he was in pain.

Fastening the necklace, he let it fall against her

skin and rubbed his hands on his shirt front, struggling to control his body and instincts. Her rose scent swirled around him, making his body rock hard.

One kiss, that was all he needed—for now.

He brushed his lips over her tender skin, breathing in her scent, spooning his front to her back.

Kate gasped but held perfectly still.

Encouraged, Seth wrapped his arms around her tiny waist and pulled her tightly against him, leaving no doubt of his state.

She moaned and pressed her bottom against his hardness, wiggling from side to side. Seth feared he'd explode, and this wasn't the time or the place. He was filthy, and the bastard who'd tried to hurt Kate was locked up in his jail. Besides, anyone could walk in and catch them rubbing against each other.

He kissed the back of her neck one more time, strained against her backside, then let go and moved away. "I should walk you back to the boarding house." His voice was so rough he hardly recognized it.

Kate cleared her throat. "That's probably a good idea. That man is finally locked up, but Jeb could be right behind him. Do you think he was the one who spied on us in the woods?"

Seth shook his head then tilted it toward the cell. "The clothes don't match up. The man I saw was rigged out in an expensive suit."

Should he tell her about the men Kerry saw? No, he'd hold off. She'd had enough scares lately. "Let's go." He took her arm and led her to the door. His hand on the knob, he hesitated and looked at her. "You know, I live at the boarding house."

Kate's mouth softened and tilted into the smile that made him want to throw his ethics to the wind, and make love to her right there. "I know."

He dragged in a deep breath, then let it out. "I don't want you to go anywhere without me. Is that understood?"

"Yes." She nodded and gazed up at him with her big, green eyes.

"I mean it, Kate. I can't protect you if you're wandering around without me."

"I know."

Seth opened the door and gestured for her to step outside ahead of him. He didn't intend to let her out of his sight until he found out who was in town. Trouble was in the air, and the crooks weren't going to waltz off with the only woman he'd ever come close to loving.

Kate stayed close to Seth as they walked to Mrs. White's. She found his concern over being too dirty to be close to her, charming. It showed that he may be a western sheriff and preferred the country to the city, but he had class, and he really did care about her.

All she had to do was recall their closeness in his office, her bottom pressed against his hardness, and goose bumps scattered from head to foot. She'd wanted to melt into him and truly become one. Just because she'd never been with a man, didn't mean her twenty-four year old body didn't know what it needed.

Kate moved closer and laid her hand on his arm. Seth hesitated mid-step and glanced at her. What kind of women had made him think he wasn't as desirable wearing trail dust, as he was in crisp, clean clothing? The man looked wonderful no matter what he wore.

"You'll get dirty touching me." He voice was gruff.

"I'll take my chances." Kate was finished with games. She couldn't forget how they'd kissed—more than once. They knew the intimacy of their bodies straining against each other. The time to cling to propriety had passed.

Seth patted her hand then opened the door to the boarding house. He might be attentive to her needs, but Kate could tell his main focus was on the people around them. He was on alert for Jeb, or whoever could grab her at any time.

Mrs. White's plump face broke into a wide smile when they walked in together. "Fresh scones just out of the oven, Sheriff." She ran a gaze from his mussed hair to his dusty boots. "You look like you could use a pot of coffee."

"Sure could. Mind if I take them to my room?"

"Not at all. Allow me to make a tray for you. I'll be right up."

Kate shot Seth a knowing smile. Even the older married women noticed and approved of Seth Morgan.

Together they climbed the stairs. Kate pointed out her door.

"Damn, I'll never get to sleep tonight. You're right next door to my room."

"Hmm." Kate tried to look surprised. "I had no idea."

"I'll just bet. You're a wicked woman, Kate McShane." He touched her jaw with his fingertips. "I love that about you. Now, remember, no going out without me. We can't take any chances until I know what we're dealing with."

"I meant to tell you this in your office, but...I became a bit sidetracked."

Seth's smile held more than a hint of satisfaction. His male ego no doubt ate up the fact that he could distract her. "What is it?"

"On my way to your office, I picked up a new telegram. Leland said Ross is looking for Jeb."

Seth glanced around, distinctly uncomfortable.

Kate frowned. "What is it?"

"You're right; it's strange."

"He's trying to trap Jeb, but for him to just drop out of sight isn't like him."

Seth rubbed the back of his neck. "Are you worried something's happened to Ross?"

"I don't want to think along those lines." She fingered the buttons on the front of her dress. "Seth, I don't know if it's important—if it means anything in light of what's happening, but since my father died, Ross has suggested marriage several times. When Jeb started proposing to me, Ross became more adamant."

Seth's brows shot up and he moved closer. "Yeah, that's important information. Williams is in love with you?"

"Don't sound so surprised. There have been several men who've claimed to love me."

Seth's expression turned to something she couldn't quite read. He slipped his hands around her waist. "Oh, I can believe it all right. I just don't plan to let any of them have their way."

Footsteps echoing up the stairs made them step apart. Butterflies fluttered in Kate's midsection. She wanted to be alone with Seth. But that would have to wait.

"Here we are." Mrs. White carried a large tray, complete with a coffee carafe, an entire plate of scones, a sugar bowl and cream pitcher. "This and a bath will put you to rights. My hired man is bringing up hot water right now."

Seth moved to his bedroom door and opened it, then took the tray from his hostess. "Thank you, ma'am. They look delicious."

Elena White fluttered her thanks, then returned to her domain in the kitchen and dining room.

Kate grinned at Seth and shook her head. "Have you always had this effect on women?"

"I'm not sure what you're talking about." He

winked and took a bite of a flakey scone. "Want one?"

"I don't think I can swallow at the moment." Everything he did made her think of intimate things.

"Don't worry, darlin'; it'll all work out. I just want you to be safe." Seth winked again and backed into his room. "I'll see you shortly."

Kate waited until he closed the door to his room before slipping into hers. Footsteps sounded on the stairs, and Mrs. White's hired man appeared, lugging the water up for Seth's bath.

Before coming to Hope, Kate hadn't given a thought about how hard her staff worked. After hanging dripping wet clothes on the line and helping Janet in the kitchen, she had a whole new appreciation for what they did. Watching the hired man lug the buckets of steaming water for Seth's bath made her back ache.

She sighed, walked into her room, closed the door, and locked it. Leaning against the hard panel, she marveled at how much she'd changed since leaving New York, since her father died.

She'd come to realize how much he'd protected her from life's harsh realities, even though she had worked in the office with him and attended the board meetings. He still stood between her and the outside world. His name, his security, and his money had created her life style.

Funny how living with the Malones had demonstrated money and influence weren't the most important things in life. Janet's contented expression as she cooked and cleaned for her family; the angle of Kerry's shoulders when he brought home the living, testified to what mattered. Kate fingered her gold pendant, another example of how the simple things could bring the most happiness.

The sound of water being poured into the tub

and the rumble of male voices came through the thin wall separating her room from Seth's. The footsteps of the handyman passed her door and echoed down the stairwell. An image of Seth stripping off his clothes and sinking in the tub floated through her mind, sending heat and tingles through her body.

Her obligation to Ethan was over, and she longed to be back in Seth's arms with no restraints.

She cautiously pushed aside one of the floral sprigged curtains framing the window.

The street below bustled with activity. Railroad officials walked toward the depot. Chinese farmers pushed their wheel barrels of late vegetables to the mercantile and the train, where they'd sell them to supply Sandpoint and the other lakeside towns. A few women of varying professions milled from the tea house to the mercantile, some alone, some with companions.

She lifted her attention from the street to the lake dominating the view. No matter how many times she looked at it, the large body of water entranced her with its sparkling, blue surface. The heavily treed islands intrigued her, and the mountains shot straight up out of the water. It took her breath away. She'd been born and raised on New York Harbor and always found comfort in the ever changing Atlantic, but here, she found a different kind of peace.

Sighing, she started to turn from the window, then froze.

Jeb Walker.

Her heart raced, blood rushed through her head. He was here.

She stepped back, then pivoted and pressed against the wall. The mixture of beauty and danger reared its ugly head.

She fingered the locket Seth had given her and vacillated between staying or running away, until she was somewhere Jeb couldn't find her. She took a stabilizing breath and looked out the window. A man in an expensive looking suit, stood across the street, his back to the line of buildings. Something about him struck a chord. He turned and looked up, toward her very window.

"Ross!"

Ross was here! At the moment, Jeb was nowhere in sight. She had to let Ross know she was here and warn him about Jeb!

Racing from her room, Kate hesitated at the top of the stairs and glanced at Seth's door. Should she alert him? No, he'd insist she wait for him, and if she didn't hurry, Ross could be gone, or Jeb might see him and leave town.

She slipped down the stairway and out the door. From the boardwalk, she looked both ways. There he was. Ross slowly walked down the street toward the sheriff's office.

"Oh, no." She pressed her hand to her throat. He didn't know the henchman Jeb had hired to kidnap her was locked up in jail. She had to update him.

Hurrying down the street, she caught up the moment he stepped off the boardwalk onto the dusty road leading to the Malones.

"Ross!"

Ross slowly turned toward her, irritation, then impatience crossed his aristocratic face and made her step falter. Time slowed. Seconds ticked by until he smiled.

"Kate. For heaven's sake, what are you doing here?"

Kate took a hesitant step toward him; Seth's skepticism rang through the back of her mind. Seth didn't trust him, but she always had. "What am I doing here? You didn't know I was in Hope? When did you arrive?"

"Of course I knew you were here. I came to bring

you home."

"Ross, I saw Jeb on the street a few minutes ago." Kate glanced around. Where had Jeb gone? Was he watching them, waiting for his chance to grab her?

"Yes, I followed him from New York." Ross looked up and down her dress. "My God, Kate. You look like a ragamuffin. What happened to your clothes?"

Two weeks ago, Kate would have agreed with him, but now—now she saw nothing wrong with wearing this simple dress around the dusty streets of Hope.

"It's good to see you, too." She made no attempt to cover her sarcasm or irritation over his condescending look. "I had the mistaken idea you'd be glad to see I'm alive and well."

Ross glanced around. "Of course I am, but can we discuss this somewhere private?"

"I'm staying at the boarding house, we can talk there." Kate turned and walked toward Mrs. White's assuming Ross followed.

He caught up and took her arm. "The boarding house? Why aren't you staying at the Hope Hotel?"

Kate cast him a side look and blinked. "For one thing, I'm there because I want to be. For another, aren't I supposed to be keeping a low profile?" How had she thought of Ross as handsome and charming?

They left the sunny, dusty boardwalk and stepped into the cool, fragrant café. Kate's attention drew to the stairs, as Seth walked down, a thunderous expression on his handsome face.

"Kate, I told you to stay in your room."

"I'm sorry. I should have tapped on your door, but I saw Ross from my window." Kate glanced back and forth between the men. Their chests expanded; their chins lifted like a couple of Janet's roosters.

"Excuse me, Morgan. Do you know who Kate is?"

Ross stepped forward and laid his hand on Kate's arm.

Seth also stepped closer to Kate, hands propped on narrow hips, and one booted foot slightly in front of the other, as if braced for a fight. "I do."

Kate moved from Ross' touch, put her hand on Seth's tense forearm, and squeezed. The fresh scent of his clean skin wrapped around her, making her legs weak. He was clean-shaven and dressed in crisp clean clothes, much more presentable than Ross' dust coated and slightly off kilter appearance.

"Sheriff Morgan has been taking very good care of me, Ross. Without him, I would have been kidnapped on the train."

Seth glanced at her and blinked. Kate left out the other attack very likely resulting from his past. Deep inside, she wanted to protect him. That little boy on the streets whose mother didn't care if he ever returned to the brothel.

The tension became palpable. Kate raised her chin and glanced at both of them in turn. "Gentlemen, I realize you have some kind of history, but right now, I'd appreciate civility and a plan to handle Jeb's presence."

Seth's gaze held hers and reflected an emotion she couldn't decipher. His chest drew in and his shoulders back. He extended his hand to Ross. "Williams."

"Morgan." Ross accepted Seth's handshake but didn't relax his shoulders.

Someone entered the front door and sat at a table. Mrs. White hurried to wait on her new customer.

"Why don't we take a table and have tea?" Kate didn't wait for a response, sitting at a table near the stairs. A few short weeks ago, Ross had been her advisor, her beacon of safety. Now she took charge and mediated for him, her old friend, and the man she'd fallen in love with.

Seth nodded and followed, his manner as cold and abrupt as a stranger.

Not to be outdone, Ross joined them, his movements jerky, his eyes guarded. Something about him shook Kate. He wasn't the suave, self-assured lawyer she'd known and admired for years.

"My imagination must be running wild." Ross sat but didn't scoot into the table.

"Why, Ross?" Kate settled in between the two men.

"What possessed you to come here? Our plan was for you to stay with your uncle in Chicago until I sent for you."

"I had a good reason for not getting off the train in Chicago." Kate recounted her time from first meeting Seth to present. She of course left out most of the details, like her feelings for Seth, their private meetings.

During her accounting of the last few weeks, Mrs. White arrived with tea. She placed cups and saucers in front of them and a plate of sandwiches in the center of the table.

Kate smiled and laid her hand on her arm. "Thank you, Elena, I think we'll be fine for a while."

The older woman nodded and hurried away.

Kate turned back to the men at her table. Seth's jaw was set, his body tense. He clearly didn't trust Ross. He'd told her he didn't, but seeing it in action was disconcerting. Ross had always been such a trusted advisor; she couldn't imagine him doing anything to hurt her.

Ross pursed his lips and fingered the delicate handle on his teacup, then looked at her. "It sounds like Sheriff Morgan has been your constant companion since you met on the train."

"Seth and the Malone family have met all my needs since I arrived in Hope."

Ross cleared his throat and shifted in his chair, his shoulders stiffening them more. "Well, from now on, I will see to your well-being."

Kate frowned. "Once we've made a plan to apprehend Jeb, I won't need anyone to ensure my well-being."

Seth rolled his lips and then looked from his cup to Kate. "I'll find Jeb and question him. That's my job."

"Question him!" Ross scrambled from his chair. The other guests turned to stare. Mrs. White fluttered.

"Ross, for heaven's sake. Sit down." Kate stood and pressed his shoulder until he resumed his seat. "What is the matter with you? Sheriff Morgan is right. It's his job to question and arrest people who break the law."

"Possibly arrest." Seth glanced at Kate, and his mouth softened a degree. "I'll find Jeb and get his side of the story. If it doesn't add up, I'll arrest him. If it does, Kate, you'll have to accept Jeb might not be the guilty one."

Kate huffed. "Not the guilty one? Of course he's guilty. Who else could have killed my father and kidnapped me?"

One corner of Seth's mouth tilted in a smile so sexy Kate struggled to maintain her exasperation. "I have to look at all sides, Kate. I want you to be safe."

"Excuse me, for breaking into this revealing conversation, but I fully intend to confront Jeb and then take Kate back to New York."

"Not until I've questioned him. This is my jurisdiction, Williams, and I'm not in any body's pocket."

"Are you insinuating I am?" Ross leaned forward and bumped the table, rattling the tea set.

"Really, Ross." Kate glanced around, embarrassed over his lack of control. She pinned him with a stare she hoped expressed her impatience. "This is a small town. I'd prefer not to have everyone listening to our business."

"What does it matter? You'll be leaving this burg very soon."

Kate hesitated, surprised how much the realization hurt. She really was leaving Hope. She'd always planned to leave, but it suddenly didn't seem as appealing. "When I leave, it'll be on my terms."

"I hope the good sheriff hasn't used you like he did Trisha Walker." Ross pulled off an innocent look and glanced from Kate to Seth and back. "Or didn't he tell you about courting Trisha?"

"He told me all about it. He got close to her in order to gather more information on Allen Johnston, and they parted on good terms."

"According to Morgan, or Trisha?"

Seth's mouth tightened. He pushed his teacup back and started to stand. "Williams, I don't know what your game is, but my private life is none of your business."

"Gentlemen, please." Kate glanced around the room. Curiosity had turned to fascination. "If we can't stay civil, we need to take this conversation to a less public place." Her nerves twanged, and her hands trembled. Shifting in her chair, she knocked her cup from the saucer. Tea splashed across the table staining the white tablecloth.

"Don't worry, dear, I'll see to that." Mrs. White appeared, a damp cloth in her hands.

"Please, Mrs. White, allow me." Kate took the cloth and mopped up the tea. Her heart pounded, and tears clouded her vision. Seth had closed himself off from her, and Ross acted like a stranger. Nothing was going right.

"Williams, how long have you been in Hope?"

Ross blinked and his mouth gaped. "Since yesterday. Why?"

"Why?" Seth leaned forward. "You arrived yesterday, but you didn't check in with me or attempt to find Kate?"

Ross shifted and stared at his cup of tea. "I resent this line of questioning."

"Seth has a point, Ross. You must have known I was in the area from my telegrams."

"You didn't tell me where you were. I followed Jeb to Hope."

"You didn't ask for the origin of my messages?" Kate couldn't believe he'd be so remiss, not to try to track her down.

For the third time, Ross straightened his tie. "Well, I uh, of course I did."

Kate's chest tightened with a sense of dread. Something was wrong. "You knew I was in Hope, yet you didn't seek me out."

Seth's face tightened and his lips narrowed. Kate feared a fight between he and Ross. No matter how much Ross disconcerted her, she didn't want things to end up this way. Two of the most prominent men in her life, fist fighting.

Ross sucked in his cheeks and blinked. "I had no intention of leading Jeb to your doorstep."

"So what did you propose to do?" Seth shifted in his chair and folded his hands on the white linen tablecloth.

Ross scooted away from the table and crossed one leg over the other. "I plan to question Jeb. I don't want this case botched with a small town lawman."

Seth drew on every bit of restraint he possessed to keep from dragging Williams outside to beat the hell out of him.

Kate's face went from flushed to pale, her lips tight to her mouth gaping. She fidgeted in her chair until he expected her to bolt and leave them both in the dust. Despite all the dangerous situations he'd been in over his life, having Kate between Ross

Williams and the law, twisted his gut in a knot. Her safety was on the line, but so was her presence in Hope and in his life. Ross had the power to take her away. Seth would still be breathing, but there'd be pain with each breath.

Seth shoved back his chair and stood. Mrs. White glanced toward them, her hands fluttering nervously. Ross' bravado cracked, but he was quick to mask his uneasiness.

Kate stood and crossed her arms over her breasts. "Where are you going?"

"I'm going to check on my prisoner."

"You haven't outlined a plan yet."

"I've said what I mean to say right now. You have what you want, and I have a job to do." He didn't want to leave her in Williams' slimy care, to have more lies fed to her, but he knew a losing battle when he saw one. There was no getting to the truth as long as she had a shred of trust in Ross.

He strode from the boarding house on a mix of anger and frustration. He might not have the chance to tell Kate everything about his time in New York. The train was leaving in the morning, and he was sure she'd be on it.

Chapter Eighteen

Kate stomped her foot and huffed at Seth's retreating back. How dare he walk out in the middle of such a serious conversation?

"Dear, are you all right?" Mrs. White laid her hand on Kate's arm, making Kate realize she'd just lost her temper in the middle of the boarding house café.

"I'm fine, Elena." She patted the older woman's hand and smiled at her and the curious customers, their necks cranked from their meals to watch the drama.

"Excuse me, Ross. I have to talk to Seth."

"Don't be silly." Ross grabbed her arm before she reached the door. "He said what he had to say. Things happened in New York, and I'm sure he doesn't want you to know about them."

Kate tried to shake off his grip. "What do you mean? About what?"

"Your father for one, and the night he died."

Ice ran through her veins. "Why are you bringing it up now? Why didn't we discuss this before I left?"

"What were the odds of you ever meeting the illustrious Seth Morgan?"

Kate struggled to breathe and escape this crazy version of Ross Williams. "Let go of me. What's wrong with you? I want to know what happened in New York with Seth."

Ross didn't budge.

"Dammit, Ross, let go of me."

Ross loosened his hold. Kate jerked away and

hurried out the door.

Her heart pounding in her ears, she ran to the sheriff's office. First Seth walked out on her, then Ross started spouting accusations about Seth. She didn't understand why Ross and Leland hadn't mentioned Seth before she left New York.

She slammed into the sheriff's office. Seth wasn't there. He must have stopped somewhere on his way back. Well, she'd wait for him. A bump sounded on the other side of the door leading to the two small jail cells. The henchman was on the other side of that door. Chills skittered up her spine. She backed around Seth's desk, putting it between her and the door.

She ran her hand over the desk top. The curiosity of what Seth kept in his desk reared its head again. She touched the drawer pull and glanced at the door Seth could come through at any moment. The clock on the wall ticked away.

Kate opened the drawer. Nothing. She opened the next one. A jumble of writing supplies, extra badges, and a stack of wanted posters greeted her. The latter sent a shiver up her back. The faces were hard edged, the eyes filled with hate or daring. Kate slammed the drawer shut.

She moved to the right hand bank of drawers, glancing at the door and out the window facing the street before she opened the first one. Kate frowned. Several small pieces of paper lay crumpled on top of a past edition of The Pend Oreille Press. She absently picked up one and smoothed it out.

Sick disbelief curled in her stomach. They were her telegrams! Both sent and received. Rage built as she smoothed one after the other to chronicle her time in Hope. How long had he been collecting them?

Her legs wobbled. She sank into the big chair behind the desk, the telegrams clutched in her hands. Her fists tightened, and her eyes burned.

"How dare he?"

The door opened and Seth strode in.

"How dare you?" She pounded her clenched fists against the desktop "How dare you collect my telegrams, my business, as if you had a right!"

Seth stopped just inside the door and quietly closed it, his hand on the knob. "I'm the sheriff of this town, and you were a suspect."

Kate shot out of the chair. "Suspect of what? I was a victim, Sheriff Morgan, or have you been in law enforcement so long you can't tell the difference?"

Seth's dark gaze narrowed on her. "I didn't know what you were up to, but I knew you were lying."

She threw the missives at him, then walked around the desk to face him, toe to toe. "And how did you know I was lying?"

"You were, weren't you?"

Seth stood straight and staunch. Kate fought the urge to hit him. "About some things! That's beside the point! Oh, damn you!" She sputtered in frustration. "Ross said something more happened in New York. Did you ever plan to tell me?"

Seth bracketed her arms with both his hands. "Are you going to let Ross ruin everything we have?"

"What do we have, Seth?" Kate wanted to sink against him but held back. She'd known Ross since she was fourteen; he'd been a trusted friend of her father's. Seth, she'd only known for a few weeks. Ross's strange expressions and manner since seeing her this morning flashed through her mind. Ross wasn't the solid voice of reason anymore. Her world was topsy-turvy.

"I love you, Kate. Laugh at me if you want, but I love you."

Kate's throat tightened with a need to sob. "Oh Seth, I've waited all my adult life to hear those words, but something's threatening to divide us.

Trust is formed by honesty, and you haven't been completely honest with me about your time in New York. About my father."

"Honesty? Kate, you lied to me from the beginning."

"I did lie—out of need—but so much of what I said and did was plain old me."

Seth feathered his fingers over her cheek. "Ah, Kate. There's nothing plain or old about you. Please trust me to tell you everything when the moment is right."

Her eyes burned and her heart ached. "I don't know who or what to believe anymore."

She looked at the floor, the way the tips of their boots nearly touched; hers so much smaller than his dusty, worn ones.

"Kate, don't do this."

She couldn't look into his dark eyes and retain any dignity. "My mind is in turmoil. I have to leave." She stepped away and started for the door.

"What do you mean leave? Where are you going?"

"I'm going back where I belong, where I know how to act." The doorknob felt as hard and cold as her heart. She stepped out onto the street and into the warm afternoon. Seth didn't follow.

Had she wanted him to chase after her? Try to stop her with more empty assurances? She glanced up and down the dusty street. The sun still beat down with unseasonable heat, but Kate shivered. Strange, but deciding to leave Hope seemed more like leaving home, than when she'd left New York.

Before she lost her nerve and ran back into Seth's arms, Kate hurried toward the depot.

Twenty minutes later, she returned to the boarding house with the train ticket tucked in her pocket. Ross was nowhere to be seen.

Once in her room, she sat on a small chair next

to the window and gazed over the main street and scenic vista. She hadn't bothered to unpack, so she was ready to leave at a moment's notice. The train didn't depart until five-forty the next morning, so now what? If Kerry or Kyle didn't deliver her trunk today, she'd just leave it for Maura and Janet to use. None of the contents were hers anyway. Especially the wedding dress. She'd probably never need one.

Watching the teaming activity below made her feel even more alone. She despaired over how much had changed since earlier that day when she'd seen first Jeb, then Ross on the street. Seth's kisses and caresses had teased and taunted her, but reality crashed around her when she found the telegrams in his desk. She fingered the gold locket he'd given her. The geography separating them was nothing compared to the secrets he didn't wish to share.

She needed to talk to someone. With Erin still so far away, Janet was her next logical choice. Janet was a wise woman with a good heart and would help her sort out her confused feelings

Kate glanced at the small clock on the dresser. Janet and Maura might be back from Ethan's ranch. With luck, Ross wouldn't be downstairs, and she could slip out and up the road to the Malone's undetected. She couldn't handle another confrontation today.

The café was empty and Mrs. White could be heard humming from the kitchen. Her heart racing, she hurried out the door and up the street. The sheriff's office edged the road to the Malone's. She paused and glanced around. A narrow alley ran between the mercantile and post office. Leaving the main street might not be the wisest choice she'd made, but she needed to talk to Janet.

Wading through the tall, dry grass, chills smattered up her shoulders and the back of her neck. The henchman could be watching her from the small window in the jail; Jeb might be tracking her, waiting for her to emerge from the alley. The man who attacked her, possibly Allen Johnston, was still on the loose.

Her life had been safe and secure until the kidnapping attempt in New York. The fear returned and swept over her. Weakness and vulnerability filled her and it made her angry.

Leaving the protection of the buildings, she hurried up the second street which made up Hope, and toward the road. She instinctively patted her dress pocket, drawing some security from the hard shape of the derringer.

Out on the road, she shook the dust from her skirts and patted her hair, taking a moment to catch her breath. Below her lay the roof tops of the rustic town and to the right and down a level, the railroad depot.

Tomorrow, she'd leave on the train and return to her life. Since escaping the henchman on the docks, she'd been running away. She'd resented every decision she'd had to make to keep moving and hiding, yet here she was, planning to run again. This time, leaving the only man she'd ever been able to love. What had happened to the strong woman she'd believed herself to be? Had she ever really existed?

Taking one more glance at the town, she marveled over how it looked less rough and untamed than it had a few weeks ago. The spaces between the lumber on some of the buildings were wide enough, Janet claimed you could throw a cat through them. Kate chuckled. She'd never forget Janet's colorful sayings.

Life in Hope, Idaho Territory might not be refined, but the napkins Mrs. White served with her tea and scones were edged in lace. Mr. White's Mercantile carried floral sprigged cotton. Janet Malone always had fresh flowers on her kitchen table and managed her house with a class Kate had found missing in many a New England estate.

Hope might be rustic and backward in fashion, but something special dwelled there, a substance, a determination she hadn't seen at home and she liked it. Possibly the same determination led her father to build the shipping company.

Wasn't she cut from the same cloth? Lord, she hoped so. She didn't want to be some wilting flower, waiting for a man to rescue her.

Lifting her chin, she squared her shoulders and turned toward the hillside, and the remainder of her trek.

She no sooner walked into the kitchen before Janet and Maura surrounded her.

"Kate, you're back! We were so worried!"

Kate glanced toward the table. "Didn't you see my note?"

"Of course, but it made us worry all the more." Janet glanced around her. "Seth should have come inside." Janet looped her arm through Kate's and led her to the table. Kate wasn't about to admit she came alone. "Now sit down while I cut us some of the pound cake you helped me bake yesterday. It seems we have a lot of catching up to do."

"Yes, I want to hear all about the visit to the ranch. What did Ethan say?"

Maura's face took on a glow. "We're getting married Sunday."

Kate laughed. "You must have impressed him! You were only there for a couple of hours."

Maura blushed, and a small smile tilted the corners of Janet's mouth. "They went for a walk to see a newly cleared field. They were gone quite a while."

Images flashed through Kate's mind; her episode with Seth in the woods not far from here; the day he brought her home from the picnic to change.

Heat climbed its way up her throat.

"Oh, Mother," Maura said, giving Kate a moment to gather her emotions. "Ethan and I are getting married. Aren't you happy?"

"I'm elated." Janet hugged her daughter.

"What about you, Kate?" Maura laid her hand over Kate's. "Are you happy for us?"

"Of course I'm happy. It's what I've wanted since the first time I saw you and Ethan together. Now my mission is done, and it's time to say goodbye. I bought a train ticket for tomorrow."

"Goodbye? You can't leave before my wedding!" Maura, bless her heart, truly looked devastated.

"I don't want Kate to leave either, Maura, but she has a company to oversee in New York."

"Part of why I returned was to thank you. Your entire family has been more than gracious to me. Even when you found out I wasn't who I claimed to be, you didn't throw me out on my ear. You stood by me."

"Of course we did. If anyone else had responded to Ethan's advertisement, we might not be planning our wedding. That's what makes it even more important for you to stay. Just for a few days?" Maura's mouth turned down in a pucker.

Janet's jaw dropped, and she pressed her hand to her forehead. "Oh my, you're right, Maura! It's only a few days away! We have to plan your wedding! My goodness, what will you wear?"

"The dress is something I can help with." Kate grasped Maura's hand and winked at her. "It's only right for you to use Mary Catherine's wedding dress." Kate laughed with the pure joy of doing something so right. "It's traveled some miles, but was meant for Ethan's bride. I'm sure Mary Catherine would agree."

"Oh, Kate!" Maura folded her hands over her mouth, excitement and tears brimming in her eyes.

"I'd love to wear the traveling dress."

"I propose we all go up to my old room so you can try it on."

"You could stay, you know." Janet's expression went from gratefulness to sadness.

"I couldn't impose on you a minute longer. Except for my trunk, I'm settled in at the boarding house."

"Just because you've revealed your true identity, doesn't mean you're safe. The man who attacked you is still on the loose."

Kate sighed. "You're right, I'm not safe. Since I moved into town this morning, I've seen Jeb Walker, and my attorney, Ross Williams. Ross and Seth already had a standoff in Mrs. White's dining room."

"They're all here? I can't believe Seth didn't stay to see you back!"

Kate cringed. "He doesn't know I left my room. I promised him I wouldn't go out without him, but after the way he behaved with Ross, and then—then I went to his office and discovered he'd confiscated all the telegrams I've sent and received."

"Dear, he is the sheriff. He must have had a good reason."

"Oh he gave me the reason. He thought I was a criminal when we first met."

"Seth's a good man and a good sheriff. He probably got the telegrams from Mr. Smith before he really knew you. There's something special between you and Seth." Janet calmly sliced a large piece of cake and placed it on a plate, handing it Kate.

"That's far more than I can eat, Janet."

"Fiddle. Now back to Seth."

Kate squeezed her lips together to keep them from trembling, then smiled softly. "Seth is so different from any man I've ever met."

"You're a beautiful woman. I'm sure you had plenty of men courting you in New York."

Kate tilted her head to one side and absently picked at the firm, but delicious cake. She'd been amazed at how many fresh eggs it took to make it. "I had several proposals, but they were for position and money, not for me." She shrugged. "Even when my mother left my father, I still believed love was the only reason to marry."

"I agree." Janet's smile held deep satisfaction. "Kerry and I both came from modest immigrant families. Money has taken care of the necessities, but the true bond in our marriage has always been love."

Kate glanced at Maura, envious of the glow on the younger woman's face.

"Seth and I are two different creatures. He loves his life here and never wants to leave, but I'm born and bred, New York. Although I have to admit, despite its rustic building and dusty streets, I've come to love Hope. It's so different from what I'm used to; I didn't expect to like it at all."

"It's very different from Boston, too." Maura smiled. "The air is cleaner, and it's so quiet at night."

"You're right." Kate sighed. "There's something here the big cities don't have. The lake, the beautiful mountains and trees. Heavens, I've never seen so many trees, and there's a charm to the town I didn't expect." She stopped speaking and glanced around the homey room, the row of nails in the wall by the back door, holding Janet's aprons and shawls. The shelves filled with jars of dried herbs for seasoning and medicinal uses. "Chester" the shotgun hanging over the door.

Seth's image flashed through her mind. Seth and his handsome strength. The way his dark gaze bore into hers like he could see her soul. Yes, he had taken her telegrams and still hadn't revealed his entire time in New York, but her instincts said Seth couldn't have done anything wrong, so why was she worried about it?

Ross bothered her. He acted so strangely. In New York, he'd convinced her that Jeb killed her father to gain full control of the company. Marrying her would seal the deal. But wouldn't marrying him accomplish the same thing? Put her company in the hands of a man who'd take the management position away from her?

She nibbled at her bottom lip and drummed her fingertips on the table. "Seth and I argued over Ross, but to be honest, I don't trust Ross anymore. He arrived in Hope yesterday, yet made no effort to find me. He had to know I was here."

"But last night, you told us Ross was helping you." Maura's glow from a few minutes ago turned to pallor, her blue eyes large and filled with apprehension.

"He has been, Maura. But this morning—he was different."

"Follow your instincts, but don't see a threat around every corner." Janet scooted her chair closer to Kate and took her hand.

"I'm trying to stay calm, but it isn't easy." She shook her head. "Things have become so convoluted. I'm not sure about anything anymore."

Janet leaned toward Kate. "You can trust Seth, and all of us."

"I do trust you." She crossed her arms under her breasts and rubbed her arms. "You should have seen Seth and Ross this morning. They were so busy accusing each other of everything under the sun. They completely forgot they're supposed to be on my side." She shook her head.

"I'm sure you're the reason they were squaring off." Janet raised a brow. "Two roosters, one hen."

"Exactly!" Kate pursed her lips. "They're so busy posturing; it's disgusting. Something Ross said really disturbed me."

"What?" Maura asked, her eyes wide.

Chills ran down her body. "About a week ago, Seth told me about being in New York and meeting many of the people who work for me. Ross said Seth was involved with more than I knew. He made it sound shady, illegal or something."

Janet slammed her fist on the table. Kate and Maura jumped then looked at each other with raised brows.

"Ma, what is it?"

"Seth Morgan is a good upstanding man. Kate, don't believe a word this Ross character tells you. Sounds to me like jealousy. A person would have to be blind not to see what's between you and Seth."

Kate covered her eyes with one hand. "I'm worried about staying here even a few more days, fanning the sparks into an explosion. Seth's searching for Jeb but said he'll only lock him up if he has a good reason. Isn't my father's death a good reason?"

Janet smiled. "Kate, Seth's crazy about you and will do what he has to do to protect you. Ross sounds like the threat. We'd better get you back to the boarding house before Seth discovers you're gone." Janet stood and covered the cake.

"He can just stew for a while." Kate stood and carried her cake plate to the dishpan. Trouble was, she did care if Seth worried about her, and it irritated her. "I want Maura to try on the dress."

"Don't play with his feelings, Kate. He cares about you." Janet swiped the dishrag over the table and brushed the crumbs off her hands.

"He does care about me," Kate drew out her words. "He said he loved me, but he had no right to take my telegrams."

Maura stood and pushed her chair into the table. "And you said Seth's not like anyone you've ever met. Don't forget how I jumped to the wrong conclusions about Ethan."

Kate began to pace. "I know you're right, but my heart's struggling with my sense of reason. I'm so confused. I should get on the train tomorrow and go home. My company can't be safe without Ross there to watch over it."

"I think Ross is part of the problem." Janet fingered the course weave of her brown skirt. "Why isn't he dogging your steps, if he's here to protect you?"

Kate rubbed her face with both hands and groaned. "I can't argue with you. All right, let's go upstairs and take a look at Maura's dress, so I can return to the boarding house before Seth and Ross duke it out."

Kate led the way, her step considerably lighter from sharing her thoughts with her wonderful friends, even if nothing was resolved.

Once in Kate's former room, they giggled and cried as Maura tried on the wedding dress. Outfitting the bride was an appropriate way to end her adventure, to witness Maura and Ethan happily married.

"You look like you're thinking about leaving." Janet sat on the bed next to Kate.

"Am I so transparent?" Kate tried to smile but teared up. "What will the town's people say when Maura is the bride and I'm a guest?"

Janet smiled and patted her hand. "Things are different in the West, my dear. People are more accepting. We aren't as bound by social restrictions as where we all came from. Ah, there'll be some whispering, that's human nature, but they'll get beyond it and be happy for Ethan and Maura."

"I hope so." Kate squeezed Janet's hand. "How you can be so understanding after I lied to you and your family?"

Janet chuckled. "I suspected something from the

day you arrived. You didn't fit anything I'd heard about Mary Catherine. I understand how you did what you had to do."

The dress needed only a few quick tucks, which Janet could accomplish before the wedding.

Janet stood back and gazed at Maura and Kate. "I want you to listen to me for a moment. Kate, this is a day you'll never forget because you helped bring Maura and Ethan together. Maura, this is the day the man you love proposed to you. The day you tried on your wedding dress." Janet sighed and looked beyond the two women to the bright day outside the window.

"Life is made up of times like this. I call them, life markers. It's how most women remember what happened at certain times in their lives. They measure it by the day their love proposed to them, or their wedding day, or when the first child came and each child there after." She took a deep breath and looked at Kate. "It's what happened the day you received the news your father died, and the day you laid him to rest. It's the day you met Seth, the day you realized you love him.

"Never forget how quickly life flies by. It seems so long at first then it picks up speed and before you know it, you're my age, and your children are grown, or nearly grown. You start to feel some aches and pains, and if you're lucky, you look toward old age with the man you love and adore."

Kate couldn't control the rush of tears spilling from her eyes. Janet was so right. She would never forget those events, but what would she have to mark future days? No wedding of her own, no children.

Maura wrapped her arms around Kate, spilling a few of her own tears. "Now look what you've done, Ma. You've got Kate upset and crying."

Janet sank to her knees in front of them, her

brown skirt billowing around her. "I didn't mean to darken your day, Kate, but you know what I'm talking about, don't you? Don't make rash decisions based on confused emotions. Those markers only mean something if you take a chance and follow your heart."

"Your mother's right, Maura. Life changing events, whether they're joyous or sad, are what we remember, how they made us feel." Kate wiped her eyes with Janet's proffered handkerchief and blinked. She had to return to town before Seth found her gone. "I'll think over what you've said before I walk away from Seth and the chance to marry the man I love."

With Chester in hand, Janet and Maura walked Kate to the top of the hill, then waited while she descended the steep hill back to the main street.

Kate's outlook on life had taken on a new hue since she walked out on Seth. Spending time with the Malone women, bonding and sharing had filled her with a happiness and clarity of mind she'd never experienced. A warmth filled her heart like it hadn't since her mother left.

She'd face the people of Hope, Ross, Seth and whoever she had to, to fulfill her commitment to Maura.

Her steps faltered with a realization as she climbed the stairs to her room. She'd made a commitment to Maura, without putting her company first. Everything she'd done since her father died was to either save the company or her freedom. Staying for the wedding put both of those things in jeopardy. Unless Seth arrested Jeb and Ross turned into his old self, Kate took a tremendous chance by staying in Hope.

She curled up on her bed and hugged the pillow. Was she going to hibernate in this room for the next few days? Her other option was risking a confrontation with one of the men in town she wanted to avoid.

Seth was probably too busy to think about her.

Kate blew out her frustration over the idea of being shut in this room. Meals could be delivered, but she'd have to use the necessary.

She sat up and threw her pillow at the wall. Being forced to hide made her blood boil. The nerve of Jeb Walker, to chase her across the country. She sprawled on the bed and stared at the plaster ceiling. The trouble was he did control her present situation. Dammit, if she wasn't so confused over her feelings for Seth, she'd track him down to see if he'd questioned Jeb yet.

Her mind in turmoil, Kate paced the room, glancing out the window each time she passed. Clutching her head in frustration, her chignon collapsed and spilled her hair over her shoulders. She didn't care how she looked; she wasn't leaving her room until dark.

Over heated, she unfastened the first few buttons of her dress and fanned herself with a fan she'd carried in her satchel from New York. Her father had purchased it on a business trip to the San Francisco office, for her eighteenth birthday. She missed her father. Terribly.

The keen loss choked her, and tears welled. When had she become so over emotional?

Boots echoed up the stairs, then sounded on the landing outside her door. Her heart quickened.

"Kate?" Seth rapped on the wood panel. "Kate, are you in there?"

Her chest heaved, her throat closed up. She wanted to reassure him, but what had he done to comfort her? He'd asked her to trust him and wait until the moment was right to learn his part in her father's death. He'd built the turmoil until she thought she'd explode.

"Kate, please open the door. We need to talk. Dammit, I need to see you." His voice turned to a growl.

The emotion in his tone sent goose bumps over Kate's shoulders and breasts. She fanned herself harder. He set her on fire, an emotion she'd never known before Seth Morgan came into her life.

Janet's words of wisdom flowed through her mind. Seth was the man of her heart. If she didn't give their relationship a chance, he could give up and let her return to New York without a fight.

Her feet leaden, Kate walked toward the door and unlocked it. The latch turned, and the door swung toward her. Seth loomed in the doorway like an avenging angel; a little less fresh than he'd been earlier in the day.

The typical sprinkling of whiskers sprouted from his tanned face. His hair was marked by his hat band and furrowed on top from raking his fingers through it. She met his dark gaze and backed into the room, mesmerized as he followed her and closed the door behind them.

"I've been worried about you." He ran his gaze over her hair, pausing where the ends curled at her breasts, his breathing as uneven as her own.

"I went to the Malone's. I had to say goodbye and find out how Maura's visit to the ranch went."

"You went to the Malone's? Did Kerry or Kyle take you?" The warm sensuality in his eyes, dimmed.

"No, I went on my own." She lifted her chin and clamped her hands to her waist.

His gaze followed the direction of her hand, then traveled over her breasts until Kate thought she'd faint from pent up passion.

"You went on your own." He repeated the words, his voice low and lethal.

Kate wasn't afraid for her safety. Not with Seth.

Oh no, what she feared was her own actions when he stepped so close his boot tips touched hers. When his long, tanned fingers touched the skin left bare from her unbuttoned neckline.

"I warned you, Kate. You have to be careful until we find out who's the biggest threat." His hand slid down her bodice, feathered over her nipples and cupped her waist.

Kate released a sharp breath. She'd never dreamed a touch could start a fire deep inside her. A fire and a need to be closer to him. She swallowed and jutted her bottom lip.

"You didn't try to stop me when I left your office this morning, unaccompanied."

He pulled her against his hard, muscled body. "I wanted to lay you over my knee, so I figured I'd better leave well enough alone." He lowered his head and pressed his lips to her partially exposed shoulder. His thick, dark hair feathered her face and the side of her neck.

"You wanted to spank me?" Kate tried to sound indignant, which was difficult with his hands on her, his lips pressed to her bare skin and his masculine scent wrapped around her. "I thought you said, you loved me."

"Oh, I do, darlin', but that doesn't preclude how fired up you get me on a regular basis. I just want you to be safe, sweetheart."

His voice was muffled, as he explored the side of her neck and with ease, flicked open more buttons on her bodice. Kate raised a questioning brow. "You're very adept at that."

In seconds, the air hit her bare breasts. Kate gasped. Seth lifted his head and drilled her with hot, dark eyes.

"I need to touch you, Kate. I promise I won't hurt you." He released her long enough to lock the door.

"You seem rather confident." She pulled the bodice over her shoulders and pushed the sleeves off her arms. The dress hung at her waist.

Her nipples beaded and pressed against the thin silk of her camisole. Seth moaned. "Is that fancy underwear yours or Mary Catherine's?" He slid his hands over the silk, grimacing, when his callouses caught on the fine material.

"All mine. There are some things a girl won't sacrifice."

Kate unfastened a few more buttons, dropping her dress into a pool at her feet. She stepped out of it, thrilling when he ran his hands over her custom made silk pantalets. They reached mid-thigh, with slits up the sides, and tied around her waist with a blue ribbon. They were light weight and offered much more freedom of movement than what most women wore.

"Damn, Lady, you are full of surprises." He stepped behind her, bracketed her hips with his strong brown hands, and pulled her against him. He slid his hands up the sides of her pantalets and under the matching camisole, cupping her bare breasts.

Kate gasped, then moaned when he began teasing her nipples. She rested her head against his shoulder and bared her throat for his kisses.

"It's so good to touch you, breathe you in." He left her breasts and ran his hands over her stomach to the spot no other man had ever touched. "I'm not letting you go without a fight, Kate, and sometimes a man has to bring out the big guns."

"I think you have." Kate giggled and rubbed her bottom against his hardness, heady with power, when he moaned and buried his face in the side of her neck.

She turned in his arms and looked into his dark, passion-glazed eyes. "You may not let me go without a fight, Seth, but you will have to let me go." Her breathy voice and tingling body belied her words and made her wonder how she could ever stand by her decision and leave this handsome, rugged man. She pressed her mouth to his whisker-roughened jaw, breathing in his spicy, musky scent. Everything was still uncertain, in turmoil, but she'd relish these moments in the lonely days to come. McShane Walker was a big company, but other than paying for her big feather bed and the coal to heat her mansion, it didn't keep her warm at night.

Seth slid down her body, covering first one breast, then the other with his mouth, dampening and heating the silk that covered them. Kate moaned, leaned against him and ran her fingers through his thick hair.

He moved down her body, stroking her hips and legs, until he kneeled before her. Through a fog of sensations, she looked down to meet his gaze. Being with him exceeded any fantasy she'd ever had.

His gaze holding hers, he moved toward the juncture of her legs and opened his mouth over it. A pleasure she'd never imagined shot through her. Her face flamed with heat, but she couldn't move away, couldn't stop the building emotion, taking her somewhere she'd never been.

Fire roared through her body, seeming to lift her off her feet. She gripped Seth's shoulders and hung on, fighting the weakness in her knees.

She lost the battle. Sensation after sensation raced through her, wrapping her in a world of stars, weightlessness and a pleasure so intense she never wanted to leave it.

Her knees gave out. Kate sank into Seth's arms and wrapped her arms around his neck when he lifted her and carried her to the bed.

"Lordy, woman. You don't know what you do to me." Seth laid her on the bed and sat beside her. He ran his hands over her silk covered skin, dipped to kiss her lips, then her throat and breasts.

"Oh, Seth."

"I know, darlin'."

"You know?" She opened her eyes and glanced at the bulge in his pants. "Did it happen to you, too?" She stretched her arms over her head and wiggled on the bed in delicious abandon. "Isn't it incredible?"

"It is sweetheart, but I didn't feel what you did. Not this time."

"But—"

He laid his fingers over her lips. "It's all right. We'll be together soon, and when we are, Kate, it'll make this time seem like nothing." He stood and covered her with the quilt.

Kate propped her body on a crooked arm. "Can't you stay?"

"If I stay, I'll throw away my scruples and join you in bed. You wipe away my control, Kate, and push me over the edge."

"I don't understand, Seth. Why can't we do that now, so you—" she struggled for the right words.

"So I explode into a million pieces like you just did?"

"Exactly."

"I won't risk a baby until we have the certificate making us man and wife." He gazed at her another moment and backed from the bed. "I won't do to my child, what my parents did to me."

Kate was speechless. He wanted to make complete love to her, but not until they were married?

"Stay in your room. I mean it, Kate. I'll check on you in a couple of hours."

"A couple of hours?" Reality crashed in around her. Nothing had changed. Ross was still somewhere in town acting like a stranger. Jeb was doing who knew what.

"Wait a minute." Kate rose on her knees in the middle of the bed. "Have you seen Jeb?"

Seth fumbled with the doorknob behind him, his chest heaving in and out like he'd been running. Kate was amazed how he could stare at her crumpled, damp, underwear like a man who hadn't eaten in days but not stay and finish what his body must be craving.

"I haven't seen Jeb, but I will. I have trustworthy people watching for him, too." He turned the lock and opened the door. "I'll see you later."

Before Kate could ask another question, he was gone.

"Lock it now," he said, from the hallway.

Kate squirmed off the bed and locked the door. She leaned against the wood panel, her blood still humming. No wonder Erin glowed most of the time, if she and her husband shared what she'd just shared with Seth.

She moved to the vanity and gasped. She'd been so caught up, she'd left on her boots and stockings! "Good heavens!" She glanced in the large oval mirror, her eyes wide. "What was I thinking?"

Her underwear bunched in damp spots over her womanly areas, and her hair stood out like she'd been in a wind storm. She resembled a picture in a book she'd smuggled into the house years ago, where the heroine turned out to be a woman who bordered ill repute.

Was the spinster business woman really a loose creature? Was Seth repulsed and reminded of his childhood and the type of woman who worked in the bordello?

Kate blushed with shame. How could she do that to him? He seemed to enjoy everything he'd done and wanted to do more, so maybe she wasn't a disappointment.

Maybe making love in daylight wasn't a good thing. She did remember Erin talking about it when she and her husband first married, and how she asked him to extinguish the candles before they shared the intimate act.

Maybe only women of ill repute did such things in the daylight.

Kate stared at her reflection. Despite the surge of embarrassment, she also felt awe. Awe of what her body was capable of, of the emotions Seth could evoke in her. She'd thought, based on the two times they'd been close and kissed, it couldn't possibly be any better. She'd been wrong. What would it be like when Seth enjoyed it as much as she did?

As promised, Seth returned in two hours to accompany her to the necessary and walk around town for exercise. People nodded and greeted them but looked very curious about her relationship with the sheriff.

Seth wouldn't discuss Ross, or Jeb, so Kate finally gave up asking him.

She couldn't help but look at him with a whole new awareness. He'd seen her in her underwear, touched her bare skin, and did things she'd never be able to share with anyone; not even Erin. Her life would never be the same.

Returning to her door, Seth stopped in the hall. "I'll say goodnight out here. If I step foot in your room, I might not be as strong as I was before." He framed her face with his strong, capable hands. "I need to know what you're planning to do. About leaving." His voice grated like sand against Kate's heart.

"I promised Maura I'd stay for the wedding. I'll catch the train the morning after."

"Just like that? Your life's still in danger. We have unfinished business, but you're leaving and on your own. What about the circumstances of your father's death?"

Kate fingered the silk of her purse. "You don't want to talk about it, and I can only draw the worst conclusions. Ross and Jeb are in Hope, so I'll sneak out of town and be home before they realize I'm gone."

"Strange Jeb hasn't tracked you down, if he's such a bad guy."

He stared at her so long, goose bumps trailed up Kate's back and over her breasts, recreating the sensations from her moments of abandon. She wanted to step into his arms, but he'd been clear. They wouldn't be intimate again until they married, and that could never happen.

"Seth, I have very strong feelings for you, but I can't commit to anything when so much stands between us."

Seth raked his fingers through his hair. "I want to tell you everything." He glanced around the hall and landing. "We can't talk in your room—or mine. Let's go to my office."

"I suppose that terrible man is still in your jail."

"He is." Seth tapped his black Stetson against his thigh. "We'll take a walk toward the depot, but it's getting dark fast. I won't compromise your safety, Kate, just to satisfy your curiosity."

"Satisfy my curiosity?" Kate mimicked his words. "Considering my father died unexpectedly, I don't think curiosity is the right word."

Seth blew a frustrated breath through his lips and took her arm, leading her down the stairs and out the door. Town was settling down for the night. Kate had never been on the main street in the evening and it looked so different.

They walked toward the depot, her hand firmly on his arm. From the street, they could see Mr. Smith still at work in the glow of the telegraph office.

Kate turned to Seth. "Please talk to me."

Seth lifted his black Stetson and resettled it. "Ever since you told me who you were, I've wanted to talk about your dad, how I met him—and liked him. Hell, I respected him more than any man I'd ever met, except maybe Griff."

Kate's heartbeat increased. "He was a great man."

"I met your father when I went to New York after Allen Johnston."

Kate's breath caught and her heart fluttered. She could picture Seth and her father talking, discussing the case. "I can't believe no one mentioned you when I returned."

Seth gave her a side smile. "I was a Texas Ranger tracking a criminal, nothing more. Why would they mention me?"

Because he was the most incredible man she'd ever met, except her father of course, but that was different. She shrugged, struggling to appear casual. "You were new to our circle. Allen Johnston worked for us. It just makes sense someone would mention you."

"Your father and I met several times while you were in Europe. Leland and I had dinner with him at your house one night."

Kate pressed her hands to her chest. "You were in my house?"

Seth grinned. "Well, it's more of a mansion. No wonder Hope seemed so foreign to you." He brushed a curl off her forehead. "Your father was very interested in the case and wanted Johnston brought to justice. He had no use for one of his employees breaking the law."

"So what did he do?"

"I don't think he had a chance to do much of anything. He died two nights after our dinner. Darlin', I don't think Jeb's guilty of murder.

Johnston could be, but at the risk of offending you, Ross isn't as innocent as he claims."

"You think Ross had something to do with my father's death?"

Seth shrugged one shoulder. "Ross has dirt on his hands. He fooled you and your father for a while. In my last meeting with your father, he admitted he had evidence of Ross double crossing him and was just waiting for the right time to trap him."

All the air and strength left Kate's body. She stumbled forward and laid her head on Seth's chest. The black leather vest cooled her cheeks; his beating heart soothed the turmoil in her head. "I don't know what to believe anymore." She lifted her face to look at him square in the face. "Thank you for telling me. I never believed you were involved with my father's death, but not hearing everything from your lips shook me."

Seth clasped her arms in his hands and held her against him, gazing through the twilight into her eyes. "I won't allow Ross, or anyone, to come between us. I love you, Kate. I understand your need to go home, but it doesn't mean we're through. I've waited a life time for you; I'll wait until you come back."

Kate bit back tears. Once she left Hope, she had no intention of returning. It'd be too painful to see Seth again and not be able to blend their lives. "Oh Seth, it will never work."

Seth pressed his face into her hair. His breath warmed her scalp and sent those familiar goose bumps over her body. Her heart ripped into shreds. She'd wanted a man she could love; she'd found him. She'd wanted to experience love making, to hang onto the memory through all the lonely nights to come. She'd done that.

Now, the future stretched out in front of her, filled with memories of the man she loved with all her being, and how she couldn't have him.

****

Spending Saturday shut in her room all day nearly sent her into the streets to challenge, Jeb, Ross, and the man who'd attacked her.

The only relief from her boredom came when Kerry delivered Mary Catherine's trunk. She passed some time, packing and unpacking, then debating over what to wear to the wedding. She settled on the traveling suit she'd worn from New York and sent it to the Chinese laundry to be cleaned. A smiling Asian with a long queue down his back delivered it early Sunday morning, looking remarkably good.

Over the long hours of seclusion, she came to several conclusions—she wanted to kill Jeb with her bare hands, and Ross too, and she truly loved Seth. Each time his boots sounded on the landing outside her door, her heart ached. She wanted to throw away her pride and open the door, pull him into the room and wrap her arms around him. But he wouldn't give in. Not about making love without a marriage certificate and not about being unable to blend their life styles. She belonged in New York, running the shipping business, and he belonged here, keeping the peace.

Kate bathed and put on the clean suit. Today she could be herself.

The ceremony was scheduled for noon, right after church services ended. It seemed in the West, weddings were held right after church, since everyone was in town on Sunday. She felt guilty about missing Mass but didn't want to stir up trouble. Attending the wedding might be scandalous enough.

A luncheon, provided by numerous women from the community, would follow in the Hope Hotel. The large hotel, large for Idaho Territory standards, normally closed in September for the winter, but with the railroad officials back in town, and the influence Ethan Howland carried, the owners were more than happy to host the reception.

Her nerves jangling, Kate slipped from the boarding house and hurried to the church. The townspeople were milling around, waiting for the signal to begin the wedding.

Finding a place on the bench behind Kyle, Kate tapped him on the shoulder. "Is your mother with Maura?"

"Yeah." He grinned. "Maura acts like she's going to be sick, so Ma's staying with her until Da comes for her."

Kate smiled at the teenager, who after all that had happened, seemed to look at her with even more interest. "Weddings can do that to people. It's a big decision."

"When I get married I won't be sick, just eager to get the ceremony over so I can have my bride to myself."

"Kyle!" Kate tried to look serious, but laughed. Kyle wasn't a boy anymore, but not quite a man either.

Kyle chuckled and turned back to the buddy sitting next to him.

Kate glanced around the church, trying to keep her senses sharp and not succumb to panic. She prayed Jeb and Ross would stay away. Today was about Ethan and Maura saying their vows, not Kate's problems.

Several of the guests looked familiar, many didn't. They were squeezed, shoulder to shoulder on the rustic benches, and lined the back and side walls of the church, with still more people standing outside, hoping to listen to the ceremony and join the celebration afterward.

She glanced around for Seth. He hadn't stopped at her door that morning but had sent Mrs. White's handy-man to escort her to the necessary. Maybe he'd finally given up. He'd start his new life without her mystery plaguing him.

A lump lodged in her throat, and tears pricked her eyes. This was the way it should be, she'd return to her life and Seth to his. Why couldn't her heart accept it?

Mr. Smith from the post office sat across the aisle from her; Mr. and Mrs. White a few pews back. Twisting on the hard bench to glance at the doorway again, she froze.

Jeb Walker. Her chest tightened, and the room seemed to tilt. Something told her he'd bided his time until they were somewhere she couldn't escape.

She tore her gaze from her nemesis and looked at the line of people standing against the back wall. Ross was half a dozen people from Jeb. She motioned with her head urging him to look toward Jeb. Ross kept staring at her; a strange expression on the face she'd once thought handsome. The same expression she'd seen the day she discovered he was in Hope.

Kate gripped the edges of the bench. Where was Seth when she needed him?

She struggled not to faint. Her best protection was to stay at the wedding among people. After the ceremony, she'd slip out through the milling crowd and hide until time for the morning train. She patted her pocket, relieved she'd carried her derringer.

The pianist began to play, and the minister entered from a corner door, followed by the priest, Ethan, Travis, and Seth. Two things hit her at once. The marriage ceremony would be in both religions, and Seth was standing with Ethan and Travis. Her heart fluttered until she could swear she was floating.

The dark suit hugged Seth's broad shoulders and draped along his long, well-muscled body ending in tails touching the back of his thighs. The white shirt, crisp with starch, contrasted sharply with his dark, handsome looks. The thought of leaving him tomorrow, of never again seeing him, was too much to think of. Right now she'd drink in the sight of him for memories to hold later.

Chapter Nineteen

Seth followed Ethan through a side door at the front of the church. In a strange twist of fate, he'd asked Seth to stand with him, along with the best man, Travis Connor. It evened out the two young ladies standing up with Maura.

Seth was happy for them and even happier Kate wasn't becoming Mrs. Howland.

The woman drove him crazy, and knowing she dressed, bathed and slept on the other side of the thin wall between their rooms didn't help. Sleep was impossible with the fire raging through his body.

Shaking off the frustration, he turned his attention to the over-flowing church. His instincts had to stay sharp and alert. There were at least two men in Hope who could use this event to cause trouble: Ross and possibly Allen Johnston.

"Damn." Seth spoke under his breath, but Ethan elbowed him all the same.

Jeb Walker and Ross Williams were in the line of guests standing against the back wall. Several people separated them. Had they seen each other?

Good thing Kate's kidnapper, Arlie Thompson, was locked up. An itch traveled up his back. At least Arlie was behind bars when Seth checked the jail before coming to the church. He fidgeted with the urge to drag Jeb and Ross out of the wedding, lock them up until the ceremony was over.

His eyes strayed to the woman who plagued his thoughts, day and night. She sat toward the front, right behind the Malones.

Beautiful as ever in the tailored suit she'd worn

on the train, the memory of her landing in his lap, crashed around him. Most likely she still planned to leave tomorrow, but there was tonight and if he had his way, they'd make memories she'd never forget.

Hell, he'd never forget them.

Shaking his head, Seth turned to the crazy man in the back of the church.

If Kate would just sit there like a good girl until Maura and Ethan were pronounced husband and wife, he'd escort her out of the building. It certainly wasn't his best plan, but all he had at the moment.

By the set of her shoulders and the tightness of her mouth, she must have seen Jeb and Ross. Her perception of Ross had changed. Otherwise, he'd be sitting with her right now.

He'd trailed Ross over the past few days waiting for him to slip up so he could throw him in jail with Thompson. Other than making it clear how much he disliked Seth, Ross hadn't broken the law.

Kate knotted the strings of her purse, her breasts rising and falling in agitation. Seth didn't want to disrupt the wedding, but he'd do whatever he needed to keep her in the church and in his sight.

The traditional wedding march sounded. He glanced toward the back of the room as Maura, a vision in lace, came up the aisle on Kerry's arm. He leaned around Travis, toward Ethan, whose eyes were firmly fixed on his bride.

"Gentlemen, go with me if I do something strange. It could be life or death, so protect the ladies."

Ethan frowned and opened his mouth to reply, but Maura stopped in front of him, and Kerry placed her hand in his.

Jeb stayed by the door, but Ross moved up the aisle. Seth didn't like it. The evidence he'd uncovered in New York, plus the telegrams he'd received over the past few days, confirmed James McShane's suspicions of Ross, and established enough motive for him to kill James.

Ross was three pews from Kate.

"Is there any reason this couple should not be united in marriage?" The pastor asked first, then the priest.

Silence.

Ross reached out to lay his hand on Kate's shoulder.

"I object." Seth's voice boomed through the church.

The guests gasped in unison and began whispering amongst themselves. Startled, Ethan raised his brows. Maura's mouth dropped open.

"Please state why this marriage shouldn't take place." The pastor held his hand up. "Quiet please, and let this man speak."

"Seth?" Maura squeaked his name.

Ross's hand stilled and fell to his side.

Seth looked hard into Kate's eyes. She sat perfectly still, her hands clenched in her lap, no longer worrying her purse strings. "I object because this should be a double wedding. Pastor, I'd like to marry Kate McShane."

"Now?" Kate gasped.

"Yes, now." Seth glanced at the back of the room. Jeb had moved through the crowd and was halfway up the aisle. Seth left Ethan's side and moved toward Kate, drilling Ross with a look that said he'd shoot him if he tried to take Kate.

"Now see here." Ross ignored the warning and stepped toward Seth.

Kate twisted on the pew to look up at Ross. Her mouth parted and her eyes went wide. That cinched it for Seth. Kate was leery of Ross and hadn't known he was standing so close.

"Mr. Williams, please step away from my fiancée."

"I object, Pastor." Ross laid his hand on Kate's shoulder, his cold blue gaze drilling Seth with hatred.

"The sheriff already has." The pastor sighed.

"I object to the sheriff marrying Miss McShane. She's my fiancée."

"What?" Kate squealed and stood, squaring off with Ross. "I am no such thing, Ross Williams and you know it!"

"Excuse me, sir." Maura turned to Ross, her chin up. "Ethan and I are honored to have our good friends share our wedding day."

"Kate?" Seth wanted to bend on one knee in front of her, but he was afraid Ross would stab him in the back. He kept his peripheral on Williams while he waited for Kate to consent.

One part of his mind yelled, what in the hell are you doing? While the other part knew, this wasn't only to keep Kate safe. He loved her and he wanted her in his life; forever. One night would never be enough.

Kate glanced beyond Ross to Jeb. The room was filled with innocent people who could get hurt. Because of her.

She looked at Seth. He was offering his protection, but she'd get more than protection. The memory of his arms around her, his lips caressing hers, flashed through her mind.

The reality of Seth always in the line of fire, twisted her stomach, but she'd never change who he was, she'd never want to. She wanted Seth for who he was and what he could give her—love.

"I object," Jeb yelled from three pews back.

"What are you objecting to?" The priest stepped to Maura's side and laid his hand on her lace covered arm.

"Kate McShane is my fiancée; she can't marry Ross Williams." Jeb shoved his way through the crowd who had surged up the aisle in excitement. He pushed against Ross.

Ross pulled back his shoulders and lifted his chin. "You are not engaged to Kate." He removed Jeb's hand from his shoulder, as if distasteful.

"I certainly am." Jeb straightened his jacket. "I'm her fiancé and half owner of McShane Walker Shipping."

"Forty-nine percent owner." Kate stepped past Seth, her eyes narrowed at the man she'd known for a good share of her life. She'd been running from Jeb for weeks, suspecting him of killing her father; attempting to kidnap her to force her into a loveless marriage.

She gripped the back of the pew to steady her shaking body. "Furthermore, Ross has reason to believe you killed my father!"

Jeb's jaw dropped open, then he whooped with laughter. "That's rich coming from Ross Williams. He failed to tell you he was the last person to see your father alive."

"Wrong." Ross shouted. "Seth Morgan was."

Jeb tilted his head at Seth but looked into Kate's eyes. "I traveled to New York with Seth Morgan. We met with James to plan the trap for Allen Johnston. Seth, here, had strong evidence pointing to Johnston's involvement with the stagecoach and train robberies in Arizona." Jeb took a deep breath through his nostrils, the sound whistling through the silent room.

"Kate, the night your father died, Seth and I found him slumped over his desk."

Kate shook from head to foot, and her knees threatened to buckle. Jeb had been the villain, Ross her guide. The tables had turned and her head spun. Seth had found her father dead. What had seemed so straight forward became very complicated.

The ugliness of her life had spoiled Maura's

wedding day.

Kate turned to Ethan and Maura. "I'm so sorry. Gentlemen, can we postpone this discussion until after the ceremony?"

A smile curved Maura's full lips. "I believe Seth asked you something my friend, and you haven't answered him."

"No!" Ross stepped forward and pushed Seth. Seth's jaw hardened, and his hands curled into fists, but he straightened them and pushed Ross backward past Jeb.

"Kate isn't marrying anyone but me! She's mine!" Ross screeched, struggling against Seth.

"I belong to no man." Kate's shouted over the roar of voices. The weakness of moments ago left, to be replaced with fury over being manipulated by a man she'd believed she could trust.

"Ross, you've gone mad! I made it clear on several occasions. I'm not interested in marrying you!"

"You will marry me."

Kate shivered at the insane tone in Ross' voice. What had happened to the steadying force he'd been for so long? The coldness in his eyes chilled her to the bone.

She tore her gaze from Ross to find Jeb staring at her. Despite his testimony for Seth, she still didn't trust him. She only had one choice.

"Yes, Seth, I will marry you."

"No!" Ross pushed around Seth to grab Kate's arm.

"Release me, Ross. I don't know what happened to you, but you're not fit to be my advisor any longer."

"That's ridiculous! You can't function without me!" His eyes and hair were wild.

"No, the fact that I trusted you for so long is ridiculous, but I can't fault my misjudgment." She lifted her chin. “My father was an excellent judge of character, and he trusted you, too.”

“Let her go, Williams.” Seth’s teeth were clenched, his tone deadly.

Kate jerked her arm away from Ross and laid a hand on Seth’s chest. His muscles were bunched and ready for a fight. The Texas Ranger he’d been for most of his life had kicked in to protect her and his town. Kate deplored the violence but thrilled at the upright man she was about to pledge her life to.

“Wait!” Ross shouted again.

The pastor held up both hands. “I believe there have been enough objections, and none of them have to do with Ethan and Maura saying their vows. If they want the sheriff and Miss McShane to join them, then let us continue.”

A deafening cheer followed the pastor’s words, and the guests who’d left the building during the confrontation, cautiously walked back in and sat down. Kate expected the roof to tumble down from the racket, but if she’d doubted the sentiments of the townspeople toward her, those doubts were erased.

Seth enveloped her hand in his and led her toward the front of the crowded church.

He cleared his throat. “Pastor, we attend the padre’s mass, but we’d like both of you to say the words. I don’t have a marriage license, but I’ll file something at the county seat. Will you marry us?”

Ethan smiled and turned to the officiating leaders of the two church services in Hope. “I’ll vouch for Seth’s word.”

The pastor motioned for Seth and Kate to join them at the altar. “Regardless of what denomination you belong to, it’s better to marry.”

Kerry stepped forward and took Kate’s arm. “If you two are getting hitched, it’s going to be proper. Seth, go stand beside Ethan, and I’ll give Kate to you.”

Kate blinked against a flood of tears. "Kerry, I put you and your family through so much."

Kerry pulled her against his side. "Nonsense. We care about you, Kate, and we're grateful for how you helped bring Maura and Ethan together."

"Thank you." Kate patted his arm. "Let's go."

The ceremony was a blur, but she managed to respond at the proper times despite Ross staring daggers each time she glanced his way. If only this ceremony was real and binding, instead of a ruse to protect her until they could safely leave the church. She'd be marrying the only man she'd ever love. A man who'd been attracted to her before he knew she was a wealthy heiress.

No, the pretend wedding only solved the immediate problem. There were too many issues, east and west; money or not. Nothing and everything had changed in the past few days, heavens, in the past few minutes.

First the pastor, then the priest faced Ethan and Maura, then Seth and Kate. "In the name of our Savior, Jesus Christ and the Territory of Idaho, I now pronounce both couples—"

A gun shot rang through the air, rattling the rafters. Everyone clamped their hands over their ears. Women shrieked and children whimpered.

Seth pivoted, drew his gun, and stepped in front of Kate. Kate peeked out from behind his broad back to find half the men in the room standing; guns drawn.

Ross waved a smoking pistol toward the front of the church.

"Kate, come with me, or I'll shoot your boyfriend and anyone else who gets in the way." He waved the gun over the heads of the guests.

Panicked mothers shepherded their children toward the back of the church, while their men stood guard. Kate had never experienced such a scene.

Dizziness swept over her; she stumbled against Seth. “Ross, no! These people have nothing to do with us!”

“You’re coming with me, no matter what I have to do.”

“Listen to Kate, Williams.” Jeb held his hands in the air and walked toward Ross. “No sense in hurting innocent people. Let’s take this outside.”

Ross sneered. “Why Jeb, when did you become a man of such principles?” He turned back to Kate. “I wonder if the good sheriff has a deal with Jeb, since he courted Trisha Walker?”

“Gentlemen, please leave this church and settle your dispute outside.” Mayor Ellis finally spoke but visibly shook.

Kate pursed her lips. “The mayor’s right, and for your information, Ross, we already had this conversation.”

Seth ran his hand down her side and pressed her back behind him, his Colt still aimed at Ross. She had to stop Ross before blood spilled and completely ruined Maura’s wedding day. Seth’s readiness to protect her at any cost warmed her heart and strengthened her determination.

“Mayor, please sit down and let me handle this.” Seth’s tone brooked no interference. The mayor sank back to the bench.

Kate moved away from Seth and backed toward Ross and Jeb.

“Kate, what are you doing?” Seth stepped toward her, his free hand extended, the Colt still trained on Ross.

“Seth, I can’t let anyone get hurt. I have to go with them.”

“No!” Maura shrieked and started toward her, but Ethan pulled her back. “Ethan, we can’t let this happen!”

Ethan murmured something to Maura and

tucked her firmly into his side. She stared at Kate, her blue eyes wide, tears flooding her cheeks. Kate's heart warmed at the true friendship she and the younger woman had formed and how far they'd come in just a few weeks.

"Williams, if we weren't in the middle of innocent people I'd shoot you dead." Seth's voice held the hard determination of the Texas Ranger he'd been for most of his life.

"That's exactly why I chose this moment to take the little lady off your hands." Ross raised a brow. "I know your reputation as a Ranger. Given the chance you'd kill me, but you have a crazy sense of honor, and you won't risk other lives."

Seth glanced at Kate, his eyes softening for just a moment. "Be careful." He shoved his pistol back into the tooled leather holster.

Kate nodded, then took a deep breath and turned toward the door.

Once outside, she slowed her step while the townspeople scattered for safety. Soon they'd all be out of the way, and she could make her move.

Jeb hovered behind them, making it difficult to tell exactly whose side he was on. He'd stood up for Seth and revealed a relationship Seth had never mentioned. There appeared to be more about her Ranger she didn't know. She just hoped they lived long enough to unravel the unexpected parallel in their lives.

Her legs shaking, she pushed to keep up with Ross. They passed the rustic stores and businesses and headed toward the sheriff's office, where the path to the train station cut down the hillside. She blinked rapidly, fighting the lightheadedness when her surroundings wavered and faded.

In the time since she entered the church, the weather had changed. Instead of the shimmering blue green she'd seen since arriving in Hope, the lake had turned a steel gray. Heavy dark clouds burgeoned over the far mountains. A breeze rustled the colorful autumn leaves in the birch and cottonwood trees and fluttered the curls escaping the chignon she'd carefully wrapped her hair in that morning. The world took on a surreal cast

"You're out of luck, Ross. The train doesn't leave until tomorrow." She infused her voice with a strength she didn't feel.

Ross jerked her arm and laughed. "Of course not. Before I attended that mockery of a wedding, I freed our friend, Arlie Thompson, from your sheriff's jail. He's at the stable with horses. I've paid off the captain of the barge down there." He pointed toward the lake shore where two steam boats were moored waiting for passengers and supplies. "We'll take the boat to Lakeview, then ride to Spokane and catch the eastbound train."

Air rushed from Kate's lungs. "My God, I thought Arlie worked for Jeb."

Ross's mouth stretched in an evil smile. "Convincing, wasn't I?"

Nothing was as it had seemed. It had been Ross all the time. He was the threat to her and her company. He'd killed her father. She rubbed her face against her shoulder, refusing to let him see her tears.

"What was your plan if I'd stopped in Chicago?" She had to distract him long enough to pull her derringer; take a chance to escape.

"The moment I saw you off at Grand Central, I wired your uncle with the news of our engagement. He replied within the hour, elated. If you behave yourself, we'll stop in Chicago and get married at the country club, with your family present. My God, Kate. What were you thinking? Marry the sheriff of a backwoods town in a rustic, to say the least, sad excuse for a church?"

Anger over rode her fears. "You haven't a clue, do you Ross? These people are real and genuine. Besides, I wouldn't marry you under any circumstance." She twisted to glance behind them, but Ross jerked her before she could clearly assess the situation.

She had seen Seth, as he fanned out to her right, his hand on the butt of his gun. Wedding guests hovered around the church, staying back as Seth had no doubt instructed them. All except the men, including Ethan, who walked behind Seth and Jeb, with either drawn pistols or rifles at their sides.

The anger she'd harbored for Jeb was mild compared to her fury for Ross. The man was a traitor and a murderer. He'd used her and her father, pretending to be their friend and advisor. Kate glared at him, wishing looks really could kill. The man deserved to die after the pain, grief, and misery he'd put her and her father through.

She turned just enough to catch Jeb moving to their left. Seth stayed to the right, his eyes never wavering from her and Ross. Did he suspect she'd make a move? If only she could signal him.

Her heart ached over how this could all turn out. One of them could be killed, and she'd never have the chance to tell Seth how much she loved him, regardless of their backgrounds. She wanted to be the one to help him heal the wounds of his childhood and realize what a good and deserving man he was.

Wind whipped up the hillside, sending a dust devil spinning toward them. Kate turned her face and covered her mouth and nose with her free hand. The storm was moving fast, dark and ominous. Rain scented the air, coupled with the metallic tang of lightning. Thunder cracked and rumbled over the lake.

The very thing the town had prayed for, added to the backdrop of this nightmare.

"Ross, this is insane, you'll never get away with it."

They'd reached the stables and Kerry's blacksmith shop.

Ross shoved her in front of him. "It's gone too far. You're going back to New York with me whether you marry me or not. I'll control the company and keep you for my pleasure."

Kate dug her toes into the dusty ground and pulled against his hold. "You can't be serious! No one on the board would let that happen. They may not think a woman should run the company, but they won't allow you to, either. They're decent, upstanding men."

Ross tightened his grip. Pain shot up her arm. "Keep it up, and I'll have my pleasure and dump you off the train somewhere between Spokane and Chicago. By the time they find you, your bones will be bleached."

Faintness swept over her. Her knees weakened. She had to make a move before he put her on the steamboat. Kate glanced around.

Lightning flashed, striking somewhere on the mountain above them. Thunder cracked, and rumbled like a freight train.

Seth stood close enough to draw fire. Jeb waited in front of the group of the men, who risked their lives to protect a woman they barely knew.

Perspiration beaded her skin, and her blood ran cold. They were there to protect her, but any one of them could be killed in the cross fire.

She had to make a move; distract Ross. "What about Leland?" Wind whipped up the bank and roared through the tall trees. Waves crashed against the rocky shore below. "I can't believe Leland would agree with your plot at any price." Her voice cracked as she yelled over the wind and thunder.

Ross laughed. "Always questioning aren't you,

Kate? If you must know, Leland is ignorant of my plan. He'll be disposed of before we return to New York. He's not progressive, Kate. He's one of the guards who must go."

Kate's stomach roiled. "My God, you plan to kill Leland?"

"Progress, my dear. He'd never agree to my plan. He fancies himself your second father."

"He is my second father," Kate screamed. Her hand shook with rage as she shoved it into her skirt pocket. "I won't let you hurt another person in my life, Ross Williams."

Ross barked a maniacal laugh. "You have no power over what I do, Kate."

Kate pulled out the gun and shot at him.

Surprise widened Ross's eyes, and blood bloomed from his side. He looked at her, then at the wound.

"You bitch!" He released her, stepping back to cup his hand over his side. "You'll die for this!"

Thundering hooves took her attention from Ross long enough for him to rip the gun from her hand and throw it over the bank.

Arlie rode around the stable, two saddled horses behind him. He dropped the leads and dismounted to help Ross. The panicked horses raced up the street, scattering the group of brave men.

Before Arlie could draw his gun, a hole appeared in the center of his forehead, and he fell like a tree. His horse reared and pawed the air, then raced off, knocking Jeb off his feet.

Seth stood in the dusty street, his legs braced; the Colt in his hand still smoking. He'd killed Arlie and didn't waver. Kate's heart leaped into her throat. She was so far from her New York City drawing room.

"Step away from Kate, Williams. It's over." Seth kept the Colt trained on Ross, visually unaffected by what he'd just done, what he was prepared to do to protect her.

Far out of her element, Kate couldn't move. Ross wrapped one arm around her, his gun in the other. His breathing rough and rapid, he waved his gun at Seth. Kate's heart pounded against her breast bone and her head swam.

"Thanks, Morgan. You just saved me the bother of shooting that piece of scum. Now stay back or Kate's next."

"Listen up, Williams." Seth stood tall and strong, his dark eyes as hard as flint. "You hurt Kate, and killing you won't be enough."

"Ha!" Ross dragged Kate toward the bank leading to the shore. "The big shot Ranger, kill someone in cold blood? You're too upstanding for that." He spit out the words and wrinkled his nose.

His gun hand shook. "Get out here and help me, for god's sake!" He jerked Kate with him toward the top of the stairs leading to the shore.

A man stepped from behind the stable, his gun drawn.

A sharp breath tore from Kate. The man who'd attacked her on the hill!

Seth's expression only flickered.

"Greetings, Morgan." The man stopped beside them and lifted his hat at Seth.

"Johnston. How long have you been taking orders from Williams?" Seth stepped closer, his shoulders tense, his gun still trained on Ross.

"I don't take orders from anybody." Allen Johnston ran his palm over the chamber of the large pistol, spinning it like a nervous habit. "So Jeb, when did you hook up with Morgan?"

Jeb had managed to get up off the street. Covered with dust, he limped toward them. "If I'd known what you're capable of, Johnston, I'd have taken care of you long ago."

"If Jeb didn't, I would have." A new voice joined the fray, shouting over the storm bearing down on them.

Kate shifted in Ross's hold, her eyes searching for the owner of that oh, so familiar voice. The man himself stepped out from between the post office and the sheriff's office.

"Daddy!" Kate's knees buckled. She collapsed to the ground.

Something whizzed over her, followed by a crack.

"Stay down, Kate!" Seth's voice reached through her fog. Her father? How could that be? She wanted to stand, run toward him, but she heeded Seth's warning. They couldn't stop Ross if she was in the way.

She went against her instincts and cowered, covering her head. Another gunshot whizzed close by. Something heavy landed on her and knocked the breath from her. Twisting on the rugged ground, she looked into Ross William's lifeless eyes.

The world went dark.

Chapter Twenty

Kate came to when the heavy weight was lifted from her and she could take a deep breath.

"Kate, are you all right?"

Seth's voice reached through the grayness. His spicy scent wrapped around her along with his arms. She cuddled close and buried her face in his neck.

"Come on, Seth. Let her breath won't you? There's plenty of time for that."

The soft Irish lilt penetrated the horror and shock of what she'd gone through and reminded her of the face she'd seen before she fainted.

"Daddy?"

"Yes, Katie Rose, it's me."

Kate opened her eyes and looked at the man who'd been everything in the world to her before she met Seth Morgan. "Daddy, how can you be here? Alive?" With Seth's help, she scrambled to her feet and into her father's arms.

"I'm sorry about that, Katie. Not good timing, but there you have it." James McShane stroked her hair back from her face. "There were things that had to be done without even you knowing about it."

Over her father's silver hair, the sky was black with rain clouds. Lightning continued to strike and the thunder hammer. But right now, the earth could split in two and she wouldn't care. Her father was alive, and well, by the looks of him.

"I don't understand." The first drops of rain splattered on her face. One, then two, then the clouds opened and pelted them with their bounty.

"Let's get inside. We can talk at the boarding

house." Seth shouted over the storm, then took her arm. Her father took her other arm, and they ran up the street toward Mrs. White's.

Mrs. White met them the moment they stepped into the tea room. "Oh, my dears, are you all right? I was so afraid for you."

Kate looked down at her rain soaked skirt. The dust was now mud, and she must look like a homeless ragamuffin. She glanced at Seth, then her father and Jeb, who came in right behind them. "Mrs. White, I appreciate your concern. I'm afraid we're going to dirty your boarding house."

James gave a hoot of laughter and wrapped his arms around Kate. Seth chuckled. "What's so funny?" Kate looked at the three men who played such important parts in her life. Yes, even Jeb, who had redeemed himself.

"You are, Katie Rose. You could have died out there, but you're more worried about Mrs. White's housekeeping. You're a prize, Katie, my dear. I've missed you so."

Kate hugged her father, smiled, giggled, then laughed, tears streaking down her cheeks, adding to the smears of mud on her jacket. She struggled between humor and sadness, until her father led her to a chair and settled her with a cup of Mrs. White's tea. Elena White bustled about in her element, ordering a bath be sent to Kate's room.

All the while, Seth stood a respectable distance away, his gaze never leaving her. Kate longed to tell him about the revelation she'd had when they'd both faced death, but with her father and Jeb, and the well-meaning Mrs. White hovering, it wasn't the time or the place. Oh, but she wanted to talk to him, hold him, kiss him. Torn, she glanced from her father, to Seth, and back to her father.

A smile tipped one corner of James McShane's generous mouth. He stepped back and motioned to

Seth.

Seth hesitated, then stepped in front of her and kneeled. Kate looked into his dark eyes, her chest tight with emotion. "So much has happened." She set her teacup on the side table and pressed her hands against his whisker roughened jaw.

Seth turned his head and kissed each of her inner wrists, sending thrills up her arms. She wanted to pull his head against her breasts and hold him close. "You could have died out there."

"We both could have." He gasped her hands and looked down at her left hand. "I want a ring on that finger, Kate. My ring. My proposal wasn't just to save your life, but to save mine too. I need you."

A breath of wonder rushed through her. "Seth, I love you too, but there's so much to talk about before we—before we can truly commit to each other."

Seth's mouth turned up in that sexy smile she loved. "Kate McShane, your father is standing here as my witness, I want to remain your husband. The rest will come with time. Will you stay married to me?"

Mrs. White sighed and tittered. Jeb chuckled and slapped his hand against his thigh. "Answer him, Kate, so we can get cleaned up and head to the hotel. I hear tell Ethan has some fine Scotch whiskey, and I'm ready for a drink."

Kate wanted to say yes, but there was so much to settle. What about her home in New York? The company? She looked at her father, her brain still not believing what her eyes saw. Her father alive and well!

"Katie Rose, if it's me you're worried about, there's a train track out there, running both ways. We can afford the tickets, my dear."

Kate sputtered, then laughed. "Oh Daddy, it's so good to have you back. I have to hear all about this plan you and Jeb devised."

"Yes, but now, Katie Rose, there's a man kneeling in front of you, who loves you very much. You have my approval, if that's what you're waiting for."

Kate threaded her fingers through Seth's, looked into his dark, dark eyes and sighed. "Yes, Seth Morgan. I want to stay married to you. Forever."

Seth stood and swept her into his arms. "In that case, Mrs. Morgan, I'm with Jeb. We need to clean up and join the reception. There's a marriage certificate to sign, good food and drink, and a wedding night to get to."

"Seth!" Kate swatted his shoulder, her face hot with embarrassment. She couldn't help but laugh with pure joy.

Her father and Jeb chuckled and James patted Seth's back. "Jeb and I took rooms at the hotel yesterday and had a devil of a time avoiding you before we were ready to confront Ross. This town should feel secure with such a thorough Sheriff. We'll see you at the reception?" He cocked one eyebrow at both of them. "Don't keep us waiting too long."

"We'll be there, Daddy." Kate threw him a kiss and waved at Jeb, as her husband carried her up the stairs.

Chapter Twenty-One

At her bedroom door, Seth gently set her on her feet letting her slowly slide down the front of his firm, muscled body. Heat flared through Kate. Later that evening, she'd see his body completely unclothed for the first time.

Seth pressed his lips to hers. "I'm not stepping into your room, Kate, until we're truly husband and wife."

Kate buried her face against his wet shirt, afraid to have time to herself, time to think about the horrific scenes of the day. "I don't know if I can be alone yet."

"You'll do fine. You're a strong woman." Seth backed away, toward the door to the room he'd slept in since arriving in Hope.

"You sound like my father." Kate's heart swelled and her throat closed. Her father was alive, and cleaning up in his hotel room at this very minute.

"I'll take that as a compliment. Now, get cleaned up so we can join them." Seth winked and disappeared into his room.

Kate slowly turned the doorknob, pushed open the door, then stepped inside. Seth was right, she'd faced many things and survived. She'd come to terms with what happened today, too.

A bathtub filled with steaming water sat in front of the hot stove, a stack of fresh towels on her bed. Kate dipped her fingers in the water and moaned with pleasure at the clean, lavender scented bath. She peeled out of her cold, muddy clothes, heaping them in a pile in the corner. So much for her traveling suit. She'd have to wear one of Mary Catherine's dresses home.

Home. Which home? Her father had given her permission to stay with Seth. Her husband. He'd assured her frequent visits. What more could she want? James McShane didn't need her help to manage the company he'd built. He was relatively young, vibrant, and handsome. He might even meet a nice woman, if Kate wasn't hovering in his life all the time.

The thought of having her father back in her life, then saying goodbye so soon, sent a sharp pain through her heart. He'd been the man of her life, well, her entire life. They'd always been close, but even more so since her mother left.

With a sigh, she lowered herself into the copper tub. To be clean again. Warm again. With Seth again.

It all flashed back and forth in her mind as she washed away the mud and blood. Through all the years of denial, she'd longed to meet a man she could love completely, and who loved her, for herself; not her money and prestige.

She wanted a home with a husband and children. Everything Erin had. Now, it all rolled out in front of her like a red carpet.

Could she adapt to Seth's way of life? He'd been a lawman since he's turned sixteen. When he'd shot Arlie Thompson, she's seen the look in his eyes. They were darker, shielded from what he had to do. He didn't kill people in cold blood. He did it to protect innocent people. Was the shield over his eyes how he remained so sensitive and gentle? The man took her breath away. He was so handsome, so masculine, and so caring.

She slid farther into the water and dunked her head, scrubbing at her scalp before she surfaced and grabbed the bar of lavender soap. People were waiting for them, she'd think later.

Slipping into fresh underclothes, and a dark green, taffeta dress, Kate toweled her hair, then wound it into a chignon.

Knuckles rapped on the door.

Kate jumped and pressed her fingers to her throat.

"Ready, darlin?" Seth's deep, welcome voice sounded from the hall.

Her heart sang with the excitement of being with him and seeing her father again. She opened the door and basked in his admiring gaze.

Seth crooked his arm. "Ready?"

The moment Kate and Seth entered the hotel lobby they were surrounded by well-wishers and the beaming Malone family.

Kate returned their hugs. They were all concerned over how she'd survived the episode with Ross and filled with congratulations for her marriage to Seth. Kate was no stranger to large events and managed a façade of politeness even while her mind was on seeing her father again.

She finally spotted him, angling his way through the crowded room, a glass of Scotch in his hand. James glowed with health and happiness.

Kate's heart swelled with joy, and tears pricked her eyes. "Daddy!" She hurried toward him and wrapped her arms around his middle.

"Darling Katie. You look radiant." He tipped her chin up and gave her a look gone serious. "I want you to put away the ugliness of today. Ross was sick, Katie. I saw it happening a couple years ago but had to wait to catch him in the crime. I should have told you, but I couldn't imagine he'd harm you." He pulled her toward one of the couches, lining the wall to make room for the large reception.

"You have to believe, my dear, if I'd had an inkling of Ross hurting you, I'd have shipped you off myself."

"I know, Daddy. Ross mainly played with minds. Until today." She covered her face with both hands and shook her head. "I never imagined someone could change into such a horrible monster." She looked at her father. "Then to find him involved with Allen Johnston. Was Ross working with him all along?" She gasped and pressed her fingers to her throat. "Allen Johnston. What happened to him? I fainted, then when I woke all I could think of was Seth safe and were you alive."

James glanced toward Seth, then back to her. "Allen's in jail, Katie. When Seth shot Ross, Allen turned his gun on Seth. I shot him in the shoulder."

Kate shivered. "What now?"

"Jeb and I are leaving in the morning. If Johnston makes it through the night, he's going with us to stand trial."

"You're leaving so soon?"

"I have a company to run, Katie Rose. Working together to stop Ross and Allen helped Jeb and I bury the hatchet. We plan to make McShane Walker even stronger."

Kate swiped at the incessant tears. "I'm going to miss you. Again. Do you really think I should stay here?"

James nodded. "Seth's a good man, Katie. I couldn't have chosen a better husband for you if I'd hand picked him. He loves you deeply and will take good care of you, and my grandchildren."

Kate smiled through her tears. "I can tell you're determined to have grandchildren."

"They're the riches of a man's life. Through all this craziness, you've found the perfect father for them. Speaking of which." James looked across the room and lifted his chin.

Kate followed his line of vision and met Seth's dark, intense gaze. Even across the room, his look sent goose bumps and heat racing over her body. She could hardly believe how far they'd come since the train journey west when she'd devised the plan to fall into his lap.

"I think your husband's chomping at the bit to have you to himself." James helped her off the couch, then kept a firm grip on her hand, until they reached Seth. "I was jealous when Kerry Malone gave you away at your wedding." He smiled at Kate's raised brows. "Oh yes, I was there, hidden just outside the door. Now is my chance to give your care over to Seth and give you my blessing." He placed Kate's hand in Seth's.

"Thank you, sir." Seth pulled Kate against his side and wrapped his arm around her. "It means a lot to me. Rest assured, Kate will visit you as often as weather permits." He smiled at her, a glint in his eyes. "And when it's safe between babies."

A few weeks ago, Kate would have considered his statement sexist and very old-fashioned, but coming from Seth it warmed her and made her feel cherished. "We'll discuss my traveling plans later." She might enjoy having a wonderful man like Seth as her mentor and husband, but she wasn't going to let him know how much power he had over her.

As darkness settled in, the reception guests thinned. There were chores to be done before bedtime. More than once, Seth sent her a side glance, his dark brows raised in suggestion. Kate's emotions bounced between anticipation and nervousness over completing the act they'd started on several occasions.

She visited with Maura and Ethan, hugged Will a couple of times, and talked to Ruth. Ruth had already bought a train ticket and intended to leave for Boston in a couple of days.

No doubt, her confidence in Maura's abilities as Ethan's wife and Will's mother accelerated her plans to leave. If Ethan had married Mary Catherine, or any other woman, she would have stayed longer.

Sometime between the heaping plate of food, and her second glass of champagne, Seth met with the priest to draw up a marriage certificate and presented it to her with a pen.

Her hand trembled and her heart pounded as she added her name to Seth's, tying them together forever. As always, he sensed her inner turmoil and pulled her into his arms.

"I'll make you happy, Kate."

She slid her arms around his trim middle and splayed her hands against his strong back. She tipped her chin and gazed at him. "Oh, Seth. We'll make each other happy. Our wedding was unusual to say the least, so I want to say something now. Something I couldn't say then.

"You are such a worthy man. Through all the soirées and balls I attended in New York and Boston, all the men I met at social and business functions, none of them hold a candle to you, Seth Morgan. Next to you, they are all mealy mouthed and lack integrity. I'm certain, no matter what happens, you'll protect me and our family with your life."

Seth's dark eyes misted. He cupped the back of her head in one strong hand and pulled her face against his white shirt front. She breathed in his clean, spicy scent and smiled. He didn't want her to see how greatly her words moved him, how close the strong, former Texas Ranger was to crying.

His chest expanded and contracted several times, while he slid his other hand up and down her back. The remaining guests glanced their way but didn't intrude. Kate stayed in his arms until he was ready to loosen his hold, and let her look into his face.

"Kate McShane, I don't know what I ever did to

deserve you, but thank you for loving me and for being my wife."

"Oh Seth, you deserve the best." She blinked with the realization of how her remark sounded, then giggled and patted her hair. "What more can I say?"

Seth roared with laughter. "There will never be a dull moment with you, darlin'."

"Oh, and by the way." Kate pressed her index finger against his chest. "My name is, Mrs. Morgan now, and don't you forget it."

Seth chuckled and pulled her against his firm body. She gasped at the clear evidence they needed to say goodnight to the guests.

"Oh, don't you worry, Mrs. Morgan." He pressed his lips against her ear, then laved it with his tongue.

Kate gasped again. "I think we need to say goodnight to everyone, don't you?"

****

Kate hesitated outside her room at the boarding house. "Wait a minute. Which room should we use?"

Seth glanced down her in disbelief. "What does it matter?"

Kate shrugged. "I guess it doesn't, but my things are in here and yours are in your room."

Seth shook his head and swept his bride off her feet. "I don't care about my things, what I care about it making love to my wife." He leaned down, turned the knob to Kate's room, and carried her inside, shutting the door with his foot.

Kate giggled and looped her arms around his neck. "I hope no one else heard that!"

"I don't care if they did. I have a piece of paper, your father's blessing, and I think, your love, saying I can make love to you whenever I want."

"What do you mean, you think, you have my love?" Kate forked her fingers through his hair.

Seth had never seen anything more beautiful than Kate's face filled with emotion. It planted a huge lump in his chest and sent him into a realm much deeper than physical love. He planned to cherish this woman all the days of his life.

"I heard the words, but I guess it's still hard to believe." He gently set her on her feet and pulled her against him. Sliding his hands up her back, he buried his fingers in her hair and began to remove the snood holding it captive. Damn, he'd never get tired of seeing her hair tumble around her shoulders and down her back. The fire dancing through each strand fascinated him more than gold ever could. "Your hair is so beautiful. Did your mother have auburn hair?"

"No, my hair color came from my father. He's just much older and turning white." Kate threaded her fingers through his hair. "I imagine your mother had dark, shiny hair like yours."

The joy thrumming through him, dimmed just a touch. "My mother had beautiful black, shiny hair. She was beautiful."

Kate framed his face between her soft hands. "Seth, I want to make love too, but first, can we talk about your mother? I sense how much she influences your feelings about love." She glanced away, her lips quivering. "The day we almost made love—" She nibbled at her bottom lip. "I worried you stopped and left because you didn't want me to be like her. Alone, with a child." She looked in his eyes. "I could never be in that situation, Seth. My father built an empire to protect me and keep me safe. Please tell me why your father left?"

Seth backed away. "First of all, we did make love that day. I just left the completion for when we made things legal. Hell, tonight will be my first time to love the person I'm with." Seth walked toward the stove, staring at the bright red glow through the crack around the door. "You're right. My mother did shape my feelings on what happens between a man and a woman. I swore I'd never use a woman, get her pregnant then leave. She claimed he loved her but had obligations in Kansas. He was a cattleman. She swore he had money and would eventually take care of us.

"When I was three, she heard he'd been killed in a stampede. The little bit of money he'd left her ran out. There were no other options, so we moved into the brothel."

Kate leaned against his back, slid her arms around him and held tight. "A woman knows when she's loved. If he hadn't died, I believe he would have returned for you and your mother. It's all so sad."

Seth unclasped her arms and turned, pulling her against him. "You've had a hell of a day, darlin'. Are you sure you want me to stay?"

She rolled up on her tiptoes and pressed her lips to his chin. "Only every night for the rest of my life. I'm sorry I asked about your mother when we should be making love, but I wanted to clear the air. We don't need ghosts in our bed. No second thoughts."

"You're one amazing woman, Mrs. Morgan."

Kate slipped her thigh between his legs. Seth moaned. Damn, the woman switched gears so fast she made his head spin and his blood race right to the spot he'd contended with since the first time he kissed Kate McShane. Tonight, he'd please Kate and himself; seal their marriage.

"One thing my mother's life did for me, Kate." He trailed kisses down the side of his throat.

"What?" Her voice sounded pinched, but her body was pliant and warm in his arms.

"It made me wait for you."

"Oh, Seth, I can't be sorry for anything that made both of us wait to meet each other."

Kate rocked against him, sending Seth over the

edge. The conversations would have to wait until later. He lifted her off her feet, and laid her on the bed, slipping his hands down her legs to take off her boots. Sliding his hands up her thighs, he unhooked her stockings, smiling when her special made, silk under pants brushed the back of his hands. Hot damn, the fire she started in him would never burn out.

Kate moaned and wiggled, somehow removing his tie and opening the front of his shirt. Her soft hands stroked his bare chest and sent flashes of heat through his groin. He was so hard he feared he'd hurt her. For all her spunk and business knowledge, Kate was a virgin and would have some pain, but he didn't intend to frighten or ruin her first time.

When she slid her fingers under his waist band, Seth gave up on moving slow and methodical. He shucked off his boots and pants then shook off his shirt.

He almost panted when her green gaze devoured his naked skin and settled on the bulge in his underwear. "Darlin, I don't want to frighten you, but I have to take off my drawers."

Kate slowly nodded, her eyes fixed to his bulge, her chest rising and falling in excitement. At least he hoped she was excited and not afraid.

The glow of the lamplight bathed them in its golden light, as he pushed the cotton drawers over his hips and down his thighs. Her intense stare made him feel like a prospectus on the board room table. She touched his aching body, feathering it with her fingertips.

Excruciating pleasure flashed through him when she wrapped her slender fingers around him and pressed her thumb against the tip. A droplet of moisture appeared, and she looked up at him in wonder.

"Darlin', I hate to stop your exploration, but this

will be over before it starts if you don't stop that."

She blinked and her eyes widened. "I'm sorry, I thought you would like for me to touch you."

Seth growled and moved over her, flicked open the buttons down the front of her dress. "Yeah, I love it too much. We need to get to the next step."

In moments, her clothes were in a heap beside the bed, her pale skin gleaming in the lamp light. The contrast between them, their shapes, their skin colors, their size, made coming together fill him with wonder. She was so delicate, he was afraid he'd break her.

Amazed, Kate floated on a thousand sensations. Seth Morgan was one beautiful man; making her recall the statue she's seen in Florence, on her European tour. But Seth was flesh and blood, not marble, and he loved her.

Their scents mingled with a new one, musky and warm, and acted like a potion to make her forget her inhibitions and allow Seth to take her on this journey into marriage and intimacy. He stroked her inner thighs and feathered his fingers over the feminine parts he'd pleasured the day she'd moved to the boarding house.

His hands were everywhere and his large body, somehow didn't squash her. She loved how his skin glowed a rich bronze in the lamplight, contrasting with her paleness. When his fingers delved inside her, she closed her eyes and began her ascent to the stars. He played her like an instrument, making her body hotter and wetter.

"Oh, Seth, it's happening again." She panted and rocked against his hand.

"Let it go, darlin'."

Pleasure mounted and mounted then broke into a million, glittering pieces. She was weak, exhilarated, and all his.

Seth moved over her body until that gleaming

tip pressed against her auburn curls.

Unable to look away, Kate stared, as his mysterious part, disappeared inside her, stretching her until she thought she'd rip in half, then a sudden sharp pain.

Kate gasped and tried to move away.

Panting, Seth stilled, his hands framing her face. "It'll pass, sweetheart. It's your first time, but it'll pass in a minute. Then you'll know."

Know? Kate trusted him and lay still, waiting for the pain to pass. It did and was replaced with a pleasant ache. Testing the waters, she moved her hips.

Seth moaned. "You all right, darlin'?"

"More than all right." She moved again, relishing the sensations so similar to what she'd experienced when he kissed and stroked her, but so much better. "Seth, I want it all." She wrapped her arms around his chest and hung on, while Seth showed her what knowing meant.

Later, wrapped in each other's arms, Kate sighed and stretched, running her toes up and down her husband's hair roughened legs. "Now I know why Erin always blushed when I asked her about marriage." Her voice pierced the darkness, only filled with the breath of sleep and satisfaction. The fire in the stove snapped, and a piece of wood rolled over.

"Yes, Ma'am." Seth rolled to his side, and stared into her eyes, his hair dark against the white pillowcase. "I know I'm going to thoroughly enjoy marriage. Coming home to you every night, sometimes during the day."

Kate pulled her head off the pillow and opened her mouth. "Seth Morgan, you're going to create a scandal!"

Seth grinned and pulled her down beside him. "Every man in Hope will understand, and every woman will be jealous."

"That sounds rather arrogant."

"You're the one who said those things when I made you—"

"All right, I understand." Kate laughed and leaned on her elbow, stroking his hair with her other hand. "I'm going to thoroughly enjoy each time you make love to me, Seth Morgan, but I'm not going to hang around the boarding house waiting for you. Tomorrow, after we see my father and Jeb off on the train, we're going to plan our house."

Seth groaned and rolled onto his back, folding his hands over his chest. "Here we go, married only hours and you're planning our life and all the work I'm going to do."

Kate rolled on top of him. "You better believe it, Sheriff. I plan to keep you really busy."

Seth threaded his fingers through her hair and pulled her face to his for a long, deep kiss. "Your wish is my command, Mrs. Morgan. I want a home, too. We'll start planning tomorrow, because tonight isn't over and neither is this hunger I can't seem to get past."

"I'm hoping your never get past it."

"I won't, not with you, darlin'."

A word about the author...

Tesa lives in the Inland Northwest, with her husband, Don, and close to their married daughters, charming sons-in-law, and seven adorable grandchildren.

www.ingramcontent.com/pod-product-compliance
Lightning Source LLC
Chambersburg PA
CBHW070539260626
47161CB00002B/452
9781612170251